Monarch in the Flames

Modutan Empire, Volume 2

S.V. Farnsworth

Published by Stone Wolfe Press, 2020.

MONARCH IN THE FLAMES

First edition. October 10, 2020.

ISBN: 978-1733859943

Written by S.V. Farnsworth.

Also by S.V. Farnsworth

Modutan Empire
Woman of the Stone
Monarch in the Flames

Standalone
A Rare Connection: Inspirational Romantic Suspense

Watch for more at https://svfarnsworthauthor.com.

Table of Contents

Monarch in the Flames is dedicated to my mother, Deb Clark, a fiery redhead with green eyes. She has inspired me all my life with her love, courage, tenacity, and unfailing kindness.

Chapter One

Once you've been burned, everything is fire. Gray winter clouds drifted like ash over the flattened, yellow grasses of Frenland's plains. Ice shards hurled by the wind seared like cinders on Stephan's tortured skin. Would there be no end to his suffering?

"Sir." Helen leaned from her saddle to touch his arm where he sat astride a forbearing warhorse.

The weight of Stephan's fledgling reign as the king held him bound to a hollow pit of despair in his chest. "Have you secured Cairn?"

"Yes, sir. The town is peaceful and there is shelter to be found here. They've done the work you've asked and captured two fugitives. We have a reason for cheer."

Stephan focused his gaze on her. "Cheer?"

Helen flinched. "Justice is good news. I only wish you would stay your hand and hire an executioner."

"What difference would that make? It's my judgment that has sentenced them to death." Stephan scowled, remembering the past.

A remarkable woman with soulful brown eyes and dimples floated before him as if Valerie were close enough to touch. She would die by his dutiful hand when apprehended for her crimes. His stomach twisted. He had agonized over issuing the warrant.

Stephan leaned forward in the saddle. His mount carried him toward the image of her. The ice crust on his cloak to cracked and fell away.

The irrational action startled him. He returned to the harsh reality of his dilemma. He hadn't realized how long he'd stared toward the ghosts of Sion. Compulsion drew him to witness the ashes of the village Valerie had torched in Salicor's name.

"Come with me. Warm yourself in town." Helen's horse whinnied invitingly.

Stephan gazed to the west. "Don't you need to see the remains of your home?"

She followed his line of sight and the hopeful expression on her face collapsed. "No. I'll never return to the charred remains of my people. Their ghosts haunt the place and rightly so. It is unsafe...even if the weather permitted the journey which it decidedly prohibits. We must leave for Soniashi in the morning, or we'll be snowbound." She leaned over to caress the unmarred side of his scarred face. "Stephan, come with me. You're far too young to freeze to death."

He snorted a laugh and shook off her hand. The warmth of her touch scalded him. "Fine. You owe me a story."

That was their agreement. When he sank into depression, she shared a personal story to break him free. She had made it clear she didn't particularly like to share. But then, he loathed leaving the numb place he had created to protect himself. That made the trade fair.

"I will tell you a story just as soon as you move." Helen caught his attention.

He urged his mount to walk toward Cairn.

Helen maneuvered her horse to walk along beside him. "I was a little girl of three years when a stranger dressed in blue rode through my village. His cheerful expression sat in contrast with his battle-scarred face."

She glanced at Stephan. "I did not consider the man frightening because of his kind eyes. He noticed me staring. But instead of being angry he dismounted and withdrew a carving from his purse. He whittled one last bit and handed me the figurine of a horse."

Stephan realized the purpose of the story was to remind him that his actions spoke with more force than his hideous appearance. Part of him resented Helen's presumption that he needed to hear this story. The other part of him longed for a balm to soothe his insecurities.

Helen leaned forward to pat her mount on the neck. "His generosity surprised me. I ran inside my family's hut to show the toy to my siblings. We shared it, though I always held it at night, unable to sleep without it in my hand." She passed Stephan a well-worn, wooden figurine of a horse.

He stared at the carving in the palm of his hand. The animal looked happy. The unfortunate beast Stephan rode today walked glumly in stark contrast. A celebrated warhorse like Marcin should not be treated with such disregard.

"Thank you. I needed to hear that story. Is there a livery stable for our mounts? Marcin deserves some special care after a day like today." He handed Helen the carving and allowed her to lead him through Cairn's unpaved streets.

The grooms ran from the livery stable to take the horses in the gloom of evening's darkening influence. Somewhat disappointed because he would have liked to make it up to Marcin himself, he reluctantly handed over the reins. Helen grabbed his arm and pulled him around the side of the structure toward the rear entrance of a two-story building. He let her have her way.

"This is the Clarion Inn. The food is rumored to be the best in the province. You need a good meal to warm you, sir." Helen held open the door.

Stephan strode inside. The prospect of more than hardtack and dried meat enlivened him. The interior bustled with activity. Servers carried heaping platters to waiting patrons. It was a common-looking fare that smelled delectable.

The conspicuous exception to the plain food was the bread. It was finer than any he'd seen elsewhere. He couldn't resist grabbing a braided loaf from a young girl hurrying past on her way to a corner table. The first bite tasted of butter and garlic. It was delicious and made his mouth water.

The child returned from the corner table. She met his gaze without flinching at the sight of his scars. Expectantly, she held out a hand for payment.

"Bring us the house specialty, please." He dropped several coins into her outstretched hand.

The girl nodded and hurried into the kitchen.

Helen shook her head and chuckled under her breath.

"What? Shouldn't I be polite?" He understood her mirth and the censure that triggered it.

The servant girl hadn't realized he was the king. Stephan preferred it that way. Others considered it improper for him to live in a lowly manner. Little did they know, he had been raised by the humblest of monarchs to live a self-reliant life. Emerald Stone of Danalan never burdened her subjects. Instead, she served them tirelessly.

Helen beckoned him toward the last available table in a sea of blue uniforms. With the town secure, the soldiers had thought first of their stomachs. Stephan didn't blame them.

He took another bite of bread and sat opposite Helen. A woman carrying a tray of ale steins passed their way. Helen flagged her down with a shiny coin. The woman glanced at Stephan next. He shook his head.

He saw no benefit to the prevalence of alcoholic drinks in Frenland. He witnessed daily proof of the evils of intoxication. How could he change the hearts of inebriated people?

The degeneracy of those who excused themselves because of strong drink made him long for Danalan. Life had been straightforward there. Even after months in the north, he still thought of Stone Castle as home.

Helen sipped ale and watched him. "One won't harm you." The foam on her upper lip must have tickled her because she wiped it away.

Stephan's mood soured. "I don't give fair wages to have it spent on such things. Wouldn't that coin have been put to better use feeding the hungry?"

"They don't serve water here, my king." Helen swigged the ale. "Besides, I'm thirsty and in need of refreshment. A musician is setting up. Perhaps we could dance."

Stephan searched the place for the musician and found a boy holding a fife. Disappointed, he sighed and returned his attention to his friend. What had he been hoping for? Thus far, he had not had the heart to sing and play in this country. There had been no dancing either.

The people who lived south of the Impenetrable Mountains liked ballads of virtue and adventure. This northern people of Frenland preferred raucous tunes with lewd lyrics. He hadn't yet mentioned to anyone he sang and played. Sarialla knew, but she was gone in search of her daughter.

Thoughts of Valerie were always close at hand. She had captured his heart the night they met last summer. He'd been burned and was close to death. She had saved his life.

Not knowing who the other was, they had let down their guard. In those innocent hours, he'd learned she was much more than her wicked reputation had taught him to believe. Unfortunately, his impressions of her stood in stark contrast with the evidence of her guilt.

He'd had no choice other than to condemn her to death when the facts were presented in court. It was the hardest thing he'd ever done. Holding out hope for her redemption was a curse. He needed to concede that his impressions of her kindness were in error. However, the memory of her scorched hands as she selflessly tended his burns haunted him.

"Your meal, Majesty." The little serving girl laid a platter on the table.

She curtsied awkwardly. Stephan smiled at her. It was the first genuinely happy expression he'd given anyone since Sarialla took a message to the mountain people weeks ago. Affairs in the kingdom were awry and allies were essential if his rule was to survive the plots of his enemies.

"Thank you for your good service." He handed the girl an extra coin.

She hurried back to work.

Helen laughed. "You do realize, she forgot about me, right?"

He slid the platter of steaming meat and tubers topped with savory onions into the middle of the table. "We'll share."

Helen didn't require a second invitation.

The fife music commenced and the roar of conversation in the room lowered to near silence. The server girl climbed atop a stool. Her singing voice was clear and her ballad heartfelt.

Helen stabbed the table with her knife and stalked out of the inn. Stephan watched her go confused by her response. The song was lovely and the heroine of the epic praiseworthy. The tale was about a horse named Clarion and the woman who rode her into battle. He carefully memorized the tune and lyrics. Then he heard the name of the rider. Valerie.

The hostility of the soldiers around him focused on the girl and the musician. A subcommander snatched the fife from the boy, tossed it to the floor, and trampled it. The girl cowered before the act of violence.

Stephan rose to his feet. "Pay for the fife and ask forgiveness of the girl. You've frightened her." Stephan's voice boomed and the room hushed.

The subcommander's red face darkened to a shade of purple. He tossed coins at the fife player, then departed from the inn. With the slamming of the door, the remaining soldiers returned to their meals and conversations.

Stephan strode over to the girl. He offered a hand of friendship. She took it and stepped off the stool. He noticed Valerie's brand on her forearm as he escorted her into the kitchen. His curiosity was piqued.

"Tell me your name."

"Lily, sir." She curtsied.

"You may call me Stephan." He delighted in her dimples because they reminded him of Valerie. "May I sing your song to the orphans in Soniashi? I think they'd like it."

Lily smiled. "I don't mind. Jane of Appleton wrote the song."

He relaxed. "How did you come by your name?"

"My mother named me for the lost child of the general who owned us." The girl sat on a straw mat in a corner out of the way of the busy kitchen staff.

"The general had a child?" Stephan hadn't heard this shocking bit of news about Valerie.

"Oh, yes, a twisted baby girl." Lily's voice held sadness.

Stephan frowned in pity for Valerie. "The child was deformed?"

"Yes, but no one knows why. It didn't matter to the general. Everyone says she loved Lily more than life." The solemn look on the girl's face told of the truth of her convictions.

"How did the general's daughter die?" Stephan's heart went out to Valerie.

"King Salicor hurt her. I don't know in what way. No one will tell me." The little girl shook her head slowly. "He was a bad man."

Stephan nodded in grieved understanding because he had heard extensive testimony regarding the way Salicor abducted children. Stephan had not suspected the tyrant capable of doing such an abhorrent thing to members of his own family. If he had harmed Lily, then he may have committed the same atrocities against his niece. Could that be why Valerie was so damaged?

"Anyway, I'm glad he's dead." The little girl whispered this last bit.

"I am too." He leaned against the wall. "Tell me about the general."

"She saves people. She's very brave and," the girl cocked her head, meeting his gaze, "she loves the prince."

A ray of sunshine burst in his heart. "She does?"

"Oh, she never said so. She doesn't talk about her feelings. My mother tells of how she pined for him and forsook all others." Lilly giggled. "We were shocked when the general gave up ruling the kingdom to support him."

Stephan wanted to hear more about the pining, but he didn't quite understand the giving up the kingdom part. "She was in line to rule Frenland?" Why hadn't he realized this?

Lily nodded. "The general was the crown princess until Salicor cast her off."

"He denounced her?" Stephan hadn't heard this either.

"Because of the woman," Lily whispered.

"What woman?" His curiosity had him completely enthralled.

"I don't know. It's a secret. General Byron took the woman away. Salicor was so angry he turned over command of the army to Danielle of Trent. She was his spy." Lily scowled.

"What happened to the spy?" Stephan had never met Danielle. When the Valkyrie army had joined him to take Soniashi, they had been led by Ashlyn of Cairn.

"The general slaughtered Danielle in mortal combat at Archtown. Mother says it was glorious." The little girl beamed with enthusiasm making gestures to illustrate the story.

"Why didn't the general stay with the prince?" He wished Valerie had not gone to the mountains.

"That's a sad tale. General Byron sent her to help the woman." Lily nodded solemnly.

"Who is this slave woman you speak of? Do you know her name?" Why hadn't he been informed of the significance of any of this?

"Stone. She is the Woman of the Stone." Lily met his gaze.

Emotion hit him hard in the chest. Emerald had been in Frenland? She had known Valerie and Byron? That explained why the twin generals had turned against their Uncle Salicor.

"Did you ever see the Woman of the Stone?" He hoped Lily had more to tell.

"No, but mother did. The woman has red hair." Lily pumped her eyebrows with a twinkle in her eyes.

"What is the significance?" He couldn't fathom the look.

"Intercourse." Lily had lowered her voice.

Stephan choked a bit because nearly everyone in the south had red hair and it did not mean anything inappropriate. "Really? I wasn't aware that people in Frenland had red hair."

"Of course not. It isn't natural. Only highly skilled trollops dye their hair red. Anyway, the woman is worth twenty gold pieces. At least that's what Prince Byron paid the general for her." Lily looked sad. "Salicor was so angry the general hadn't given the woman to him that he tortured her and took away the army."

"Torture?" None of this information had come to light during his interviews with the people.

"The bad kind." A tear slid down each of Lily's cheeks.

Stephan's heart reared to a halt, stomped once, and then quivered. "Are you sure?"

Lily met his gaze with mournful eyes. "He did it all the time. She took it to keep the rest of us safe."

Stephan's lower lip trembled as his heart broke.

Chapter Two

Valerie of Bluebird Vale sought forgiveness that might incrementally wash clean her blood-stained soul. Guilt drove her to seek a peaceful end while mortality stalked her with each weakened heartbeat. Drawing breath had become an agonizing battle she no longer desired to fight.

She crossed the majestic Imperial City recently discovered inside the Sacred Mountain. She sought the tranquility of the Temple of the Creator. Bowing deeply at the shrine of the unnamed son, she paid respects to the dead.

The unmarked blade of a freshly forged copper sword was all that remained of Emerald's premature baby. Sorrow for lost children weighed on Valerie. She grieved for her daughter, Lily. The passing of years had not diminished the pain.

Strength fading, Valerie slipped through the silver doors of the temple. She removed her riding boots in a recessed area and stepped onto the polished granite flooring. A concentrated beam of focused sunlight entered the sanctuary through a crystal of grand proportions. The crystal shafted downward through the cavernous ceiling and extended upward to the highest peak of the Impenetrable Mountains. Within the light grew an ancient tree on a mound of earth surrounded by water.

Peace poured into Valerie's troubled heart.

Water flowed over the raised edge of the pool. It exited the temple to the right and the left. She knelt, stretched her arms forward, and bowed until her forehead touched the floor.

With her hands in the cool water, she symbolically washed away the filth of her former life. She closed her eyes and prayed for wisdom. The Creator spoke to her mind.

Restore my peace and forgiveness is yours.

She doubted her physical ability to make a quest. Mortality loomed like a light into which she wished to step. She gritted her teeth and rejected the resignation to quietly enter the beyond.

She could have been the queen of Frenland. Stephan reined in her stead. She was partly responsible for winning the throne for the young man. Yet, she hadn't realized she'd be giving up everything that bound her to this life when she did.

Why had she sacrificed so much? The feel of Stephan's innocent lips caressed her memory. Her entire body warmed.

The sensations were unbecoming of a woman poisoned by disease and hopelessly untouchable. She hardened her heart to protect it. Stephan had sworn out a warrant for her arrest. He must have overcome the feelings he had professed last summer.

An ache commenced inside her chest. If Stephan had learned about her obedience to Salicor, then his condemnation made sense. Even so, the tender feelings she had for the young king would not be denied. In her increasingly cold body, her connection with him radiated warmth to her soul.

"I thought I'd find you here, Ree." Her mother's voice held reverence for the sacred setting.

Valerie cupped her hands in the water and rinsed the tears from her face. Reverently, she backed away from the tree until she stood beside the royal counselor and sage, Sarialla.

"I have many regrets, Mother." Valerie dried her face on a cloth from a pocket.

Sarialla touched Valerie's shoulder. "If it wasn't for the fires of Scion, then the people of Frenland could forgive you."

Valerie stared at the tree. "Scion..."

There was nothing to be said about Scion that would not lead to tragedy if revealed. She had cultivated a daunting reputation by artfully embellishing and enhancing her exploits the night the village had burned. The purpose had been to create a haven for the jewels of the crown and shield them from Salicor's cruelty.

The stories had spread until they reached outlandish proportions. Terror was a double-edged sword and cut both ways. Valerie stood condemned to die by the lies that continued to spare innocent women and children from suffering. She would not betray them.

Sarialla stared at her daughter. "Won't you defend your actions? I heard the same testimony King Stephan did. Everything about Scion is hearsay. None of the witnesses saw how the fire started. Helen commands the king's ear and she believes the things she was told by the people of her village. I have my doubts because the accounts are not consistent."

Valerie waved off her mother. "Leave it alone. You cannot absolve me of responsibility for the things I've done in Salicor's service. I must live with the guilt."

Sarialla stood her ground. "My brother was an evil dictator. Many people fell under his influence during his time as the illegitimate king of Frenland. Most of them paid with their lives."

Valerie's heart broke to think of her brother Byron. Twins, their combined suffering had been doubled. Salicor had played on their sympathies for one another.

Sarialla swiped at her tears. "My only joy is that you survived his cruelty. I wish Byron had as well."

Valerie closed her eyes against the pain. "Do not speak his name. My feelings are too raw. He sent me to safety while he planned to murder our tormentor. If he had told me his intentions, then I would have helped him."

Sarialla embraced her. "You both did what you had to do."

Valerie accepted the comfort of her mother's embrace by wrapping her arms around her. "I didn't think you understood."

Sarialla stroked Valerie's hair. "Perhaps there is a way for you to return home."

Valerie shook her head and released her mother. "You know I'm not long for this life."

Sarialla took Valerie's hand. "If there were a cure for your illness, then you could come home."

Valerie's breath caught in her throat. Cured, she could be with Stephan. "Have you discovered treatments?"

Sarialla sighed and squeezed Valerie's hand. "I'm looking into the matter, but it remains to be seen. Do you harbor feelings for Stephan? I've heard rumors."

Valerie scoffed because as far as she knew her mother wasn't a mind reader. "Why would you think so? He's too young, and I'm too tainted."

Sarialla's expression grew pained, but she did not look away. "Stephan loves you."

Valerie's heart thumped against her chest as a reminder of her condition. "He condemned me to death. I think he's moved past his infatuation."

Sarialla chuckled. "He would abdicate the throne to follow you."

"Ridiculous. I don't believe it." Valerie slipped into her boots. "No one ever gives up power once they've taken it."

"You did." Sarialla sat on a bench along the wall to put on her boots. "Regardless, he's coming here for Emerald's coronation. It would be a good time to speak to him."

Valerie shook her head. "He's coming to honor Emerald. She is his foster sister. He's not coming for me."

Sarialla stood to meet Valerie's gaze. "I know his heart, Ree. I sat by his sickbed as he spoke in delirium without restraint. He has passionate feelings for you."

"Passionate?" Amusement caused Valerie's eyebrows to rise. "He's innocent. What does he know of passion?"

Sarialla smiled. "Oh, I'm not saying he hasn't tried to talk himself out of it. He has no intention of marrying. That goes double for a woman wanted for war crimes. He is working to transform the monarchy into a republic and cannot afford to continue his bloodline for fear the people will follow his heir. Nevertheless, his heart always wins the argument." Sarialla touched her daughter's shoulder.

Valerie stared into her memory. She had shared a single night with the future king of Frenland. It was a completely innocent encounter...except for the kiss.

"I can't explain the connection between us." Valerie touched her lips.

"For all our sakes, I hope you do not covet the throne that would have been yours had things gone differently. I only say this because I want you to marry him." Sarialla's face expressed profound sincerity.

Valerie frowned as a means of hiding her hurt. "I pledged my Valkyrie Army to Stephan's cause. Isn't that enough? You know I cannot lay with him unless I pose him no threat." Physical proximity to Stephan would be an agonizing temptation if she remained diseased.

Sarialla nodded. "You could be together if there is a cure. You established a bond that cannot be refuted by supporting him with your army. Many on both sides of the debate continue to hope for your return. They will kill him without you by his side."

Valerie scoffed. "His supporters are eager for a blaze."

Sarialla's face pinched in concern. "You think they will burn you at the stake?"

"Rest easy, Mother. I will not be returning to Frenland. There is no hope. It's too late." The painful beating of the heart in her chest intensified with longing for things that could never come to pass.

"Perhaps the East Icers will support the union." A twinkle lit Sarialla's eyes.

Valerie blinked away her surprise. She shook her head in disgust at the thought of them as potential allies. "No. I will not play this game with you. I wish to die in peace."

Sarialla hugged her daughter fiercely. "I can't let you go."

Valerie succumbed to tender emotions. "I would have been a better ruler than you believe. I wish you understood that. Despite the circumstances involved in my disgrace, or perhaps because of them, I don't deserve to die by fire. If I return to Frenland, then they will burn me alive. Go back to Stephan. Save him if you can. But leave me be."

Sarialla took Valerie by the shoulders. "No, Ree. I will not leave you to suffer alone. Salicor coerced your actions by committing unspeakable crimes against you. I cannot rest until your honor is restored."

Valerie laughed as a dark expression of the torment she still suffered. "I'm not worth the effort. You must let me go because I haven't the strength to fight you."

Sarialla swiped great tears from her wrinkled cheeks. "If not for Scion, then you could have been exonerated."

Valerie faced the tree of the Creator, seeking the courage required for absolute honesty. "Scion isn't what you've been told."

Sarialla touched Valerie's face. Deep concern crinkled the crow's feet at the corners of her aged eyes. The old woman shook her head.

"Daughter, come with me to the imperial residence. Emerald will want to talk about her walk with Darrin. I saw them arguing in the statuary gardens." Sarialla walked toward the silver temple doors.

Valerie swallowed her grief at her mother's dismissal of the confession. She had not committed the atrocities that had occurred in Scion. However, despite her mother's earlier assertions to the contrary, it seemed she would rather believe her guilty.

Valerie allowed the mental image of Emerald and Darrin to absorb her attention. "He is immature. Arguments were bound to happen once they finally held a candid conversation." Valerie pushed open the temple doors.

Sarialla passed through. "He loves her. That is all that matters. It would be the same for you and Stephan."

Valerie met her mother's gaze, reassured by the surge of love and deep concern emanating from the woman who had given her life. "It's good to have you here. I wish you didn't have to return to Frenland with Stephan after the coronation."

Sarialla met her gaze. "I'm not going with him unless you do. I will never abandon you."

Valerie sighed. "Then let's hope I die before that becomes a problem."

Chapter Three

Valerie stepped out of the Temple to see the Imperial City gleam in the refracted evening sunlight that shone through the crystals in the dome of an enormous geode. The awe-inspiring proportions of the cavern were a marvel. Even so, she would have gladly forgone the privilege of living in the Sacred Mountain to return to everyone and everything she loved in Frenland.

"Ree, the sword is missing." Sarialla pointed at the shrine where the blade forged on Emerald's son's funeral pyre normally rested.

The sound of the palace gong drew both women's attention.

"That is the least of our concerns." Valerie pointed to the upper tunnel entrance where white-clad figures flooded into the stone city.

"The East Icers have come at last." Sarialla's wistful expression held hope.

"Mother, what have you done? They're horse killers." Fury laced fingers around Valerie's heart and squeezed out wrath.

She didn't wait for her mother's objections. This was a subject on which agreement was impossible. Anyone who murdered horses deserved to die.

From the sheath on her belt, Valerie drew the ancient sword of Dana the Stonehearted. She called upon the unnatural strength it offered. Energy surged from the hilt like twin vipers curling up her arm to sink fangs of power into her flesh. She sprinted across the city to meet the invading forces.

Clothed in funeral white, they resembled harbingers of death. She welcomed a glorious end. The warriors shed their shaggy white fur coverings to reveal loose-fitting white clothes. They drew their swords and met her halfway across the city in the granite statuary gardens.

She charged ahead and raised Dana's sword to strike down the leader. Her aged green blade met with his fresh copper weapon in an explosion of radiant light. Both wielders blasted backward. The man landed on his back-side. Valerie maintained a defensive stance, stunned, but uninjured.

The attackers kept their distance as they assisted the fallen man to rise.

"You wield the sword of the ancient queen." The man stared at the blade. "Who are you?"

"I am the avenger of the horses slaughtered by your people." Turmoil raged inside Valerie's chest as she warred with the unusually peaceful impulses coming from the sword.

The man scoffed, softening it with a genuine smile. "You are mistaken about my people. We do not murder your sacred beasts. You must be Valerie of Bluebird Vale. I am surprised the esteemed Royal Counselor Sarialla did not explain the truth to you."

The man waved at the others to continue infiltrating the city. They obeyed his hand command with swiftness. He sheathed his sword.

Valerie faced her mother. "Does he speak the truth?"

Sarialla's expression closed. "I cannot say."

"I will ask you again in private." Valerie sheathed Dana's sword in eagerness to remove her hand from its intrusive influence.

The man from the East Ice extended a hand. "You have nothing to fear from me, General Valerie. You saved the lives of my children and myself three years ago. I owe you a great debt."

Valerie accepted the handshake. "I had no idea you spoke the language of Frenland. I remember your face from the skirmish on the glacier. Tell me your name, sir." She had been compelled to kill her subcommander when bloodlust compelled the woman to disobey orders and pursue a group of loyalists onto the forbidden ice flow.

"I am Trelan of Litton on the Green Way. It is my pleasure to meet you."

Valerie nodded. "I nearly lost my life defending you four years ago. Will you return the favor now by sparing the lives of those I love?"

He bowed his head and led her toward the Imperial Palace. East Icers engaged a man in fierce combat at the foot of the steps. Darrin fought a dozen men with his inferior steel blade. It sparked and chipped with each blow.

"He is a friend of mine." Valerie resisted the urge to go to him.

"Then I will grant you his life." Trelan clapped his hands.

The East Icers took notice of his command and eased backward. Darrin continued to wield the damaged blade in a cavalier fashion. A heart-wrenching cry of anguish burst forth from his throat.

"Darrin of Wolfe Mountain where is your betrothed?" She spoke the mountain language so he would fully understand, fearing the worst had happened to Emerald.

"Valerie?" Darin eyed her standing with Trelan. "Have you betrayed me too?"

"No." She held his gaze. "What do you mean?"

He clenched his jaw as a bitterness darkened his features. "Emerald is a liar."

Valerie laughed with the irony of it. "You know her better than that. She is incapable of deceit."

His eyebrows raised before crashing downward as did the tip of his sword. "I will never forgive her."

The soldiers from the East Ice urged the defeated Darrin toward a gathering of people of the West Wind at the foot of the palace steps. A dozen soldiers from Frenland were sequestered off to the side. Everyone was surrounded by East Ice guards. Sarialla joined the blond-haired men.

Valerie scanned the crowd. Emerald was not in the mix. Anxiety clenched her middle to think that her friend may have been killed.

Trelan escorted Valerie up the stairs to stand beside the quartz statues of the ancient queen and her king. "How is it that you wield the sword meant for the Creator's child, General Valerie?"

Valerie did not understand the layers of implied meaning in the question. "The sword fell to me when I captured the Woman of the Stone on the plains of Frenland last summer. I know not why it chose me."

A surge of warmth emanated from the blade. It invited her to touch the hilt, but she had never liked being controlled. Trelan glanced at the weapon as if he also felt the radiating heat. He took a step away.

He faced the crowd with a somber expression.

Chapter Four

Rage caused Darrin's fists to shake. He stood by his mother at the bottom of the Imperial Palace steps. The East Icers' invasion had been the excuse he needed to die defending his people. He preferred that than confessing his act of treason regarding his broken oath to Emerald. The invaders had spared his life. Why?

Valerie.

What reason did they have to listen to her? Considering the recent hostilities between Frenland and the East Ice, he could think of no motivation. Sarialla and her small contingent of guards had been segregated from the people of the West Wind. Why was Valerie standing with the leader of the East Ice?

Darrin ground his teeth and scanned the crowd. Emerald was not among the captured and the conquerors. He refused to worry about her. However, habit proved a hard taskmaster and he caught himself looking a second time. He closed his eyes in frustration.

"Bring forth the enemies from the north." The East Ice leader spoke from the top of the palace steps beside the statues of the ancient queen and her king.

Gruff captors with stern expressions forced the people of Frenland forward to the bottom of the steps.

The leader surveyed the group. "State your names and affiliations."

Sarialla spoke for them in favorable terms. She gave her name and position as a royal counselor last of all.

"A message must be taken to King Stephan." The leader met Sarialla's gaze. "For your service as a messenger, Royal Counselor Sarialla, you shall be spared. The rest must die. If your king meets the terms, then peace will be restored. Otherwise, we remain at war."

Swordsmen moved in from all angles to take the lives of the Frenland soldiers. The efficiency stunned Darrin. Blood showered on everyone nearby. Sarialla's hands dripped with it. Her clothes were stained, but she did not flinch.

"Deliver this message." The leader handed a scroll to another who carried it to Sarialla.

The elderly woman received the parchment with a bow. "Commander Trelan, I will deliver the message to King Stephan."

Sarialla strode through the crowd in a swirl of cloak and skirt. She looked longingly at her daughter as she passed the steps with only a slight hesitation. A pair of East Ice guards escorted her in the direction of the stables in the lower passageway beneath the city.

"Bring forth the steward." Trelan's voice boomed.

Celeniurisa stepped forward with her head held high. Darrin's hand twitched for his sword. What if they killed her? He couldn't lose his mother.

Not wanting to provoke the East Ice invaders, but unable to do otherwise, he followed her without drawing his blade. All eyes tracked him as he ascended the staircase at her heels. He kept his head bowed, though his hand lay on the hilt of his sword.

"Steward, where is the Creator's child?" the man asked.

"I do not see the future queen among us, Commander." Celeniurisa boldly met the gaze of the man who had ordered the deaths of a dozen Frenland soldiers.

Trelan took a step toward her. "When did the Creator's child depart from this city and by what method?" He drew a sword and placed the point at the lady's neck.

Darrin drew his sword to defend his mother. The men on either side of him poised their blades to slay him. He lowered the tip.

"I'm unaware of Emerald Stone's departure. She was well and here in this city only moments ago. Many saw her walking with my son among the statuary." Celeniurisa faced Darrin. "Son, where is your betrothed?"

Darrin squared his shoulders and unclenched his jaw. "I have no answer, my lady, except to say that she and I are not to be wed. I have refused her." He lifted his chin, unashamed to have rejected the woman he had loved since he was twelve.

The surprise on his mother's face was absolute. "You are no son of mine." She flushed and faced away with a finality that hushed the crowd.

Shunned? The chilling implications echoed inside Darrin like a rock bouncing down a chasm. He glanced at Valerie in time to see her sun-bronzed northern features blanch. Her reaction implied censure. Mortification emblazoned his cheeks with heat.

The emissary addressed the other prisoners. "Has anyone an answer to the question?"

The chaperone who had escorted Emerald and Darrin on their walk in the statuary gardens stepped forward a half-step before collapsing to his hands and knees in a tremulous full-bodied bow.

Trelan eyed the man. "Speak."

"The future queen accepted the dissolution of the marriage agreement. She commanded that Darrin of Wolfe not be harmed. Then she declared her intention to return to Stone Castle in Danalan." The chaperone's voice quavered.

"So be it." Trelan met Darrin's gaze with blistering animosity. "Surrender your weapon, oath breaker. Descend these hallowed steps to take your place below."

Darrin sheathed the sword. He unfastened the belt, dropped it, and backed down the steps in humiliation. Emerald had commanded that his life be spared yet again. This time, his honor was in tatters. Whatever status he had, and it had never been much, was gone.

"Steward, take me to the Hall of Records." Trelan waved Darrin's mother toward the doors of the palace and held out his hand for Valerie.

To Darrin's surprise, she accepted it.

Chapter Five

Valerie took the hand Trelan offered because it was a sign of unity. She felt no loyalty to these invaders, but having an ally could mean the difference between life and death for those she loved in Frenland. Why had her mother sent for these killers?

Emerald had departed for Danalan. That left Valerie in a precarious position. With her mother sent north and the soldiers who had defended her dead, Valerie needed new allies for her people. The matriarchs of the West Wind had once ordered that Valerie be executed. Would they do so again? That left Trelan as her only possible advocate with any influence

"Speak your name, Steward." Trelan's tone softened.

"I am Celeniurisa of Wolfe Mountain." She inclined her head in deference.

"I am Post Commander Trelan of Litton. What will we find in the Hall of Records, Celeniurisa?"

She paled. "A shameful history. The ancient story of Queen Dana's disgrace was a lie fabricated by her enemies to discredit her. You will also learn that the current Matriarchal Council acted against the Creator's child. I regret to inform you that my objections were overruled and the foreigners' executions were ordered. I accept full responsibility."

The lady's admission shocked Valerie.

The party entered the hall to find a group of white-clad figures bent over tomes of ancient writing. Oil lamps brightened the room. The smell of smoke and dust threatened to make Valerie sneeze.

She stifled the impulse because she had no desire to break the tension in the air. It held Celeniurisa on a knife's edge. Since the execution order had been directed at Emerald and Valerie, she enjoyed the moment of retribution. Killing Emerald would have been nothing short of blasphemous.

Trelan left Valerie standing with Celeniurisa to join those studying the records. Valerie glanced at Darrin's mother. She stared at the expression of disgust on one researcher's face. The man waved Trelan over to the table. The two conferred over an enormous leather-bound volume with gold-edged pages.

"I made those entries. If these people worship Emerald as the Creator's child, then it will likely mean my death. Tell my son I'm..." Celeniurisa shook her head as tears clouded her blue eyes.

Was that remorse for turning her back on Darrin?

Valerie scrutinized the woman. "There are many things about this realm I do not understand. Unfortunately for you, it is easy to recognize betrayal when I see it."

The steward winced, then lifted her chin. "The future queen spared his life by decree. It is up to you to save his soul from the bitter consequences of his actions."

Valerie scowled. "What responsibility do I have? He is childish and in need of a thrashing. He's in love one moment and overtaken by hate the next. What woman could educate such a man?"

Celeniurisa's expression hinted at amusement. "He listens to you. Besides, it is because the future queen did not name her premature baby that Darrin has responded with such anger. You see, he loved the boy. Since Emerald's son was never honored with a name and given a blessing, Darrin believes she didn't love him. I've tried to soothe him, but he must have revealed his resentments to Emerald."

Valerie frowned as the implications rippled through her mind like a large stone dropped into a pond. "The baby's death nearly killed Emerald. Why can't Darrin forgive her for grieving according to her own culture? Would he rather die than overlook a perceived slight?"

Celeniurisa sighed. "I should have simply married them without the delay of a formal courtship. He needs to be bedded. That is the whole of his problem."

Valerie stifled a bawdy laugh. "I attempted to do just that last summer, but he would not be seduced. You're not suggesting I take him now?"

The lady looked sideways at Valerie. "Was this before you contracted crypt's disease?"

That set Valerie's teeth on edge because there was no way this woman should know about the illness. "You mean before the monster with crypt's disease took me against my will? Well, yes, it was. I'm sure you are aware that I have not bedded a man in this city. I did not suspect you knew why."

The torture she had endured at the hands of the sadistic and grotesquely disfigured man who had held her captive seared Valerie's mind. Darrin had saved her life against her wishes by cleaning her torn body and treating her festering wounds. She had not been grateful to live, not with the knowledge that she would die an even slower and more painful death in the end.

Celeniurisa touched Valerie's shoulder. "I did not realize the circumstances. Forgive me for misjudging you."

Valerie took a deep breath and shook her head once. "You are not far off in your condemnation. The things I've done could be called worse than defiling the dead. At least the dead do not suffer."

The lady looked pained. "How did you, an attentive nurse and talented baker, commit the atrocities attributed to you? I have trouble believing it after knowing you these past weeks."

The words touched Valerie deeply. "You are the first to suspect me of duplicity."

The lady's eyes twinkled and a flash of a smile graced her lips. "The most effective lies are those mingled with the truth. I have underestimated you, crown princess of Frenland."

Valerie had not been the crown princess since her uncle had disowned her last summer. The steward's use of the title caused Valerie to question her previous assumptions about the woman's information gathering abilities. Not even Emerald had realized the implications of Valerie's position in the former regime.

Sarialla knew of Valerie's fall from power, as did the soldiers from the north whose blood now soaked the stones at the foot of the palace steps. What else had the steward of the West Wind discovered? Considering what she had just revealed, perhaps the assassination attempt had simply been an aggressive form of diplomacy with Frenland's new king.

How badly did Stephan want her dead?

Chapter Six

The crowd of dark-haired mountain people stood in silence. Everyone waited for the steward to emerge from the palace. No one looked at Darrin. His skin crawled with them not looking. He forced himself to think about something else.

Silver moonlight shone through the crystals in the cavern above their heads, softly highlighting the polished stone surfaces of the Imperial City. Emerald would have enjoyed the exquisite beauty of this moment.

The realization further dampened Darrin's spirits with something akin to guilt. In all the weeks Emerald had been recovering, she had never seen outside the palace until today. He remembered her surprised expression when they walked through the doors and she realized they were in this ancient city.

The steward and her captor returned to the top of the stairs. Valerie stood shoulder to shoulder with him. Darrin chewed his bottom lip. Her solidarity with the stranger unnerved him.

Trelan called for the counsel of matriarchs to come forward. The stately women ascended the steps in a line. Celeniurisa avoided eye contact with them. They glared at her in hostile silence.

"Step backward as I call your name." Trelan read a list.

Two-thirds of the council complied.

Relief poured over Darrin when his mother's name was not called.

Trelan signaled, and the East Ice guards mercilessly slew the offending matriarchs.

The people of the West Wind cried out in shock and horror. Children wept as they struggled to reach their mother or grandmother. The guards that surrounded them held them back. It was too late. The women's blood cascaded the steps in a display of stomach-wrenching gore.

"Perhaps you wonder what they did to deserve their fate." Trelan distanced himself from the stain and strode to the far edge of the stairs. "They condemned the Creator's child to death. She is our hope and our future. In treacherous fear, these matriarchs did as their ancestors of old had done before them. But these things can never happen again." He clenched his jaw. "Do any of you stand in opposition to the Creator's child?"

Not even Darrin dared to speak against Emerald.

Chapter Seven

Stephan stood at the door of the Clarion Inn. A fresh blanket of snow greeted him as he stepped into the ankle-deep ground covering. He had slept well and enjoyed a breakfast of warm porridge and sausages.

Snow swirled from the housetops as the sky threatened more. Clad warmly, Stephan trudged toward the modest meeting house in the center of Cairn. He discovered several women clad in Valkyrie parade uniforms of red and black waiting inside. The women saluted. Two cages sat on the floor behind them. Each contained a bruised and battered man.

Stephan returned the salute. "You may speak freely."

The women glanced at each other.

The leader stepped forward. "My king, I am Sheriff Ashlyn of this village. These are my deputies. We enforce your laws and keep the peace in Cairn. Our citizens reported strangers walking into town last week and we questioned them. These men are two of the murderers you seek. I present them for your judgment." She bowed.

Stephan bowed his head to Ashlyn. "It's good to see you again, Commander." He glanced at the men. "How did you determine their identities?"

One of the deputies flushed crimson and ducked her head.

Sheriff Ashlyn stood a little straighter and met his gaze. "There is a witness to their atrocities."

"A victim?" Stephan dreaded the tale he would soon hear.

Emotion strained the sheriff's face. "Yes, sir."

Stephan nodded in grim understanding. "May I speak to the witness in private?"

Ashlyn glanced at the blushing deputy who gave a curt nod.

"Of course, sir." Ashlyn led the others out of the building.

Stephan regarded the young woman. "Please tell me your name."

"Deputy Joan of Cairn, sir." She bowed.

Stephan nodded. "Forgive me for asking you to relate to me something so personal. I know it must be difficult to speak of how you have been hurt. Tell me only what I need to know to execute these men."

The woman handed him notices of arrest issued from his court. "This is the first man and the other one the second."

"You can read?" he asked. Literacy was a rare skill in Frenland.

"Yes, sir. I'm a Valkyrie. The general honored all of us with an education." She bowed her head.

It surprised him that Valerie had taken the trouble to teach an army of slaves to read and write. No other master in Frenland had done the same. Byron certainly hadn't. But if the Valkyrie were this serviceable, then they could be employed in the new representative government.

He returned to the task at hand and looked at the first man. "Are you Cal of Orton?"

"No, sir. I've never been to Orton." The man held the bars of his cage.

Stephan faced the other man. "Are you Fener of Bluebird Vale?"

"I am. Everyone knows it. But I didn't do anything I wasn't ordered to do by my superiors. I'm a good soldier and I could serve you well, my king." The man bowed his balding head.

"Deputy, is the first man Cal of Orton?" Stephan spoke to her gently.

"Yes, sir. There can be no mistake. I was tasked as a recruit with carrying a message from General Valerie to King Salicor. These men attacked me on the road. They never served in the king's armies. They are robbers and rapists. I heard them refer to one another by name as I lay near death from my injuries. I must admit that their place of origin was not mentioned." The deputy did not look at the men.

"She lies, sir." The man reached his arm between the bars. "I've never hurt anyone. I'm from Scion. My name is Horton. I'm a cart maker. Please spare my life."

"Scion?" Stephan's lip curled in disdain. "Let's settle the matter." He strode to the door and opened it. "Sheriff, will you send for Commander Helen of Scion? I require her testimony. Please come in out of the cold."

The sheriff sent a deputy to fetch Helen. The rest of the women entered the meeting house. Everyone stood in awkward silence until Helen strode through the door in a swirl of snow.

"Sir, the weather is closing in. We must leave at once." Helen dusted herself off.

"Commander, do you know this man?" Stephan pointed toward the accused.

Helen brought a lantern from the wall to peer at the man. "No, sir."

"He says he is a cart maker from Scion named Horton." Stephan came to stand beside her.

Helen shook her head. "I saw Horton burn to death in the fire that destroyed my village. I attended his funeral. This man is a liar."

Stephan drew the ancient copper sword of King Krelor. Darrin had once carried this blade. It was the same weapon Byron had used to slay Salicor. It thrummed with power as Stephan thrust it between the bars. The pulse of the man's heart quivered to a stop.

Stephan removed the blade from Cal's chest. Fener cried out in panicked pleading. Stephan killed him anyway. The men's faces as they died filled Stephan's mind with grotesque emotions. Blood dripping from the blade, he stood trapped by his inner-darkness until Helen touched his shoulder. She drew him toward the light when she captured his gaze.

"We must ride, my king." Her voice was soothing.

"Give me a moment with the sheriff." He glanced at Ashlyn.

The other women in the room nodded and departed into the storm.

"Thank you for capturing these men. Your deputy is one of three victims who have testified of their guilt. Many more could not do so because they are dead. I hope Deputy Joan will rest easier now that these murderers are no longer a threat."

The sheriff nodded. "Thank you." Her eyes clouded with mist. "You are a just king."

"I deliver justice so that you can be merciful." He cleaned the blade with a cloth from his pocket and sheathed it. "Protect the children of this village. We need an untouched generation if we are to heal as a nation."

She nodded. "My cousin and his wife own the Clarion Inn. My daughter works there. Lily said you were kind to her. Thank you, sir."

Stephan met her gaze and his heart softened. "She is a good girl. You have done well in raising her." He thought that ended the conversation.

"She isn't mine." Ashlyn met his gaze.

He analyzed her expression. "The dimples... You don't have any."

"I am Lily's guardian and hardly old enough to be so. But I took over for another woman who had assumed the task before me. It is a secret. I'm telling you because I see goodness in you." Ashlyn turned away and shook her head. "I want to trust you. Yet, you have condemned to death the noblest woman I've ever met. If you truly seek justice, then there is something you must see."

The intensity of her gaze cut him to the core.

"Ashlyn, I have condemned no one who hasn't been proven to be the most heinous of offenders. You have my word. I judge according to the evidence and testimony." He had no stomach for the name he feared she'd give, especially after learning of the abuse Valerie had endured at Salicor's hand.

"What if the evidence and testimony are misleading? There are times when a reputation is the only defense one has against retribution. This is especially the case when merciful conduct is punished in unspeakable ways." Ashlyn's weather roughened features looked older than her youth should have allowed.

"Who are you referring to?" Stephan angered at the Sheriff's avoidance of candor because it frightened him that his judgment may have been in error.

Ashlyn's aged honey eyes met his gaze. "Someone who deserves to receive the mercy she has so often shown to others."

Stephan ran his hand through his close-cropped hair. "A name."

Ashlyn frowned. "Come with me and I'll give it to you."

Agape, he stared at her. "Alone, and in this weather? No."

Ashlyn shrugged it off. "I would never lead you to harm, sir. Not when the woman of whom I speak loves you." She strode toward the door of the meeting house and held it open.

He followed with his heart in his throat only to be met by Helen. He couldn't go. The horses were ready and the snowfall had intensified.

"I will return in the spring, Ashlyn. Take care of your charge." He mounted and led his forces toward Soniashi.

Chapter Eight

Morning light entered the kitchen through the glass-like stone panels of the ceiling. Valerie braided bread dough on a table in the center of the room. The oven burned hot enough to make even her cold body comfortable. It was part of her enjoyment of the occupation.

Allowing the dough to rise, she slid another loaf out of the oven. The aroma made her stomach growl with hunger. She didn't wait for it to cool. She cut it and slathered a slice with butter. The first bite made her moan in ecstasy.

Trelan entered the kitchen from the bakery's storefront. "I see there are other things than men that please you. Do you mind sharing?"

"Help yourself." She leaned against the counter and finished her breakfast.

Trelan cut a slice, buttered it, and took a large bite. "It's delicious, General."

"You may call me Valerie while in my kitchen." She continued working.

"There's enough dough here to feed everyone in the city. How early do you rise?" He looked under a cloth-covered bowl.

"I awaken before dawn. I'm the city's baker." She kneaded a ball of dough.

"I suggest you take on apprentices and teach them quickly. Royal Counselor Sarialla will have delivered the terms of peace to King Stephan within a few more days. If he returns with her as soon as possible, then there isn't much time." Trelan poked a lump of dough and smiled as it retook its shape.

"It's winter, Trelan. Snow may interfere with their ability to travel." She wished she knew what he was plotting.

"I'm sure King Stephan will see the wisdom of the bargain in time." Trelan looked confident.

A restless night of tossing and turning on her cot hadn't resolved Valerie's conflicted emotions about the people of the East Ice. However, she was eager to know if they had a cure for crypt's disease.

"My mother thought your people may have a cure for my illness." She was unsuccessful at sounding casual.

"You may visit with Doctor Blythe whenever you choose. I've been told you tend the horses in the stables below. Please instruct my people in their care. Allow them to perform the physical labor." He faced her direction gazing at her chest.

"Why?" Sweat dripped from her temples. She wiped it with the back of a flour-covered hand.

"Because you are wheezing with the efforts required in a kitchen. I can only imagine your state by the end of cleaning a single stall let alone a dozen more." He met her gaze.

"The men who owned those horses had been doing their part of the task." She shrugged. "You should try kneading bread. It isn't as easy as it looks."

He smiled as if she'd made a joke. "I wouldn't know where to begin doing what you do."

"I imagine your interests lay elsewhere." She rotated one loaf out of the oven and slid another inside.

"My talents run in a different direction. I served in a far-flung outpost in my younger years and worked my way up to the rank of commander. I have political ties on my mother's side of the family. My education and language abilities are part of the reason I'm leading this expedition." His eyes saddened. "I'm doing what must be done."

"Are you saying that executing dozens of people out of hand was not your idea?" She placed smaller balls of dough into baking pans to make rolls.

"The parliament determined that all people from Frenland should be executed for unlawful trespass. I petitioned the empress to vie for an exception to be made for you and your mother. Three members of Parliament traveled with me. They are the ones who researched the documentation and put forth the names of the matriarchs who were to be executed." He sliced another piece of bread, drizzled it with honey, and stared at it instead of eating.

She didn't seek his gaze. "You have earned a dark reputation with your work here." Experience had taught her where that path led.

He nodded solemnly. "I do not delight in death, nor do my people, Valerie."

Chapter Nine

The heat of embarrassment climbed to throb in Darrin's face with each reminder that his mother had disowned him. Without her protection, he no longer had any status among his people. Having no other option, he did whatever he was told.

The East Icers honored Emerald's wishes and left him alone. However, they didn't seem to care one way or the other what became of him. Furthermore, none of his people had status in their society. That left them vulnerable, but none as much as Darrin.

The city had been searched for weapons and the people cordoned off in a crowded section of residences. Assignments were given for menial labor. East Ice overseers made sure the work was done.

Darrin marched with a dozen men and women to the mushroom farms. He picked sacks of mushrooms all morning and carried them to dry in direct sunlight outside the mountain's upper entrance. He carried buckets into the dark caves to water the fungus all afternoon.

The overseers announced it was time for the evening meal. He trudged along a rough trail in a dark cavern to enter the shining city. The whispers of several women caught his attention. Their glances in his direction didn't bode well.

He hurried toward the kitchens in hopes of a loaf of bread and a glimpse of Valerie. One of the whispering women followed him. Something about the way she leered made him worry she might claim him as a husband. Any unmarried woman could do so. They no longer needed to ask for permission now that his mother had disowned him.

In his haste to escape from the woman pursuing him, he ran smack into someone. "I'm sorry." He bowed and backed away.

The woman he'd collided with caught him by the shoulder in a firm grip. "I think you owe me more than an apology."

"I meant no disrespect." He tried to run.

She dragged him into a narrow alley away from the busy street. The woman who had been following him watched the situation. But she didn't pursue them.

"Do you remember me?" the aggressive woman asked.

"You are one of my mother's guards." He bowed his head to his chest. "You escorted me up the mountain after I was wounded in the final battle in Danalan."

"My name is Kalia. I mentioned to you then that I needed a husband." She clutched his crotch. "Are you intact?" Her voice remained casual.

He was so shocked by her actions that he knocked her backward. She came at him with a knife and held it to his throat. He had no weapon.

"I won't hesitate to kill you." She stepped forward to press him to the wall. "No one will complain. You have no advocate. But if you please me," she pulled his belt until it came loose, "then I will claim you." She slid her hand inside his pants to fondle him but pulled away quickly. "You're filthy." She took a half-step away but kept the blade at his neck. "Go bathe."

Darrin's hands trembled as he hitched up his dusty pants and fastened his belt. He had no legal recourse since she planned to take him as a husband. He stumbled as his body went numb.

He headed toward his quarters to retrieve a change of clothes. Kalia shook her head and waved him toward the hot springs at the far edge of the city. The sunset faded in the quartz crystals overhead as the lamplighters performed their task.

"Don't take long." She followed him with a lecherous gaze as he approached the sulfurous smelling hot springs.

He went behind a stone wall and stripped off his filthy clothes in privacy. A waterfall lay at the edge of the pool and provided a convenient place to wash. Dirt continued to come out of his hair and he scrubbed more ferociously. How could this be happening?

"Come out now." Kalia's voice boomed through the cavern.

Darrin slowly emerged from the water. He could run deeper into the cave, but there was no escape. He had no choice.

Even if this was to be his fate, he didn't regret rejecting Emerald. He hated her for what she had done. Furthermore, his life would be no different now than it would have been when he was twelve. It was as if he had never served in the office of royal shadow.

He squared his shoulders. At least this way he would be a father. Kalia wasn't ugly...outwardly. He shuddered.

"Don't make me cut you," she said.

Her voice sent a chill along Darrin's spine. He grabbed a drying cloth and wrapped it around his waist. Several men watched him as he gathered his dignity and walked out to meet her. He was unprepared for the audience who awaited him.

"Let's see it." Kalia waved her hand toward his crotch.

Darrin's eyes went wide and his face drained of blood. "What?"

Five women laughed under their breath to one another, but none took their eyes off him. Kalia pulled the cloth away. He managed to keep ahold of it and bring it back to cover himself, but not before being exposed.

"Drop it." Kalia's voice held a threat.

She fingered the hilt of the knife tucked in her waistband where she had concealed it. All other weapons had been confiscated by the East Icers. It was forbidden to bear arms.

Darrin wished he could report her. He hoped the penalty would be high, but there were no East Icers here. Calling for them would not bring them quickly enough to avoid death. So, he let go of the cloth.

The women ogled him. One brought a candle lantern closer to further illuminate his body. Several of the women frowned.

"I was hoping he would be," a young woman cocked her head, "bigger."

Kalia laughed. "You have never had a husband. Let me show you how to encourage a man." She placed the flat of her knife on Darrin's belly and knelt before him. "Don't move."

He trembled. Would she cut him as she had threatened? He didn't dare watch, but he couldn't look away.

Kalia captured him with her mouth. He pulled away. She pinned him against the wall. The knife drew blood until he held still.

She took him again. The unwelcome sensations sickened him. Faint from the long day's work, his knees trembled. Shame flooded over him as her actions aroused him in front of the other women.

"What goes on here?"

Valerie's voice caused the crowd to part. She gasped at the sight of him. Kalia released him and stood to face her.

"I plan on claiming this man as a husband." Kalia paled.

"No, Kalia. You will not." Valerie's tone held a dangerous edge.

"You have no right to stop me." Kalia glared.

"I have other rights." Valerie's voice held terrible power as her hand came to rest on the hilt of Dana's sword.

Darrin fled into the hot spring cavern.

Chapter Ten

Darrin washed Kalia's saliva off of his body in the hot spring pool until he felt raw. His mind shied away from thoughts of what had just happened. It could not have happened.

He trembled all over and thought of drowning. He contemplated the nearby rocks. If he hit his head, then he would slip beneath the surface never to rise again.

He swam into the depths of the pool. He punched the lava rock at the far side. Hot blood oozed from the ragged wounds on his knuckles.

Emerald had caused this. She had betrayed him. He wished she were dead. He trembled with hatred for her until he realized that she had never done anything remotely as horrifying as Kalia.

"Darrin?" Valerie's voice echoed in the cavern, but she wasn't close yet.

He jumped from the pool and stumbled in the pitch darkness to the end of the cavern. He felt around for a way out and discovered a narrow vertical opening in the volcanic rock. He slid into the crevice.

Light angled through the gap. Valerie appeared with a lantern. He shielded his body from her view without touching himself.

Darrin held Valerie's gaze for a long time as he listened to the sound of water. She didn't make a move. Of all the people in the city who might have happened upon the situation with Kalia, why did it have to be her?

"How did you find me?" He shivered despite the warmth of the hot springs cavern.

"Wet footprints." She gazed at him through the crevice.

"My mother has disowned me." Emotion choked him.

Her expression grew dark. "And this leaves you vulnerable to women like that?"

He ground his teeth to quash the bitterness threatening to spill forth from his insides. "Kalia needs a daughter to lead her sons if she is to continue her house."

Valerie extended a drying cloth toward him. He eyed it but didn't want to expose himself to take it. She looked away.

He grabbed the cloth and wrapped it around his waist, scraping his forearm on the rock in the tight space.

Silence prevailed until Valerie spoke a tender question. "Why would you reject Emerald?"

Resentment clouded his judgment. "She betrayed me. I hate her."

Valerie didn't say anything at all. In the end, she simply sighed.

He thought she would say something. He thought she would argue with him. He wanted to fight. His anger faded as the silence persisted. He took a deep breath and leaned against the crevice wall. His eyes closed as fatigue overcame him.

"You need to rest. I'll keep you safe."

He trembled. "If you touch me...I might kill you."

"I won't. Just talk to me." She met his gaze.

Darkness had entered his soul and he needed to expel it. He rubbed his face with his hands. He didn't know what to say as his mind spun with thoughts.

"Have you ever put your mouth on a man's...?" His voice choked off.

His entire body flushed. How could he have asked her that? Intelligent, she would guess at his full meaning.

"Not by choice."

He could hear the faded horror in her voice. It spoke of past trauma. His trauma remained raw and he didn't know what to think of her answer.

"Who was he?"

"I said it wasn't by choice." Her voice held an angry edge.

"Why would a man force you to do that? What did he...? I mean, why would he want you to do it?" His voice cracked.

"Sadistic pleasure." She expectorated on the cavern floor. "He seemed to enjoy it."

"Why didn't you bite him?" Darrin felt stupid asking.

"He held my life in his hands. He promised to save me if I did what he wanted. I wasn't ready to die."

"Was it your uncle?" Darrin had long suspected the former king of Frenland was capable of such things.

"No."

"What was the man's name?"

"I don't know the demented monster's name. He was simply a diseased wanderer capitalizing on my weakness. Did you ask his name before you ran him through?" She slammed the rock near the crevice with the palm of her hand.

Darrin remembered the grotesquely disfigured face of the man he had slain for raping Valerie. His feelings hardened even further. He had never regretted killing that man.

An odd trickle of mania bubbled inside him. He almost laughed. With a shudder, he pushed the feeling away.

He wouldn't go mad. He'd seen that happen to someone before. Emerald had been pushed beyond her ability to endure. She had been lost. Valerie had found her...had saved her.

"I need help." His entire body trembled and his voice shook.

"Eat this." She rummaged in a knapsack and handed him a roll. "Now tell me what you need."

He chewed the bread and thought for a while. "I need a wife who won't rape me."

"Emerald raped you?"

"No!" He struggled to swallow the bite in his mouth. "Not Emerald. You saw what Kalia did. She forced me to..." He shifted and squirmed as he found the words. "I allowed her to suckle my..." He flushed wishing the darkness would cover his shame. The fact that Kalia had been armed didn't alleviate his humiliation. "I'm a warrior. I should not have permitted her to do it in front of all those single women. I tried not to let it happen, but her ministrations aroused me." He faced away and wept great raucous sobs of mortification.

Any other woman might have said the wrong thing. Most women would have tried to touch him. Some women might have laughed.

"I will take you under my protection."

Darrin fell silent, stunned by her declaration. Tears wet his face. He wiped them away. He had been inconsolable a moment ago. Now he wondered if this was the answer he sought.

Valerie had offered to marry him. Would that keep him safe? She had harbored feelings for him at one point. Would she exploit his weakness?

He shook his head. He had no good options. The one thing he knew about Valerie was that she had honor. She had been hurt before and would understand his needs. He trusted her not to force him to do anything he didn't want.

"You would do that for me?" It was hard to control the emotion in his voice.

"I believe your custom states that I merely need to claim you. So, if you consent, I will keep you safely out of other women's reach." Valerie's voice stayed calm almost to the point of dispassion.

"What are you hiding?" He knew her too well not to recognize her tactic of concealing her feelings.

"This is permanent. There's no changing our minds. If I die, then you are treated as property and subject to my dying wishes. I can give you to anyone I please."

"Can I trust you?" He folded his arms across his chest.

She held his gaze. "Do you trust me?"

He didn't want to think about the problem, but it plagued his mind. He craved a modesty he might never feel again. One thing was for sure, he could not endure such vulnerability any longer.

The words he needed to say didn't come easily. "Claim me, Valerie."

"Darrin of Wolfe, I claim you and offer you my protection."

Her voice held a heavy solemnity that sank deep into his chest. She had concealed a personal cost from him. He sensed her loss because he felt it too. Emerald was forever out of his reach now. He ground his teeth, hating her. This was for the best.

Chapter Eleven

Valerie led Darrin out of the hot spring cave by lantern light. His dirty clothing was not where he had abandoned it. They walked through the sleepy streets of the city toward his dwelling. A shadowy figure moved to meet them. Valerie drew her sword.

"You are too late, Kalia. Darrin is under my protection." She adjusted her stance to guard him as the woman walked closer.

"You have claimed him?" The voice of the woman belonged to Steward Celeniurisa.

"Not in the way you think, but yes. He belongs to me now and I can give him to whomever I choose." Valerie's only intention was to preserve him for Emerald.

Celeniurisa studied her with subtle scrutiny. "There is no way to undo this. Are you certain you wish for me to record your claim?"

Something about the way she said it raised the hairs on the back of Valerie's neck. "Yes, but only because you will not take him back."

"I cannot." The lady looked at Darrin with mournful eyes.

"Darrin, what would you have me do?" Valerie felt trapped.

"Honor your promise." His voice reverberated like a growl.

She met his gaze. "I will."

"Then I will record it and declare it for all to know of your commitment." The lady walked toward the Imperial Palace.

Darrin stalked toward his living quarters. Valerie followed him up the steps to a second-story room. He ducked through a curtain to enter a bedchamber. She held the curtain open and extended the lantern so he could see to find his clothes.

Slashed canvas and a splintered wooden frame littered the floor. Enough of the image remained for her to be sure he had destroyed his latest painting of Emerald. The crocks that held his paints were smashed. Color splashed the stone walls and floor. When had he done this? After the argument with Emerald in the statuary garden?

Valerie raised her gaze. His eyes held a desperate kind of anguish. She had felt as he must on many occasions as a child.

"I need you to drive her out of my mind." Tension locked his musculature in well-defined splendor as he loosened the towel and parted it for her to see his body.

Valerie glanced behind her, but no one was there to observe the display. "Whom should I banish from your mind, Kalia, or Emerald?"

He looked taken aback and deeply pained by his recent trauma. "Both. I am tormented."

Valerie had waited a long time for a good look at him. He was a modest man. Even though they had lived close to one another for some time, he had never permitted her so much as a glimpse. As things stood, however, it felt completely wrong. She stepped inside the room and allowed the curtain to fall closed behind her. It afforded some privacy. He was uncut. Perfect.

"I have often wondered..." She met his gaze. "I've never seen a man who is..." she switched to the language of Frenland, "uncircumcised."

"I don't know that word." He grabbed a pair of trousers and slipped into them.

"My uncle required the men of Frenland to prove their dedication to him by having their foreskin cut away. It's called circumcision and is practiced on the steps of the far north by the nomads." She considered how much she should tell Darrin about female circumcision.

He'd seen her body when he'd treated her wounds last summer. That was still a sore point with her. She hadn't consented. He'd never said anything about it. He probably didn't understand what he'd witnessed because of his innocence.

He frowned. "You don't want me because I'm not mutilated?"

Surprised caused laughter bubble from her. "You want me to take you right here? Right now?" She sobered. "I'm sure you do not. I know you better than that. Why would you offer yourself to me?"

He held a somewhat paint-stained tunic in his hands. "I trust you to be generous." He faced away and pulled on the long-sleeved tunic.

She took in a breath and let it out slowly. "I've nursed a few fantasies about you, Shadow, but you are not mine. Even if you are exquisite."

He met her gaze. "I'm not Emerald's shadow anymore. She means nothing to me."

The declaration crushed Valerie with sorrow for her friend. "So be it."

Darrin found socks and boots. She descended the steps. He trailed after her.

She led him to the bakery. The cot in the corner of the kitchen called to her. The bath she had sought earlier tonight would have to wait for the morrow.

Darrin would have to wait forever.

Chapter Twelve

A harsh knock sounded against the kitchen door and it burst inward to crash against the wall. Valerie startled awake in her cot. Darrin leaped from the floor beside her with his fists raised.

Trelan carried a lamp and entered the room. "Deceiver."

Valerie had slept in her clothes. She had no qualms about rising just an inability to do so. Rest had not come easily and she'd had too little of it. Why was Trelan calling her out?

"What do you mean?" She couldn't focus her eyes.

"You married this man." Trelan shoved Darrin.

"No. I did not. You don't understand the culture of the West Wind. Darrin needs a protector. That's all I've agreed to." She yawned and wished Trelan would go away so she could sleep.

Trelan scoffed. "General, it is you who does not understand. Celeniurisa was in the process of recording your claim. I stopped her before she affixed the official seal. She has been stripped of authority. Regardless, she says you are married."

Valerie met Darrin's gaze in disbelief. "Is this true?"

He looked surprised. "You claimed me."

"And that is what it entails?" Her voice climbed as her heart pounded in shock.

"Yes. I thought you knew." He puffed up his chest and frowned deeply.

Her anger surged to meet her fear at the unforeseen turn of events. "Trelan, close that door and leave me to him. He owes me an indecent bedding."

She stood and walked away from both men. Why had Darrin asked this of her? Why had Celeniurisa been so eager to accept it?

Trelan cleared his throat. "You haven't consummated the union?"

"No, but I'm about to." Valerie hadn't been this angry in a while.

Darrin often had that effect on her. She charged at her would-be husband intending to knock him on his backside. He scrambled over the table. She pushed past Trelan in pursuit.

Trelan laughed. "Take him if you must. I don't care if the coward dies. But the marriage is absolved by decree of the representatives of Parliament."

Valerie breathed heavily and glared at Darrin. "He is still under my protection and soon to be beneath me in pleasurable ways. You may watch my technique if that sort of thing excites you."

Trelan chuckled and departed.

She listened to the sound of his footsteps as he retreated through the bakery's storefront. With him went all the light except the glow of the embers in the open oven.

"I thought you wanted me to be your husband." Darrin backed away and his body sagged against the wall. "I would never have shown myself to you outside the bonds of marriage."

She closed the distance between them with a growl and slammed the meat of her fist against his chest in frustration. "I never agreed to marry you. Do you understand me?"

Darrin clasped her elbows. "You have a choice."

She realized he was the only thing keeping her from falling to the floor. She couldn't catch her breath. Motes of light swam in her narrowing vision.

Darrin lifted her in his arms and laid her on her cot. "What's wrong? You seem unwell."

She barked a raspy laugh. "Leave me alone."

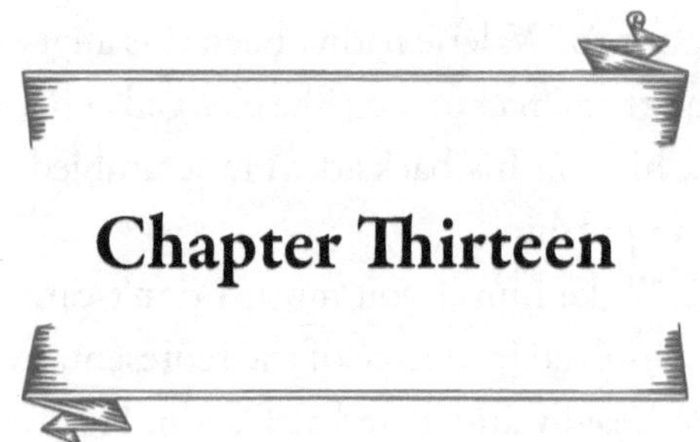

Chapter Thirteen

Darrin let Valerie rest until she awoke naturally. Her breathing had returned to normal while she slept. He hoped she would consent to see a physician about her health.

"You look worried." She rolled from her back onto her side.

He had sat on the floor beside the cot watching over her for so long he couldn't feel his legs. "Who can help you, Valerie?"

"Death will not be unwelcome." She closed her eyes and the dark circles under them stood out in stark contrast to her pale skin.

"I thought the same thing, but it isn't true. Don't let the sadness take you...not you." He leaned closer to her.

Her dark brown eyes opened and held him in her sorrow. Tears welled in his eyes to block the view. The wetness slipped down his face as he realized the depth of her pain and the need for release.

"My mother sent for the people of the East Ice in hopes of saving my life. Perhaps it is time to receive their gift." Valerie stirred from the cot.

"I will not leave you." He had never been a friend to her the way he could have been, always holding her at arm's length because his attraction to her had been inappropriate.

Darrin followed Valerie as she left the bakery and approached the guards. They patrolled the perimeter of the section granted for use by the people of the West Wind. They held their ground.

One man's eyebrow rose fractionally. "General, how may I help you?"

"I request a consultation with Doctor Blythe." Valerie inclined her head.

Darrin had no weapon. He wished he had a weapon even though he knew full well it would do him no good. He could not defend Valerie against these men and their curved copper swords.

"The man must stay." The guard turned.

The others parted so she could follow him.

"No. He comes with me."

Darrin's heartbeat was so loud he thought they would hear it. The angle of Valerie's chin and the lack of tension in her body spoke of her years of leadership. She must expect to be obeyed. He envied her confidence.

The man looked her in the eyes and nodded. Valerie strode after him. Darrin tried to match her dignified pace.

The guard led them up the steps of the palace. They walked past the statues of the ancient Queen Dana and King Krelor. They passed through the open doors of the great hall to enter the Imperial Hall.

Chapter Fourteen

Darrin watched the guard pulled a silken cord hanging near a wall in the Imperial Hall.

No sound occurred, but the man took an attentive stance facing the opposite entrance. Those doors led to the imperial residence and the many rooms there. Darrin stood straighter.

The doors swept open and Trelan walked into the hall. He scrutinized Valerie.

"It is good you are seeking medical attention, General." Trelan frowned at Darrin.

"She says this unfaithful dog is with her." The guard bowed and departed.

Trelan's eyebrow arched. "Why is he still with you, General?"

Trelan walked across the marble floor with its inlaid mosaic of a tree. He stopped in front of the dais that held the imperial throne. Large cushions had been placed there.

"I claimed him for a reason. Darrin needs protection because his mother has disowned him." She followed Trelan to the cushions. "The laws and traditions of the people of the West Wind left him at the mercies of a culture bereft of the quality...at least concerning men and monarchs."

Trelan seated himself and indicated that Valerie and Darrin should follow suit. "He was to marry the Creator's child. I understand that he rejected her and broke the oath. Why would you help such a man?" One side of Trelan's mouth lifted in a momentary smile. "At least not in such a binding way."

Darrin wondered just how much Trelan knew about Valerie's sexual proclivities. He seemed to know her all too well. Darrin's surprise must have shown on his face.

Trelan bowed to Valerie in an apologetic gesture. "Forgive me if I was crude."

Valerie's emotionless expression did not alter. "My reputation belies my motivation in this instance. I misled you earlier because I was angry. I have not lain with Darrin and have no plans to do so.

"Emerald Stone is my friend. I have no intention of betraying her. She loves Darrin deeply and did not reject him. She simply respected his right to reject her. I know she would want him protected. I have done what I must to preserve him for her."

The thought chilled Darrin. His resentment for Emerald deepened. He hadn't suspected Valerie had taken him under her protection out of a sense of obligation to her friend. His hands curled into fists and he concealed them in the pillow. He clenched his jaw to keep from voicing his objection to being preserved for a woman he hated.

"The chaperone stated the Creator's child's wish that Darrin not be harmed. Who disobeyed her?" The dark line of Trelan's eyebrows crashed together.

Valerie frowned. "Emotional harm to a man is not often taken into consideration among the women of the West Wind. I doubt their callous infringement on his sensibilities, nor the violation of him in intimate ways, was thought to be against Emerald's wishes. It is more likely that Emerald was not considered to be a threat since she is not present.

"She never threatened anyone when she resided here. Emerald does not seek power, nor authority, only justice tempered by patience. Her capacity for mercy is unlike anyone I have ever met." Valerie held Trelan's gaze and did not relax into informal postures and tones.

Darrin held his tongue and avoided looking at either of them. He had trouble holding still. The desire to pulverize something warred within his chest like two quarreling wolves snapping at one another. He could not overcome his anger toward Emerald and he could not forgive Kalia.

He had hoped Valerie respected him. She had not indicated it here. His behavior wasn't something he felt prepared to evaluate so coldly. He couldn't reconcile his feelings with Emerald's actions. He still didn't understand her rejection of her innocent son. He couldn't comprehend her refusal to claim, name, honor, and love him.

Darrin had wanted Emerald to grant him similar things. His most tender hope had been to be cherished by her. But now his disappointment and dis-illusionment made his stomach twist with resentment.

He could not forgive Emerald, nor could he go back to her. He would try to be with Valerie. He evaluated his wife's guarded expression for clues regarding her true feelings.

Trelan sat in an attitude of deep contemplation. "I have considered the evils of the laws and culture of the West Wind. However, I had not imagined the kind of abuse I have discovered here."

Trelan looked up. "Abuse happens in every culture, of course. The laws of my people as well as our philosophies and traditions protect the victims and punish the perpetrators." Trelan faced Darrin and put a hand on his knee. "I'm sorry for what happened to you. Name your attackers and I will have them brought to justice."

Darrin's brows raised in surprise. He hadn't thought of retaliation. Bitterness made him speak her name.

"Kalia."

Trelan nodded and withdrew his hand. "There is no place among my people for such individuals. The others will learn from swift justice that sexual violence and intimidation are against our laws. We do not tolerate crimes of this nature. I understand these women take boys into their beds when they are only twelve years old." Trelan shook his head with an expression of deep disgust.

"It will not be tolerated. Such thinking will not be permitted to corrupt my people. I fear many women will perish and many years will pass before our two peoples can become one." He frowned. "I had wished it could be different." He looked at Valerie. "I see now why the Creator's child left this place."

Valerie took Darrin's hand. "I believe Steward Celeniurisa is different in some regards. She may prove an ally in your efforts to enlighten these people and bury their detrimental traditions. They are not all bad, nor are they without redeeming qualities."

Valerie sat back a little. "My experience under Salicor's rule was worse. I hope King Stephan's laws will align with his foster sister, Emerald's. If so, then they will bring the Creator's peace to their lands. I supported Stephan for this reason. My mother has informed me that great strides have been made in the direction of freedom."

Valerie frowned. "I am wanted for war crimes by Stephan's new government." She met Trelan's gaze. "I am guilty of most of the accusations, but not all. Times were different before Stephan became king. I had special...motivation to obey my uncle's commands." Valerie's eyes held the ghosts of horrors within them.

Darrin set his jaw and took her chilly hand. He met Trelan's gaze as a second witness of Valerie's traumatic past. Perhaps it did not fully absolve her of guilt. But he wanted Trelan to understand that her actions over the past few moons had redeemed her in his estimation.

Trelan's frown deepened as did the lines of sadness around his eyes. "What exactly could motivate you to behave dishonorably, General? My knowledge of you is a personal one. You saved me and my children from your soldiers on the ice flow. I owe you my thanks."

Valerie nodded. "You owe me nothing. I acted to prevent a war with your people. I am sorry for the loss of your wife."

Trelan bowed his head and closed his eyes. "Four years has not lessened my sorrow, nor has it diminished my gratitude, General. I will not forget my debt."

"Sparing my mother is repayment enough." Valerie relaxed somewhat on her cushion.

"Your mother's epistles over the years painted a poor picture of you. Celeniurisa's answers to my questions elevated my estimation of your character." Trelan cleared his throat. "My only other knowledge of you is from long-distance observations. Your scarcely secluded acts of intimate conquest with random men baffled me. Other acts led me to believe you to be ruthlessly cruel. I assume your battlefield conduct was ordered by Salicor. Why would you obey him?"

Valerie blinked. Her whole body quaked. She turned a tortured gaze on Darrin, stood, and drew him to stand beside her.

"Will you help me show him?" Her voice trembled.

Darrin's sympathy solidified into resolve. Valerie unbuckled her belt and pulled her shirttail out of her pants. She faced away from Trelan. Darrin lifted the shirt to reveal the scars on her back and lowered her trousers on the right side to reveal the brand on her buttock.

Trelan's intake of breath indicated that his long-distance observations had not uncovered the secrets these marks revealed. Darrin could see that he still did not fully understand the implications. He covered Valerie.

"Salicor killed Sarialla's husband and kidnapped her children. The twins were five years old when he sodomized them. The marks on Valerie's back tally the violence. He held them bound by fear and lies. Emerald freed them with the truth...and her compassion for their suffering."

Valerie remained facing away from Darrin and Trelan.

Trelan stood and walked in front of Valerie to embrace her. "I had no idea your uncle had such a savage nature. Sarialla spoke somewhat of it in her epistles. But I doubted the veracity of her words."

Trelan released Valerie. "My people should have acted against this evil. We are skilled in defense but are not a warlike people. We have not engaged in a largescale conflict since the Fracture War four-hundred years ago."

Trelan frowned and paced the room. "I'm sorry we didn't stop Salicor. Sarialla asked for our help many times over the years. Unfortunately, we thought it was none of our business." He shook his head. "We were wrong."

Valerie tucked in her shirt and buckled her belt. "Why did you aid Stephan?"

Trelan stopped as his eyebrows shot up. "We did not aid him. He is our enemy. By impersonating us, he caused Salicor to send his armies onto the ice to destroy us. Sarialla informed us of Stephan's plans to bait them into conflict with us. We never left the ice until coming here."

Color climbed Valerie's neck. "You did not slaughter the great horses of my people?" She shook her head. "I don't believe it." She clenched her jaw before speaking. "If not you, then who ended two of the five sacred lines of the ancients?"

Trelan looked saddened. "I think you know the answer."

She swallowed. "All reports from the front indicated your involvement. Are you saying that Stephan ordered the murder of horses?" She shook her head as if she didn't want to believe it and could not face such an idea.

Her eyes filled with tears. Even so, her face remained taut with fury. She crumpled on a cushion and rubbed the tears from her face.

"What will you do to him?" she asked.

Trelan remained visibly moved and his posture open. "Parliament has not yet decided. I had hoped you would temper him...teach him his own culture...make him more acceptable to the people of Frenland. Sarialla fears he will be executed if the citizenry discovers his crime."

Darrin sensed something important. "Valerie, how do you know King Stephan?"

She glanced at Darrin. "I—" she avoided his gaze, "—I thought I loved him." She squared her shoulders. "I had not thought the boy I knew capable of this level of evil. To murder a horse is a sacrilege."

Darrin frowned deeply. Valerie loved Stephan? When had they ever met in such a personal way?

"How does the king feel about you, General?" Trelan asked.

Valerie glared at the man until her brows rose in curiosity. "How can his feelings for me be of service to your people?" Her brows drew together momentarily.

Trelan met her gaze. "Your mother wants you to marry him. Our people have agreed to the idea in a hope that you will stabilize the fledgling government and unify the factions within the populace. The message your mother carries states the conditions of peace as a union between the king and the former crown princess."

Valerie's jaw hung open. "I do not consent." She grasped two fistfuls of her blond hair. "That sniveling child ordered the deaths of Halcornin, Shilblatha, Mistorthal, and so many more. I cannot forgive him." She shook her head slowly and stared into nothing.

Trelan frowned. "I'm sorry that Stephan's actions grieve you, but I must know the king's feelings toward you."

Valerie frowned. "He declared himself to be in love with me. I can't understand why he would say anything like what he did. All I know is that I felt a deep connection with him." She wouldn't meet Darrin's gaze. "No one has ever connected with my soul the way he did."

Darrin stood straighter. He hadn't suspected Valerie capable of such intense romantic inclinations. He didn't regret her rescuing him from Kalia, but he didn't want to hold her to a marriage she didn't want.

"I don't know what laws to follow." Darrin glanced at Trelan and then stared at Valerie. "I accepted your protection because I needed it. I never considered that you loved someone else. I thought you had feelings for me. I hoped our feelings for each other would mature." His face flushed with heat.

"I respect you, Valerie. I trust you." He focused on her intensely. "I will not be responsible for keeping you from the man you love."

Valerie laughed and shook her head as she rose from the cushion. She strode toward him with a smile on her lips. "Have no fear." She met his gaze. "I'm not long for this world." She patted her chest right over her heart. "The man you killed for me last summer made me unfit for...romance."

She glanced at Trelan. "I carry a deadly disease. It has gone to my heart. I'm not sure how long I have left, but..." she faced Darrin, "I will not share certain intimacies with any man. That is how crypt's disease spreads." She held Darrin's gaze as if seeking his reaction to the news.

Darrin's breath caught in his chest. He had killed the grotesque man that had held Valerie captive to his perversions. He had suspected disease and watched for signs in her, but had detected none.

Darrin took Valerie's hand. "I had no idea you were ill. There is no known cure. I'm sorry. Crypt's disease was eradicated from among my people, but I've read about it. Not all of my time in the wilderness protecting Emerald was spent painting. My mother is the greatest physician of our people. Have you asked her for help?"

"General," Trelan drew both of their attention, "I believe we have a cure." He smiled a sorrowful expression. "It cannot restore the deterioration that has already taken place, but it can prevent further damage. You will be a threat to no one after you receive an injection of medicine."

Valerie blinked and gave her head a quick shake. "I had not dared to hope for such a possibility." She looked at Darrin. "I don't regret my decision to help you."

"You don't have to honor your commitment." Darrin wanted to be clear. "You love Stephan and should be with him."

Valerie's gaze darkened with anger. "I don't know what the connection between Stephan and I means. All I know are the facts. He is the king. I'm a war criminal condemned to execution. He signed the order. The tender feelings he declared last summer have ended."

Darrin heard her heartbreak and did not wish to add to her sorrow. "I know Stephan well enough to be sure that his loyalties do not shift easily. These people will protect me. You don't need to keep me safe. We are married, but I will not hold you to it. You have the right to put me away. That will allow you to marry Stephan."

Valerie's jaw gaped slightly. "You wanted me to be your wife?"

He relaxed enough to smile in a bashful sort of way as he avoided her brown-eyed gaze. "We have a history."

Valerie blushed.

Darrin stared. She was lovely.

She tugged his tunic and drew him closer. "You think we have a future then? Perhaps a tumble is finally in order." She stroked his midsection with the back of a finger.

Darrin considered her words and dismissed her flirtation. He sensed it was her way of making him uncomfortable enough to reject her. She seemed to believe that would be the best course of action.

The choice proved more difficult than he first thought. She could be his wife fully after she received the cure. He had expected that eventuality when she had accepted him. He trusted her ability to overcome his newly formed insecurities regarding intimacy.

He would never go back to Emerald. His hatred of her actions prevented him from forgiving her. Valerie had known she was dying and had offered her protection as a temporary measure to save him for Emerald. She had never intended to betray Emerald by taking him into her bed. He drew Valerie closer until her hands rested on his chest.

"I won't go back to her. If you don't put me away, then you must be with me. Love me if you can. Share your life with me and create," he smiled, "as many children as the Creator grants us."

Her eyes widened and flooded with tears.

He knew she wanted children. He had contemplated what their children might look like. The possibilities pleased him.

Her gaze drew him in and held him in the dark wells of her soul. Eventually, she found his lips with hers. Her kiss conveyed tender hope, desperate need, and the deepest respect. He returned her affection until his passions rose too high. He broke away before he embarrassed himself.

Breathless, she said, "I want to be with you."

She glanced toward the cushions and startled at Trelan's presence. Had she forgotten he was there? The flush of her cheeks deepened.

Trelan walked closer and put his hands on their shoulders. "I respect your choice. I'll fetch the physician. I only hope she has carried the proper medicine with her." He departed from the hall.

"Are you sure about this?" Valerie asked.

Darrin knew she desired him because her kiss had told him so. He had known she wanted him ever since their first kiss in the tall grass of the northern plains early last summer. She had surprised him then, and his feelings for her surprised him now.

His desire for her wasn't new. He had fought his feelings for a long time, but that had been easy because of his obsession with Emerald. Holding Valerie in his arms felt wonderful, powerful, and sensual in the extreme.

"I need you." His voice came out low.

She giggled.

Seeing that for the first time made him unreasonably happy. He nearly laughed out loud. She let him hold her in his arms.

"That feeling I understand." Her expression sobered. "It's other things I worry about."

He inhaled a deep breath to calm a surge of anger. "Emerald isn't a factor. She shouldn't matter anymore."

The chill of his own words sent a shiver down his spine. He couldn't believe the depth of his resentment. He'd never hated anyone like this before.

Valerie's expression saddened. She stared into his eyes for a long time. Her chin quivered.

"Emerald will never forgive me for this."

He took Valerie in a fierce embrace. "I don't care."

She held him for a while with her head on his chest. "You will."

Chapter Fifteen

"Whoa there Dusty."

Emerald Stone's eyes flew open at the sound of the man's voice. She must have dozed in the saddle. Two militiamen stood in the middle of the rainy road. One held Dusty's bridal and smiled as he offered a hand.

"Let me help you dismount, Madame."

Dusty had brought her nearly home. They were at Stone Bridge. A newly constructed guardhouse had been built on the southern side.

"Jeff Hill, we've known each other since we were babies. Why are you calling me, Madame?" Emerald took his hand and stiffly dismounted.

Jeff chuckled and hid in his two years' growth of beard. He kept ahold of her hand to steady her as he guided her toward the guardhouse. It had a window on the east side and a door on the northern wall. The back had a lean-to stable and the roof looked like a hayloft.

"Come inside and warm yourself." Jeff released her hand.

"I'm almost home. I might as well ride on." Emerald protested in word only.

She was relieved to be out of the rain. She wasn't overly cold since her dress was made of thick wool, but she was still miserable. Furthermore, she was heartsick over Darrin's angry decision to end their engagement.

Jeff's expression sobered and the corners of his eyes creased in concern. He urged her to take a seat on the bench beside the coal brazier. It was warm and the room smelled of cinnamon tea. She didn't protest further.

"You're soaked to the bone without even a cloak to warm you. Have something to eat and drink. I have biscuits and goat cheese along with some hot tea. Please help yourself or my wife will have my hide."

Jeff opened his lunch pail and handed her a cloth-wrapped parcel. The other militiaman poured her a cup of tea.

"I couldn't eat your supper." Emerald's gaze fixated on the food. She hadn't eaten in three days.

"Of course, you can. I ate my fill earlier." Jeff looked toward the western wall of the structure.

"Thank you, and thank Aimee. How is she?" Emerald ate with as much decorum as possible despite her eagerness for nourishment.

"Oh, my Aimee is round and rosy." Jeff laughed. "We have two sons and another child on the way. That woman is a joy to me."

Emerald took a sip of tea to cover her surprise. "Congratulations."

The number of children was shocking, considering the two-year term of the marriage. But she was pleased to hear Aimee was well. She'd always been a hardy girl.

"Allan, do you have anything left in your pail?" Jeff asked the other man.

"No. I'm sorry. Let me pour you more tea, Lady Stone." The young militiaman filled her mug again.

Emerald shivered at the mention of Allan's name given her history with Darrin's brother. However, the tea warmed her hands and soothed her nerves. This Allan was the harpist's son. He looked barely old enough to have joined the militia.

"Thank you. Allan Harper, am I right?" Emerald asked.

Allan smiled and nodded as he set the teapot on the floor and placed a pan of water on the brazier to warm.

"I'm surprised you remembered me. But my dad tells a story I'm sure you will have heard before."

Emerald sipped the tea.

"The way he tells it, your mother traveled three days' journey from Humetown to hear him play the harp. She waltzed into our shop decked in city finery on a perfect spring day and asked to see 'the famous Arthur Harper'. Well, my dad nearly fell off his stool. He'd never put on airs about being important and 'Arty the harp maker' was not exactly famous to most folks." Allan smiled.

"You're being too modest. Your dad is Meadowgren's most famous resident. Even the chief judge stopped by to hear him play when he was in the village last year. Um, beg your pardon, Madame." Jeff ducked his head.

Emerald's expression froze and her hand stopped in mid-air with the tea mug giving a little wobble. It was clear that Jeff hadn't meant to remind her of her murder trial last spring, nor what Hubert Carpenter and his two sons had done to her to cause it to take place. Though it took some effort, she forgave Jeff without a word, quietly sitting the mug in her lap.

"Well, ugh, my dad played his harp for Miss Ellora Hume. It wasn't until she started to sing along that a ruckus broke out in the street. Your father, my lady, stopped his wagon right in the middle of everyone's way and rushed inside to hear her. It was love from that moment on. Gaining your grandfather's permission to wed her was another story, or so I've heard." Allan bowed his head. "I'd better tend to your horse." He gathered up the pan of warm water that would doubtless be used to make a mash for Dusty.

"Thank you for the story, and please thank your father again for me." Emerald had always loved the story of how her parents met.

Allan nodded and hurried outside.

"Would you like more tea?" Jeff lifted the kettle from the floor.

"Thank you, no. I've had enough. It's excellent cinnamon tea."

Emerald couldn't figure out why she was all politeness when she needed to be going home. Perhaps she'd learned more from her time as the future queen of the West Wind than she had thought.

"Your man started everyone at the barracks drinking it years ago. It costs some shiny coins to import, but he has connections that reduce the expense. His relatives in the islands send him cinnamon by the cask full." Jeff laughed.

"My man?" Emerald blanched with shock. "If you're referring to Sergeant Hume—"

"I know you and Liameo have had your disagreements over the years, but everyone knows he's your man and always has been. That's why no one was surprised to find out he'd beaten Roger Carpenter to death."

Emerald gasped. She dreaded the consequences of such an action.

"Well, nearly to death. Doctor Platt testified at Liameo's trial that Roger had died from an improperly healed wound on the leg. It had broken open during the fight and spread infection. I guess you dealt him that. All of us think he deserved his fate. It cost Liameo a dishonorable discharge from the militia, but that was all. None of us hold it against him."

"He did that for me?" Emerald was stunned by the gesture of loyalty.

"Liameo would do anything for you, Madame. When I heard about the things that Roger said to bait him, I completely understood." Jeff clenched his jaw and the look in his eyes hardened.

"What did Roger say?" She needed to know because the answer had long-reaching ramifications.

"Oh, well, he said he'd put you with child and you'd agreed to give him the baby. I knew he was lying, and here you are with no child. The braggart deserved his fate. He should never have betrayed his friend, let alone done what he did to you."

Emerald had gone faint at the first mention of Roger. Motes of light floated before her eyes despite the fortification of the tea. Jeff draped a wool blanket around her shoulders. The sound of Allan riding away on horseback echoed in her ears.

"I'd best be going too. We're supposed to report your arrival to Captain Hammond and Judge Porter immediately. Stay, sit, and warm yourself. I'll let Liameo know you're here after I tell the judge." Jeff left the guardhouse.

Soon the sound of horse's hooves on the gravel road let Emerald know Jeff had gone. Roger was dead. She had miscarried the baby. Liameo had nearly been executed for defending her honor.

The weight of it crushed her. She had no honor. Indeed, she had promised to give the baby to the very man who had begotten the child by raping her.

She hadn't understood how her heart would change toward the little one as it grew inside her body. She had never dreamed she could love her tiny son...especially not a son. But she had loved him deeply and long before the premature infant died in her arms.

Regret plagued her over the foolish promise she had made to Roger. It had cost her Darrin's respect when he'd found out. He hated her for it. Her face contorted in agony and a flood of tears.

She needed to go home to her orphans. Seeing Nina and hugging that sweet girl would make her feel better. Marta would have grown so much in the many moons since Emerald had gone away.

She imagined seeing each of the children again after so many moons. She sprang to her feet in eagerness. Leaving the mug behind, she wrapped the blanket around her more tightly and stepped outside into the rain.

Allan had stabled Dusty. He'd removed the saddle, brushed him down, watered, and fed him. She didn't have the strength of heart to take the old horse into the soggy weather.

She took nothing except the sword forged to honor her unnamed son. She crossed Stone Bridge and ran her fingers over the weathered granite railing slick with rain. Her soft leather boots sank into the muddy gravel road. She hardly noticed and slogged onward.

The sight of Stone Castle caused her to breathe a sigh of relief. Home. More tears spilled from her eyes as exhaustion wrung the strength from her spine.

She didn't notice anything amiss until she walked through the open gates. There was disarray in the courtyard and an absence of livestock. No smoke came from any of the chimneys.

Emerald ran to the stairs of the keep, mounted them, and cast the partly ajar door wide. Grief overwhelmed her and she collapsed to her knees in the entryway. The place was cold and desolate. Leaves swirled in the breeze blowing in the doorway behind her. No one had lived here for quite some time.

The children were gone.

Shock halted her tears. What had happened here? She looked into the darkness blinking in disbelief.

The sound of a horse's hooves on the cobblestones of the courtyard and a dog's bark roused her from dark contemplations. The dog would be Eugenia. Emerald remembered the large, blond Wolfhound from years ago when she'd first met Liameo Hume and his son Liameo the younger.

Eugenia nuzzled her nose into Emerald's hand. She petted the dog's wet head. Eugenia smelled, but not terribly. Liameo had always kept her well-groomed.

Liameo's massive frame blocked the light coming in the doorway. Emerald had tried to forget about him. Now everything belonging to him came back to her recollection.

When she was fourteen, Captain Hume senior had traveled with his son from the coast. He'd been seeking her grandfather's consent to a betrothal between Emerald and Liameo the younger. A ship's captain in his own right, Liameo was eighteen and her half-second-cousin on her mother's side.

Their great-grandfather had remarried after the death of Emerald's great-grandmother. Liameo's great-grandmother was an islander and the exotic blood showed in his tall, broad build, and darker skin. Liameo's line were seamen. Emerald's line had continued with farming out of Humetown west of the Capital City of Andolin.

Liameo's father was rich and owned a fleet of ships. What he had wanted out of the union was land. Marrying his son to Emerald had been a means to that end. Grandfather had refused to give his consent, but it was too late. Emerald had become enamored with the young man and pleaded for permission to marry him.

Jacob Stone had sent the men away despite Emerald's feelings. Two days later, Allan Wolfe had murdered her grandparents and ravaged her soul. When Liameo returned alone and against his father's wishes, she ignored his petitions at the castle gates, avoided him in Meadowgren Village, and tried to forget him.

"Em..." Liameo's voice was even deeper than Darrin's.

She stroked the soft hair between Eugenia's eyes.

"I'll bring in wood for the fire." Liameo went outside.

A dim light shone through the entryway. The rain kept falling. Emerald slowly climbed off the floor.

Cold, stiff, and emotionally empty, she walked further into the room that had been full of life and activity for many years. She righted a chair and ran a hand over the dusty surface of the table. Meals had been enjoyed here. She almost wiped the dust on her white, wool dress, but pulled an embroidered handkerchief from her pocket instead.

She still wore the clothes she'd chosen for the walk in the statuary gardens with Darrin. Memories of the ancient Imperial City inside the Sacred Mountain were tainted by his rejection. How could it only have been three days ago?

Liameo strode into the room with an armload of wood and tossed it into the fireplace with a clatter. He knelt to split a piece into kindling with an ax from his belt. Emerald stood motionless as she watched him build the fire. Eugenia trotted around the keep with her tongue lolling out of her mouth as she investigated the place.

The fire glowed and started to bloom. Liameo went to shut the door. Firelight did little to soften the harsh reality of the situation for Emerald. The children were gone and nothing mattered without the ones she loved.

Liameo crossed the room and mounted the stairs to the barracks-like bedchamber above. He returned with clothes and a blanket. Emerald stared at the honeybees embroidered on the quilt. Her mother had made it for her long ago. Tears welled in Emerald's eyes.

Liameo took a chair from beside the table and dusted it with his great hand. He put the chair in front of the fire and laid the quilt and clothes on it. Clearing his throat, he shuffled his boot on the hearthstones and then headed outside.

"Gene, guard."

His command absorbed all of Eugenia's attention. She circled the room searching for danger. Emerald walked to the chair and touched the soft stitching of the quilt. She wished her mother were still alive for the hundredth time today.

Not wanting to be caught unclothed, Emerald changed quickly into the dry trousers and shirt. She hung her dress, silk slip, and stockings on pegs beside the fire to dry. She put her son's sword on the mantle. Touching the smooth leather of the scabbard, she thought of her tiny boy.

Eugenia's panting brought Emerald back to the here and now. She took her muddy boots over by the door. Eugenia followed her every move.

Liameo burst into the keep. Startled, Emerald dropped the boots in the entryway. Rain poured down in sheets outside. It ran off Liameo's three-cornered, leather hat in streams.

He pushed the rest of the way inside and shut the door. He hung his hat and greatcoat on pegs by the door and just stood there looking at her. She looked at him too.

"Why does everyone think you're my man?"

He slouched and shuffled his foot. It seemed like a strange gesture from a man so large and normally confident. What was he keeping from her?

"I thought you were going to ask me about the children." He searched her eyes.

She went to stand beside the fire. He followed her. Eugenia lay down on the rug between them.

"I know what happened to the children." She had known it could happen for a long time. "Judge Porter had them removed from Danalan. I'm guessing they've gone somewhere else now and are quite beyond my reach. I suppose this makes the judge happy." She was too tired to let bitterness influence her tone. The words were bitter enough.

"The law—"

"Hang the laws of Andolin. The children were safe and happy here in Danalan." Her anger flared with an intensity that spoke of her deep resentments toward the neighboring country's intrusions.

"You left and took far too long coming back." He leaned his arm on the mantle and stared at the blade before he gazed into the fire.

"I did what I had to do." She used the handkerchief to wipe the cushioned chair free of dust, wrapped her quilt around her, and sat with her feet tucked underneath her body to warm them.

She was guilty of everything Liameo said and so much more. But there was nothing she could do at the moment to make amends to anyone. Furthermore, she was too wrung out to carry more blame tonight.

Tomorrow she'd find the children. Tomorrow she'd rebuild her life...somehow. She leaned her head against the side of the chair and closed her eyes.

Chapter Sixteen

Valerie and Darrin watched the doorway until Trelan returned with the physician. Their expressions held concern.

"Let me introduce you to Doctor Blythe of Cauldron Proper. She is the physician on this expedition."

The woman bowed. Valerie and Darrin reciprocated.

"I regret to inform you that the vaccine I carried with me froze on the journey and rendered it inert. A dose is available at our nearest outpost on the Green Way. If you will allow me to examine you, then I will know more about the urgency of your condition." Blythe took out a long tubular contraption from her valise.

Valerie stiffened. "What type of examination do you require?"

Blythe smiled openly. "Nothing invasive, I assure you. I simply wish to place this," she pointed at the flared end of the device in her hand, "on your chest and listen to your heart. It only requires you to unbutton your shirt a little." She faced the men. "Will you please provide us with privacy?"

Trelan nodded. "Of course."

He and Darrin walked across the room keeping their backs to the women.

Valerie unbuttoned her shirt. The doctor listened to her heart by sliding the device around her chest. Blythe repeated the exercise on Valerie's back. The look of concern on her face intensified.

"Your heart is weak. Does it pain you often?" Doctor Blythe put away the listening device.

"I've had shortness of breath and regular pains for several days. Before that, I simply tired easily." Valerie buttoned her shirt.

Doctor Blythe seemed to be considering the words. "This concerns me.

I'm recommending you be taken to the outpost to receive an injection immediately. Your heart could suffer damage if we wait. You must avoid stress. I will prepare a litter and bearers to carry you. Do not overexert yourself. Rest while I make preparations."

The grave nature of the words struck Valerie in the center of her chest. "I appreciate your aid, Doctor Blythe."

The women walked over to the men. Valerie took Darrin's hand and led him away from the others. She met his gaze.

"I may not survive the stress of childbirth even if I receive the medicine as soon as may be." She swallowed hard and looked away. "I'm willing to risk it, but that's not fair to you. Choose someone else."

His expression darkened with devastation. "It isn't fair."

He clenched his fists and pounded the wall. His already split knuckles gushed blood. The act seemed to drain him and he fell to his knees. To Valerie's surprise, he wept like a child.

"You've been through so much with your uncle. You deserve to be happy." He clenched his fists. "I deserve to be happy. Believe me when I say I don't want anyone except you." He bowed his head against the wall. "I wish I could make the men who hurt you suffer a thousand deaths."

Valerie didn't shed a tear. Her grief was passed that. She prepared herself for his rejection. He would conclude that it was foolish to involve himself with her the moment he thought this through.

She couldn't change anything. She could never make it better. The injustice and terrible unfairness of the situation defeated her.

Darrin's expression grew resolute. "I won't be the one to kill you, but I will stand with you to the end."

Surprise caused her hands to flutter. He stood before her and took them.

"I don't want your pity," she focused on his face, "and I won't be your wife without the hope of children." She looked into his eyes. "If I die, then I die a mother."

Silent tears coursed her cheeks. "I trust you to raise our child if I don't survive. I promise you I'm not easy to kill." She squeezed his hands. "I will fight. I won't give up." She looked away as she realized that he might blame himself. "It isn't your fault if I die."

He kissed her neck. His breath caressed her ear. Her body reacted as if he'd tickled her. Gooseflesh rose on her skin. He leaned in and nuzzled her neck. She smiled and squirmed away.

He held her close and kissed her lips. She surrendered to her passion. Nothing else existed except the two of them. She had saved him and now she needed saving.

Her breathing became shallow and forced her to part the kiss for air. "Not yet."

Chapter Seventeen

Darrin ran behind the covered litter that carried Valerie. The East Icers had wasted no time. They traveled through the harsh environment of the mountains in the fading daylight. She needed the cure before further damage to her heart shortened the time she had left to live.

The men carrying the litter remained sure-footed despite the driving snow. They wore the white suits of fur they had worn when they invaded the Imperial City. Darrin wore one as well. It amazed him to discover how warm and comfortable he was even in the most inhospitable conditions.

Valerie's health concerned him. But his thoughts focused on their life after she received the medicine the East Icers promised. He hoped their first time together would be as good as he imagined it could be.

His reservations about intimacy were new. Hers were deeply ingrained. He didn't want it to be like he had observed her actions toward her conquests last summer.

He needed her to be genuine. He feared that she would misjudge what he expected because of her past experiences with men. He formulated what to say to convey his thoughts, but couldn't find the right words.

He sighed in the icy air and stopped trudging. The litter continued along a trail he couldn't see. He would figure out something to say when the time was right. Just as he determined this, she disappeared into a whiteout.

He hastened to catch up. Where had she gone? He slid into an opening in the mountain.

A light flared and a lantern ignited to illuminate the cavern in which they stood. He climbed off his behind and looked around. Two merry green doors with brass knobs adorned the end of the cave.

The men carrying the litter each took a handle and opened them. Warm air whooshed out of the tunnel. Darrin followed the litter onto the Green Way. Plants grew on both sides of the stone-paved road.

"Close the doors, Darrin." One of the men smiled as he spoke.

Darrin shut the doors tight. He turned around to find the men stripping off their suits and shaking them free of snow. They untied the flaps of the litter so Valerie could come out into the warmth. She emerged with an expression of awe.

The men stowed their suits in the litter. Darrin followed their lead. They foraged for food among the lush plants growing within reach. Both of them pulled weeds and tended the plants as they ate. An amicable conversation expressed their enjoyment of the place.

Darrin's mouth watered. He hadn't had fresh vegetables since he'd been in the north last summer and then only when he'd stolen them. Stolen vegetables didn't taste as good as those obtained through industrious effort. One man handed him a red tomato.

Darrin took a big bite. It tasted sun-ripened. Juice ran down his chin and he wiped it with the back of his hand. He ate the rest of the tomato and looked for more.

The men handed Valerie as much as she could hold. She stowed most of it in a knapsack slung over her shoulder. Pale, she didn't seem to have much of an appetite.

"How is this place possible?" Darrin spoke around a mouthful of a green vegetable he'd never seen before.

The nearest man laughed. "Look up." He pointed to the ice ceiling.

Darrin squinted. It wasn't ice. It couldn't be. He'd seen slabs of stone that looked like that in the Imperial City.

"Is that quartz?" he asked.

"Yes. The sun shines in and leaves its heat. The Green Way is warm year-round. On days like today, it would grow cold if not for the steam vents located periodically along its path. The mountain heats the road and our cities. The heat melts the ice and fills the cisterns that water the gardens. It is a perfect system. Though it does have a few weeds and we have to replant after harvests." The man walked away but turned back. "I hope you will not tell anyone about the Green Way. We depend on it for nearly all our food. We wouldn't survive without it."

Valerie took Darrin's hand. "You have our word. We will never betray your trust."

"Come then." He smiled broadly. "The outpost isn't far."

They left the litter there. Everyone walked at a leisurely pace down the slope of the mountain on a perfect road. The two men weeded the garden beds on each side as they went.

Darrin held Valerie's cold hand to warm it. A rush of heat thrilled him at her touch. They strolled along together. He grinned as he tried to identify the plants. He recognized some, but others were new to him. He had been north and south of the mountains, but he'd never imagined anything like this.

"Is this medicinal." Valerie inspected a pointy leafed plant.

"Yes," one man remarked. "Many of the plants we grow are used to concoct medicines and treatments." He continued with his work.

"Does the cure I need come from any of these?" she asked.

"No. It's made from bread." He looked at her more intently. "Well, not exactly from bread, but from bread mold. I'm not quite sure how they do it. I'm a duck farmer. I know a little about vaccines because they are sometimes created inside eggs." He returned to weeding.

From Valerie's look of confusion, Darrin gathered she understood as little of what the man had said as he did and that wasn't much. He knew the words except for 'vaccine'. It had been mentioned before.

"What is a vaccine?" Valerie asked.

The man scratched his head. The humidity made everything itchy. "Well, I'm not exactly sure, but it's alive. It can't be allowed to become too hot or cold, or it dies." He frowned. "I don't know if you need a vaccine, but the medic at the outpost will fix what ails you. Have no fear." He returned to his task.

The men were studious in their gardening. They didn't throw the weeds on the floor either. They wore satchels and stowed the refuse in them.

Darrin felt guilty for not helping. The trouble was that he didn't know a weed from a plant. He could only identify one in five of them.

A smell increased the closer they came to whatever caused it. The temperature increased as well. Valerie scrunched her nose. He remembered reading in a medical text that women possessed a keener sense of smell than men. It had said that in many cases this was particularly true when they were pregnant.

His feelings for her warmed at the thought of her conceiving a child. He had no qualms about becoming a father. This relationship would be different than it had been with Emerald. Emerald had been...untouchable.

Valerie would be his wife. He could create a life with her. The baby would be part of him and he intended to be involved in every aspect of the child's development.

He grinned. She noticed him looking, squeezed his hand, and stopped. He swung around to face her. She stood on tiptoes to kiss him briefly. The light advanced with the rest of the party.

He placed a palm on her belly. "Will you let me experience it with you?" He didn't know how to ask what he meant, yet the earnest question made her smile.

"I'll try." She looked away. "I'll certainly make you pay for it when the child is born. Lily hurt me worse than anything I had anticipated. I didn't think I was going to live."

Her easy conversational manner disappeared when she seemed to realize what she'd revealed. Her face paled.

"Lily?" He tried to sound casual.

She had just admitted she'd had a child. That was news to him. Her rate of breathing increased and her lips took on a blue tint. She blinked as if she couldn't see clearly. Her knees buckled. He caught her.

"Valerie?" He adjusted her in his arms and her head lolled. "What's wrong?"

She struggled for breath.

The men ran back with the lantern.

"What happened?" the duck farmer asked.

"I don't know. I upset her." Darrin laid her on the stone floor. "She passed out. How far is your medic?" He withdrew the letter from Doctor Blythe from Valerie's satchel and handed it to the duck farmer. "Give this to the medic."

The two men ran ahead and soon returned with the medic, blankets, and a stretcher. They loaded Valerie onto it and the medic injected something into her buttock with a needle tipped vile and plunger. She flinched at the puncture wound and moaned. Her intense expression of pain remained otherwise unaltered.

The two men lifted the stretcher and carried her to the outpost. They brought her through an archway, across a courtyard, and into one of several multi-level buildings. They continued through what looked like a waiting room for patients, down a hallway, and into a private room.

They transferred Valerie onto a narrow bed and took the stretcher away. Darrin stood by her side and held her hand. The medic put the device used to hear her heart on her chest. His expression brightened somewhat.

"Will she be all right?" Darrin hoped for the best.

The medic withdrew his instrument and fastened the buttons on Valerie's shirt. "She will have incidents like this from time to time. But she is young and will recover somewhat now that she has received the cure for the disease."

Darrin pulled the blanket over her even though the room wasn't cold. Color had returned to her lips. But he couldn't forget the terrible hue they had been only moments earlier.

"What happened?" Darrin couldn't take his eyes off of her.

"Her heart has been weakened by the disease. That means she must be careful not to overexert her body. She should avoid strenuous labor and stressful situations. She needs peace and rest. Not to say that she should not engage in mild exercise because that is good for the heart." The medic placed the stethoscope in the bag he had brought with him.

Darrin frowned as he brushed the hair away from Valerie's forehead. "How strenuous is lovemaking?"

The medic chuckled. "She should be fine as long as you do most of the work." He patted Darrin's shoulder but squeezed as the humor faded from his demeanor. "You should use contraception. Pregnancy is stressful for a woman. She's not likely to survive childbirth."

Darrin could see the medic's concern. "What is contraception?" He had never heard of such a thing.

The medic frowned at the question. "I forget you are not one of us. Contraception is the employment of various means to prevent pregnancy. There are several methods the two of you should consider before becoming intimate. I take it you are newlywed?"

"Yes." Darrin looked at Valerie. She would not wish to delay having a child, but new options presented new dilemmas. "Is your medicine not able to lessen her stress? She wants children. We both do. I just don't want her to die. How long does she have to live?"

The medic patted his shoulder. "We can lessen her pain. We can ease her delivery. We cannot lengthen her life because we can't repair her heart. She has years to live if she meditates, exercises, eats right, and maintains a low-stress lifestyle." He squeezed Darrin's shoulder. "If she becomes pregnant, then the cost could be dire."

"Tell me about contraception." Darrin couldn't risk losing her.

Chapter Eighteen

Emerald awoke to the sensation of warm, bare skin beneath her hand and the feel of an enormous man's arms around her. She jerked awake and backed out of bed. She startled Liameo from a sound sleep. He grabbed for the blankets as she fled, but missed them and ended up completely uncovered.

"You're naked." She couldn't take her eyes off of him.

He didn't even have a pair of socks on. He scrambled to dress in his now dried clothes. But she'd seen all of him and more than she'd imagined existed of him because it was morning.

He turned his back to her as he fastened his trousers. Light from the high windows bathed his back. She gasped. Ugly scars crossed his skin. One was particularly wide and jagged.

Liameo spun around to face her. He grabbed his shirt, put it on, and quickly buttoned it up wrong without noticing. He tucked it in and searched for his socks and boots.

The shock of waking up next to one more unwelcome man made her dizzy. She inventoried her aches and pains. She had none and hadn't felt this rested in days.

Why had Liameo stayed? Why hadn't he found something to wear? What made him think he could do this?

He moved in her direction to reach for a sock. She reflexively backed away. The idea of closeness repulsed her. He met her gaze and seemed to realize he'd broken trust with her.

"A man may sleep beside his wife. You need not fear me, nor what anyone will say."

Her jaw fell open. "Your wife?"

"Read these letters and you'll see. You've been my wife for nearly seven years." He handed her two folded letters from his trousers' pocket. One was faded and had a large, dark stain on it.

She pushed the letters back into his hand with a crunch.

"No. This can't be right." She paced away. "Grandfather never consented. If the blood on that letter is his, then I don't want to know what it says." She walked to the stone wall of the keep and placed her forehead on the cold surface.

Married? Liameo wouldn't lie. It had to be true.

The other letter must be from her mother's father, Albert Hume. When faced with the proof in the first letter he must've relented to Liameo's claim. It was the law.

"I belong to you?" She faced his direction with her head bowed.

She slid up the sleeve that covered her right forearm. She stared at the scars left by Valerie and Byron's brands. A permanent form of slavery trapped her now.

Liameo strode over to gently take her hand. He frowned deeply. His thumb rubbed across the scars.

"You belong with me." He emphasized the word with.

She backed away until she bumped the wall. Unable to speak, she swallowed to clear the lump in her throat. He did not release her hand.

"No, Liameo." She glanced at the bed. "I don't love you and I never did. What we shared was infatuation. I was a foolish child. You are not bound to me." She pushed past him to pace the room as she struggled to make sense of this.

"I adopted four of the children." He stayed where she'd left him.

"What?" She wheeled around to face him from across the room.

"I adopted Tarah before she married George. They adopted the three little brothers you saved from the Wolf Clan last year."

She locked eyes with him. "Who are the others?" Her voice was flat and held an edge.

"Nina, Andrew, and Marta." He took a wary stance.

"And because you are a man, the judge allowed this?" She charged and pounded her fists against his massive chest.

He caught her wrists. She broke free. Tears coursed her face and sobs racked her frame.

"If only I were a man." Grief overwhelmed her and she fell to her knees.

The judge had denied her repeated requests to adopt the children. Without fail, he had told her it was because she wasn't married. The man was cruel.

Liameo scooped her up in his arms. She punched him in the jaw. He dropped her. She landed on her feet and slapped him solidly.

"How dare you?" She seethed with anger and wished she had a weapon.

His eyes flew wide and his nostrils flared as color climbed his neck. He grabbed her before she could escape and hauled her to bed. Throwing her on it, he menaced over her.

"I could have you if I wanted. The law supports me. But I will never hurt you. I've taken your name. I've forsaken my citizenship in Andolin. I'm your husband and that's all I've ever wanted." He grabbed his boots and slipped them on without bothering to find his socks.

"Why have you done this?" She couldn't understand.

He faced away as if to go.

She chased him, grabbed the crook of his arm, and spun him around. "Why do you think you have the right to do this?" Her anger intensified.

"I'll be back with the children this afternoon. George wants to come home too. Can I bring his family with me?" He looked at the toes of his boots.

She stared at him slack-jawed.

The dark emotion lifted from his face. "Please?"

"Yes." She wanted them here desperately. It was Liameo she didn't want. "Why would you force me to marry you?"

He met her gaze without a cloud of deception. "I'm the only one who could restore your honor after what the Carpenters did to you. You need me, and I still love you."

"I need you?" She scoffed at the idea. "No, indeed. What I need is justice. Furthermore, I require control over my life." She broke eye contact. "All I want is to be left alone by every man who thinks he can do a better job of managing me than I can." Her hands flailed. "I need to choose!" She paced further away from him before skewering him with a look. "And as for love," her voice trembled and her fists shook, "love without respect is not love at all."

Her words echoed in the open room. Much to her surprise, he didn't react. The nasty accusation seemed to ricochet off of her intended target to pierce someone dear to her heart.

Darrin had lost respect for her and walked away. He had given up on her. The scene of what had happened the last time she saw him turned her stomach.

How many times had Darrin said he loved her and failed to prove it? Whatever held him back remained between them. Now, this impossible barrier would keep her from him forever.

"How could you do this?" Her voice was a whisper.

Liameo drew close enough for her to feel the heat of him. He touched her face. She prepared for the worst, clenched her jaw, and shook her head. Tears coursed her face as she glared at him.

"I love someone else." She confessed though she knew it was hopeless.

Liameo's dark brows crashed together. "Darrin?"

Her eyes went wide. "How do you know about him?"

Liameo dropped his hands to his sides. "Andre told me. Nina thinks I made a mistake by marrying you. She said you would never return." He pressed closer.

She tried to run.

He caught her by the shoulders with his enormous hands. "Answer one question, Emerald Stone. Have you given yourself to him?"

Her jaw fell open and she stared at him in shock. "No, you fool. We were engaged to be married, but he broke it off because of the baby. We only kissed on one occasion." She planted a foot on Liameo's midsection and violently shoved him away. "What kind of a woman do you think I am?"

Liameo's gaze dropped to her belly. His lower lip trembled as the color slowly blanched from his face. His reaction enraged her and she swung again to slap him. He caught her arm in midair. The sudden tension in his body and the half-crazed expression on his face spoke of guilt and shame.

"There was no baby. It never happened. You are my wife. If you speak of this again, then I will turn you over my knee and take my belt to you." He released her arm, crashed down the stairs, and slammed the door as he departed from the keep.

Emerald shook with rage. She should run away. Nina, Andre, and Marta were the only reasons to stay. They were enough. She rolled up her sleeves and went to work. There was much to do in preparation for the children's return.

Chapter Nineteen

Darrin stayed by Valerie's side as she slept through the night and most of the morning at the outpost hospital. Her face had more color when she awoke. He explained the need for contraception, but that proved to be more challenging than he had anticipated.

"So, this is what you want, is it?" She lay in the hospital bed puffy-eyed and with her arms folded across her chest.

She jerked the blanket away and tried to sit up, swaying as if she were dizzy. He steadied her. She shoved his hands aside.

"I don't want your help." She stood and wobbled a bit as she looked for something. "I need my boots."

He'd taken them off so she could rest comfortably. "Please, you shouldn't exert yourself."

He didn't know what to do with his hands. He didn't dare touch her. But he wanted to force her to return to bed.

"The medic said to rest." Darrin ran a hand through his hair.

She jabbed him in the chest with a finger. "I'm not an invalid. We talked about children. I thought you understood what I want. Perhaps you don't know what I'm willing to do to have a baby."

Darrin stiffened. "You will die, Valerie." His voice went a long way toward expressing just how much he didn't want that to happen. "We can be together without hurting you."

She glared at him from her full, yet diminutive, height. "I'll find someone else." She slipped into her boots. "I've never had any trouble finding a man. It doesn't matter who it is." She stifled a sob. "I can be persuasive." She wiped her tears. "Any man would be lucky to have a go at it with no obligation."

Darrin took her in his arms. Despite the seriousness of it all, he had to chuckle. He knew she didn't mean it.

"I want more time with you." He rubbed her back. "The medic said none of the options prevent pregnancy without fail. A baby will come eventually." He kissed her neck and breathed on her ear the way she liked.

She snorted an unwilling laugh, shoved him, and gave him a halfhearted slap across a buttock. "How long does the medic think I'll live? Won't I become weaker as time passes? What if we wait too long and our child dies with me?"

The pain in her expression moved him. "You might have years if you avoid stress and are careful with your health. He expected you to recover to a certain extent."

She took a deep breath and let it out before arching an eyebrow. "How stressful do you think it is to be with me?" Her tone implied more than a casual encounter.

Darrin blushed. Being with her in any capacity had never been easy. "I was told to do most of the work." He couldn't meet her gaze because he had no idea what that entailed.

"Oh?" She wrapped her hand behind his neck. "I'm not planning on being on the bottom." She captured his lower lip in a gentle bite before kissing him long and deep.

He sensed her fear and attempted to soothe her, but her tension persisted. She thrust her tongue into his mouth, dominating him until she bit again. In pain, he pushed her away, tasting blood.

She wiped his blood from her lip. "I'm sorry." She walked to the other side of the room. "I don't know how to be with a virgin. You're making me break my rules."

He realized she was still trying to put him off. "What are your rules?"

She maintained a considerable distance between them. "No first-timers. No married men. No perverts. No diseased monsters." She spat the last word. "Oh," she faced him, "and I never kiss a man twice."

He nodded as he walked toward her. "And you're always on top." He suddenly realized what that meant and a lopsided smile tugged at his face. "You've kissed me a few times."

She shoved him playfully. "If I've broken one rule..."

"Then you might be persuaded to break another?" He drew close and took her in his arms. "I need to be patient. Is that what you're saying?"

She pulled out his shirttail and slid her hands along his back. The feel of her touch aroused him. He drew her closer and tipped her head to the side as he bent to kiss her neck. She captured his lips instead, sliding her hands around the front of him and up to his chest. She ran her fingers through the sparse hair there and found his nipples.

He laughed and backed away involuntarily. He'd never been touched like that before. Her surprise at his response seemed heavily laced with amusement because she smiled a genuine expression of delight.

"I thought you were the ticklish one." He wanted to move in for more but feared she would capitalize on his newfound vulnerability.

She shrugged and put her arms in the air as if she surrendered, but her smile told him otherwise. "If you want to stay a virgin, then there's nothing that I can do about it."

"Ha." He dove in to embrace her and lift her off her feet. He swung her around once and sat her on the narrow hospital bed. "Is that right?" He worked his hips between her knees and kissed her slowly. "There's anything I can do?"

She gave him a peck of a kiss on the lips and leaned against the wall. "Not here there isn't."

Chapter Twenty

Emerald dusted, washed, swept, and mopped the entire castle keep. She started in the Library, moved to the dormitory, then cleaned the common room. Last, she scrubbed the kitchen floors, including the bathing area behind the curtain. She was still on her knees with a brush and bucket when the door upstairs flew open.

"Em! Are you here?"

She recognized Andre's voice, even though it was deeper and had cracked. She flew up the kitchen stairs to the common room and swept the boy into an embrace. Holding him tightly, his giggles turned to gasps.

"All right. Enough hugs." He laughed and his eyes sparkled with delight.

She kissed both of his cheeks and let him go.

Marta had been holding up the others as she climbed the narrow stone staircase into the keep. The little girl was dressed in velvet and lace with her auburn hair curled in ringlets and tied with ribbons.

Emerald fell to her knees. Marta was beautiful. Emerald held her arms wide in anticipation of the little girl running into them.

It took a moment for Marta to spot Emerald in the dimness of the firelight. It had stopped raining and the sun shone brightly outside. Marta paused, then ran toward Emerald.

A pair of hands caught her. Nina held the child tightly to her skirts. Her lips compressed into a thin line.

"Em*ma*!" Marta said.

Emerald rose to her feet and strode toward the girls. Judge Porter hurried past them into the large room. His presence brought Emerald up short. He had no right to be here.

"Ah, Madame Stone," he extended a hand to take hers, "everyone is glad you have returned in good health." He released her hand and surveyed the surroundings.

She'd never allowed him on her land before let alone into her home. She clenched her jaw and watched him closely. After a moment, he seemed to become aware of her silence.

"I see you're already putting things in order. I apologize for what had to be done in your absence. But the law is the law, and I—"

"You should go." Emerald balled her hands into fists and turned her back on him.

"I have one last duty here before I depart. The ritual of the razor. Shall we gather in the courtyard?"

"No." Liameo's voice boomed.

Everyone faced him as he entered the keep with an armload of firewood.

"But we must." The judge looked from one face to another as his hands fidgeted. "Unless you haven't joined yet, then I'll come back tomorrow. I just assumed since you spent the night together that all was well. Emerald dear, you haven't kept Liameo waiting, have you?"

What kind of perverse pleasure was this man taking at her expense? She glared at him. It took a moment for her to gain enough self-control to speak.

"You assume too much, sir." Emerald struggled to keep her tone moderated.

The judge's eyebrows shot up. "Then you have not—"

"I have not and I will not."

"I knew you would ruin everything." Nina shot across the room, leveling Emerald with a slap that echoed throughout the keep. "You should never have come home. I hate you!"

"Nina." Liameo dropped an armload of wood with a clatter.

Nina ran upstairs. Liameo moved to follow her. Emerald stood in his way. She placed her hands on his chest and braced to block him, sliding across the floor until he pulled up short.

"I'm not going to hurt her, Em. I'm going to talk with her. She can't do that to you," Liameo said.

Emerald involuntarily lowered her gaze to the painful bruises now darkened on her forearm. His gaze followed hers and his posture crumpled. Shuffling over to lean against the mantle, he stared into the fire.

"You are a foolish and spoiled child, Emerald Stone." Judge Porter stood his ground with one fist trembling. "Liameo has restored your honor. Now you repay him with dishonor, but not upon yourself alone, but upon these children as well. You know the expectations inherent in the marriage bargain. I'm sure you are aware of the legal consequences of disobedience." He strode toward her. "Will you yield to him, or not?"

Emerald's met the gaze of the people in the room. The judge stood in self-righteous indignation. Marta hid under the table crying. Andre stared, wide-eyed and pale. Liameo still would not look at her.

She'd rather be flogged in the village square than let him have her. Unfortunately, she'd lose the children and possibly her life as well. Undoubtedly, she'd become a pariah, an outcast, a whore to be respected by no man. The realization crushed her.

"I choose," Emerald gathered Marta from under the table and soothed her tears, "to keep my family." She hung her head until her chin touched her chest.

"Then you will yield to your husband?" the judge asked.

"Yes." She wished she didn't sound defeated.

"Shall I return for the ceremony of the razor tomorrow?" asked the judge.

"The queen," Liameo stepped up from behind and took Emerald by the shoulders with both hands, "will observe only those customs she chooses to keep. If you recall, she has asked you to leave, sir. If we need you again, then we will send for you." Liameo spoke over the top of Emerald's head.

The weight of his hands held her cowed.

The judge frowned but held his tongue. He inclined his head in acknowledgment and marched out of the keep. The taps of the leather soles of his shoes as he retreated were the only sounds.

"Shut the door, son," Liameo said.

Andre obeyed.

Chapter Twenty-One

Darrin encouraged Valerie to rest until the medic felt it wise for her to resume normal activities. She slept on her side in the hospital bed. He leaned his head and shoulders on the edge. They held hands. The medic cleared his throat and Darrin noticed his arrival.

"We have a more comfortable place for you. She should be well enough now." The medic smiled a knowing expression as he handed Darrin a paper envelope. "I brought what you requested. Are you sure you know what to do with them?"

Darrin flushed as he accepted the package. "Yes, I think so."

"Wake her, then I'll take you to your quarters. The location is secluded and no one will bother you." The medic stepped out of the room.

Darrin snuck a look inside the envelope and shut it just as fast. Mortification washed over him in waves. He needed to put the tube on his... He took a deep breath. He had been nervous excited, but now his doubts crept in.

What if she was too forceful with him? She frightened him sometimes. He felt like a child to admit that even to himself because men weren't supposed to be afraid.

He'd never done this before. What if he did something wrong? She'd been hurt many times before. What if he injured her? What if she never trusted him again?

Valerie yawned and stretched. Her hand bumped into him and she startled awake. Her apprehension disappeared from her expression as she recognized him.

A crease formed in her brow. "What's wrong?"

"Oh," he looked around the room, anywhere except at what he held in his hands, "well, nothing, exactly. I'm just, well, um, I don't know." He started sweating.

"Is this about Lily?" Her expression held raw vulnerability.

His jaw dropped open. He shut it. "Yes."

"I had a baby when I was thirteen. My uncle tricked Byron into doing it." She looked away from Darrin to stare at the wall. "My uncle sodomized my daughter when she was only a year old and destroyed her tiny body. I was the one who ended her suffering after the surgeons said there was nothing they could do. So, it is clear to me that you hate Emerald for far less than what I have done."

Darrin couldn't breathe. Unable to do anything else, he stared. No words could express his shock and dismay.

She faced him. "You should know that before we do anything you will regret."

He dropped the envelope on the floor. Heart pounding in his chest, he walked out of the clinic, through the courtyard, and along the Green Way. At that point, he started running.

He ran until his heart felt like it would explode. Part of him wanted it to explode. He couldn't face Valerie's confession regarding what she had been forced to do, what she must have gone through, and the risk she had taken to trust him with the secret.

He stopped and braced his hands on his knees. He wept for her and cried in anguish for the child she had lost. The echoes of his grief rebounded on the Green Way, soothing him as if he were not suffering alone.

Valerie had endured it alone.

She trusted him. She wanted a child with him because she didn't worry the baby would be hurt. She knew he would protect them.

His hands shook as he realized he had to tell her he would be there for her in every way she needed. But how could he promise her nothing bad would ever happen? How could he know it? Iron resolve straightened his spine. He could do it because he would die before allowing anyone to harm her and their baby.

Returning to the woman he wanted above all others, Darrin ran through the archway, across the courtyard, and into the hospital. Valerie hadn't moved from the bed, but she had covered her head with the blanket. The pillow muffled the sound of her sobbing.

Panting, he said her name, "Valerie," he breathed in and out, "I will never let anything happen to you and our child." He wiped the sweat from his face. "I promise."

She hesitantly lowered the blanket. Her face was swollen from crying. She looked at him and her lower lip trembled. Questions and fears played across her features. Words worked inside her throat, but she didn't voice them.

He took her hand and laid a kiss on her lips, tasting her tears. "I promise you, Valerie. I will never leave again, not even for a moment. I'll always be with you."

She kissed him in an agonized, painful sort of way, then desperation seemed to overtake her, but finally, she gained enough confidence to relax. She smoothed his hair and took his head in her hands.

"You'd better keep that promise. I'm trusting you." She looked deep into his eyes. "Never leave me."

He met her gaze. "I need to know you won't push me away. I want to be a part of everything. It can't be like with my people where a man is only for pleasure and reproduction, but little else." He blinked twice as he tried to articulate his thoughts. "I want to be your partner, not your property."

She didn't smile in the slightest. Instead, she opened her soul to him. He saw her heart in the depths of her brown eyes.

"You have my word."

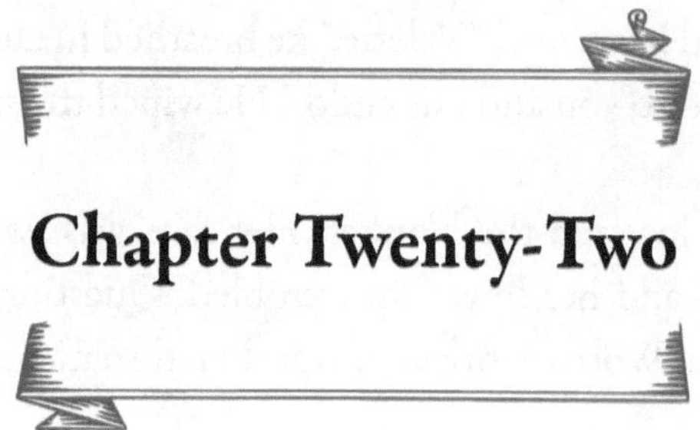

Chapter Twenty-Two

Emerald made quick preparations for dinner and bed. Nina sulked around the keep in silence. George and Tarah finally arrived with their three boys and a wagonload of possessions. Everyone helped unload it into the castle keep. Tarah's round belly was a surprise to Emerald.

"Welcome home." Emerald brought a kettle of cinnamon tea to the table and poured Tarah a cup.

Liameo came over to the table. Emerald poured him a cup as well. She handed it to him and sloshed a little on her fingers. She couldn't hold it steady.

He took the cup from her without a word. He'd seen her tremble. George must have seen it too because he looked away and his neck turned red. Part of her wanted George to save her from the fate awaiting her tonight, but she knew better.

George was big and strong and brave and good. However, he was no match for a trained soldier. Liameo was far more mature of frame and muscle, not to mention taller and broader than George. Her tiny hope of rescue died. It had been a fool's hope anyway.

"Time for bed," Liameo said.

George's head snapped around. Emerald caught his eye and gave an infinitesimal shake of the head. He unclenched his fists, but not his jaw.

She hurried about her final preparations. There was no avoiding it any longer. She followed the others upstairs to bed.

Curtains had been hung to divide the room into quarters. Tarah sat on the side of the three little boys' bed in one quarter and sang to them. She and George would share a bed in another quarter.

Andre had a bed next to the bed Nina and Marta shared in another quarter. In the final area, Emerald assumed she'd find Liameo waiting for her in the bed they would share. She didn't bother to conceal the terrible dread that threatened to crush her chest.

Tarah stopped singing. Everyone stared at Emerald where she stood immobile at the top of the stairs. Marta crawled out of bed and padded across the floor with bare feet to take Emerald's hand. She tugged her toward her bed and the warm light of a lamp on a small table beside it.

"Bedtime," the little girl said.

"I love you." Emerald gathered Marta into her arms and hugged her close.

"I love too." Marta smiled and wrapped her arms around Emerald's neck.

Emerald smiled through her tears. She kissed the little girl's cheek before tucking her into bed. She sat on the edge of Marta and Nina's bed, hoping Nina would look at her. She didn't.

"Come to bed, Em." Liameo's voice came from behind the curtain.

The sound of it caused her to flinch. His command had startled Nina too. The girl understood what must happen.

Emerald kissed each girl on the head, gave Andre a reassuring smile, and parted the curtain. In her nightgown and stocking feet, she walked to the edge of Liameo's bed. She let the curtain fall closed behind her. It was scant privacy. She must not scream.

Liameo lay in bed and held up the covers for her to enter with him. To her relief, he wore a nightshirt. She lay beside him on her back. He lowered his arm and the covers over her.

He lowered his hand to pull her nightgown up to mid-thigh and he slid his knee between hers. She shuddered. He rose over her and lifted the other side of her nightgown to match.

She looked away to block out her terror. Liameo leaned in to kiss her neck. She squeezed her eyes shut as the stubble on his chin scratched her skin.

He placed his other knee between hers. Flashes of memory assailed her mind. His fingers traced her bare leg and he lowered his weight upon her. She bit her lip until it bled, but when the horrifying memories of the past subsided, she realized something.

Emerald stilled his fingers on her leg and met his gaze. Much to her surprise, the sparkle in his eyes indicated she'd done what he expected. Frowning, she pushed him off of her.

He yielded and lay on his back. He wasn't aroused. That was the difference from the others.

Liameo could've taken her. She would've let him. But that power did not excite him.

"Why?" She spoke in the barest of whispers.

"You gave me something I didn't intend to take. I need you to take it back."

"What?"

"Your dignity." With that, he adjusted his head on the pillow and stared at the ceiling.

Emerald lay for a long time pondering what had happened and what Liameo had said. She didn't dare trust him, but he seemed to want her to. Circumstance had made them both behave poorly today. Perhaps...

Her thoughts were interrupted by a steady squeaking coming from George and Tarah's side of the curtain. Emerald frowned and looked, but she could see nothing. The sound intensified and Tarah moaned softly. Heat flooded Emerald's cheeks. She turned away only to see that Liameo wasn't asleep either.

The sounds of passion increased and Emerald curled into herself. She tensed until her ears rang and sparks floated in her vision. Liameo drew her alongside him and placed her head on his chest.

He covered her exposed ear and held her tight. She could hear nothing save the beating of his heart. When at last he relaxed, the room was silent. She didn't move away and fell asleep to the beating of his heart.

Chapter Twenty-Three

Darrin and Valerie followed the medic to a secluded subterranean home in the mountainside. Darrin had picked up the envelope he'd dropped when he had run away from his wife after the disturbing news about her daughter. He hadn't shown her what was in it yet because he didn't know if she would want to be with him anytime soon.

She seemed frail after her episode yesterday. Had it only been a day? Exhaustion made him rub his eyes. He'd watched over her most of the night and hadn't slept well.

The medic unlocked the door and departed. The man was very generous to have arranged this. Darrin was grateful for the private residence with a living area, a kitchen, and a separate bedroom.

Objects belonging to a household surrounded the newlyweds. Through the open bedroom door, Darrin spotted clean linens folded on the mattress. A meal lay on the table, steaming with heat.

"Are you hungry?" Valerie watched him.

His stomach growled. "No." The food smelled good. "Not if you aren't."

The hint of a smile played across her features. "I'm hungry."

"All right then."

He walked over and helped her with a chair. He sat opposite her at the table. Out of habit, he bowed his head to the Creator before he ate.

She took a bite and watched him as she chewed. "What is your religion, exactly? I understand the Creator is your God. He's mine too. But there's more than that, isn't there? Don't men of the West Wind worship the moon?" She took another bite of rice, chicken, and vegetables.

"You think the Creator is a man?" Darrin took a drink of water from the full cup beside his bowl.

Her eyebrows shot up. "Well, yes."

"Emerald is a woman. Doesn't that prove that God is a woman?"

Valerie nearly choked. She coughed for a while before she finished with a laugh.

"You think Emerald is God?"

He looked away at the wall hangings. "My mother does." He met Valerie's gaze. "These people do." His anger revealed itself in his voice.

Valerie laid her spoon on the table.

"She's supposed to be perfect." He curled his hand into a fist. "Why do you think I hate her so much?"

Valerie placed both hands on the table and stood. The chair squeaked on the floor as it moved backward.

"She's just a woman, Darrin. You expect too much of her. No one is perfect."

He glared until her fire put out his. He blinked as the idea sunk in. Did he believe Emerald was the Creator of everything in the sky above and the earth beneath? He'd always thought so, yet wondered why she struggled to simply survive this life.

Had he held her to an impossible standard? He knew she bled. He knew she cried. He knew she'd been injured emotionally and in other ways. But she had endured. She had remained... He wanted to say unbroken, but that would be a lie.

She was resilient, not invincible. She was human. She had betrayed him, but God never had. No, Emerald was not God, just a treacherous woman.

His mood crashed in with his brows. He clenched his jaw and tightened his fists until they bled again from the splits in his knuckles. He had earned those injuries punching unyielding surfaces like the wall of the Imperial Palace. It was Emerald's palace, or rather her ancestor's palace of treachery.

His anger ebbed as the truth hit him.

He had always believed Queen Dana had betrayed her husband, King Krelor. But the accounts found in the newly discovered Imperial City archives had set the record straight. It was Darrin's ancestor who had betrayed Emerald's.

Had he made a mistake with her?

No, he couldn't accept that. It couldn't be true. Had history repeated itself? One of the matriarchs had asked that question in his presence once. Was it possible?

Darrin looked at Valerie. His deep frown lifted fractionally at the sight of hers. He shook his head.

"No, Valerie. I didn't expect too much. I simply expected her to love her son, to name him, to honor him, to prove to me that she wouldn't cast me off. She didn't do that. She never loved him, nor did she love me. I will not forgive her. Don't try to make me." He glared at his bowl of rice. "I just want to eat."

Valerie harrumphed. She continued to glower at him, but he wouldn't relent. Eventually, she gave in and sat.

"After everything you know about my flaws, it makes me wonder what trifling thing I might do to make you hate me just as much." She picked up her spoon. "I mean, what if I inadvertently say or do something that upsets you? Will you break your oath to me?"

Her fist shook the spoon at him. "How can I prevent that from happening?" She dug the spoon into her bowl of rice. "You're a stupid hothead." She spilled rice all over the table and the utensil clattered to the floor. She tossed her hands with a cry of exasperation.

He watched her antics. When he met her gaze again, he couldn't help laughing. She cracked half of a frustrated smile. He laughed until his sides hurt.

He shook his head. "Never." He finished laughing. "I'll never leave you, Valerie." He met her gaze. "I love you."

His words stopped her. She looked as though she might say something in return, but she seemed to swallow the impulse. He knew she cared, but a declaration of love couldn't be withdrawn.

He didn't regret saying it first. She needed to know before they were intimate. She may question love, but he knew she felt something, and it could be love too.

Valerie shook her head. "Men often say that to me. It's never been true before."

She bent to retrieve the wayward spoon and tidy the spilled rice. When she popped back over the edge of the table, Darrin came to stand beside her. She froze before looking at him. Her eyes were wide. She dropped the spoon and it nearly missed the table.

"Enough of this." He took her by the hands.

The rice fell from her fist when her fingers meshed with his. Her expression slid into a frown as she looked at their hands. They had become one.

"Darrin, I—"

He stopped her with a kiss. Tenderness filled him with a desire to feel of her softness. He led her to the bedroom and closed the door. The only light came from underneath. He made the bed.

"You forgot that envelope of yours." She watched him without moving.

"It's here." He pulled the envelope from where he'd tucked it in the back of his waistband.

"Oh," she said. "What's in it anyway?"

"It's a sleeve that inhibits conception."

"Oh?" She still hadn't moved.

He pulled his tunic over his head and dropped it on the floor. "It goes on here." He pointed down on his body. Heat rose in his cheeks, but he was sure she couldn't see.

"What does it do?" She visibly struggled to say the words.

"It catches the tiny children before they can begin to grow."

Her laugh broke the mood for him, but it spurred her to embrace him. When she stopped laughing, she kissed him. The laughter had put her at ease.

Her lips roved his jaw, nipped his earlobe, and caressed his neck, stopping at the hollow of his throat. Her hands found their way across his chest and slid to his belt. Panting, she lifted her head to meet his gaze.

"May I?"

"Yes."

Chapter Twenty-Four

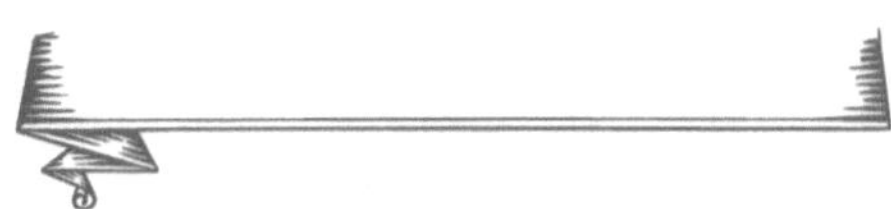

The dream was upon Emerald just as Allan Wolfe had been. She struggled and screamed as she looked into her grandmother's lifeless eyes. A shining personage of light stood above the body. It was Grandmother's spirit and her eyes shone with strength. Emerald fought Allan with the only weapon at hand.

Someone shook her awake.

"Em, wake up. It's all right. You're all right."

Her eyes flew open, dispelling the nightmare from her past. She ceased struggling and made efforts to calm her breathing. Glancing around, she remembered where she was, with whom, and why.

Liameo hugged her close and kissed her forehead. "You scared me."

Her heart continued to pound with fright. His embrace wasn't welcome. She rolled away from him to hug the edge of the bed.

"Em..." He put his hand on her hip.

She pushed it away.

"Em*ma*?" Marta's voice came from the other side of the curtain. She must still be in bed.

"I'm here little one. Everything is fine. Please go back to sleep." It was hard to control her voice.

"I be good," Marta said.

"You are a good girl, Marta." Emerald had trouble speaking past the lump in her throat. "Sweet dreams."

"Sweet dreams, too."

Emerald wept in silence.

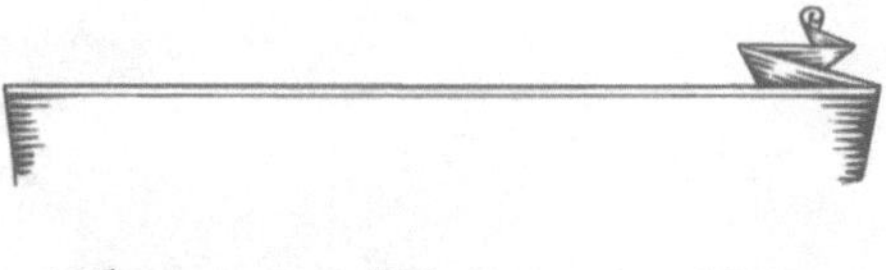

Chapter Twenty-Five

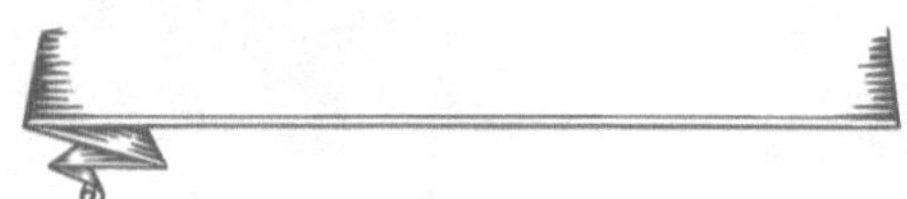

Darrin held his wife in his arms. They lay in the bed they shared. She had long since fallen asleep.

He treasured the feel of her lovely curves. He hadn't dreamed it could be this good. He hadn't hoped for the intimacy she had shared with him.

He marveled at her trust. He marveled at how she inspired him to trust her. Everything else had faded away. All fear had departed.

His only regret was that they had not attempted to create a child. But then a greedy desire to be with her for the rest of his life surged within his chest. He almost wept at the knowledge that she would die. She, this generous lover, this vulnerable woman, his wife would one day ascend to the heavens. He would be left behind.

He hugged her closer. She stirred but didn't awaken. He kissed her brow.

"Valerie." He couldn't be without her for another moment. "Wake up, love." He kissed one cheek and then the other.

She leaned back. "Is there something you need?"

He could hear the smile in her voice.

"I need to find the envelope." He leaned away to reach for contraception.

She pulled him to her. "Once was enough with that thing."

Darrin's heart quailed. "Please," he caressed her face with his fingertips, "I can't lose you...not so soon."

She took his hand in hers and kissed the palm. "All right. I'll be patient."

Chapter Twenty-Six

Emerald awoke reluctantly. The noises of children rising and the light on the other side of her eyelids compelled her to leave her comfortable spot in bed. Her eyes flew open. Once again, she was wrapped in Liameo's arms and resting her head on his chest. How?

She tried to rise and realized what must've happened. She'd fallen onto him. She hadn't wanted to, but he was so big and took up so much of the bed that once asleep she relaxed and simply fell into the arch of the mattress caused by his weight.

He was awake. Initially, his expression held wide, sparkly eyes and a silly grin. She frowned. He laughed, sat on the edge of the bed, pulled on his trousers, stripped his nightshirt, and continued to dress.

She watched his every move, absorbing each detail of his body. Before he turned around, she realized what she was doing and climbed out of bed on her side. Her feet grew cold immediately, but she didn't dress in front of him.

He flashed her one more smile before going through the curtain.

"Good morning children. Would you like griddle cakes and bacon for breakfast?"

"Yes!" Marta said. "Oh, daddy you make the best bwekfas."

Emerald could hear them kiss.

"Then dress and come down to help me."

The sound of his boots going downstairs let Emerald know she could dress in peace. But peace didn't come. So, she hurried because he shouldn't be making breakfast.

On the other side of the curtain, Nina stood with her hands on her hips. No one else seemed to be in the room. Emerald's eyebrows rose in surprise.

"Good morning, Nina."

"You didn't do it, did you?"

Emerald broke eye contact and tensed. "It's none of your concern."

Nina scowled and bared her teeth. "I'll kill myself if you make him leave."

Emerald's jaw dropped. Nina headed downstairs. That left Emerald scrambling to know what to say.

"Nina, wait, please," she caught the girl's arm, "you don't understand. These things take time."

Nina looked up at her. Resentment reluctantly released its hold, exposing a fragile hope. Nina was so easy to read. All of her pain washed over Emerald.

"Promise?" Nina asked.

"I give you my word." The oath cut Emerald so deep that it felt like being stabbed, almost as if hot blood throbbed from her heart to scald her spirit.

Nina hugged Emerald, clinging to her desperately as she sobbed out her grief.

"Oh, my sweet girl, I've missed you." Emerald held her tight, stroking her hair and rubbing her back. "Everything is going to be all right." She kissed the top of Nina's head.

"Don't ever leave again…, Mother."

Chapter Twenty-Seven

Valerie lay in Darrin's arms as he slept. Mid-morning's light shone through the stone panels in the ceiling of the bedroom they shared. She lifted her head to watch his foreign features relaxed in peaceful repose.

He had become dear to her over the past several moons. But after last night, the sight of him brought her joy. The feel of his body quickened her pulse.

An ache intensified in her belly. She took a cleansing breath to dispel the impulses she battled. She'd never craved anyone quite this way before.

Darrin stirred, stretched, and opened his blue eyes. Smiling, he wrapped his arms around her. A shadow of concern flitted across his face and he released her to roll from the bed.

The used sleeves lay on the floor. Naked, he bent to tuck them in the envelope. She enjoyed watching him.

He blushed. "We used them all, so don't ask."

She flashed the dimples in her cheeks and drank in the view of his body. He was uncut perfection. She'd never been with a man who wasn't circumcised. Was that what had made the stunning difference? No. It was him and him alone that had performed a miracle.

Darrin slipped into his trousers and took the package out to a trash receptacle in the kitchen. "I thought six would last longer than one night." He talked over his shoulder as he washed his hands.

She watched him find a fancy brush and powder to scrub his teeth. She wrapped a blanket around herself and came up behind him. Unable to resist, she caressed his behind. He faced her, and she leaned into his arms.

He held her. "Are you all right, Valerie?

"You don't know, do you?" She rested her head on his bare shoulder.

His breathing rate increased. "Did I do something wrong?"

She leaned her head back to look into his eyes. "Wrong? No."

Confusion played across his features.

She shook her head and smiled briefly at his lack of understanding. Looking away, she tucked the blanket tighter and walked over to the kitchen table. She sat in a chair and crossed her legs. The blanket gapped.

He stared at her bare leg.

She lowered her gaze to his middle, watching him through her lashes. His excitement heightened, but he didn't move. She wanted what he wanted.

He cleared his throat. "What did I do?"

She took a sip from her dinner glass. He watched her lips and throat, taking an awkward step back to lean against the countertop. The stone surface seemed to snap him out of his fixation.

"Perhaps it was a onetime thing. If I tell you, then you may never do it again." She was toying with him, but not in a bad way.

He frowned even as he smiled. "How can I do it again if I don't know what I've done? What if I forget how?"

She laughed. "That's not likely."

"Well, hmm," he turned halfway around as if in thought.

She giggled at his bulging profile.

He blushed from head to toe. "Please, I'm trying to think."

"That looks difficult for you at the moment...maybe even hard." Her emphasis on the last word left no doubt about why he couldn't think.

"You're not helping." He faced away completely.

She enjoyed that almost as much.

He faced her. "I don't know, love. But if you allow me to finish dressing and go to the medic for more contraception, then I'll let you explain it to me."

She smiled. "You mean I should explain it to you in terms that you understand?"

He nodded innocently. "I would like that very much."

She stood and walked over to him. She didn't touch him but came close to it. She leaned forward to whisper in his ear.

"It was my first time." The confession caused her to flush with something akin to embarrassment.

He was so near. She could feel the radiant heat of his skin. He almost touched her, but hesitated. She knew if he did, then he'd lose his resolve to delay impregnating her and take her straight to bed.

He swallowed. She stood on tiptoes to kiss the lump that bobbed in his throat. He exhaled an unsteady breath. She enjoyed exercising the power to mesmerize him.

"That's good." He didn't seem to have any idea what he was saying.

"Now you know how I felt when it happened." She dropped the blanket and caressed his chest. "Helpless in the most amazing way." She met his gaze. "I didn't think it was possible." Her thoughts drifted to a dark memory, but she turned from it and shone her light on him again. "Thank you."

Tears clouded her vision. She had believed herself incapable of enjoying a physical relationship. Until last night, she'd never experienced anything except pain. There had always been the hope of pleasure, but there had never been the fulfillment of intimacy's promise.

When she was five years old, Salicor had mercilessly cut delicate parts from her body. He had sewn closed much of what remained, preserving her flower. Female circumcision wasn't common in Frenland. Her uncle had reserved the ritual for jewels of the crown.

"I don't understand," Darrin hugged her tight, "but I'd do anything for you."

Her tears splashed his chest. "Why do you think you succeeded where no other man had?"

He gently shook his head. "I still don't know what you mean. But I'm guessing it has something to do with the gift you gave me after that last time."

She had said she loved him. "It happened right before that, but the reason is the same." She looked into his eyes. "I do love you," she smiled, "even if you don't know anything about women."

He sighed. "I thought I'd learned something, but apparently not. Perhaps I need to start all over again." He leaned in to kiss her, exercising impressive skills. Then he groaned in aggravation. "Not without contraception."

She smiled with her eyes closed. "I'll make breakfast while you obtain it."

He kissed her cheek, dressed in a hurry, and ran out the door.

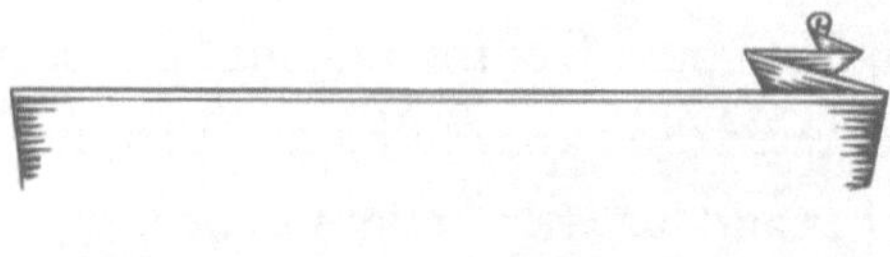

Chapter Twenty-Eight

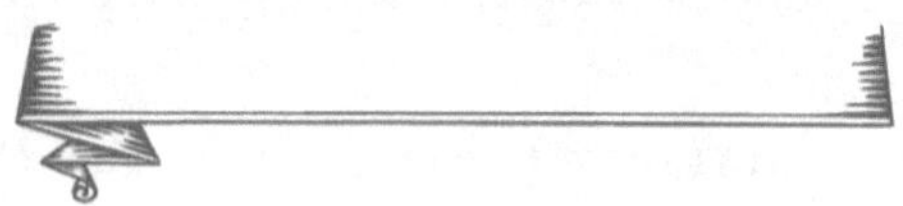

Stephan had ridden hard with his troops on his heels. They reached Soni-sashi before the snow became too deep for travel. The trip had taken three days and it was late in the afternoon.

He was exhausted. Riding past the Royal Hall toward the palace gates, he realized there were dozens of petitioners waiting in the snow. It wasn't fair to leave them there.

He dismounted and handed Marcin's reins to Helen. "I will hold court."

"No, sir. You should rest." Helen gave him a stern expression.

He chuckled. "Have the grooms rub down his right front leg, he's favoring it."

Stephan's royal guard surrounded him as he entered the Royal Hall and took his seat on the throne. The day wore on in an endless litany of complaints. One after another, he issued warrants for the arrest and questioning of man after man.

The last rays of daylight faded outside the high windows as a storm closed in. An old woman wrapped in a cloak approached. She bent over a crude cane to walk the length of the hall. Snow and ice clung to her clothing. Fires roared in the fireplaces, but the frigid gusts of wind buffeting the structure drew the heat up the chimneys. The marked candle to Stephan's right indicated the hour to be early in the evening. Time passed slowly in his court, especially when his subjects' grievances never ended, or when they walked as slowly as this old woman.

"Please, state your complaint." He spoke before she'd even come halfway to the dais.

She did not stop moving forward, nor did she speak. But her hand trembled on the cane. She came to a halt a little too close to him. The guards did not seem alarmed. A whisper had gone around the room at the woman's entrance.

"Madame, who are you?" Stephan rested a hand on the hilt of Krelor's sword.

"I am your humble servant, my king." Sarialla straightened enough to look him in the eyes.

He rushed forward to gather her in his arms as she collapsed. "I'm taking the counselor to my residence for care. Send for a physician." He carried Sarialla toward the exit on his right. "Admit all petitioners to the courtroom for shelter and bring them a meal while they wait."

He hurried out the door. Four guards in box formation surrounded him with security. The other guards hurried to complete his orders.

He carried the counselor through the palace gates. The incline to the courtyard had him winded. Sarialla was a sturdy woman.

He took Sarialla to his second-story bedchamber because the fires would be lit. "Pull back the covers and fetch the warmers." He attempted to stand Sarialla as he patted her cheek to rouse her. "Counselor, can you hear me?"

Her eyes roved without focus. He felt her hands. They were as cold as her face. Stephan unfastened her cloak and the coat underneath it. He sat her on the edge of the bed and stripped off her boots and stockings. Her feet were perilously cold, but not frostbitten.

"Fetch warm broth for the counselor."

One of the servants ran after it.

Sarialla wasn't shivering. Another servant carried in the warmers. Stephan helped Sarialla into the bed, placing the metal containers filled with hot coals in beside her. Fearing it wouldn't be enough, he sat at the bottom of the bed and lifted the down comforter to rub warmth into her feet.

The servant with the broth arrived, propped Sarialla upright with pillows, placed a napkin beneath her chin, and commenced spooning the liquid into her mouth. Sarialla gradually regained her senses and consumed the broth. When it was finished, she looked up and immediately pulled her feet out of Stephan's hands.

"My king," some color rose in her cheeks, "forgive me." Her hands fluttered as tears flooded from her eyes. "I have become a burden and I bare bad news."

"You've never been a burden." He stood, walked to the corner of the room, and brought a chair to the bedside.

The servants bowed and departed. That left four guards. Two men stood inside and two outside the open doorway to the living area of the cozy suite of rooms.

Stephan took Sarialla's hand. "Tell me your news."

She tearfully related the encounter with the invaders from the East Ice and the deaths of her men. She handed Stephan a message from within a buttoned pocket.

"The worst part is that I don't know if my daughter will survive. I was forced from the Imperial City without a chance to say goodbye. Emerald must have escaped because Dusty wasn't in the stables when I saddled Lightning." She met Stephan's gaze. A look of concern deepened the wrinkles on her elderly face.

Stephan leaned backward in the chair and waived to a guard. "Please, request a tea be brought for the counselor and me." He faced Sarialla. "You know very well how resourceful Emerald is. She'll be fine. As for Valerie, it sounds like she has allied with this Commander Trelan."

The emotional response he felt every time Valerie's name came up baffled him. He loved her. Yet, because of her atrocities, he needed to harden his heart. The only thing that stopped him was the dilemma of justice versus mercy that gnawed his conscience.

He couldn't reconcile his impressions of Valerie with the facts. He'd been presented with her crimes in session after session of court, yet Ashlyn had spoken so warmly of Valerie. His mind turned to Lily for a moment before he put away the line of thought.

"How did Valerie behave in the Imperial City?" He fidgeted with the seam of his trousers near the knee. "I mean, how did she conduct herself before the invasion?" He couldn't meet the counselor's gaze.

"She baked loaves of bread and pastries every morning. She tended Emerald and the horses each afternoon. The steward was distrustful of foreigners at first, but she came to value our service over time. Celeniurisa expended a great deal of effort in learning our language. I saw the sadness in her eyes when our men were executed."

"Yet she did nothing." He scowled.

Summary execution unsettled Stephan. How could one be certain the right decision had been made. Did the East Icer commander care?

Sarialla's head bowed. "There was nothing any of us could do. The people of the East Ice are fierce warriors. We were vastly outnumbered. Resisting their ruling would have led to more deaths."

Sarialla reached out to him. "I know nothing of what happened after I was forced to leave. It is a miracle Emerald escaped before they came. How does she always know?"

Stephan harrumphed and released Sarialla's hand. "If Emerald knew, then she would have saved herself from the Carpenters on the Border Road last spring." He stood and paced the room. "I think she follows her feelings. Her intuition is uncanny. She is inspired, but by no means all-knowing."

He rubbed his close-cropped hair with both hands. "Her conscience guides her. Her traditions inform her. Her faith in people may yet be the death of her."

He shook his head. "Her luck runs hot and cold, but she somehow survives and I'm not sure how she does it." He stopped pacing and stared at Sarialla. "She is the Woman of the Stone."

Sarialla sat in bed as a servant placed a tray of tea on her lap and propped more pillows behind her. "The people of the East Ice call her the Creator's child. I've never heard it phrased that way before." Sarialla sipped the tea, eyeing the letter in his hand.

A second servant placed Stephan's tray on the bedside table. He didn't touch it. Instead, he sat beside the bed and drummed his fingers.

He broke the wax seal and read the letter while the counselor ate. The message declared him, Stephan King of Frenland, to be a warmonger and an enemy to the people of the East Ice. They blamed him for seventy-two deaths during recent incursions of their sovereign territory. They warned against any more invasions, stating that the mountains were sealed and trespassers would be killed. Strangely, they invited him to come to the Imperial City to negotiate a peaceful end to the hostilities.

Stephan frowned and leaned back in his chair with the letter in his lap. "Seventy-two deaths."

Sarialla met his gaze, sipping her tea.

He sighed. "They only lost seventy-two people. Salicor's commanders sent their entire army onto the ice. They lost thousands of men."

She nodded.

Stephan lifted his eyebrows. "I believe you when you say they are formidable."

She set down the teacup. Weariness lined her pale features. She didn't look well and her eyelids drifted shut.

He shook his head. "How can they be negotiated with? I certainly never meant to start a war with them." He stood and paced. "I admit I used their reputation to intimidate my enemy. I knew Salicor might retaliate, but I never imagined a full-scale invasion, especially when my forces were easier targets and more relevant."

Sarialla sighed. "It was because of the horses that were slaughtered, my king. It is well that the people—" she glanced at the guards in the living room, "—do not know your secret."

Stephan looked at his guards in the far doorway. He walked toward them, bowed his head, and put a hand on their shoulders.

"These men know many secrets, including the shame of their king. I was once a man who thought horses were merely animals."

Chapter Twenty-Nine

The next day, Stephan sat beside Sarialla's sickbed. He'd moved her from his room to the other bedchamber in the suite this morning. She now rested in the room she had shared with her long-deceased husband, Arlon.

They had raised their twins in this suite of rooms when they served Stephan's parents as a royal counselor and king's baker. Even as an adult, Valerie had occupied her childhood bedchamber whenever she visited Soniashi. Stephan had claimed it soon after he took over the kingdom.

Sarialla's health had taken another downturn. She lay motionless and her breath rasped. During her waking moments, she asked for her daughter.

A knock sounded at the living room door and a messenger entered the suite. "Sir, the Representative Council has finished their deliberations over the letter from the East Icers. They request your presence during the vote."

Stephan released Sarialla's hand and tucked it under the comforter. She believed her daughter would come. He hoped she wouldn't. If Valerie returned to Frenland, then she'd be executed. There was nothing he could do.

"I'll be right there." He walked across the living room to his bedchamber, donned his official uniform, and departed the elaborate palace.

He crossed the beautiful grounds that glistened with snow and exited the gates. Across from the Royal Hall lay the Hall of Representatives. Four guards accompanied him at all times in box formation. Threats to his life were frequent. Attempts to kill him had been executed by various means and inventive ways.

Stephan approached the newly renovated building in the weakening light of the early evening. The representatives conducted the business of the kingdom over the winter because their pursuits, mostly farming, took place in more productive seasons of the year. That meant, they boarded in Soniashi, spending time away from their families to serve the people of their provinces.

Stephan had permitted them as much time as they required to discuss the message from the East Icers. They had debated the course of action the nation should take regarding their adversarial neighbors. It would have been better for Sarialla to have testified before the representative body, but she was too ill.

Stephan entered the large room and absorbed the grim mindset of the assembly. The arguments stopped and everyone bowed as he crossed the central area to the far end. He was a guest among them with a position of honor in an ornately carved, high-backed chair. He gave them a nod before he sat.

Plentiful windows let in the gray rays of winter daylight to illuminate the contrasting glares and downcast expressions of the women and men in the assembly. Their looks were sour enough that Stephan could almost smell their displeasure. Though, the odor may have been caused by their fear.

The hall had three entrances. He had come in the main doors, but the female representatives usually entered a private entrance on one side and the males on the other. Thus, the genders remained separated by a central area.

Helen stood at a lectern on the female side as she conducted the meeting. Stephan had come in at the tail end of a passionate exchange. The deaths of Sarialla's guard seemed to have driven them into shouting matches.

Helen pounded a staff on the wood floor of the council room. "Honorable representatives, please, be seated."

Grumbling, they obeyed.

"The king has come to address us. I turn the time over to him." Helen took a seat.

Stephan stood and recited the letter from the East Ice Nation in full. "I take responsibility for the war footing on which we now stand. It is an unfortunate turn of events."

"Sir, why would our allies during the war deny the alliance now?" Commander Gentry leaned forward in his seat.

Stephan tread on dangerous ground. "I have given this much thought, Commander. While at the mountain fort, we received horses from time to time. We know they came from raids on Salicor's army. Only a handful of men were ever seen. It stands to reason, given this letter, that those men were not sanctioned in their actions by the government of the East Ice."

An eruption of discourse ensued between the representatives. Stephan resumed his seat to wait out the debate. Helen met his gaze. She knew the truth, as did Commander Gentry and several others. Thus far, their loyalty to him held. By offering this information, Stephan hoped to ease the people's shock when they inevitably discovered the reality of what their king had ordered to be done.

"And what of the horses? Slaughtering the noble bloodlines, ending two of them, is unpardonable. These regal animals cannot be permitted to have died in vain. Their bodies were placed on pikes!" Walter, the provincial representative from the northern foothills stood red-faced and shaking a fist.

"Foreigners do not understand our ways," Stephan interjected.

"Then, how did they know which horses to murder?" Jarales, the representative of the capital stepped to the podium on the male side of the room. "I contend that the crime was artfully executed and must be punished."

"If you require blood, then let it be mine," Stephan spoke with a firmness that silenced them all. "These acts were done in support of my rule by those who could only be called loyalists. Thus, I am to blame. Exact whatever revenge you crave on me."

A low and dissonant chorus of voices answered in the negative. All eyes were upon Stephan. One by one the delegates determined their stance, quieted, and took their seats.

"We supported you then and we support you now, your majesty. How can we appease the people of the East Ice and end the hostilities?" Commander Gentry's gruff voice carried to the farthest corners of the room.

"Peace talks," Stephan said.

"What if they demand reparations? Should we not do the same?" Hilda, representative of the plain's province asked.

"I will not give them a thing!" Cloe, a representative from the forest province stood and moved between the others on her way out of the hall.

"We know nothing about them." Rudra, a female representative of the northern foothills blocked Cloe's exit.

"That is why we need to have talks with them," Helen, who represented Soniashi, spoke up. "I say we don't send you, my king. I propose we extend an invitation for them to come here."

"But where would we host the villainous diplomats?" Kent, a representative from the forest province, asked.

"The old whore house could be made into an embassy. We could keep an eye on them there." Jarales, the Soniashi representative, took a seat.

"I motion that we vote to extend the people of the East Ice an invitation to negotiate peace here in Soniashi and do not send King Stephan into the mountains to be slaughtered," Kent said.

"I second," Gentry said.

Helen pounded the staff. "Proceed forward to make your mark either in the affirmative that we invite an ambassador from the East Ice Nation to participate in peace talks, or the negative that we do not open said exchange."

Helen set a legger on a pedestal in the center of the room. She wrote the motion heading on the page and made two columns in the book. She signed in the affirmative.

"So be it." Hilda came forward to sign in the affirmative.

"I vote yes." Jarales strode forward and with a flourish of the quill made his mark.

Others came forward to sign the tally in the law book Helen had prepared.

Stephan observed the votes of the representatives from his vantage point. It was noteworthy to see how the group settled. In the end, those in favor won.

"The count is tallied and the motion passes. Meeting adjourned." Helen slammed the staff on the floor.

The acoustics in the large building allowed Stephan to overhear several men in deep conversation on their way out of the building.

"Two of the eternal bloodlines have ended."

"The sacred trust with the Creator has been broken. We are under condemnation."

"No, the ones who committed the act are."

"No, we as a people are responsible. It is our wars that brought this upon us. We deserve the calamities that will follow."

Chapter Thirty

Stephan waited for the entire assembly of representatives to empty from the hall. The weight of his near confession held him pinned to his seat in contemplation. The representatives were savvy enough to eventually unravel the secrets he'd hitherto carefully concealed.

"You may have said too much, sir." Helen pulled tight the door on the women's side as she reentered the hall. "They will question everything now."

Stephan sighed and took to his feet. "I hate deceiving them. They are the future of Frenland."

Helen shook her head. "I disagree. You are my king, and I believe in your goodness, but too many of them are not worthy of our trust."

He laid his palms on the wooden railing that separated him from her. "Do you think the people will choose better representatives in the summer solstice vote?"

Helen laid a hand beside him, her thumb touching his. "You have to live long enough for that to happen. Do not voice your insecurities to them again."

Stephan frowned. "What aren't you telling me?"

A crease formed in the center of her brow. "One of them is behind the latest assassination attempt."

He pressed against the railing and lowered his voice. "Three of my best men died that night. Who is it?"

Helen's expression saddened. "I've done everything I can to find out who could have done it, but losses continue to mount, and I still have no witnesses. How are they moving around the city? How did they enter the palace undetected?"

Stephan brushed his hand over hers. "Secrets and lies."

He thought of Valerie, guessing she would know the answer to Helen's questions. She had grown up in Soniashi. Children always discovered things adults overlooked.

"I know who we need to ask. Let's go." He grabbed Helen's hand and jumped the railing.

She gave him a quizzical look. "Where are you taking me?"

The four guards with him scrambled to follow them through the door on the women's side. None of the men looked pleased. Stephan didn't care.

"The curiosity of children may save the kingdom." He led her to the orphanage.

The building lay nestled along the outside of the palace wall. It was out of the sight of travelers on the Grand Road and had a spacious yard to play in. A high stone wall with barbs on top prevented anyone from approaching them without being admitted through the front gate.

Many of the children were innocent victims of abuse. They needed to feel safe. The wall also corralled the youngest from escaping their caregivers. Not that the orphans were prisoners, they were free to come and go as long as they were supervised.

Helen pulled up short, dragging him to a halt. "No, my king, not the orphanage. Last time I went inside with you, I came out crawling with lice. You have no idea the misery I went through."

Stephan chuckled. "Why do you think I trim my hair unfashionably short?"

She squeezed his hand. "It's not funny. I had to cut my hair. I look like a boy."

Stephan grasped both of her hands. "You do not look like a boy. In fact, in Danalan they would say you look like a newlywed bride."

Helen blushed. "It is unlikely I will marry. No man has ever...expressed an interest in me."

He raised his eyebrows. "That's not true. I paid you a compliment once."

She met his gaze with a warm intensity. "I'm sorry for the way I reacted then. I fear I made a mistake by not encouraging you."

He shied away, dropping her hands. "My intentions were honorable, Helen. Furthermore, I meant what I said. I come from the south. Well, at least I grew up there. Your sturdy attributes are attractive in my culture. I wish the men of Frenland saw it my way."

She stood unmoving. "Did I miss my chance with you?"

He glanced at her and was captured by her gaze. "I...I'm sorry, yes, you did." The memory of Valerie's kiss warmed his lips.

Helen's pain was plain to see.

"Forgive me," he said.

Stephan walked to the iron gate of the orphanage. He regretted hurting her, but there was no help for it. He planned to escape from the responsibility of ruling Frenland by handing over the kingdom to a representative government. Then he would pursue Valerie into the Mountain Realm.

A smile crossed his lips. He decided to sing the epic tale of Clarion and her rider for the children. The words of Valerie's song lifted his spirits enough to face living again.

Chapter Thirty-One

Emerald's new family had settled into a routine. The day had filled with work and fellowship, but being Liameo's wife hurt. More than anything, Emerald wanted a way out of the marriage. Yet, she owed him a great debt for restoring many of the orphans to her. The bitter-sweet emotions spoiled her appetite for dinner.

She climbed several flights of stairs to the library. Running her fingers along the spines of the leather-bound law books, she wished they held an answer. She took one from the shelf, laid it on the table, and opened it to a random page. The words blurred into a soup of letters as she blinked back tears.

Emerald looked away to stare into the fire. Trying to figure out how to make things right had only given her a headache. Loneliness clawed at her with longing for Darrin. She gritted her teeth to endure it.

Valerie would know what to say at this moment, something inciteful and humorous. If Stephan were here, then he'd have a plan. But what would he think? He had read these law books many times.

Was this marriage truly her only option? Was she trapped? It felt like her heart would fall from her chest.

"Em." Liameo stood in the doorway.

"Yes." She didn't look directly at him.

He closed the door and came to stand behind her.

"I missed you." His breath warmed the side of her neck as he laid a soft kiss on her skin.

She blinked back the sensation.

"I'm glad not to have to cut this." He unraveled her braid. "It's beautiful long. Why don't you ever wear it loose?" Once released the curls sprang to life.

"You shaved this morning. Everyone knows we didn't..."

"Let them think whatever they will. It's a foolish tradition anyway."

He was referring to the ceremony of the razor. She'd never thought of it as foolish. As a girl, it had seemed romantic. A new husband cut his wife's hair with his razor and bequeathed the blade to a younger man for luck in finding a wife.

"Who would you have given your razor to?" She focused on the flames in the fireplace.

"Rick, I think." Liameo kept playing with her hair. "He's apprenticed in town with the blacksmith."

She faced Liameo and met his gaze. "Not Rick, please. Nina's too young."

"Nina?" Liameo's forehead creased in the middle.

"She admires him. I think he feels the same way. Wouldn't his apprenticeship prohibit marriage for seven years?" Emerald searched Liameo's expression.

"Indeed," his brows rose in amusement, "but you should see the boy, he needs a razor."

Emerald avoided Liameo's gaze. She had something to ask. If he forbade her this, it would be unbearable.

She swallowed her trepidation. "May I see him? I'd like to see each of the children who were adopted out. I need to be sure they're safe. Please?"

Liameo's hands stilled. "You don't have to ask my permission, Em. You rule this land. I am subject to you."

Surprise opened her eyes. "Really?" She'd never imagined he would submit to her wishes.

"Yes." He held her gaze. "I'm a Stone because of you. All of us have a future in Danalan because of you. We're free because you are our queen."

She absorbed the words with a degree of sorrow. "I don't want to be a queen. I don't think I believe in it."

He chuckled. "Someone has to lead."

He walked to the library table and picked up the book laying there. Gazing along the shelves, he placed it in the empty spot.

Emerald watched him. "I'm not sure I'm suited for ruling a nation." She had seen what a dictatorship looked like during her time in Frenland. It had not been pleasant.

"Leaders don't choose their followers." his words came casually.

She had never thought about it like that. "I'd like to go tomorrow. Will you show me where they live?"

"I'd be happy to." He smiled brilliantly. "Gael will be harder to find than the rest. He was fostered by the traveling merchant who coveted his carving abilities. You know, the man who buys your wolf teeth and furs."

"I hope Gael is well." It was a lot to think about. "Thank you, Liameo." She walked past him on her way downstairs.

Chapter Thirty-Two

Emerald departed from the library and descended two flights of steps to the main room of the castle keep. Nina played blocks with Leland while the other little ones ran around chasing a rag ball. George sat in the padded chair with Tarah across his lap. Their faces were close together as they spoke softly to one another. The sight of them that way made Emerald's tangled emotions ache for resolution.

She crossed the room, grabbed a cloak, and went out for a walk. The evening would soon darken into night. She breathed deeply of the cold air as she walked across the courtyard and through the castle gateway.

Appreciating the sights and sounds of home, she glanced into the dark waters of the moat. The echo of her footfalls on the wood of the drawbridge gave her a thrill. The wind whipped down from the Impenetrable Mountains in a harshly familiar greeting, causing her to pull the hood over her loose hair.

She had guessed that the white-clad figures that had poured into the Imperial City were East Icers. She assumed that they now held the mountains, had captured her friends, and would bar her way back to Stephan. If they sent an envoy to her, then perhaps a resolution could be reached and an ally gained. If they provoked Stephan into war, then they would come to understand on whose side she stood. Unfortunately, her opinion would make no difference. Furthermore, Danalan was vulnerable to anyone who wished to claim it because she could not defend against invaders.

Liameo's heavy-handed arrangement of marriage had sidetracked her from thinking about these problems. Nonetheless, she had a great deal of business to attend to and plans that must be formulated. Once again, she had a family, a land, and a home to manage. Yet, the greater issues persisted. Many people expected her to lead them to prosperity and peace as their empress.

The citizens of each nation in the ancient Modutan Empire counted on her to restore the former glory.

Impossible.

Emerald walked the gravel road leading from the castle to Stone Bridge. It relaxed her to be outside. She breathed fresh air, watched the first stars come out, and listened to an owl hoot.

The road bisected a field. A handful of deer entered the tree line on the eastern edge as she approached. Even if she could still hold a bow steady, which she could not since her shoulder had caught an arrow at the final battle, the deer were out of range. It didn't matter anyway because Liameo provided ample food and supplies for the household.

Tea and bacon had been rare treats in times past. Now the children enjoyed their favorite foods often and in abundance. They wore nice clothes and had toys to play with. It made her wonder about the price of her marriage.

Men had offered enormous fortunes for her hand. Liameo had been disinherited by his father when he had returned for her nearly seven years ago. Bits of overheard gossip had informed her of this. For years, her maternal grandfather, Albert Hume, had denied all suitors. How could Liameo have convinced him to permit the marriage?

Emerald's mouth went dry. The murder trial and its revelation that she'd been raped explained it. More than likely, the letters Liameo had presented to Albert had offered a welcome excuse to end his patriarchal duty concerning her.

Liameo might be the only man who still wanted her.

No, numerous men coveted her lands. Roger Carpenter's declaration to his brother when he thought no one would hear suggested as much. Yes, some men wanted Danalan enough to do anything to obtain it. They would even marry a woman who had been defiled.

Had Liameo presented the letter from Jared Stone and demanded a dowry in exchange for honoring it? The law said he wasn't bound if she wasn't pure. Would he tell her if she asked? She shook her head and walked into the gathering darkness, not wanting to know.

The texture of the weathered granite railing at the bridge comforted her. It was gritty and enduring. Stone River rushed beneath her.

Before she relaxed any further, she looked over at the new guardhouse on the opposite side for any sign of occupation. It stood empty. Its purpose had been fulfilled now that she had returned. The trap had caught its prize.

A fish jumped. She focused her attention on the water. Inhaling deeply, she sighed. This river wound a course throughout her life. Many meaningful moments connected with it.

The hairs rose on the back of her neck. She sensed someone nearby. Her emotions descended into turmoil once again.

The sound of a man's heavy footfalls on the gravel road and a friendly bark from Eugenia let Emerald know for certain that Liameo approached. She clenched her jaw and waited. Why had he been the one to come?

Part of her had hoped Darrin would appear. She wanted to tell him what had happened. She hoped he would say something unexpected that would help her understand her predicament. She needed a way out of the marriage to Liameo, so she could be with Darrin. She swallowed a lump in her throat.

Eugenia trotted over to place her head beneath Emerald's hand. She petted the dog, taking comfort in the animal's affection. Nothing more than simple love was required to please the creature. It made Emerald long for a resolution to the complex problems in her life. If only things were as simple and people were as trustworthy as this dog.

Liameo came to stand beside her on the bridge. He oppressed her with his height, bulky musculature, and nearness. She hoped the darkness concealed her resentment.

"What will you tell him when he comes?" Liameo asked.

Emerald frowned, then her frown doubled. A multitude of possible answers flitted through her mind before settling with a thud.

"I'll tell him you won. I'll tell Darrin that I never had any say in the matter of my marriage. Though, I thought I did. I'll apologize for making promises I couldn't keep." Her voice quavered and her lower lip trembled. "I'll tell him I still love him."

"And then you'll leave me." Liameo stood ridged, but not hostile.

Emerald's jaw dropped open and she gaped at him.

"No," she blinked, "I'll never do that. He wouldn't take me anyway. I'm angry and I don't trust your motives, but I understand that I'm bound to you. I will not leave unless the law allows it, and I know the law will never make such an allowance. Therefore, fear not because I am yours."

Liameo hunched over the railing of the bridge. The moon shed some light on his inner struggle. His jaw clenched and relaxed as he shuffled his feet.

"You don't trust my motives?" He swallowed, his tone emotional and not only with anger.

She took a step away from him. "Everything you've done may have been for your benefit."

"But it wasn't." He straightened and faced her. "I didn't do this alone, either. The children and I built this family because we want to be with you. You're the reason for everything."

She squared her shoulders. "And the land meant nothing to you? The possibility of power means nothing to you? Possessing me didn't tempt you?" The pitch of her voice elevated.

"At first, yes. When I was younger, you were a prize to be won. My father plotted and planned for every contingency. He wanted this land for me. When I first saw you, I wanted you to be my wife.

"From the moment we met, you admired me and did all of those girlish things to let me know you loved me. Em, you made me sachets of rose petals to put in my travel trunk. You knitted me socks that didn't fit. You looked at me like I was someone special and hung on my every word." He met her gaze.

"I'd never been treated so sweetly by anyone. I felt responsible not to let you down." He looked into the river. "When you kissed me, I knew I'd be a cursed man if I broke your heart."

Emerald didn't know what to say. She stood stock still with a hundred shredded thoughts churning through her mind. They mingled with another hundred emotions swirling in her heart.

The river ran beneath them.

"You didn't break my heart, Liam." She could barely speak past the emotions that choked her. "I release you from your curse."

He took her in his arms and kissed her desperately. To her surprise, she allowed it. His tears fell on her cheeks. He kissed her until he was breathless, then pulled her close and rubbed her back.

She wished he'd stop.

As he wept, he shook his head. "You haven't called me Liam since I asked you to marry me. I've been bitter all these years." He kept rubbing her back. "You never told me you'd been raped. You should've told me." His body trembled and he hugged her tighter.

"You wouldn't have understood." She firmly pushed against the muscles of his lean belly.

He released her.

She backed away from him. "Who could understand it? I didn't?" She shook her head. "I hated everything and everyone for a very long time."

Liameo clenched his jaw. "Perhaps you hate me as much as I hate myself for what Roger and his father and brother did to you?" His hands formed fists. "My foolish pride caused that to happen. You almost died because I couldn't accept that you wanted me to go home to the sea. I resented all the lost years with my family, not to mention my occupation as a ship's captain. I thought you owed me an explanation. And all because I still loved you."

"Obsession isn't love." She squared her shoulders.

He laughed. "I know. Don't you think I've figured that out by now? Your grandfather wouldn't have allowed me to marry you, not for anything, if he hadn't believed I truly loved you.

"I went often to see him. For six long years, I offered him every coin I'd saved. I told him you loved me once. Over and over again, I told him I was the right man for you. I swore an oath that I'd honor your leadership and I believed what I said. But I was deceiving myself, and he knew it. He knew, and every time he refused his consent.

"Haggard from my illness and weighed down with the knowledge of what the Carpenters had done to you, I went to Albert Hume one last time. I carried with me the letter I'd found in Jared Stone's pocket in the mausoleum. I sat in the same study I'd sat in many times before. I waited for hours until your grandfather arrived. When he spoke to me, he surprised me with his wise words.

"He made me realize my mistake. I hadn't respected your history. I hadn't comprehended your future. It was then that I understood what I'd missed. You are destined to change everything for everyone.

"I knew you couldn't do it unless I restored some of what had been taken from you. When I told Albert, he wrote a letter of consent." Liameo sighed. "And then the real work began, convincing Nina to go along with my plan."

He shook his head and chuckled.

Emerald's resolve solidified. "How much money was I worth? Did he pay the price, or did you?" Her voice held bitterness.

"There was no price, except a lifetime with a resentful wife." Liameo's tone resembled a growl. "Perhaps I should've asked for compensation. Coins may be cold, but you're frigid." He stalked toward the castle.

Eugenia trotted from a clump of trees with a fox in her jaws. She followed Liameo with her tail wagging in the moonlight.

Chapter Thirty-Three

Emerald didn't hurry back to the castle. When she did return to the keep, she took her time bathing. She'd missed dinner, but she wasn't hungry. Guilt at not being there to help prepare the meal and tend the children piqued her discontent.

When at last she went upstairs to bed, everyone had already settled in. Nina hadn't fallen asleep, but she didn't say a word. Emerald slipped between the curtains to find Liameo lying in bed with his arms folded behind his head and a defiant expression on his face. The blanket covered him from the waist down, but it was plain to see that he was naked.

The sight of his bare chest and all of its many muscles and contours brought her up short. Blinking the vision of him from her eyes, she slid beneath the covers. With her back to him, she hugged the edge of the bed. That wouldn't last because the instant she fell asleep she'd roll onto him. Nothing to worry about, she couldn't sleep anyway.

Liameo took a deep breath behind her and moved. His hand slid over her hip and along her thigh where he grabbed her nightgown and pulled it up. She rolled onto her back and pushed his hand away, meeting his gaze with anger.

He gave her a wicked half-smile and pulled her on top of him. He drew her into a kiss as he placed her hands on his chest. Her thigh rested in the center of his hips. The lack of imperative she felt there let her know he was not attacking her.

"What kind of game are you playing?" She kept her voice low, attempting not to sound alarmed.

He didn't answer except to work the lacing of her nightgown open at the neck. He looked at her breasts where they pressed against his chest. She tried to stop him. But he prevented her from drawing the gown closed. All the while, he smiled and shook his head.

"I want to see," he said.

Her eyebrows shot up and then plunged downward. She shook her head. He nodded his head. After a long staring contest that nearly made her eyes cross, she braced her hands on the bed and raised her body upward. The gown gaped, allowing him to ogle her as she scowled at him.

He curled up to kiss the top of each breast. With a grin on his face, he relaxed on the bed. This exercise had aroused him, but it seemed to be all he wanted for now.

She slid off of him onto her side of the bed. Shaking her head, she gathered the gown to draw it closed. His hand shot out to still her fingers.

Startled, she met his gaze. It held intense concern. She glanced down to see what he looked at and saw the ring of scars on her left breast.

Heat flushed her skin. She brushed his hand aside, pulled her gown closed, and lay shoulder to shoulder with him. Her nostrils flared to draw in enough air to vent her angry shame. It wasn't working, so she turned on her side to face away.

He wrapped an arm around her middle and pulled her backward, holding her from behind. His arousal had disappeared, so she permitted the embrace. After the initial aversion wore off, she took comfort in his sympathetic gesture.

"I didn't know." His tone was gentle and his mouth right behind her ear.

She laid her arm over his and laced fingers with him. The tension eased out of his body. He sighed and laid a kiss on her shoulder.

"I'm sorry," he said.

She turned to look at him.

"You shouldn't have married me." A sob escaped her. "I'm not worthy of it. Everyone knows what happened. They just don't know how many times it has happened. Even you don't know." She couldn't bring herself to tell him about Byron. She didn't dare mention Roger's baby again.

Liameo's arms encircled her. His expression held deep concern, but not regret. With one hand, he moved a strand of hair out of her face and smoothed it behind her ear. For an instant, he gave her a sad smile.

"You don't have to explain, though I'd like to know someday. You're not the kind of woman to do things worthy of reproach. I know it, and you know it. I don't regret marrying you." His gaze lowered to her breasts.

He eased her gown open to look at her body. "I still think you're beautiful." He met her gaze. "I want to be your husband." His pupils dilated in the dim lamplight until they were deep pools.

She relaxed onto her pillow as she looked into his eyes. Sadness threatened to crush her, but she believed him. Somehow, it made things a little better.

Inevitably his gaze lowered to her breasts, but she didn't hurry to cover them. To her surprise, he didn't leer at her. He relaxed his head on his arm and simply looked at her body in a way no man had ever admired her before. At that moment, she knew he respected her right to choose.

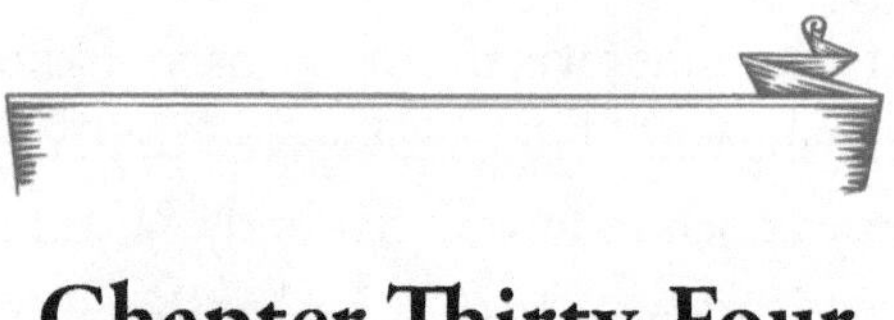

Chapter Thirty-Four

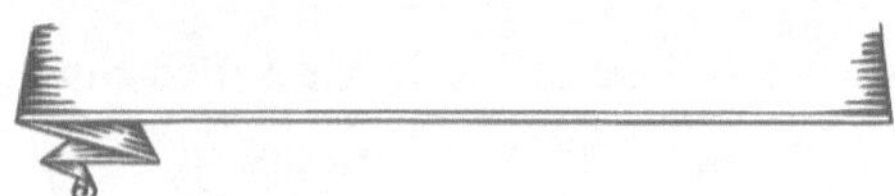

Darrin opened his eyes. Early morning light shone through the bedroom ceiling. Valerie lay beside him in bed. He often found her gaze upon him. This time, concern tinged with sadness creased her expression.

He looked into her beautiful brown eyes. The joy of everything about her made him want to smile, but he understood what she must be feeling. The threat of death hung over their relationship.

He touched her bare shoulder. "It's too late to spare me." He looked into her eyes. "I love you too much for losing you to be made easier by you leaving."

She shook her head and sighed. "How do you know what I'm thinking? How do you know you wouldn't be better off? I have no right to be the one here with you...the one..."

Darrin rolled onto his side and leaned in to kiss her nearest shoulder. Tracing along her arm, he found his way to caress her midsection. He wouldn't consider her words. If he did, then he would be angry. She was talking about Emerald and that wasn't allowed.

"You are the one I love, the only one." He kissed closer to her neck.

She rolled away from him.

He stared at the scars on her back. "Lay on your belly."

She looked over her shoulder at him. "Why?"

"Please," he said.

She lay as he asked, but the tension in her muscles doubled. She wouldn't look at him. He noticed her measured breathing, an effort to calm herself.

He smoothed her blond hair away from her neck and slid his hand down the scars on her back, moving the sheet off of her body. He had never thought to count them before, but he did now. There were one hundred and forty-three scars. His disquiet increased.

He slid his hand over the brand on her buttocks. She trembled. He continued lower to uncover her legs and the burn scars, including the pattern of the rope charred into her ankles.

He'd missed something. He ran his hand back to just below her right knee where he found a deep scar. He felt the bone. It had once been broken. She'd nearly lost the leg.

"You have many stories to tell." He lay beside her. Both of them were naked. "Perhaps I will leave no mark on your soul."

He looked through the transparent ceiling. What if he meant only little to her? What if she loved the pleasure he gave and not the man who gave it?

"The marks on my soul are being erased by your love, Darrin." She faced him. Laying on her side, she traced the scars on his body one by one. "I wish I could do the same for you."

His gaze snapped to meet hers. Service to Emerald had given him every one of his scars. Resentment over the cost he's paid hardened his heart. He clenched his jaw against a surge of rage, nostrils flaring.

Valerie slid over him, touching every bit of him as she left the bed. "That is why you would be better off without me."

The feel of her body distracted him from his ire, as she must have known it would. "I need you, not her. You want me to forgive Emerald, then what? Do you expect me to go back to her?" He stood up. "I will never do that."

Valerie didn't face him as she dressed. "Who will raise our child when I am dead?" She let the silence pervade the conversation for a while before she faced him. "Who should I trust with the two people in the world I love the most?"

His jaw hung open. He could see the anguish of her decision. She had to do it because his law demanded it. She would not leave him and the baby unprotected. Who could she choose? He clamped his teeth.

Valerie walked over and put a hand on his face. "Who could love a mixed-blood child, our child, the way Emerald can? I want you both to be loved...when I'm unable to do so."

He looked into her eyes and saw the tears there. She believed she was doing the right thing.

"Don't do this, Valerie." His fists shook with rage, but he opened them and came down to kneel before her with his head bowed. "I beg you."

"As you wish, Darrin." She lifted his chin to look into his eyes. "You choose your next wife."

Chapter Thirty-Five

In the morning, Emerald dressed warmly. Liameo made breakfast in the kitchen of the castle keep. She couldn't stop him. He said his years in the militia had ingrained the habit.

Emerald lifted Marta onto her hip with one hand and carried a stack of plates with the other. The little girl took a plate in both hands and leaned over the table to put it in place. The two of them repeated the exercise until the table was set.

Liameo carried two heaping platters from the kitchen containing sausages and round cut biscuits. Nina followed behind him with a pitcher of milk and freshly churned butter. Both of them were smiling. Emerald couldn't remember the last time she'd seen Nina carefree.

Everyone took a seat around the table. George skewered sausages for each of the little boys and passed out biscuits at the same time. Emerald poured Marta a cup of milk. How had Liameo afforded milking goats?

How much had he gone without to save his meager wages these seven years? Grandfather had done the family a great service by not taking any money for her. The thought of being bought and sold still galled her. However, she'd been bought without a price and paid for with sacrifice.

Emerald lifted her gaze to find Liameo watching her. He seemed to be in a very happy mood this morning. She glanced at Nina who watched them both from beneath her lashes as she buttered a biscuit.

"Please, pass the sausage," Emerald said.

Liameo complied.

"Thank you."

He smiled openly and passed her the biscuits as well.

Before long the platters were empty. Tarah helped Leland eat while she only nibbled her breakfast. Emerald sympathized, remembering exactly how difficult pregnancy was. Suddenly Emerald's plate of food didn't look appetizing.

"Are you all right, Em?" Liameo asked.

Faint, she blinked away the unsettling idea of becoming pregnant again. It would happen. She needed to face that.

"I'm fine."

She forced herself to eat, set Marta on the floor to play, and gathered the dirty dishes. Liameo followed her downstairs to the kitchen. She commenced washing the dishes. He leaned against the opposite counter, watching her. The silence lengthened until she discovered him looking at her hips intently.

"Liameo Hume, go find something better to do." She scoffed at the absurdity of his absorption.

He laughed and came behind her, putting both hands on her hips.

"I'm not a Hume anymore. I'm a Stone and that seems fitting at the moment." He bumped his front into her backside playfully.

Instantly, she knew what he meant. Scandalized, she turned around wet hands and all. He pulled her into his embrace for a kiss. She merely allowed it at first. But his skin smelled inviting and his lips were silky smooth and firm. She began to participate with increasing abandon.

A gasp at the kitchen door caused her to retreat. Nina stood wide-eyed on the top stair. Liameo kept Emerald pressed against the counter, concealing his excitement against her midsection.

"You did it?" Nina asked.

Emerald blushed.

Liameo faced away from the girl, hiding a grin.

"No, sweetie, not yet." Emerald could barely speak the words. She too found the situation humorous, but couldn't quite explain why. "Perhaps a little privacy would help."

"Oh, absolutely!" Nina backed out, shutting the kitchen door.

Emerald and Liameo's eyes met. On impulse, she laid a quick kiss on his lips, wanting to taste them again. He didn't allow her to retreat as she nearly did in embarrassment at her brazen act.

It was all she needed to overcome her nervousness. She drew him into a passionate kiss. The pleasure of the sensations he elicited throughout her body ached so painfully that she broke away in confusion.

"I want to be with you," he said.

His gaze held her captive. His breath came fast and ragged. She ran her fingers through his dark, wavy hair.

"I'm not ready."

With obvious effort, he calmed his breathing. He nodded, released her, and mounted the kitchen steps, leaving her alone.

She returned to the task of washing the dishes. As she did, she searched her heart for a resolution to the dilemma she faced. It stubbornly refused to come.

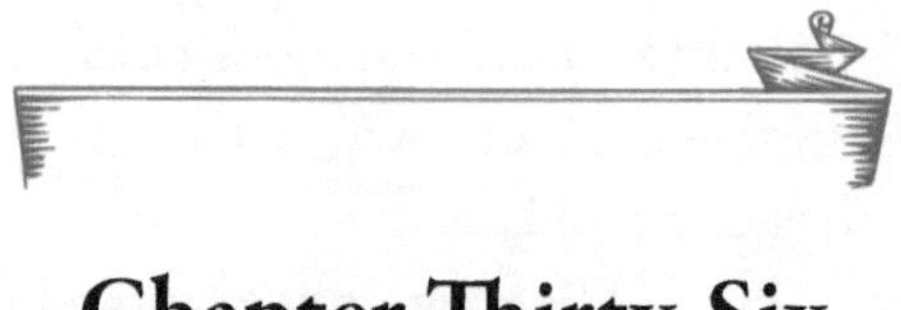

Chapter Thirty-Six

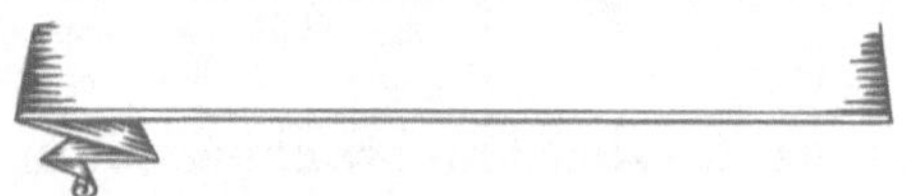

Darrin followed Valerie's litter as they traveled deeper into East Ice territory. She had been invited to see Cauldron City before returning to the Sacred Mountain. The Green Way hadn't lost any of its charms. Before long, he gave up being angry about Valerie forcing him to choose a replacement wife.

He ate his fill of vegetables as he walked. It felt like summertime. The late afternoon sunshine warmed his face.

The litter bearers had insisted on carrying Valerie to the city. They said she would have plenty of exercise exploring the wonders of the ten-story plaza of businesses that gave the town its name. They had stripped the fur coverings from the litter and were carrying her in the open air.

Darrin could see her frowning. He frowned back, but he didn't mean it. She just wanted to protect him and their child.

He thought about their baby and smiled. Valerie noticed. She noticed everything.

Her expression lightened. He stared in admiration, enjoying her Frenland features. His smile must have betrayed his changing thoughts because she shook her head with a reluctant smile of her own and gazed ahead.

Darrin laughed.

The city came into view and the Green Way wrapped around the upper edge of the cauldron. Ten stories fell below them in rings of colorful shops. Tantalizing smells wafted from venders of every delicacy imaginable. The bustle of shoppers filled the city with happy sounds.

Darrin couldn't believe his eyes. He leaned over the railing to take it in. One of the litter bearers grabbed him by the belt and hauled him back.

"This place is amazing." Darrin hadn't realized how close he'd come to falling over the edge.

"We'll leave the litter here." The duck farmer placed silver coins in Valerie's hand. "Trelan wanted you to enjoy your visit." The man bowed and went his way in apparent anticipation of having a good time here.

The other man bowed too. "I'm going to visit my mother, but I'll be back in a few hours." He hurried along the Green Way.

Darrin walked over to Valerie. "Will you permit me to buy you a wedding ring?" He took her free hand. "It would mean a great deal to me."

She allowed him to help her from the litter. Standing in front of him, she met his gaze. He never knew what she was going to say.

It made him nervous for the instant before she surprised him with generosity he knew must sometimes be against her better judgment. What would she have been like if she had never been taken by her uncle? The thought of her without scars combined with her current proximity, exciting him.

She raised an eyebrow. "You should be looking for a woman." She walked away.

Darrin trotted after her. "I am looking at a woman, my woman."

At those words, she would probably have said something, but he stopped the words with his lips. Her eyes went wide, then closed as she relaxed. He kept his eyes open and turned her aside to keep her out of the view of others. Public displays of affection between couples were taboo in West Wind territory.

This wasn't his culture, however, and no one seemed to care. He deepened the kiss. She tasted like...well, he had no words, but she was utterly lovely.

She peeked at him through her lashes. He slid his lips down her neck and back up to nibble on her earlobe. She laughed and tried to escape, but he pulled her closer.

"Trust me, my love." He kissed her on the lips. "Just trust me."

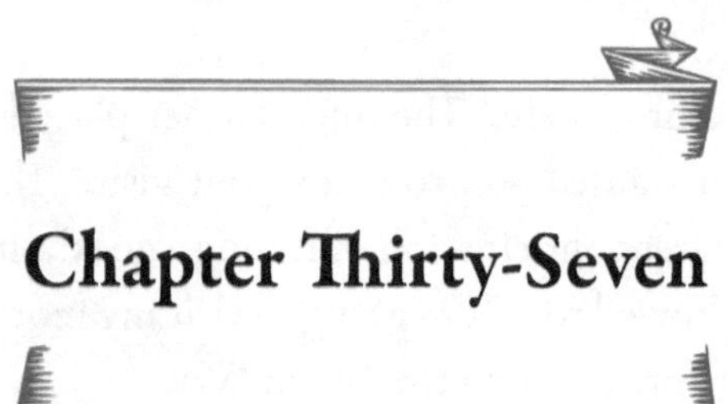

Chapter Thirty-Seven

When a man told Valerie to trust him, she instinctively did the opposite. Experience had taught her to fear men and for good reason. She suppressed the urge to push Darrin away, allowing him to caress her skin with his lips. But it had to stop.

Valerie applied enough force to his chest with the palms of her hands to distance herself from him. "The contraception failed last night. I noticed the torn sleeve in the trash receptacle this morning."

A faint line creased his brow. "I felt a change in sensation." He blushed. "Are you saying you're pregnant?"

Surprise at his naiveté dissolved her serious mood into one of humor. "How could I know so soon?"

He avoided her gaze. "If you received my seed, then you may conceive. Correct?"

She stiffened. "That was the risk we took. You should have been honest with me about not wanting a baby. I trusted you."

He grabbed her as she walked away. "Valerie, please, you misunderstand."

"Don't touch me." Seething, she clawed his chest with the fingernails of her free hand.

He didn't let go. She dropped the coins she'd been given and fought harder. Fear sliced deeper than her nails. He grabbed her wrists and pressed her against the wall. She glared at him, unable to move.

"If you want a child, I'll give you one right now." He hadn't hurt her.

She gritted her teeth, shaking her head. "Keep it." She struck his groin.

He doubled over and released her. She walked away from Cauldron City. Undeterred, and with twice the degree of panic in his body language, Darrin followed her.

The Green Way occasionally had side passageways that might afford enough privacy for them to work this out. She needed reassurance, though why she was reacting this way baffled her. She'd known it would come to this. She hadn't wanted to force him to surrender his seed, but he was just a means to an end after all. Pain tugged at the center of her chest. She had hoped for more.

"Valerie, please," limping slightly, he caught up with her, "you may have whatever you want from me. You know that."

She shook her head. "Marrying you was wrong." She faced him. "I was a fool."

Tears coursed her cheeks. She couldn't catch her breath. A cold feeling of dread washed over her.

"You're just afraid." He looked deep into her eyes. "Death frightens me too."

"But you're not the one dying," the possibility of danger made her body loose sensation, "are you? Did I make you sick?"

He shook his head. "No, not at all. I'm healthy. It's you I'm worried about."

"For a moment, I thought I'd killed you." Some of the tension in her shoulders abated. "I couldn't live with myself if that happened. I did everything short of castrating you to put you off. Why don't you listen to me? I'm no good for you and I know you'll hate me sooner or later. Having a child under these circumstances is insane."

He embraced her, pulling her head to rest on his shoulder. "You're all I have." He smoothed her hair and kissed her head. "Don't worry about me. I'm not going anywhere."

She pulled his shirt from his waistband and ran her hands up his back. Holding him in a fierce embrace, she squeezed her eyes shut. A tremor passed through her body.

"Valerie, are you well?" He cradled her head with his hand and held her close.

"How would I know? I've never been well before, not since I was little." She caressed his skin, self-soothing.

It was like children sometimes did. Darrin's closeness comforted her. But she should not take comfort from him, not now.

"You've only been ill since last summer." He held her gently.

She pulled away enough to meet his gaze. "I'm talking about my uncle and the things he did to me." She blinked and looked away. "And the things I did to others because of him."

Darrin wiped her tears with his thumb. "You've earned the right to enjoy the rest of your life. Forget about him. He's dead."

She met his gaze. Pain pooled in her chest. Did she have the strength to overcome the trauma she had endured?

"Salicor is dead." She blinked away the tears in her eyes. "He can't hurt our baby."

"Not unless you keep him here." Darrin touched a fingertip to the center of her chest and then her forehead.

She carried Salicor's poisonous words inside her mind and his actions on her skin. Making love to Darrin had been a delicate balance of give and take. It required sensitivity and patience.

She had rewarded him with far more intimacy than she had thought herself capable of. He hadn't known what to do and had taken it very slowly. He had exceeded everything she had hoped for in a marriage partner.

She drew her hands from his back to caress his midsection. Oddly, it wasn't sexual. There was a hint of possessiveness about it, but not in an overbearing way. He didn't shy away from her touch.

Fear still pinched at the corners of her perceptions. He placed his hands on her hips, relaxing his body. He was the answer to what she needed...wasn't he? Stephan haunted her recollection, intruding on so many moments.

"I'm yours," Darrin said.

Valerie knew he meant it. "Why?"

"Because kissing you is the best part of making love to you." He grinned. "You have a gift."

"I've given away many kisses." A stark emptiness hollowed out her chest.

He flushed. "Then maybe it's what I have to offer that has the power to change your outlook on our marriage."

She met his gaze. "I will never kiss another man. That is my wedding gift to you."

He moved, as if to speak the same promise to her, she stopped him with a finger across his lips. With a slight shake of the head, she took him by the hand and walked toward Cauldron City. She could not allow him to make a promise he should not keep. Yet, she desperately wished he would.

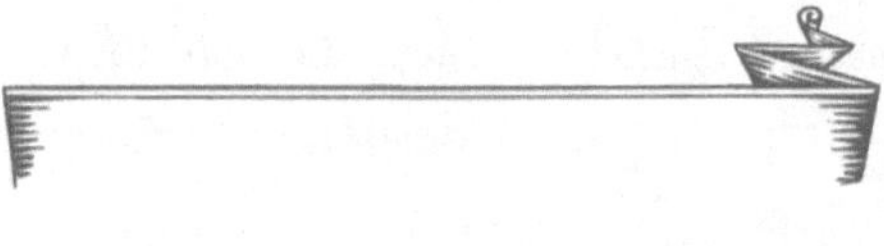

Chapter Thirty-Eight

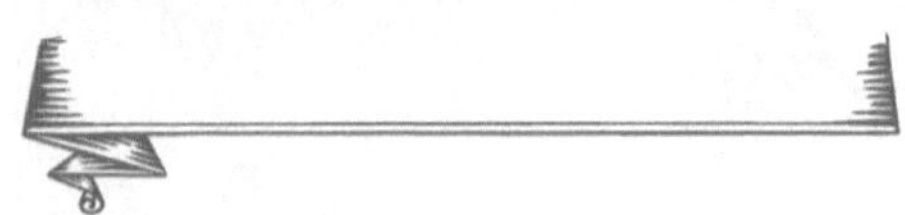

Midmorning Emerald skirted the castle courtyard, passing outbuildings at the foot of the curtain wall on her way to the stables by the gate-house. Liameo had gone ahead of her while she finished her chores. The sunny day grew relatively warm for mid-winter. She looked forward to riding out to visit the children in their new homes.

Striding through the open double doors of the stables, Emerald noticed Liameo chatting with Andre. They stood in front of Dusty's stall. The horse nipped affectionately at the boy's hair.

"Take care of your sisters while we're gone today. We'll be back in a few days." Liameo waved the horse off and smoothed the chaos Dusty had wreaked in Andre's hair.

Emerald smiled at the boy. He smiled back.

Liameo noticed Emerald then. He ducked his head and averted his gaze. He took Andre by the shoulders, bent down, and looked the boy square in the eyes.

"I need to talk to your mother. It may take a while. Will you make sure we have some privacy?"

Andre glanced at Emerald. "All right."

"Thank you, son." Liameo straightened.

Andre ran to the double doors. He slid them both shut, waving as the last of the daylight disappeared on the outside of the stables.

Emerald frowned in the semi-darkness. She let her hands fall to her sides beneath her cloak as she waited for whatever Liameo wanted to say to her. Was he offended that she'd made him wait to lay with her? The thought put her teeth on edge.

"Before we go to town, there's something I need to tell you. The villagers are aware of it, and I don't want you to hear this from them." Liameo faced her squarely but didn't meet her gaze. He grabbed at some hay that had fallen from the hayloft onto the top of Dusty's stall door. "There is a likelihood that I will not be able to have children." He glanced at her as he twisted the hay in his hands.

Stillness fell over Emerald. Her knowledge of his body seemed to indicate that he was capable of making the attempt. How did he know he couldn't father a child?

"And you know this because all of the other women you've lain with—"

"Emerald Stone!" His face and neck flushed deep hues of red. "No." He huffed and paced for a while, meeting her gaze at last. "I've never lain with anyone. I'm yours and yours alone." He looked away. "It's just that I became ill last year and the fever went low on me." He faced away. "The Doctor said there was little chance I could ever be a father."

Emerald stopped breathing. He had been faithful to her all this time. Militiamen had a reputation for finding willing women to bed. She had assumed he'd been a party to at least some of that over the past seven years.

She gasped as a thought struck her. When had he been ill? She set her jaw and lifted her chin.

"When did the fever occur?"

He turned halfway around and glanced at her. "It doesn't matter." His agitation slumped into lethargy.

She strode over and tugged him by the elbow until he faced her. His chin rested on his chest and his eyes were closed. She looked at his face in silence, but he wouldn't meet her gaze.

She unbuttoned his greatcoat, pushed his arms straight, pulled the sleeves and it slid off his back. She folded the coat and laid it over the door of an empty stall. Coming up behind him, she tugged his shirttail out and ran her hand up his back to feel the scars there. He walked away.

"It was my fault." The responsibility hit her hard. She had been the reason he was whipped for insubordination by Captain Hammond. The deep scaring on Liameo's back spoke of a savage infection. "No wonder you felt you had the right to make me pay."

Liameo closed the distance between them. His throat worked with unspoken words. His hands eventually settled on her forearms.

"I thought a lot of things right after it happened. But what I told you last night was true. I love you. I love these children. I want us to be a family, and...whatever might have been doesn't matter anymore." He met her gaze.

Emerald broke eye contact with him as emotion rose in her chest to choke her. Tears threatened to overwhelm her ability to hold them back. She knew full well that he had dreamt of a very different family than the one he had created. She had too, all those years ago, when she was fourteen years old and wanted pretty babies by the buggy load.

She had hoped to give Darrin children. However, Liameo hadn't given her a choice, and she'd resented the idea of submitting to such indignities for him. She knew it might cost her life and she'd been unwilling to pay the price.

She hadn't let herself love Liameo. She hadn't thought he deserved it, but now she knew better. He did deserve her. Indeed, he was worthy of her...affection.

Unshed tears blurred her vision as she met Liameo's gaze. His expression held deep concern. Her bottom lip trembled.

"Will you forgive me?" She wondered if that were even possible.

"For what?" He held her close, rocking back and forth. "I'm the one who needs to be forgiven. Roger was my friend. He knew exactly what he was doing when he hurt you, and I hate him for what he did. I'm glad he and his father are dead. I wish his brother would die too." Liameo released her and went to sit on a stool along the wall.

"They blamed me for your illness, didn't they?" She wiped the tears from her eyes. "The villagers blamed me too, I assume. They were right to blame me. But I couldn't accept you, Liam, I just couldn't." She strode over to stand before him. "You know why. But I can now." She spoke the truth, though it surprised her that she felt this way.

He met her gaze and sat a little straighter. She moved in to sit on his lap. In his eyes, she saw a peaceful place to invest her tender feelings. He wrapped one arm around her and raised a hand to turn her head, drawing her into the soft warmth of a kiss.

She closed her eyes and took her time kissing him. She gathered his upraised hand in hers and parted lips with him to kiss the hand she held. With a sigh, she leaned into his chest and rested her head on his shoulder.

He held her.

In the dust-filled rays of light coming through the planks of the wall, Emerald noticed Dusty watching them with his wise brown eyes. Her contentment elevated to bemusement. She felt a warmth swell in her chest and the impression came over her that her grandparents would be pleased.

The details of the world around her faded and her mother appeared. Ellora stood in a haze of white light. Her eyes bright with joy, she smiled at her daughter. She nearly touched Emerald's face, palm to cheek. Words were not necessary for Emerald to feel her mother's approval and the happiness she felt to see her daughter safe, loved, and home.

Liameo kissed Emerald's forehead and the vision receded. She breathed deeply and hugged him around the middle. It felt good to be with him, to be held by him, and to hold him in return. They belonged together. Her heart tore as she mourned for the loss of Darrin. But he had made his choice, and she must make hers.

She tipped her head to look into Liameo's eyes. He leaned in to kiss her. She enjoyed the feel of his lips, the clean-shaven feel of his chin on hers. She smiled with her eyes closed and breathed in the smell of his skin. It was different than Darrin's, but that felt right.

She parted lips with Liameo, not opening her eyes. "Would you be opposed to meeting me in the hayloft?"

"Really?" There was a smile in his voice.

"Careful now. Let me lead." She met his gaze fully. "I don't know much, but I know what not to do. We'll learn together."

"I trust you." He smiled.

The humor lessened her worry. They climbed the ladder to the loft. The slow revelation of lovemaking delighted her with its discoveries.

If children came, then she would be happy. If that truly wasn't possible, then she would simply be content to have him as her husband. His love was enough.

His body was enough. His touch...took her into the white light and warmth of her visions. Nothing disturbed her there. Only good could happen when he kissed her skin and worked his body within hers.

Lying in his arms after hours spent pleasurably engaged in forming this bond between them gave her the greatest satisfaction. Under the cloak that covered them, she glided her hand along his side, resting it on his hip. Naked and sealed together by the sweat of their exertions, she still felt at one with him.

He kissed the tip of her nose.

She lifted her head to kiss his lips. "I love you, Liam Stone." She smiled and shook her head gently. "You were right." She reached up to smooth his bushy eyebrows. "I don't know how you knew, but you were right. I am happy."

No one could explain the connection Emerald felt with Liameo now. She loved him. Incredibly enough, she loved him more for having expressed it in his arms. She never wanted it to end.

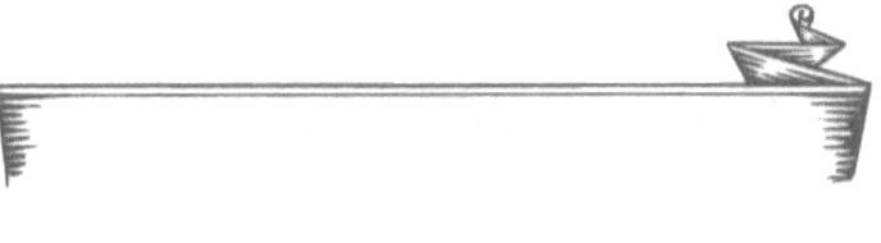

Chapter Thirty-Nine

Darrin gathered the scattered silver coins where Valerie had dropped them on the Green Way by the entrance to Cauldron City. He placed them in Valerie's hand. She looked a little tearstained, but the color had returned to her lips.

"Are you ready to see this marvel? We don't have to, you know." Concern for her wellbeing was hard to shake.

"Did you have something more interesting to show me?" Her wicked smile chased away the troubled crease between her delicate eyebrows.

He chuckled. "I'm glad you're feeling better."

They entered the ten-story spiral of shops. Valerie drew quite a few looks from passersby. He guessed that not many of them had seen a blond-haired, brown-eyed person from Frenland, but soon discovered that he was wrong. People of mixed heritage were everywhere. What was this place?

Valerie tugged his arm, leading him onward. Shaking his head, he followed her. The shop owners were gracious and perhaps a bit too generous with the pricing of their wares.

Valerie sampled their foods. "Try this."

He did, but the candy she offered wasn't to his liking. "No more, please."

The spices of most things here were foreign to his palate. Valerie took obvious enjoyment in everything she ate. He hoped she wouldn't spend all the coins before he found the hoped-for wedding ring.

Jewelry abounded, but none to suit him. He'd been thinking about it often since she had agreed to take him as a husband. What would she like?

He knew she loved horses, but these people didn't seem to have horses, so there was no horse jewelry. She loved baking. Random thoughts ran through his head as he searched for the right ring.

What colors did she like? She wore a lot of browns and creams. With her blond hair, she would look good in an elegant yellow. He imagined her in such a dress.

Of course, she noticed him looking at her. "What?" She held some kind of spiced meat on a stick.

"Do you ever wear yellow?"

"Not since I was a child." She averted her gaze. "It was my favorite color. I haven't had a reason to wear it lately. It's not practical in the army."

He could tell she was making light of it. "I'd like to buy you something yellow to wear."

To his surprise, her eyes filled with tears. She smiled through them.

"It's nice to know I married a rich man." She held out her free hand with only three coins in it.

He chuckled and shook his head. "Someday."

He turned his attention to enjoy the city's splendor. Indulging her would be his pursuit as soon as he found his place in the world. Then he could set to work providing for her and their child.

"What would you like to see next?" He realized they had only visited half of the shops.

"This way." She took his hand and led him around the circular balcony.

They explored eight of the ten levels of shops. As they approached the oddest-looking business of them all, her expression sobered. He could see her thinking about something weighty. She was staring at people as they went in and out of the shop. Several of them wore peculiar contrivances on their faces. He squinted at the wireframes holding glass lenses in front of the people's eyes.

Valerie strode into the busy shop. She watched as a young woman at the counter checked a list and ushered the waiting patrons one at a time into a hallway in the back. Plentiful seating indicated this was a place to wait.

Valerie held his hand. They sat on a cushioned bench along a wall. She observed everything around her until at last, the woman at the counter noticed them.

"May I help you?" The woman bowed and came out from behind the counter. "Do you have an appointment with the doctor?" Her smile was open and her demeanor charming.

"No," Valerie glanced at Darrin, "I was wondering what kind of doctor owns this business."

"An eye doctor, of course. Do you need spectacles?" The woman touched the rim of the contrivance she too wore.

"No, but a friend of mine has trouble with her vision. Do these...spectacles aid with vision?"

"Yes."

"What types of problems can they correct?"

"Virtually all of them, except blindness." The woman gestured toward the hallway. "Would you like to consult with the doctor?"

Valerie stood and strode forward. Darrin had to hurry to keep up. He wasn't sure what was happening yet, but he didn't dare lose her in this busy city for fear he'd never find her again. The woman with spectacles ushered them into the hallway.

"Father, a lady from Frenland has a question for you," the young woman said.

"Put her in room two. I'll be there shortly." An elderly man's voice came from within a room somewhere further down the hall.

"Please, wait here." The young woman gestured to the room on the right.

Valerie walked in and commenced to examine the tools and contraptions on the counter and in the cupboards. Her curiosity was normally more covert. But she seemed to be in a hurry to gather every bit of knowledge she could before the opportunity vanished.

"What are you doing?" Darrin was amused by her actions.

"Emerald can't read."

He frowned. It had become a habit at the mention of Emerald's name. It took a moment for him to understand the significance of the revelation. His face drained of blood.

How had Emerald made it through life without knowing how to read? Stephan was highly educated. He made an excellent king by all accounts. Emerald, on the other hand, fled from the notion of ruling the empire.

Darrin's body went limp. He closed his eyes and a sigh escaped him. He hadn't understood her limitations.

How could she rule over anyone when she didn't know how to read? She would be completely dependent on others. She must have sensed she could not rely on them. The only people she had trusted had been Sarialla, Valerie, and him.

His heart sank further. "You read my letter of proposal to her?"

Valerie glanced his way. "My mother did. I can't read your tongue." She kept investigating the equipment, poking at this, adjusting that, and probably mucking up everything.

Heat flushed his cheeks. "That's why Emerald took so long to answer."

He sat in a chair. She must be ashamed of her illiteracy. The Stones had always been famous for their wisdom and education.

He remembered the vast library at Stone Castle. He'd seen Emerald go there often to maintain the collection. What must it be like not to know the secrets those tomes held? What must it be like to have pressing questions and no one except children to inquire the answers from?

That's why she didn't ask. That's why she didn't know anything about anything. She had no hope of finding out without revealing her weakness.

He sighed. "It explains a great deal about her."

Valerie met his gaze and held it. "The fact that no one suspected her, says a great deal as well. She's more intelligent than any of us realized. Her mastery of languages is beyond remarkable. She mentioned the efforts her grandparents put forth to educate her. They worked around her disability. She knows how to read in all three languages. She can understand individual words, just not pages of them. She said the letters swim together into a mess. I think spectacles may help."

"Perhaps you are right." The elderly eye doctor stood in the doorway. "I suspect she may also need a tool like this." He came into the room and opened a cupboard to pull out a long flat piece of metal with a groove cut out of the center. He opened a book and placed the device on the page. "See how it limits the reader's view of other words? It can be slid along the pages like this." He demonstrated how one might read with the aid of such a device.

"I need to examine the lady in question. It's the only way to be sure of her particular condition. However, I expect she could be reading in no time with the right spectacles and this ruler as her aide." He held it up.

Valerie's brows knit. "Will this pay for the ruler?" She held out the three coins.

The man's white eyebrows lifted, but his eyes softened. "Of course, that is sufficient." He handed Valerie the ruler and accepted the coins. "I would like to see the woman if possible. I'm not sure the ruler alone will accomplish the task."

"She lives in Danalan. It is several days from here and the way is treacherous." Valerie sounded apprehensive.

Even Darrin could tell she was making excuses. He understood full well her reluctance because he felt it tenfold. This was important, however, and he knew they would have to go.

"I'm not as old as I look. I could make the journey. Who is the lady in need?" the doctor asked.

"Her name is Emerald Stone. Your people call her the Creator's child." Valerie followed the man's reaction.

Darrin watched them both.

The doctor smiled with obvious enthusiasm. "I suspected as much. My wife makes spectacles. We would be delighted to help." He bowed.

"And what of your business? Are you not needed here?" Valerie asked.

The doctor laughed. "Our children can manage while we are away. It would truly be our pleasure to serve the Creator's child."

Valerie didn't relax in the slightest. "We would be honored if you would accompany us. Though, we have no money and will need permission from Commander Trelan before we attempt the journey."

The doctor chuckled. "He will approve. He needed an excuse to approach the Creator's child. I've been told she wasn't in the Imperial City. It seemed logical that she would have returned to Stone Castle. Oh, what an adventure we will have." He hurried out of the room and along the hallway.

Valerie avoided Darrin's gaze and fidgeted with the ruler. "If she kills me, then so be it. I don't want you going with me."

He stood, walked over to stand in front of her, and leaned in to touch his forehead to hers. "She won't kill you. I'm going with you."

Valerie wrapped her arms around him and hugged him. "I hope this isn't a mistake."

Chapter Forty

When Emerald and Liameo emerged from the hayloft of the stables, she was surprised to see the sun lowering in the west. They'd missed lunch and the chance to visit the orphans today, but other gains had been made and she had no regrets. With their arms around each other, they walked toward the castle keep.

George came from the shadows of a structure built along the inside of the curtain wall. "Shall I fetch Judge Porter?" He met Emerald's gaze and offered a cautious smile.

Emerald grinned and squeezed Liameo around the middle. "I think that would be lovely."

George quirked a relieved expression. "I'll be back shortly." He hurried toward the stables.

Everyone else gathered in from their chores to visit with the happy couple at the large table in the main room of the keep. Tarah made cinnamon tea. Nina brought out a jar of honeyed apples.

"I know you like these best." Nina handed a mug of hot water to Emerald.

"Thank you." She dipped her spoon into the honey to retrieve a slice of apple and stirred it in the hot water.

The sweet apple-scented water soothed Emerald. Her childhood home had been near an apple orchard and her father had raised bees in neighboring fields. She didn't have many memories of her parents, but this treat brought them back.

Seeing her mother in a vision today had caused Emerald's emotions to come close to the surface. She had almost forgotten her mother's face. She squeezed Nina's hand. The girl smiled and squeezed back.

Emerald allowed Nina to brush and braid her hair. Liameo sharpened his razor on a strop. They sat in the kitchen of the keep, though Liameo was technically in the bathing area. Nina tied Emerald's hair with white ribbons. They smiled at the sound of hooves in the courtyard.

Emerald jumped from her seat, took Liameo by the hand, and led him to meet the judge. The rest of the family followed. Gavin Porter stood aghast at her smile. He had likely never seen her grin before and that made her laugh.

"Welcome to Stone Castle, Judge Porter. Will you witness the ceremony of the razor?"

He bowed to her. "It would be a privilege, Madame." He smiled a creaky expression that soon warmed into one of joy.

George took the horses to the stables. Just then, Rick rode through the castle gates on a mule. Emerald ran to him and hugged him as soon as he dismounted. Andre held the animal for him. Rick tussled the boy's hair.

"It's good to see you home, Em." Rick had grown taller.

"It's good to have you here for this happy day, Rick. Welcome." She ushered him toward the group and took her place next to Liameo.

"Is all in order?" the judge asked.

"Yes," Emerald said.

Liameo nodded.

"Then proceed at will." Judge Porter beamed.

When everyone had assembled, Liameo moved behind Emerald. He rested his hands on her shoulders. His razor was folded safely in one of them.

"Are you sure you want to do this." He stroked her braid. "It certainly seems a shame to cut it."

She looked over her shoulder at him, smiled, and winked. "Be quick now."

"All right." He sighed.

She faced forward. Liameo wrapped her braid around his hand, opened the razor, and with one swift stroke cut her braid of red-gold hair. She took a half-step forward, readjusting her balance because her head felt lighter.

Staring at his fist full of hair, she shook her head. The short strands of hair went flying. Liameo smiled at her, then walked over to Rick, folded the razor, and extended it to him.

Rick's brows shot up, but he accepted the gift with a glance in Nina's direction. Nina stared at him with a smile on her face. He blushed and looked away.

Shuffling his foot, he said, "Thank you."

Liameo clapped him on the shoulder. "Don't thank me." He looked at Emerald.

Rick followed Liameo's gaze and bowed his head.

Emerald smiled at the boy and faced the judge. "Would you care for tea, sir?"

Judge Porter's brows rose. "I'd be delighted, Madame. I'd also like to extend an invitation to you and all of your household to visit my wife and me anytime you are able. We would love to sit down to a meal with you to learn about your recent adventures abroad."

Emerald frowned, suspecting that a desire to report her activities was his true motivation for the invitation. "We would be delighted." Her tone fell a bit flat, but she led the way into the keep.

THAT NIGHT EMERALD cuddled with Liameo in their bed. She wanted more, but with people sleeping nearby, she had decided to wait for further intimacy. She sighed and he covered her hand on his chest with his own.

She tried to sleep. Slumber came for him and soon he was snoring softly. Unfortunately, she couldn't stop thinking. She needed to make plans for her household. Perhaps they should renovate a cottage near the castle and move out of the keep. It would be nice to have some privacy.

Tomorrow she and Liameo would travel to check on the welfare of the other orphans. That would inform her of their needs, then she could make better plans. Tonight, however, she floundered.

The judge had been cordial and pleasant. He had accomplished his desire. She had wanted to participate in the tradition. Though, she had modified the ceremony of the razor by declaring it to be voluntary for future men and women of Danalan. They could decide to follow it, or not, as they saw fit. Furthermore, she had not knelt before her husband as was customary in Andolin and that modification would hold.

It still felt strange to have her hair short. Nina had trimmed it neatly. The curl made it even shorter, but she loved it.

Emerald liked her new life. It was fresh, and she was happier than she'd ever been. She fell asleep a married woman in her husband's arms.

Chapter Forty-One

Emerald and Liameo rode out of the castle early in the morning. "Are you sure it will take days to see the orphans?"

"Some of them have been placed with families quite far south. I showed you on the map in the library." He met her gaze.

She smiled. "I understand the map of Danalan because I've visited the landmarks, but I've never been anywhere in Andolin except Meadowgren Village. I think I would become lost without your guidance."

He laughed. "I'll make sure we don't lose our way. Today you will see a great deal of Andolin."

She breathed the crisp air deep into her lungs. The horses' breath came in puffs of white, but the day promised to warm considerably. It was perfect weather to visit the children.

She hoped to find each of them safe and happy. If they weren't, then she would fight to bring them home. Liameo would surely allow it, but then he didn't have to allow it, the judge did. She stopped frowning and vowed to be optimistic. Liameo had assured her that the children were thriving.

It had been wonderful to see Rick the day before at the ceremony of the razor. Liameo had spoken the truth. It was high time the boy shaved. Nina had been unusually happy, though that may have been because she no longer feared losing her father.

Dusty danced as if he wanted to run. She allowed him to trot until they reached Stone Bridge where she reined him into a walk. She looked into the river as they crossed.

It saddened her to think of the children who had been drowned there over the years. It was beyond cruel for the people of Andolin to sometimes bring a child all this way only to murder them in place of giving them to someone who would love and care for them. She had never understood southern superstitions. She glanced at Liameo. Did he have superstitions?

"Em, what's on your mind?"

As they rode toward town, she contemplated an answer. "The judge seems different now."

"In what way?"

"He isn't trying to kill me anymore." She twisted in the saddle to face Liameo as best she could. "He invited us to tea." She looked forward as she shook her head in disbelief. "I thought he hated me."

Liameo laughed. "He is your great-uncle by marriage and he thinks of you much like his own child. He takes your actions personally and worries too much that you will disappoint him. He is overly proud of you, though. You need to understand that's why he compensates with discipline."

She frowned. "I find that hard to believe. Not the discipline part, but the bit about him being proud of me. I've never had that impression from him."

Liameo's expression sobered completely. "It broke his heart to believe you had committed the crimes you were accused of last year at your trial. He wept over his mistake and blamed himself when you left Danalan. He fretted that you would never return. The man was a nervous wreck. Your great-aunt nearly threw him out of the house. He spent hours in that guard shack watching the road. He paid for its construction you know."

Emerald couldn't believe her ears. She never suspected the judge would feel this way about her. He had been friends with her grandfather years ago, but they'd had a falling out. What did Judge Porter expect from her? She frowned in thought.

Liameo patted her leg. "I think you will find the attitudes of many people altered when we reach the village. There is a movement in Andolin to instate you as a monarch. Most people don't take that seriously, but I do, and Chief Judge Mason does. It's just people talking for now. However, things need to improve and many factions of the government are looking to you to bring about those changes."

The shock caused Emerald's jaw to drop. "You speak as if you don't think your words are treasonous. I urge you to be cautious. I have no desire to rule anywhere except Danalan. If things need to change in Andolin, and I agree they do, then the people of the south will have to make those changes. I simply want to work my lands and raise my family, nothing more."

He met her gaze. "That's why you are the perfect person to rally behind, Em. The Chief Judge saw that right away. He is the main proponent behind the movement. He gives it credibility and aids others to take courage."

She shook her head. "I don't see how I can help. I influence no one in Andolin. Their superstitions are intense, and I can't reason with them."

Liameo chuckled. "I think you're confusing normal citizens of Andolin with the villagers in Meadowgren. Most people further south have no such impediments."

Emerald adjusted her understanding. "Then not everyone in Andolin fears me?"

"No, not at all. Quite the opposite. There are many factions in favor of meeting with you to discuss matters." He waved to the guard at the militia fort.

The village was nearby. She worried that they should not be discussing treason where others could hear.

Liameo continued speaking. "The women of the south are polarized. However, most of them want the right to vote and need the right to own land. They envy your education and want to represent their ideas in the government. You see, Emerald, you have already altered the political landscape."

Emerald shook her head. "What you say is impossible. Everyone knows what the Carpenters did to me. There will be many who view me as a whore. Liam, whores do not influence society."

He shook his head. "You are not a whore."

"I know that now that I am your wife fully. What we shared yesterday is completely different from what happened to me before. Even so, there will be some people who will say degrading things about me because I was raped." She dreaded their remarks and feared that Liameo would react badly. "I don't want you to repay their taunts with violence."

He looked down the road and sighed. "I can't make promises, but I will try."

She captured his gaze. "Try very hard, please. I'm quite fond of you."

He chuckled. "Yes, my queen."

She rolled her eyes. "You can be so frustrating."

The baker, selling bread in the street called out a greeting to them as they rode into town. Liameo nodded with a friendly smile. Emerald waved.

"People look to you for leadership, Em," Liameo spoke softly. "The chief judge and governor have commissioned Judge Porter with reporting your every word and deed. He asked us to his home so he can question you. Everyone is curious about your adventures and what they may mean concerning the Legend of the Stone."

Emerald ground her teeth. "I will not answer his questions."

Liameo studied her, but he did not press her.

Chapter Forty-Two

Stephan stayed close to Sarialla's sickbed as much as possible. He rested little since he continued to hold court each afternoon. A knock came at the door of the suite of rooms he occupied. He hurried from his bedchamber to open the door, buttoning his coat. He didn't want another knock to wake Sarialla who slept in the other bedchamber off of the living area.

A black-haired young man with pale blue-eyes stood boxed in by a half-dozen of Stephan's guards. "I bear a message from Trelan of the Mountain Realm for the king of Frenland."

Stephan grabbed two fistfuls of the man's white tunic and dragged him to the doorway of Sarialla's room. "Look at what your people have done. She's dying because of you." He flung the man back at his guards who had entered the living room on his heels.

"What would you have us do with him, sir?" Aramis, the head of the royal guard, asked.

Stephan's chest heaved as his anger subsided. Sarialla was all he had. He feared losing her, yet the physicians had agreed, she would not linger long in her condition. The strain of exposure to the elements had sickened her lungs. Due to her age, they did not expect her to recover.

"Send for my daughter." Sarialla coughed severely.

"No, we mustn't. It isn't safe." Stephan went to her bedside.

"Read the message." She coughed even harder.

Stephan held out his hand, not turning away from Sarialla to do so.

A scuffle took place among the guards and the messenger.

"I will only give my message to the king." The messenger shook off the hands that searched him for a letter.

"He bears no parchment, sir," Aramis said.

The messenger righted his white clothes. "Only you may hear the message, your highness."

Stephan held the man's gaze. "Who are you?"

"I am Dantyn, second son of the empress." He spoke the mountain language now.

Everything the man just said, surprised Stephan. "I will listen to your message."

Stephan led the way to his chambers. He waved at the guards to leave the suite. The messenger followed him in and shut the door.

"My older brother, Outpost Commander Trelan, sends his greetings...and I know he would be grieved over the councilor's illness." Dantyn adjusted his bearing to one denoting a more formal stance. "Peace with the newly reunified Mountain Realm may be obtained only one way. You must do what is required to bring stability to Frenland. To that end, the empress has chosen a bride for you, King Stephan. Do you accept the terms?"

Stephan laughed with a dark edge. He ran a hand through his close-cropped hair, careful not to touch the sensitive scars. Considering his options, he sat on the edge of his neatly made bed.

"I assume the empress wants me to marry her daughter."

"No, your highness. My sisters are young and she does not wish to part with any of them. Trelan has a better solution and one he believes you will find agreeable. He wants you to marry the former crown princess of Frenland."

Stunned, Stephan's hands fell to his sides. "Valerie?"

"Yes. She has the power and influence to stabilize your kingdom while your republic is being fully instituted. Without her, your plans will fail."

Stephan scoffed. "My representative government will fail? And this from an empress's son, an outpost commander. What does a military man know of democracy?"

"Trelan will one day fulfill his role as a figurehead. It is an honorary title. Though, the position comes with a seat in Parliament and great influence." Dantyn relaxed.

Stephan wasn't fooled. "Why are you conveying this to me in private with no record of the request?"

"It isn't a request." Dantyn stared straight ahead.

Stephan understood the threat. "Has the crown princess agreed to this?" He couldn't imagine Valerie being willing to risk burning at the stake...unless she was seeking the throne.

"No, your highness, she's angry with you about the horses and is indulging in a dalliance."

Stephan paled. "With whom?"

The messenger flushed. "I was told not to say. Trelan is certain it means nothing."

Stephan scowled. "But he obtained her consent to marry me, correct?"

"No."

"Yet, I have no choice?" Stephan rubbed his face. "What assurances do I have that she will keep the bargain?"

"She loves you." Dantyn's demeanor softened.

Stephan stood with his heart pounding. "If that is true, then I accept the arranged marriage. But nothing must be said to her of our agreement. She's stubborn and will be defiant if forced. I must be given the chance to...woo her."

Dantyn smiled. "She is no damsel."

Stephan quirked an eyebrow at the slight. "You don't know her the way I do."

Dantyn bowed. "I meant no disrespect."

Stephan strode to his writing desk and penned a letter. He folded it, sealed it, and pressed his signet ring in the wax to make it official. "Will you deliver this to her?"

"Yes, your highness." Dantyn accepted the letter. "You have the sympathy of my people concerning Royal Counselor Sarialla. It was not our intention to cause her harm."

"Tell that to her daughter." Stephan clenched his jaw as he opened the door. "Be swift. If her mother dies before the crown princess can see her, then she will never forgive your people. Remember that and ride fast." Stephan opened the outer door, finding his guards in the hallway. "Escort this messenger to the foot of the Impenetrable Mountains on my swiftest horses. He has a message to deliver and time is short."

Chapter Forty-Three

Meadowgren Village bustled with market day activity. Emerald and Liameo rode through the crowd on the way to the Carpenter family's woodshop to check on the Miller children. It was a distasteful thing to have to do. Emerald dreaded seeing Christopher Carpenter and his spiteful mother. If it weren't for Annie Miller's children, Emerald would avoid this visit altogether. But her conscience would not allow her to neglect her duty.

Unlike in days past, the villagers showered her with smiles.

"We wish you well, Lady Stone," said the butcher from the doorway of his shop.

"Thank you. Please, send my regards to your wife." Emerald nodded.

"Congratulations, Liameo," said the cobbler.

"Thank you, sir." Liameo lifted his tricorn hat.

"May you be blessed with many children, your majesty." An elderly man bowed low.

His wife kicked him in the seat of his trousers. "Old fool." She gave Emerald a nod. "Peace be with you, Em."

"Thank you." The mention of children dampened Emerald's mood since there could be none between her and Liameo.

"Thank you, Mister Founder. Thank you, Ma'am. We are already greatly blessed with an abundance of children. They bring us joy." Liameo nodded to the older couple.

"Thank the Creator for that bit of good fortune." Madam Founder smiled a completely toothless grin at Liameo. "You're wiser than you look." She nodded approvingly.

Liameo smiled at the couple. "Are you in need of firewood?"

"No, what you laid up should last us." The old man tipped his hat.

"I'll bring the children around again in the autumn." Liameo urged Allura to walk on.

"You have our thanks," Madam Founder said.

Emerald urged Dusty after Liameo. "You work as a woodcutter?"

"Yes, but I've never required money of that couple, just like they've never charged me for a meal by their fire. The Founders are not well to do, but Mister Founder is a direct descendant of the group of men sent by the ancient king of Andolin to carve this village from the forest. Those men were Queen Dana's cousins. They established this village to provide a shield to her, so one day the Woman of the Stone could be born in Danalan. They're influential people, Em." Liameo led them down a side street toward the Carpenter's shop.

Emerald considered the information carefully. The villagers had not been overly welcoming to her growing up and they had never come to the aid of the Stone Clan as they fought for survival. It would seem their mandate had gone out of favor with them over the past four hundred years.

Liameo started singing softly. "In a meadow green and pure, eight families set up camp. With their axes in hand, they carved a village from the land. And the settlers of Meadowgren danced."

Emerald hummed along coming to a smiling finish.

Liameo sang another verse. "The old king had sent them, his daughter to keep safe. So, watch her, they did. And feed her they must. And the sacred trust never forget.

"Her sons were a mixture of race. They worked hard to make a good place. They did their part and didn't lose heart. And the Mountain's treachery they never forgot."

Emerald met Liameo's gaze after he finished the third verse. "Then you know that Dana did not betray Krelor with another man. It was he who accused her and broke his oath to marry another for power. All because she bore no daughters, only eight sons."

Liameo's jaw dropped open. "No, I did not comprehend such a tale from the ballad. Most have never heard the second and third verses. The Founders shared it with me last summer."

Emerald frowned. "I only knew the first verse."

They arrived at the Carpenter family's shop. The living quarters were on the second story. Emerald and Liameo dismounted and hitched their horses to a post.

She glanced at his grim expression. Between the pair of them, they were partly responsible for Roger's death. Would his family be willing to allow them to see the Miller children?

Emerald opened the door to the storefront. Inside were beautiful pieces of furniture on display. A cradle, complete with a cushion and blanket, caught her eye. A rocking chair of womanly proportions graced the space next to the cradle. Beautifully carved bowls, cups, and spoons lined a large table with benches. There were cedarwood chests of varying sizes.

"It's good you've come home, Em." The oldest Miller boy stood in the doorway to the woodshop in the back of the building.

"I'm happy to see you well, Ryan. I wish I hadn't needed to leave at all, but I'm home now. Are your siblings happy here?" Emerald held the boy's gaze, needing to know the truth.

Ryan nodded solemnly. "I didn't expect them to treat us well, but the family has welcomed us in as if we were their own."

Emerald understood the difficulty Ryan must face, having witnessed the late Hubert Carpenter murder his mother. "I'm pleased to hear you are being properly cared for. You can always rely on me to assist you, should the need arise."

Ryan smiled. "I think you can rest assured that we're all right."

Emerald sighed, satisfied with the answer. "Are you responsible for this fine furniture?"

Ryan walked further into the room. "No, not a bit. This is Christopher's doing and most of it is for you, Em. He's been spending one day in seven in your service as the chief judge ordered."

Emerald's eyebrows shot up. "Oh, well, I hadn't anticipated that. I mean, I know he's supposed to, but I thought caring for you and your siblings would be payment enough. Do any of you need these fine things?"

Ryan scratched his head. "My sister is marrying the butcher's son next moon."

Emerald tried not to frown at the prospect since the oldest Miller girl was a mere fifteen years old. "I don't want to be indelicate, but was the union her idea?"

Ryan smiled, his shoulders relaxing. "Yes, she's very much in love. It's a good match."

Emerald hoped that was the case. "Well, she'll need some of these things then. I imagine she's at school right now. Please, wish her joy."

Ryan nodded. "I'm afraid you caught me alone at the shop today, Em. Um, should I call you, my lady?"

Emerald smiled. "No, you're fine. I'll always be Em to you, Ryan. I'm off to visit the other orphans now, but I'll return in a few days."

"It's good to see you again." Liameo tipped his tricorn hat to the boy.

"Come again soon. It's good to see you both." Ryan returned to the woodshop.

Emerald and Liameo exited the building. She sighed because it was a tremendous relief to have that visit over with. They mounted their horses and made their way through the village, heading south on the Forest Road.

"My grandfather warned me never to travel south of Meadowgren." Her apprehension tainted the clean, close, comfort of the woods.

Liameo frowned. "Jacob Stone was wise to advise you to stay close to Danalan. It may be best if we tread carefully while traveling through Andolin."

She eyed him for a moment, weighing his response. "I have my son's sword and you have your ax. Yet, I hope to avoid conflict. It is not likely we can avoid recognition since you are a descendant of the islands. Everyone must have heard about our marriage by now." Speaking of his foreign and devastatingly handsome looks caused her to smile despite the seriousness of the discussion.

The creases of concern around his eyes eased. "Perhaps we can travel a lesser populated route. It means we will be sleeping in the homes of anyone willing to host us as opposed to finding lodging at an inn."

Emerald read the implication in his disappointed tone. It meant they would not have the privacy required to be intimate. She sighed in resignation.

"Well, it's best to be cautious." Her entire body protested the decision with an increasing desire to be with her husband.

"If there wasn't so much snow on the ground in these woods..." Liameo kept riding.

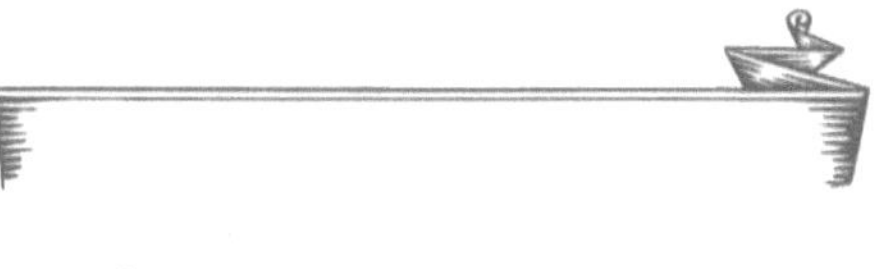

Chapter Forty-Four

Emerald and Liameo rode hard to reach the horse farm where Timothy lived before nightfall. Vast pasturelands divided by split rail fences stretched to the edge of the forests that surrounded them. Along a well-graveled branch off the Forest Road lay a cluster of structures.

Emerald spotted Timothy sitting on the top rail of a corral. A trainer performed the dusty work of breaking a fine young chestnut gelding. Timothy watched with rapt attention. He wore a warm coat and a straw hat pulled low over his ears.

"Hello, Timothy." Emerald rode along behind him, sidestepping Dusty close enough for the boy to pet him if he wanted.

"Em?" Timothy turned at the sound of her voice. He touched her face with a red wool mitten. "I thought I'd never see you again."

Tears fell from his eyes. He swiped his rosy cheeks with his other mitten. She handed him a cloth from her pocket.

"I've missed you, Timmy," She managed to say past the emotional response she too was experiencing.

He dove into her arms. They hugged fiercely for a moment before he leaned back toward the fence. She heaved him onto the top rail.

"I go by Tim now that I'm mostly grown." He sniffed and made a stoic face.

Emerald nodded torn between tears and amusement.

Liameo smiled. "Tim, how are you these days?"

Tim grinned. "Right as rain, sir."

Emerald expelled a sigh of relief. "I can't tell you how happy I am to hear that, Tim."

Timothy jumped down from the fence. "Let's take Dusty and Allura to the stables for some water and oats, then I'll take you inside to meet my family."

Emerald gladly followed the boy. "Are you the one who ended up with the brown mare?"

"No, that was Ari and Loral. They live at a dairy farm a half day's ride south of here. You'll have to stay with me going and coming." Timothy nodded soberly.

"Are you sure the Trainer family will welcome us?" Liameo asked.

"I'm sure," Timothy said.

The three of them set to work taking care of the horses and were soon walking toward the house. A woman came out on the porch to greet them. She wiped her wet hands on her apron and smiled as they approached.

"Tim, will you introduce me, please." The woman met Emerald's gaze.

"Mother, this is Emerald Stone of Danalan. Liameo is her husband, right?" Timothy looked at Emerald askant.

Emerald smiled. "Yes, that's right."

"Welcome to our home, Lady Stone." Madam Trainer flushed, attempting to curtsy. "You too, Mister Stone. Will you be spending the night? You are welcome here."

"Thank you, yes, if Mister Trainer agrees." Emerald felt awkward about not having taken Liameo's surname of Hume, though that choice was made by him and not her.

"Oh, he won't mind," Madame Trainer said.

"You have a fine log home, ma'am." Liameo tipped his tricorn hat to the woman. "We're very grateful for your warm welcome."

"It is a pleasure to have you as guests. Tim, find your father and sisters. Tell them it's time for supper."

Timothy ran off toward the barn.

"Please, come inside and wash up. The meal is nearly ready." The woman ushered them into the house.

Inside the cabin, a crystal lamp burned brightly on the table. A girl just older than Timothy set porcelain plates on a linen tablecloth. A delicate metal spoon and knife lay beside each one.

"You may freshen up in the washroom off the back of the house." Madame Trainer pointed toward the back door.

Emerald and Liameo did as they were told. The evening meal was spent in easy conversation. Afterward, they spent the night on blankets before the fire. When breakfast was ended, Mister Trainer walked them to the stables and helped them saddle their horses.

"Lady Stone, you must be careful in these parts. Do not speak to anyone on your way to the dairy farm. Hurry there and don't tarry. You must make it back here if you hope to be safe. Don't concern yourself with the hour no matter how late it is. You are welcome here." Mister Trainer held Emerald's gaze with a look of intense concern.

"I will follow your advice, sir. Will you tell me what troubles you?" Emerald asked.

"There is a revolution in Andolin. No open battle has yet taken place, but many have lost their lives for sedition. The girls you go to visit today, well, their parents were hanged for treason in Ando Bay. I do not fear you, my lady. Tim has told me much of you. He describes you as kind, humble, and not the sort of person to overthrow a peaceful nation's rule of law. That's why you are safe with my family. We may face condemnation from our neighbors when it is known that we sheltered you. Do not worry, though, we are not vulnerable to unlawful charges." His expression was grave.

Emerald's heart stirred with concern. "I hope we have not brought trouble to your family. I had no idea things like this were happening in my name. I am not behind any of these actions and I do not condone them. We will not return unless we have no other choice."

Liameo extended a hand. "If it is not safe, then what should be the sign?"

Mister Trainer shook Liameo's hand. "There is a post on Forest Road where our gravel drive branches off leading to the ranch. I will tie a red cloth to it if it isn't safe and you should ride past."

Emerald had no idea she would be endangering their family and had no intention of doing it again. "Thank you, sir. Please, do not take risks for us. The safety of your family and my sweet Timothy is of the greatest importance."

Mister Trainer bowed his head. "Farewell, Lady Stone."

Emerald and Liameo rode swiftly on their way.

Chapter Forty-Five

Emerald and Liameo arrived at the dairy farm at midday. Ari and Loral were in the kitchen with the dairyman's wife washing up after the family meal. Emerald could see them through the open window as the woman cast out the wash water from a basin.

Without warning, the dairyman and his three sons surrounded Emerald and Liameo with pitchforks.

"We don't want you here. Begone with both of you," the dairyman said.

"We have come to inquire after the Carter girls' wellbeing." Liameo had his hand on his ax as if he may draw it from the sheath on his belt.

The man looked surprised. "They're not Carters. Who told you that? I have two daughters and my name is Silace Boaire. Move along, you're trespassing."

"Ari, Loral, are you well?" Emerald called to the girls.

The dairyman's wife had an arm around each of them, though the trio had all poked their heads out the window to observe the confrontation. Both girls nodded.

"There, you have your answer. Now turn tail and ride out of here." Mister Boaire jabbed his pitchfork in Emerald's direction.

"Sir, do they speak?" Emerald had worried about the traumatized girls.

One of the Boaire boys chuckled. "We can't shut them up normally."

"Hush, boy," Mister Boaire said.

Overjoyed, Emerald wept openly. "You can't know how that comforts me. Farewell, good family." She led Liameo back the way they had come.

EMERALD AND LIAMEO did not return to the horse ranch because they took a more direct route on a path no wagon could follow. Fortunately, moonlight allowed them to travel through the night. Exhausted, they stopped at the Porter's home.

Emerald knocked on her great-aunt's front door while Liameo stabled the horses. "Auntie, it's Em."

Judge Porter opened the door in his nightshirt. He carried a chamberstick. Emerald could smell the beeswax taper. A gust of wind blew out the flame.

"Come inside. Where is your husband?" The judge grasped her by the arm and drew her into the entryway.

"He's tending the horses. I'm sorry to impose, but I feel the need to speak with you concerning the political climate in Andolin." Emerald spoke softly.

Judge Porter chuckled. "Praise be to the Creator. Child, I've waited years to hear you say that to me." He patted her arm in the dark. "But you must rest until morning. We will breakfast together and discuss matters."

Emerald stifled a yawn. "Yes, uncle." She went upstairs to the spare room, laid her cloak over the back of a chair, removed her boots, and slid into bed.

Chapter Forty-Six

At breakfast, Great-Aunt Elaine set a fine table. It was even grander than the Trainers. The cook provided a plentiful spread of bounty. In winter, that was a feat of tenacity.

"How do you possibly have fried green tomatoes at this time of year?" Emerald asked, taking a bite of the delicious breaded vegetable.

"We slice them in season and dry them in the sun. soaking them in water makes them supple again, then they can be prepared in the normal way." Elaine Porter sipped her tea, having partaken of very little of the meal.

It was at that moment that Emerald noticed the lines of care around her great-aunt's eyes and lips. "What is the matter, Auntie?"

Elaine set down her teacup and saucer. "I worried about your safety. Please, speak to us before you set foot in Andolin again."

The judge patted his wife's hand. "With your permission, we will send you supplies until the situation becomes less dangerous."

Emerald frowned. "Are you implying that we are in peril even in Meadowgren? Sir, that cannot be true."

The judge nodded his head. "I'm afraid war is brewing. Many believe that your death is the only way to prevent it."

A mad scramble of hooves on the road ended abruptly in the yard. A pounding commenced on the door. The judge went to answer it. Elaine drew the curtains in the dining room and closed the door. She stood beside it trembling.

Liameo stood and drew his ax from the scabbard. Emerald drew the sword of her unnamed son. It thrummed with powerful contentment and peace descended on Emerald's troubled mind. All would be well.

Several minutes passed before the sound of a horse could be heard trotting away from the house. A gentle knock came at the dining-room door.

"Do not be alarmed." Judge Porter entered the room. "It was an express rider with news from the governor. I wrote a reply that you had returned safely from checking on the orphans from your castle."

Emerald and Liameo put away their weapons. "There is much I should tell you, but I do not trust anyone beyond the four of us with this information. Will you keep it between us?"

"I will," the judge said.

Elaine nodded.

Liameo's brow creased. "You know my loyalty is assured."

Emerald sighed. "I have much to say regarding the state of the ancient empire. I have traveled far and wide since last spring. Are you sure you want to know where I've been and what has transpired?"

Three sets of eyebrows rose in surprise.

"Let us retire to my parlor where we may visit in comfort." Elaine led the way.

It took the better part of the day for Emerald to relate the events of the past eight moons. Her companions had many questions. The judge informed her of the political intrigues and unsanctioned executions happening in Andoshi and the region thereabout. Together, the four of them plotted possible courses of action for each of them to take to remedy the situation. Nothing seemed overly promising and every scenario held inherent dangers.

Judge Porter's wrinkled face pinched. "I'm very concerned. I don't know who is behind the troubles in Andoshi. But someone is speaking on your behalf, Emerald. Since you have convinced me that it is not you, I fear your name is being used to overthrow the lawful government of Andolin. I must advise you to stay out of it, though even if you do, there is no guarantee that you will be spared."

Emerald's anger burned bright. "I cannot sit idly by and allow my name to be used for destruction. If I do not speak for myself, then others will continue to do so. I had not intended to become involved, but now I must. I just don't know the best way to go about it."

Liameo took her hand in his. "I believe you will know when the time is right. I trust your judgment."

"You are not without great bargaining power, Emerald Stone. There is much good you could do with your influence." Elaine stood. "I have not yet congratulated you on your marriage, but I wish you both abundant happiness."

Emerald stood and embraced her great-aunt. "Thank you, Auntie. To my surprise, I am very happy."

Judge Porter shook hands with Liameo. "You've done well, young man."

"Thank you, sir. Visit us as often, um, if that's agreeable to you, Em." Liameo ducked his head.

Emerald smiled. "Of course, please, visit whenever you like." She took her husband's hand and led him from the house.

Chapter Forty-Seven

The evening sun waned as Darrin rode at the head of the procession of East Icers escorting Valerie's litter. As he approached the gates of Stone Castle a dog barked. The gates were closed, but he had spotted smoke rising from the chimneys of the keep.

"Who goes there?" Andre's voice sounded from the other side of the gates.

"Friends. Andre, allow us entrance. We have traveled far to see the future queen." What else could Darrin say?

He dreaded the sight of Emerald. Their meeting could only go badly. He dismounted the great Frenland steed he rode and held the reins.

"Em isn't home. Is Sarialla with you?" Andre peered through the crack between the gates.

Darrin stood on the drawbridge close to the gates. "No, but her daughter is. Please let us in."

Andre lifted the crossbar and Darrin pushed open the gates. "Thank you." He smiled at the boy. "You've grown since I saw you last."

"Don't be nice to me. Mother is mad at you." The boy led everyone toward the stables.

Valerie had given the party riding instructions before they left the Imperial City. Darrin had been given the honor of riding Rumsfahail, Valerie's beloved warhorse. He was high spirited, but well trained and had seemed happy to be free of the tunnels under the mountain.

"You call her mother now?" Darrin wished he spoke more of the southern language, but he made due.

"We all do. She adopted us. Well, Liameo did, but he's her husband, so we're her children now." Andre pulled open the stables door and walked inside.

Darrin stood rooted to the ground unable to move. Emerald was married? Some man had adopted her children and now she was married to him?

Rumsfahail snorted and pulled at the reins as he stomped his feet. In shock, Darrin walked the beast into the clean stall. He removed the saddle and bridle. Andre assisted the other riders to care for their mounts. Darrin brushed Rumsfahail while the horse drank from the bucket, then he shut him in the stall.

Andre brought oats for the horses. "They sure are fine animals and big," the boy said. "It makes me wish Lightning had come too."

"Did the brown mare foal?"

Darrin was curious because it had been much talked about among the boys when he'd left. He didn't even know how long a horse took to gestate. He hoped he didn't sound foolish, but he wanted to say something.

Andre looked at him sadly. "I don't know. The judge used the mare as payment so a dairy farmer along the road south would adopt two of the girls."

"You mean all the children are not here?" Darrin felt a blow to his heart.

"No, just me, Nina, and Marta. Oh, and Tarah's here too. She married George and they adopted the three little brothers from the squatter's cottage. Everyone else is gone. Liameo saved everyone he could." Andre moved to the next stall with the oats.

Who was Liameo? Darrin searched his memory. "Do you mean Liameo Hume, Emerald's cousin?" Darrin remembered a suitor by that name from years ago.

"He's not a close cousin." Andre met Darrin's gaze with a severe expression. "Don't call him Hume. He took Mother's name. He's a Stone." The boy smiled. "We all are."

"Why did she marry him?"

Darrin could hardly speak. He wasn't sure what to think. He noticed Valerie watching from nearby.

"She loved him a long time ago." Andre laughed. "She sure was mad to find out he'd obtained her grandfather's permission and not hers." He shrugged. "She came around though." The boy glanced up at the hayloft with a knowing smile. "She made him work for it, though."

Dumbfounded, Darrin looked upward at the hayloft. "She did what?"

Andre pointed up the ladder to the hay. "She took Liameo in the hayloft and didn't come down for hours. After that, George went for the judge, then Liameo cut her hair. I think they did something up there."

Darrin stared with his mouth open.

Valerie laughed and slapped her knee. She strode out of the stables still laughing. Darrin guessed she had understood at least the part about Emerald making love in the hayloft.

Valerie seemed to believe it, but he didn't want to. He couldn't understand how Emerald would willingly accept a man she didn't love. Not Emerald Stone.

The thought struck him that she may have had no choice. His mind didn't work this way normally, but he had begun to realize that different cultures required different things of men and women. Andre had mentioned that Liameo had permission from Emerald's grandfather and had adopted three of her favorite children. Perhaps she felt compelled to accept him.

Darrin shuddered. Emerald may very well hate him now...and he deserved it. He hoped she wasn't brutally injured.

"Did Liameo hurt her?" Heat and tension caused Darrin to clench his fists.

Andre walked over to Darrin. "I was worried about that too, but no. She seemed really happy." The boy clapped Darrin on the shoulder. "Come inside and eat. You look like you need...something."

Darrin walked with Andre into the castle keep. Valerie sat at the table with several of the East Icers. Tarah and George served them tea and bread.

Marta found her way onto Valerie's lap. The little girl touched her face and hair. Valerie didn't seem bothered. She spoke to the girl in the northern tongue. The round-cheeked child laughed and smiled in amusement.

"Her name is Marta." He spoke to Valerie in his tongue.

Valerie tried out the name. "Marta."

The little girl giggled at Valerie's accent and hugged her impulsively. Valerie reciprocated the embrace with enthusiasm. Marta pushed back with a frown.

"Too tight." She shook her little finger at Valerie.

"Larisa deh, yar gon." Valerie smiled even though her apology seemed sincere.

"She's sorry, Marta. She is your mother's friend." Darrin had to speak the southern language to her and this switching back and forth gave him a headache.

The little girl's frown disappeared. "Em*ma*'s friend?" She hugged Valerie around the neck and played with her hair contentedly.

The door of the keep burst open and clattered against the wall. Emerald surveyed the crowded room. Her attention rolled right over Valerie to fixate on Darrin. Her expression faltered and she fled the keep. He didn't go after her.

Chapter Forty-Eight

Emerald couldn't face Darrin. She had wanted him to come. But now that he was here, she couldn't tell him what she'd done with Liameo. Other's must have told him everything by now anyway.

Shame and grief caused her heart to sink. What must he think of her? What would he do? Who were all these people and why was Valerie among them?

Emerald flushed with embarrassment and ran from the keep. Valerie never would have agreed to a forced marriage. Darrin never would have rolled around in the hayloft with her.

"Who do these horses belong to?" Liameo had stabled Dusty and his chestnut and now walked across the courtyard toward the keep.

Emerald hurried in the opposite direction. Valerie nearly collided with Liameo as she flew down the steps of the keep. He stood stock-still, staring at her northern features. She barely came to the middle of his chest in height.

Emerald didn't watch any more. She ran to the steps of the curtain wall and climbed them. The brusque air cooled her flushed cheeks and whipped her newly cut hair behind her. Valerie followed, but Liameo stayed put.

"Emerald, please, let me explain," Valerie spoke the Frenland language.

Emerald stopped running and collapsed along the crenellations. She sat on the battlement, out of Liameo's line of sight. Great heaving sobs wracked her as guilt plagued her with remorse.

Darrin had come and it hadn't taken long. He had come and she hadn't waited. She should have had faith in him. She had always known he loved her. Why hadn't she believed he would forgive her?

"I married another man, Valerie. How can I face Darrin with news like that? I have...lain with Liameo. It's too late." Her tears started afresh.

"Darrin has not forgiven you, Emerald. He should never have blamed you for the child, but he still does. I'm sorry." Valerie shook her head and looked down at the moat.

"Then why have you come?" Emerald's heart grew heavy at the news, but it helped somehow. She blew her nose on a handkerchief from her pocket.

"The East Icers may be able to correct your vision so you can read." Valerie met Emerald's gaze.

The news further shocked Emerald to the point of silence.

"There is much to tell." Valerie's voice faltered. "Darrin's mother disowned him for breaking his oath to you. It caused...problems. He was attacked by a woman who wished to claim him as a husband. I rescued him the only way his culture permits."

"What did you do?" Emerald sensed the guilt her friend could not hide and dreaded the answer.

"I took him as my husband in the hopes of saving him for you. I thought he would overcome his hurt feelings and want to be with you. I didn't plan to take him fully, but I have." Valerie avoided eye contact.

Emerald stood, strode the two strides between them, and slapped Valerie across the face. She fell to her knees. Shock registered on her features. Holding the side of her face, she fled.

Emerald grabbed ahold of her arm. As angry as she was, she realized she had no right to judge her friend. Valerie struggled, but Emerald prevailed.

"Release me." Valerie's angry tone dissolved into tears.

"I'm sorry." Emerald gathered her in an embrace and wept great heaving sobs of grief over the loss of Darrin.

Valerie rested her head on Emerald's shoulder. "I didn't mean to..."

Emerald sensed the depth of Valerie's feelings. Ever since Emerald had made love to Liameo, she had begun to comprehend the bond that intimacy formed between two people. She had hoped Darrin would marry, eventually. She had hoped he would find happiness. She had never dreamed Valerie would be the one to fill the role of his wife.

It hurt. It hurt so much that Emerald wanted to die. But she could never hate Valerie.

She hugged her friend fiercely. "I wish you happiness."

Valerie held her so tight that Emerald thought her ribs would crack.

"I'm sorry." Valerie sobbed like a child.

It reminded Emerald of Byron and his desperation for her approval. "You are my friend. I wouldn't have Darrin be with anyone else." She stroked Valerie's hair. "I know you will give him joy." She wiped her tears. "I never deserved him anyway."

Valerie looked into her eyes. When she blinked, more tears coursed her face. "Darrin will one day forgive you, Emerald. You did nothing wrong."

Emerald released Valerie enough to squeeze her shoulders. "I loved my son." She faced away from her friend. "I just didn't love him soon enough." Bitterness poisoned her tone. "If Liameo heard me talking..."

She hadn't dared mention the baby to Liameo again. Not since the first time she'd tried had gone so horribly awry. But she needed to talk about it.

"Liameo doesn't know about the baby?" Valerie came to rest on a crenellation stone in front of Emerald.

"I told him, but he became angry." Emerald raised her sleeve to reveal the faded bruises Liameo had caused when he'd found out.

Valerie took Emerald's wrist, staring at the marks there. Lacing the two scars from Valerie and Byron's brands were yellowish bruising in the shape of fingers. Valerie released Emerald and strode along the battlement.

Leaning over a crenellation stone, she glared at the countryside. "If he has hurt you in other ways, then you must tell me."

Emerald walked over to her friend and placed a hand over hers. "He's wonderful to me."

Valerie closed her eyes and bowed her head. "He pleased you?"

Emerald sat between the crenellations to face Valerie. "You said I would enjoy it."

Valerie's eyes were haunted. "You love him?"

The question took Emerald aback. Could she really be in love with a man who couldn't face the knowledge of her son, such a basic truth about her life? She had told herself it didn't matter. The child was dead, but he had existed. He meant so much to her. She loved him even now.

She couldn't hold back the tears. Her son was dead. She would have no other. He had died in her arms; small, frail, innocent, and without a father. Would any man ever accept such a situation?

"I thought I loved him." Emerald swiped at her tears with the handkerchief.

Liameo claimed to love her. He had been tenderly persuasive in his attentions. But he had rejected the boy. Her son and his short tragic life were unmentionable, shameful. The knowledge made her grow numb.

"Is Liameo a good man, Emerald?" Valerie visibly struggled with the words. "Did he force you to marry him?"

Emerald's resolve solidified and she faced Valerie. "I have done what I needed to do. I've done the only thing I could do. I was happy for a moment. I will find that feeling again."

She couldn't imagine any degree of intimacy with Liameo while Darrin was here. She couldn't face the idea of him in Valerie's arms. She couldn't look at her friend, so she faced away, laying a hand on Valerie's shoulder.

"Come inside. You must be tired from your journey." Emerald took two steps before Valerie stopped her.

"I'm dying. The East Icers cured my disease, but my heart is damaged." Valerie walked over to Emerald. "I married Darrin to save him, but I never intended to lay with him. However, he offered me a child, and I couldn't resist. I may lose my life in childbirth, but I had to take the risk. If I die, it is my wish that you help Darrin raise the baby."

The shock made Emerald feel faint.

Valerie swallowed and looked into the courtyard below. "Darrin will forgive you, Emerald. I know it can't be the way you had planned, but he needs a protector, and I need a mother for my child."

Emerald remembered to breathe and inhaled sharply.

Valerie's lower lip trembled. "I want happiness in this life. I need to see the baby I've dreamed of for so long. I never dared to hope for a husband, but Darrin claims to love me. I know he will always love you more, at least when he comes to his senses. I know he will regret me and everything else before long."

Emerald allowed the words to sink into her heart. "I don't think he knew what love meant. I know I didn't...not really. If he loves you now, then trust in it."

Valerie faced Emerald. "I can't trust him to remain faithful to me, but please don't let him hate me. Don't allow my child to think there wasn't anything good about me. I need to know I did something right in this life and that I didn't fail my baby this time." She gasped for air as her lips turned blue. "Please, Emerald."

"You have my word." Emerald took her friend by the elbow and helped her down the steps and across the courtyard.

Valerie trembled and collapsed. Emerald caught her and carried her inside the keep. The main room full of people fell silent as she carried Valerie upstairs to bed. She hadn't passed out, but she gasped for breath and her lips were blue. Emerald loosened her clothes and removed her boots. She wiped Valerie's brow with a wet cloth and sang a lullaby until she slept.

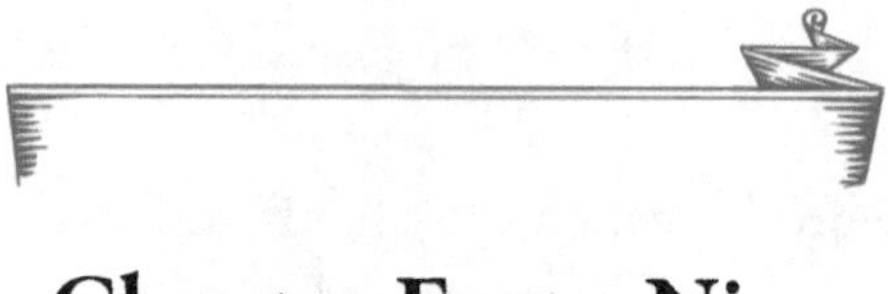

Chapter Forty-Nine

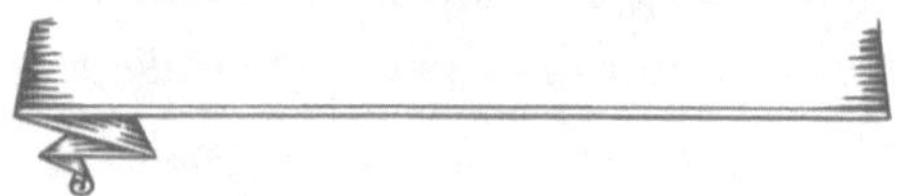

With the gray light of dawn, Emerald left Valerie asleep in bed and descended the steps to the main room of the castle keep. Darrin lay slumbering among the people of the East Ice. That's when she noticed Liameo sitting in the padded chair, staring at the fire in the hearth.

She didn't know what to say to him.

He had tried to kiss her last night at bedtime. She had turned away. He'd laid a kiss on her cheek and left her to tend Valerie without a word of complaint. But now, he looked troubled. That was how she felt as well, distanced, and apprehensive about where their relationship stood in the light of Darrin's return.

She looked at Darrin and her heart broke with unresolved emotions. He was a married man. She couldn't believe it without feeling betrayed, yet, she was betraying Liameo by feeling this way.

Fighting exhaustion after a fitful night of sleep, Emerald noticed a man in the corner of the room. He beckoned to her. She approached the mountain man, glancing at Liameo to see if he had noticed her. Not wanting to disturb those who were sleeping, she walked past the man and found her cloak on a peg. Gesturing for him to follow, she left the keep.

She had walked down the steps and crossed half the courtyard when he caught up with her.

"Creator's child, I thank you for your hospitality." The man bowed low, speaking the language of Danalan.

Emerald's brow creased in thought. "You speak the language of the south countries fluently, but I do not understand your use of the phrase, Creator's child. Aren't we all the Creator's children?"

He smiled. "Of course, we are, but the title is one reserved among my people for you, Woman of the Stone."

"Why?" She walked to the gates and peered through the crack without opening them.

"We revere you and now pledge our loyalty to you as our future empress." He bowed even deeper this time.

"I don't recognize your accent. Are you from the East Ice?" She had to be sure.

"Yes, I'm from the East Ice Territory. My name is Trelan of Litton on the Green Way. I bring a gift from my people." He bowed, though he had nothing in his hands. "General Valerie has informed us that you have difficulty reading. We can help and would be pleased if you would permit us to do so."

Emerald was so absorbed by the prospect of having her lifelong dream come true that she hardly noticed when Eugenia came up beside her. The dog lifted her hand with her head. Absently, Emerald petted the animal as she appraised Trelan's features. She concluded that he was in earnest.

"You can help me read?" Giving voice to her hope shook her emotionally.

"Yes, we believe so. Will you meet with the eye doctor and his wife? She can fit you with a device that corrects your vision. The spectacles have two lenses in a wireframe. They rest on your face in front of your eyes." Trelan smiled.

Emerald raised her eyebrows. "Spectacles?" She laughed. "Show me."

Chapter Fifty

Darrin awoke to the sound of Emerald and Trelan conversing in hushed tones with the couple who made glasses. He couldn't stand to be in the same room as Emerald and went hunting in the woods. He knew every hill and tree of this land. He loved it in every season.

This was more his home than anywhere. Yet, he had no claim to it. He didn't belong here anymore.

He killed a buck with Emerald's bow. She could no longer use it. He frowned as he dressed the animal. The blood on his hands was warm and pungent. He ripped the organs from the beast's chest cavity. The heart in his hand felt as if it were his own. Grinding his teeth, he finished the work.

He trudged back to Stone Castle. The walls loomed above him. He entered Emerald's home as if he walked on sacred ground. How could he hate her and still reverence her divine purpose? His heart ached for a resolution to his hard feelings.

Emerald had forgiven Valerie. What could it mean? He trembled to think that Emerald truly didn't love him. He had loved her for nearly half of his life.

Part of him still hoped he had meant something to her, but it seemed like she felt nothing for him now. He wanted her to beg him to return to her. He wanted to kill Liameo for forcing her to marry him.

Darrin hung the buck in the smokehouse. He hadn't been careful and was covered in filth from head to toe. Valerie stood watching him when he emerged from the small building at the base of the curtain wall. He met her gaze and knew she could read his mood.

She took his cloak and walked with him to the keep. They skirted the people in the main room and went downstairs to the kitchen. A pot of water boiled over the fire. Valerie latched the kitchen door and came to stand before him. They were alone.

"You should bathe." She hung his cloak on a peg by the fireplace.

"I will." He had no intention of bathing just yet.

She unfastened his clothes until he stood naked before her. She looked at his body but didn't touch him. Her expression held ineffectively concealed sorrow. Emerald's forgiveness carried a heavy price, as he well knew.

He lifted Valerie's chin. The dried blood on his hand matched his mood. He wanted to feel alive again. He wanted to connect with her. He tugged at the buttons of her shirt, but he lacked patience. The shirt tore open, sending buttons flying.

Her surprised expression held a flash of fear. Sorry to have frightened her, he kissed her lips until she relaxed into his embrace. He unfastened her belt and lifted her in his arms. He carried her behind the curtain of the bathing area. Laying her on the warm hearthstones by the fireplace, he removed her boots.

"I want to create a life with you." He met her gaze.

She rested her head in the golden halo of her blond hair. "That would give me joy."

"Then promise me you'll survive." He hesitated for her answer.

"I'll do my best." She drew his hips toward her.

"So be it."

Chapter Fifty-One

Emerald stared at the closed kitchen door. She had seen the look in Darrin's eyes as he and Valerie passed through the main room of the keep. She could occasionally hear the muffled sounds of lovemaking. Others noticed too.

Everyone in the room found her with their gaze eventually. She veiled her expression in defiance. She could endure this.

She lasted until the end. In the silence, however, she found herself alone. Everyone else had left the room.

She should have gone as well.

Something had compelled her to stay. She needed to see Darrin and Valerie's faces when they emerged. Emerald needed to drive home the point that she could handle their relationship.

At the last moment, however, her courage fled. She couldn't face them. She couldn't endure the glow of their joy, not when the bitterness of jealously writhed within her breast.

She stood from the table and walked quietly to the door. Taking her cloak from the peg, she escaped. Ducking around the keep, she ran through the un-kept alleyways between the dilapidated shops and homes.

She reached the wall covered with the charcoal drawings Darrin had created last spring. Pressing her entire body to the faded markings, she wept in anguish.

"Why did you let this happen?" She accused her Creator.

Darrin hated her. He had changed. The young man she had loved so desperately had perished in the fires of life's twisted cruelty.

Emerald balled her fists and sucked a breath through clenched teeth. The Creator had allowed the Carpenters to rape her. He had prompted her to grant them mercy. He knew what would happen because of it. He knew Darrin would reject her because of the baby. Yet, he had still permitted it to happen.

"Why? Don't I deserve joy?" The answer to her plea descended like a ray of sunlight to enter her heart.

The Creator had done it for Liameo because he was worthy of the blessing. He had also blessed Valerie with happiness unlike anything she had experienced in this life. Emerald found that she could not begrudge her friend any semblance of joy.

The Creator had ignored Emerald's feelings. He had permitted a wedge to form between her and Darrin. It had been Darrin's choice. Now, no hope remained. She beat the wall with her fists until they bled and her left shoulder ached from her old wound.

She faced away from the wall and looked to the heavens. Lifting her voice, she raged her whole soul toward the gray clouds that moved with the wind. The Creator's justice had thwarted mercy.

As her anger swelled, a spot of calm formed in her heart. She recognized the extraordinary feeling and heeded it as divine communication. A whispered warmth enlightened her mind and she realized that the exact opposite was true. Justice dictated that she and Darrin live a long happy life together, but mercy for Valerie and Liameo had thwarted it for a time.

How often had she done the same in the name of what was right? Her actions had been unfair to others, but they had forgiven her. Her new family trusted her. How could she not trust them too?

Her beloved Creator had not stopped all the evil in the world, but he had helped her defeat it. Frenland was a better place. She had a part in making that happen.

Emerald collapsed to her knees. She had done this. In sorrow, she wept out her heart to her God.

Once again, the feeling came that he had more work for her to do. She was the Woman of the Stone. A calm reassurance that all her sacrifices would one day be worth it, caused her tears to cease.

"Thank you." Relief washed over her soul.

She lifted her gaze to the sky. The vivid blue of a break in the clouds reminded her of Darrin's eyes. Somehow the promise of him still existed. It was far in the future and difficult to discern, but she believed he would one day be hers.

Chapter Fifty-Two

Emerald, Nina, Tarah, and Valerie kneaded dough on the kitchen table. The morning had come once again and hunger drove them to the task. There was an overabundance of mouths to feed.

Emerald wore her newly constructed spectacles. The edges of everything close up seemed sharper. She had fallen asleep in the library last night as she perused the volumes her family had treasured for generations.

She used the ruler Valerie had given her as she had been instructed by the doctor. Very slowly, her childhood lessons came back to her remembrance. She could read the words. George had come in and helped her for a while.

Liameo avoided her completely.

Emerald tossed the dough into a large wooden bowl and draped a cloth over it. She checked on the bacon where it fried in a pan hanging over the fire. Tarah and Nina struck up a conversation. Valerie couldn't understand them, so Emerald translated.

"I wonder if you will have a boy or a girl." Nina pinched dough for a pan of rolls.

"It would be wonderful to have a daughter since we already have three sons." Tarah crisscrossed the top of a perfectly formed ball of dough with a knife, so it would be pretty after baking.

Valerie braided an ornate loaf of bread and paused. "Daughters are very special."

Pain stabbed Emerald with a jealous pang. It hurt to think of her friend with the man she loved. They had made love in this room. Valerie would have his child one day.

Anger surged within Emerald's chest. She gripped the table's edge until her knuckles popped. It wasn't right to be this angry, but she couldn't help it.

She had to control it, but...she couldn't.

"Do you want a girl, or a boy, Mother?" Nina beamed.

Emerald met and held Nina's gaze as she translated for Valerie. Did the girl know? Nina paled. Yes, she knew, though she must have forgotten Liameo could not have children.

"I have two daughters and a son." Emerald reached for a baking pan.

"More children will come. I think they will be beautiful. Liameo is exotically handsome." Valerie's tone was casual as she focused on her work.

"He can't have children, so there will be none. It's for the best." Emerald worked a ball of dough with excessive force.

Valerie took Emerald by the arm. "I'm sorry. I didn't know."

"It doesn't matter. How could it matter?" Emerald refused to look at her friend as she translated.

A noise at the kitchen door, caused her to look up. Liameo stood there, glaring at her. He turned away from her with a hurt expression.

"Merciful Creator." Emerald brushed the flour off her hands and hung her apron on a peg as she went after him.

WRACKED WITH GUILT, Emerald raced up the kitchen steps to enter the main room of the keep. The sound of the door slamming let her know Liameo had gone outside. She followed as he headed to the stables. She caught his shoulder before he went inside.

"You don't even know me." Emerald's eyes filled with tears. "You haven't asked me anything. I would have told you, but you don't want to know." She shook her head regretfully. "You needed to know things before you choose me for your wife."

He took her by the wrist and raised her fist for her to see. "Are you angry with me? After what you've said and done, how dare you?"

He released her and went inside to saddle Allura. Eugenia raised her head from her bed of hay. She'd barked all night outside the door of the keep. In apparent exhaustion, she lay her head on her paws and watched them.

Fear and outrage combined to anger Emerald. "I've done nothing, Liameo. I could have done something. I should have done something. I wanted to act on my feelings, but I can't because I know," she choked on the words, "my place is with you." She shook with rage.

He finished with his horse and led Allura out of the stables. "You are the shoal upon which I have shipwrecked my life, Emerald Stone. Do whatever you wish." He opened the gates, mounted, and rode away.

She ran to Dusty's stall, flung it open, and leaped onto his back. Urging him out of the stables, she ducked as she rode through the doorway. Dusty responded to her urgency, achieving full speed soon after they crossed the drawbridge.

Liameo glanced over his shoulder. Cutting from the road to enter a field, he raced his chestnut mare westward. He had been on a course toward town but must have changed his mind. She didn't think. She just followed.

He stopped in the yard of her grandparents' cottage, dismounted, and slapped the mare's hindquarters, sending her into the meadow. He faced Emerald as she raced toward him. The look in his eyes made Dusty pull up short, causing him to dance and snort. Emerald slid off his back and closed the distance between herself and Liameo at a run.

"I'm not done talking to you, Liam. You need to ask me about the things you don't want to know. You need to look at the dust of this yard and realize that this is where you lost me." She pointed to the spot. "You need to understand how Darrin's brother broke my body and crushed my spirit."

She kicked a rock in Liameo's direction. "You need to know why I'm angry!" She clenched her fists. "I have every right to my feelings. I need to feel them for once."

She stalked to the well and shoved in the ring of crumbling stones around it. It hurt to strain against stone, but she sent the masonry down upon the bones of Allan Wolfe. Panting and furious, she nearly fell in with them.

Liameo caught her around the middle before she was lost to the dark depths of her past. She fought her way out of his reach. With Allan's defiling words ringing in her mind and his horrifying actions lingering on her flesh, she fled.

EMERALD RAN AWAY FROM the well where Allan Wolfe's bones lay.

Seven years ago, the waters of Stone River had washed her clean of his blood. Yet it had never absolved her of the guilt she carried concerning the desperate act of self-defense she'd been forced to commit to save herself from his brutal sexual assault.

Darrin's brother had been the first of many men she had killed. She had enjoyed watching them die. She hated them.

Desiring to shed the taint of that hatred, Emerald neared the banks of the river. She cast aside her clothing and dove into the frigid water. Surfacing, she gasped in physical agony at the shock, unable to see through her wet spectacles.

Liameo captured her in his warm arms. Naked he pressed his body to hers. To her surprise, she clung to him.

He kissed her breathless. The current carried them downstream. The feel of him drove out the anger of so many years and so much pain. She had missed a chance at happiness with him long ago, but she seized it now.

The current deposited them in the shallows by the shore. Liameo covered her with his body. She accepted him because the cold water had rendered him unable to deliver the message his lips conveyed.

They kissed him until their shivering forced them to stop. Surveying their surroundings, Emerald smiled through her chattering teeth. Liameo climbed to his feet and offered a hand to help her up.

She accepted his hand and led him across the pebble beach to a bubbling spring that burst from the center of a cracked boulder. Steam swirled in the air around it. She slid into the hot spring pool, submerged her head once, and stopped shivering.

He came in with her, nearly filling the pool. She marveled at the sheer size of him. He found her hands in the warm water, meshing his fingers with hers. Gazing into her eyes, he pressed her against the smooth stone to kiss her deeply.

Breathing heavily, he pulled away enough to say, "Tell me everything."

She held nothing back. To her surprise, he didn't judge her. His acceptance of the facts of her life, including her son's existence and his death, made her realize she didn't need to hold onto the pain. This time the river truly washed her conscience clean.

"I didn't understand." Liameo's voice held deep regret. "I was afraid of what other people would think. I feared you could never love me, but you did love me in the hayloft, and I thought everything had finally been set right."

He met her gaze, his torment showing in the creases around his eyes. "Darrin came back. I prayed he would never return. He had rejected you and hurt you deeply. I thought he'd missed his chance and you were mine." Terror filled Liameo's expression as the last words escaped his mouth.

She pushed off from the rock against which she rested. A desire to overcome the doubt between them emboldened her to draw her body to him until the core of them connected by touch. She removed her spectacles to lay them on the rock behind him.

"You belong with me, Liam. I don't understand the wisdom of it, but I trust the fact of it." Her pain melted away the instant she met his gaze.

She wanted him and captured his lips in a kiss. He wrapped in his arms around her and his body responded. Eager for a deeper connection, she enveloped him. He surged into her. The fervent heat of their love erased every reservation she had ever had about intimacy.

Accepting Liameo here meant more than it had in the hayloft. Making love in the Teacup held a particular significance because it was a special place. Her parents had often come here after putting their children to bed. Now she understood why.

Chapter Fifty-Three

Bow in hand, Darrin watched Emerald and Liameo talk in the Teapot. Crouched in the undergrowth at the river's edge, his impulse to kill Liameo raged. Emerald initiated a passionate coupling. She wanted the man.

Darrin closed his eyes. He couldn't see much, but he regretted watching them like this. It hadn't been his intent.

He'd been hunting in the fields near Stone Castle when the sound of horses' hooves on the gravel had caught his attention. As Emerald and Liameo had ridden past, he had run after them, guessing where Liameo would lead her. It wasn't something she was ready to confront, at least she never had been before today.

The couple had argued at her grandparents' cottage. Emerald's anger always heightened her beauty. Darrin imagined how she would look when rendered in an oil painting, her shorter hair a fiery halo of glory.

She had caved in the stones of the well and nearly lost herself to the depths of it. Allan was there, waiting to claim her life. But Liameo had held onto her.

Darrin heard a noise. Opening his eyes, he noticed movement in the brush upstream. A feeling of dread washed over him as he realized several men were closing in on Emerald and Liameo's position.

The trespassers were heavily armed soldiers from the army of Andolin. Darrin's heart pounded in his chest. They would find Emerald and Liameo if he didn't act.

Darrin moved toward the two soldiers and dispatched them with arrows to the heart. They didn't make enough noise to alert the couple. The sound of additional armed men drew his attention away.

He allowed his rage to overtake his senses as he engaged them. Two well-placed arrows felled more foes. He led the others away from Emerald.

Using his knowledge of the land, he attempted to evade them. However, the sheer number of attackers overwhelmed his escape. He didn't have enough arrows. They surrounded and beat him until he ended up face down in the dirt. The soldiers bound his wrists and ankles with cords. As they dragged him away, he remembered his promise to Valerie.

Chapter Fifty-Four

Emerald and Liameo dressed at the river's edge and walked hand in hand to the meadow at her grandparents' cottage. Their horses grazed there lazily. Emerald took a moment before they returned to the castle to kiss her husband. Their union was once again insured.

Liameo parted the kiss and rested his forehead on hers. "You amaze me."

She sighed contentedly. "That was my intention."

He chuckled, grasping her backside in his great hands. "If the children wouldn't worry, I'd—" He released her and backed away. "Well, not here. My apologies, I forgot where we were."

A blend of emotions mingled with memories. She stared at the patch of earth where she'd been assaulted. Liameo gave her a wide birth as he moved toward the grazing horses.

Blinking the haze from before her vision, she realized that with one exception her memories of this place were some of the happiest of her life. She walked to the open cottage door. Half of the thatch roof had collapsed due to neglect, but the stone structure was sound.

The memory of her grandparents' smiles and Stephan's laughter brought joy to her heart. Liameo had asked her to marry him in the far corner of the dwelling. She had been happy to say yes.

She sighed and turned away from the past. Her path lay ahead. She flushed at the sight of him bringing the horses toward the cottage. He held a fist full of Dusty's mane and led Allura by the reins.

"You are a beautiful woman, Emerald Stone." He shook his head as he walked toward her.

"Thank you for bringing me here, Liam. I needed to bury the past. I hadn't been able to do it until I realized it was truly dead. You are my future.

I'm sorry I doubted that." She'd almost lost the only man who truly loved her.

Liameo let loose of Dusty and righted Emerald's spectacles, setting them squarely on her nose. "We've come a long way since we first met. Our experiences, no matter how painful, are what inform our happiness today. I'm glad you're not hiding from me anymore."

Emerald's heart filled with sunlight, though tears suddenly clouded her vision. "I will never conceal my thoughts from you. I don't need to." She took his warm, work-roughened hand. "Thank you for helping me understand that."

He smiled at her with his happy hazel eyes. "I've missed your openness."

"You are the only one entitled to it." She grabbed a fist full of Dusty's mane and leaped onto his back.

Chuckling, Liameo followed her with his gaze. "What do you mean? Don't you speak your mind to everyone?"

She shook her head, smiling. "Speak, yes, communicate in other ways, no. I can't even look at you, or touch your hand, without wanting to..." She found it difficult to voice her need to be with him without betraying how much he consumed her at the moment.

"Wanting to what?" He mounted his horse and met her gaze.

"I've never been this preoccupied with wanting anything in my life." Her whole body thrummed with desire.

"Anything? By chance, do you mean anyone?" He grinned.

"I mean you. I can hardly keep my mind on anything else at the moment." She clutched Dusty's mane with both hands.

"Ah, well, good." Liameo urged Allura to walk.

Emerald scoffed in playful exasperation. "Good? How can that possibly be good?"

He glanced over his shoulder at her. "Now you know how I feel all the time."

She urged Dusty to catch up. "That's good to know. I'll have to find opportunities to prove my devotion."

He looked straight ahead. "I look forward to that." He grinned.

She thought fast. "I imagine you like stockings that don't fit far more now than you used to."

He laughed. "Much, much more."

"In the spring, I'll have to gather flowers to make sachets for your clothes trunk." She tried to remember anything else she had done for him as a girl.

"As long as you kiss me like you did today, then I'll be happy." He reached out to her.

She clasped his hand, enjoying her newly restored joy. "Always, Liam."

She needed him. She wanted him. She loved him.

The sadness over Darrin tugged at her heart much less now. She mourned for the life she knew was right. However, none of that made this life wrong. She let her heart rest in Liameo's devotion.

STONE CASTLE CAME INTO Emerald and Liameo's view through the trees of the forest. The bell commenced a frantic clamor. Emerald urged Dusty to quicken his pace, but Liameo grabbed his forelock, preventing him from obeying her command.

Liameo dismounted. Emerald followed his lead. They held the horses' noses so they wouldn't whinny and concealed them within the trees. Careful not to be seen by the mob, they climbed a rise near the edge of the field.

The clink of chains as the drawbridge raised mingled with the angry shouts of a mob in front of the gatehouse. Dark headed defenders manned the walls of the castle, attracting the attention of the surrounding citizens of Andolin outside the walls. Emerald didn't recognize the people in the mob.

Liameo scowled "They're not from Meadowgren. It looks like civilians from Andolin."

A cry raised above the din, "Frenlander!"

Someone must have spotted Valerie atop the curtain wall.

Hysteria broke forth among the crowd. Valerie ducked as arrows and stones hurtled in her direction. The moat prevented anyone from attempting to scale the walls in this cold weather. But the impregnable nature of the castle only seemed to incite the invaders to greater agitation.

Clouds blew across the sun, blocking its light. The wind carried the cries of the mob. "Kill them!"

Emerald started forward, but Liameo's hand closed over her shoulder.

"Look." He pointed toward the gatehouse.

Judge Porter stood atop the formidable structure. He addressed the people, but they jeered. Emerald couldn't hear most of what he said.

Captain Hammond and a handful of militiamen rode across Stone Bridge, entering Danalan. They approached the southern edge of the mob.

"People of Andolin, if you do not leave, then the governor will send troops to disperse you! This is an unlawful protest and cannot continue!" Captain Hammond's voice carried to Emerald and Liameo.

The crowd erupted into violence. People picked up rocks. They drew bows and raised blades.

"We will not leave until she is dead," one man said.

"She must die," a woman said.

"Send her out that we might kill her, then we will return to our homes," an elderly man said.

"She is not here!" Judge Porter's voice cut through the cacophony.

"Liar!" came more than one cry.

Rocks and arrows flew. Judge Porter dove for cover. Captain Hammond and his men absorbed the onslaught. Liameo moved in their direction, but Emerald held him in place.

"They'll be killed." Anguish clouded Liameo's expression.

The grim possibility wasn't lost on Emerald, but she also knew the stakes. "When they are routed, they will ride south. If we are with them…"

Liameo slumped. "We will be killed."

Captain Hammond ordered the militiamen to retreat. The fletching's of an arrow shaft protruded from his horse's flank. Several men hunched over their horses as if they were wounded, but all remained astride their mounts. As one, the militia fled toward Stone Bridge.

"I'm not worried about us," Emerald met Liameo's gaze, "but I promised Nina I would never leave her again. I cannot betray her trust."

He nodded. "Then we will wait out the siege."

Emerald took him by the hand. "Let's return to my grandparents' cottage. I know a way to pass the time."

Liameo followed without resistance.

EMERALD LED LIAMEO to the last standing cottage in the land, her grandparents' home. Dismounting, she allowed Liameo to stable the horses in the lean-to barn on the side of the stone structure while she went inside.

"Home." Emerald could feel Jacob and Estelle's presence in the moldering dwelling.

Liameo came to stand behind her with his hands on her shoulders. "It must be strange to see the place like this."

She met his gaze. He had carried his saddlebags inside with him. She opened the cedar chest, revealing quilts within it.

"At least we'll be warm." She smiled at him.

He dropped the saddlebags and righted a rickety chair. She watched him in the grey light coming in through the hole in the roof. He untied the flap of a saddlebag and handed her a biscuit. She strode over to him with blankets tucked under an arm. He patted his knee.

She shook her head and smiled. "That chair was never much. I'm sure it's not sturdy enough to handle both of us."

Being inside this cottage should have been more upsetting. But after talking things through with Liameo at the river, she felt like she'd come home at last. She regretted letting the place fall into disrepair like this.

Liameo stood, causing the wood of the chair to creak in relief. She looked into the shadows of his face. So many things might have been different if not for Allan Wolfe. She chose not to dwell on the past and let it go.

She leaned toward Liameo's chest and rose on her toes to meet his lips with hers. They breathed the same breath. She held him around the middle with both arms, cherishing the feel of him. The muscles of his body tensed in preparation to deliver more. She met him with her whole heart.

Chapter Fifty-Five

Valerie observed the untrained mob surrounding the castle from a vantage point on the curtain wall. Defending the battlements was a simple matter. But without employing offensive tactics, the occupants of the castle were essentially trapped.

George and Andre operated the gates, portcullis, and drawbridge. The East Icers held defensive positions along the wall. Tarah had gathered the young children into the keep.

From Valerie's position near the gatehouse door level with the top of the wall, Valerie crouched behind the crenellations. Armed with a short bow, she observed the happenings. Unfortunately, her understanding of the words was limited. Judge Porter addressed the people with body language that indicated he expected to be obeyed. The mob responded with violence, chasing off a mounted group of military men in brown coats.

"The Creator's child." Trelan crouched nearby and covertly pointed toward the forest at the edge of a field.

Emerald and Liameo lay concealed a safe distance from the fray.

"Have you seen Darrin?" Valerie asked.

Trelan shook his head. "A group of mounted soldiers in beige uniforms infiltrated Danalan two hours ago. When they departed, many men were tied across the saddles of their horses. There must have been a confrontation by the river. I don't know if Darrin was among the fallen."

Fatalistic dread overwhelmed Valerie. "Then he is dead."

Trelan touched her arm. "If so, then he died valiantly. There were eight men laid across their horses' backs."

Valerie's heart ached. Darrin had gone hunting to avoid Emerald. When Emerald had followed Liameo on horseback, Valerie had climbed the steps of the curtain wall to observe her actions. Darrin had run after Emerald in a westerly direction. He had never looked back.

Trelan squeezed Valerie's shoulder. "I'm sorry for considering him unworthy. I've been informed that he served as the royal shadow for much of his life. If he died in that capacity, then my people will honor him for his sacrifice."

Valerie met Trelan's gaze with watery eyes, unwilling to shed tears in front of him. "Will you translate for me with the elderly man from Andolin. I want to question him about these events."

Trelan nodded. "Yes. I have inquiries as well."

Valerie caught a glimpse of two riders in the far distance as they crossed a meadow. It was Emerald and Liameo. None of the people in the mob had spotted them.

Valerie and Trelan carefully made their way to the gatehouse door level with the top of the wall. George and the older man were arguing inside. Andre watched the mob though an archery loop with a bow at the ready. Trelan translated the heated exchange.

"I have no desire to kill citizens of Andolin, but I will defend this castle." George stammered.

The judge bent his neck backward to look the much taller George in the eyes. "Do not injure these people. The military will hear of their actions and deploy sufficient forces to take care of the matter."

George's expression held deep concern. "If they attempt to scale the walls, then I'll have no choice. You heard their threats. My family is in danger. And how will Emerald and Liameo return home with them there?"

The older man's expression grew gravely concerned. "I don't know."

Valerie stepped toward the men. "Emerald and Liameo have ridden westward in Danalan. They were not noticed by the mob."

The older man's expression of deep concern lessened and he extended a hand. "Thank you for this information. It eases my mind greatly. Allow me to introduce myself. I am Judge Porter of Meadowgren. Emerald is my greatniece."

Valerie accepted the handshake. Though it was not the custom of her people to shake hands, she had read about it. The library at the palace in Soniashi had been a favorite hiding place when she was a girl.

"I am General Valerie of Bluebird Vale."

Trelan translated, calling her, 'Crown Princess Valerie of Frenland'.

Valerie didn't speak the language of Andolin fluently, but she recognized Trelan's mistranslation. He had deliberately presented her as the future ruler of Frenland. She didn't contradict him because she was well-practiced in the art of politics.

The judge's jaw dropped. "Your majesty, I'm pleased to meet you. I did not realize Emerald had foreign guests."

"The queen is a friend. Please allow me to introduce Commander Trelan of Litton from the East Ice Territory." Valerie shifted the judge's attention.

Trelan translated fairly accurately without amendment to his title except to say that he belonged to the Mountain Realm instead of the East Ice Nation. Valerie knew Trelan's real position in the government was much more than he had yet revealed. Each time he underplayed his importance, Valerie's anxiety doubled.

Trelan shook the judge's hand. "I'm pleased to meet a blood relative of the Creator's child."

"Oh," the judge sputtered, "I'm married to Emerald's Great-Aunt Elaine. My wife is the sister of Emerald's grandmother, Estelle. I say Emerald because she is family. I should probably call her something more appropriate to her station, such as Lady Stone."

"Or Empress Stone." Trelan eyed the judge with a severe expression.

Judge Porter paled. "Do your people support her as empress?"

"King Stephan of Frenland is in favor, yes." Valerie couldn't resist participating in the game Trelan had set in motion.

"Oh." Judge Porter took a step backward.

"The people of the Mountain Realm have voted to support the Creator's child if she chooses to take her rightful place as the empress of the Modutan Empire." Trelan's tone was ominous.

Judge Porter stared. "I had not anticipated this. Emerald, I mean, Lady Stone, said nothing to me when last we sat to tea. She spoke of traveling through the mountains to Frenland, but she did not express an intention to become the empress. I had no idea she planned to overthrow the government of Andolin."

Valerie stilled the old man's fluttering hands. "She does not harbor ambitions in that regard. You know her well. King Stephan simply desires to support his foster sister in her divine appointment to reunite the lands in prosperity and peace. He knows that someone must rule the empire. I know of no one more worthy than Queen Emerald."

Despite the cold, Judge Porter took a cloth from his pocket to mop sweat from his brow while Trelan translated. "King Stephan is Queen Emerald's foster brother?"

George walked over from where he'd been looking out an archer's loop with Andre. "Yes, sir. Stephan grew up in Danalan. Sarialla, Frenland's royal counselor, brought him here when he was four years old. Emerald raised him by herself after the death of Jacob and Estelle Stone."

The judge trembled. "Emerald raised the king of Frenland?" He pulled Valerie closer. "And you are his heir?"

Valerie blushed when Trelan translated. "No, I am the prior king's niece. King Salicor overthrew the rule of Stephan's parents and enslaved Frenland. I served as one of his generals. The voice of the people supported me as his successor. However, after meeting Queen Emerald, I directed my Valkyrie Army to fight for Stephan. He is a worthy leader."

Judge Porter frowned as he listened to the translation. "Then you will never rule Frenland?"

Trelan placed his hands on Valerie's shoulders. "I believe she will rule by Stephan's side as queen. The new representative government is fragile. To maintain peace, stability is required."

Valerie shook off Trelan's hands. "I am a married woman. What do you mean, saying something like that to this man? You know I cannot rule next to Stephan in any capacity. I cannot return to Frenland. He wants me dead."

Trelan dropped his hands to his sides. "He will accept you as his wife if he wants peace with my people. It is that simple. As far as your unlawful union with the steward's son, well, it is best I do not intrude upon your grief."

Valerie balled her fists, preferring to be enraged than a mess of tears. "How dare you speak of him, either of them? Do you have no feelings?"

Trelan bowed. "I'm deeply sorry for offending you. Please take some time to mourn after the manner of your customs. I will not disturb you."

Anger shortened Valerie's breath. Her heart raced in an irregular pattern. She needed to calm down.

Trelan explained to those present who spoke the language of Andolin that Valerie had just lost her husband and was emotional about the proposed union.

The judge kissed Valerie's hand. "I am deeply sorry for your loss, Princess."

Valerie withdrew her hand. "It isn't certain. His body has not been found." She couldn't catch her breath.

George drew Andre away from the archer's loop. "Take Princess Valerie and Judge Porter to the keep through the second story door by way of the chemise wall on the northern side. Beware of enemy archers. Let Tarah know the situation. It would be best for her to keep the children inside the keep until the threat of arrows is ended."

Judge Porter offered his arm to Valerie. Needing support, she accepted it. She had too much dignity to lose consciousness and no desire to be carried to bed ever again.

Chapter Fifty-Six

Darrin struggled against the chains that bound him inside a metal box atop a wagon bed. Air entered the smelly prison through a narrow slot in the door at the back. The wagon had traveled south for two days without stopping.

People ran from their homes at the sound of the marching soldiers escorting the wagon. He could hear them speculate about who was in the box. Their awe and dismay added to his deepening concern.

He couldn't understand much of what the Andolin soldiers escorting him had said when they captured him. Therefore, he didn't know why they had taken him away from Danalan.

His only solace was that he had led the dangerous invaders away from Emerald. Seeing her in the arms of another man had stirred Darrin with jealousy in ways he hadn't imagined possible. She loved Liameo the way Darrin had always wanted her to love him.

Emerald was whole.

Darrin knew then that he was broken. Something was wrong with him. The anger was irrational, yet very real. Why?

Valerie had feared his unresolved issues would lead to tragedy. She must be worried about him. He jerked on the chains that held him bound, but only bruised his wrists and ankles further.

Defeated, he collapsed in the filthy straw. Wishing he had kept his oath and stayed by her side, he summoned his wife in his mind. The remembered sensation of her kiss caused his hands to react. Stilling them by grasping his knees, he meditated.

He breathed in, remembering her breath on his cheek. Even from afar, she had the power to calm him. She had generously yielded to him so much of herself. He mourned for the loss of her companionship. His greatest wish was to be safe in her arms, yet he was here.

Valerie would be forced to parent their child alone if he did not find a way back to her. Anger stirred him to stretch his body toward the slot in the door. There had to be a way out. He listened intently for an opportunity to petition the people in the street for help.

"I wonder if it's a black-haired devil from the mountains." An elderly woman pointed at the box, showing a child of perhaps eight years.

The girl tucked her head into the woman's ample side. The wagon rolled past and others stared. One shop keeper stepped into the street to spit at the wagon.

"I think they've captured the queen of Danalan," an old man said.

"Her army will sweep us like a plague of locusts." A young man said in a tone of alarm.

Darrin didn't know what a plague was, but he sensed their toxic fear.

The wagon rolled through a market place crowded with people. Everyone watched the box. Speculation abounded and most of it focused on Emerald. Darrin heard her name mentioned repeatedly.

A thud hit the door of the box. Two hands gripped the slot. A pair of eyes appeared between them.

"Emerald? Are you in there?" Gael clung to the outside of the box.

"She's safe." Darrin strained against the chains.

"Darrin?" Gael's brows shot upward.

"Tell her—" Darrin was cut short when the soldiers flung the boy off of the box into a cloth merchant's stand.

The sound of the wagon wheels changed to a hollow, rhythmic thumping. Abruptly, the wagon stopped. The door to the box flung open and men climbed inside.

They dropped a black hood over his head and cinched it around his neck almost too tight to breathe. Darrin struggled to escape. Someone punched him in the jaw and he fell to the filthy floor of the box.

"Be still," a soldier said.

The sound of a lock clicked. The chains were freed from the ring that had held them to the floor of the box. Darrin lunged for freedom, but the soldiers held him firmly between them. He fought them as they hauled him away.

They cast him down and he landed on his head and shoulders in a small wooden prison. Dazed, he thought it was the blow to the head that caused the world to undulate. Horrified, he realized he was on a ship to be sailed far from everyone he loved.

Chapter Fifty-Seven

Valerie wept for the loss of Darrin. Huddled in a suit of fur, she kept a vigil on the castle curtain wall during the daylight hours. Thus far, it had yielded nothing except heartache.

She had watched Darrin follow Emerald three days ago. He hadn't looked back. He had not considered his wife when he left, even though he had promised he would never leave.

His death wounded her soul.

Valerie considered her options. In the warmth of a spring-like evening in the middle of winter, there seemed to be hope in the air, but none in her heart. She had known this would be the way with Darrin. Yet, it pierced her to the center of her chest that he chose Emerald over her so quickly.

"Your lover's body must have been among those carried away by the soldiers in beige uniforms." Trelan walked over from the side door of the gatehouse. "We have been on the watch for carrion birds along the river, but there are none." Trelan sat beside her on the gray granite stones of the curtain wall.

"I married an impulsive child." Valerie hid her face in her arms where they rested on her knees.

"He died valiantly. You were the making of the man." Trelan took Valerie's hand.

Taking a breath, she looked at the sky and imagined the lonely days ahead of her. "I don't know how to live without his love."

Trelan patted her hand and released it. "You loved another man once. It would bring your mother great joy to see you become the queen of Frenland. I will send you home and all will be well."

"You want me to rule Frenland? Why?" Valerie frowned at the mysterious leader of the Mountain Realm.

"As I have said before, my people wish to end the bloodshed. Peace is possible with balanced leadership in the north. The people of Frenland are divided and will kill the young king without your protection. If Stephan wishes to end the war and save himself from assassination, then he will agree to marry you." Trelan leaned forward, looking at the mob camped at the edge of the castle moat.

"You have asked him?" She stopped breathing.

"Yes. My brother has traveled north to inform him of what is required."

Valerie gasped for air. "Required? Who are you to make such demands of a king?"

Trelan met her gaze. "I am the eldest child of the empress. The Mountain Realm requires stability in Frenland."

Valerie's blood chilled. "Or what?"

Trelan scowled. "Either your marriage to King Stephan will succeed in cleansing Frenland of evil, or we will be forced to do so by bloodshed."

Valerie blanched. "You threatened Stephan with an invasion if he does not marry me. And what are you threatening me with?"

Trelan's expression lightened. "I thought you'd be pleased. Until I presented this plan, Parliament was prepared to order the invasion without negotiation."

Blood drained from Valerie's face. "Reuniting the Modutan Empire is a lofty ambition."

He smiled a deceptively innocent flash of teeth. "The Creator's child has set everything in motion."

Valerie didn't dare to ask, but she had to. "Who will rule the empire?"

Trelan relaxed. "Emerald Stone cannot rule the empire alone."

Valerie read the implication. "She is married."

He shook his head. "Liameo forced her to marry him even though he cannot give her children. She will cast off the wicked traditions of the south and forge new laws soon enough."

Valerie shook her head in horror. "And what of your wife?"

Trelan's eyes hardened. "I lost my wife to your subcommander on the ice. Tashal died defending my children after I was gravely wounded and our guards were slaughtered. If not for you, my friend, then I would have lost everything. I reward you now with a kingdom, but I require your allegiance."

Valerie inhaled and exhaled slowly as she considered a response. "I support Emerald as the Woman of the Stone. If you do not, then end my life because I will never betray her."

Trelan's brow creased. "I had the opportunity to read the inscription on the stone. It is a noble destiny the Creator's child has before her. I hold the Sacred Mountain. She will find her way to me when the time is right. Women will do almost anything for the want of a child."

Heat flooded Valerie's skin. "Emerald isn't like me. She won't be fooled like I was. She has married a man whose ways are different than the boy I chose. Liameo will never leave her the way Darrin has forsaken me."

Trelan smiled. "Do you speak of his death? He can hardly be blamed for that. No. Death stalks us all, but I digress. The boy king of Frenland will not give you a child, Valerie. He has declared as much. Though, perhaps the task is already accomplished. I promise to assist you should your lover have failed you."

Valerie lost sensation in her hands. "Your generosity knows no bounds."

He scoffed. "Your prowess is infamous. Thus, the offer is self-serving. I have a fondness for you, Valerie. I respect you. It seems only fair that you be allowed to receive the joy that only a baby provides."

Grief crushed her like a rockslide, sweeping aside Trelan's unsavory offer as if it were nothing by comparison. "I cannot carry a child into Frenland. It isn't safe for anyone connected with me. They have plans to burn me at the stake."

Trelan leaned closer, his blue eyes boring into hers. "I will slaughter the entire kingdom if they do."

Valerie huddled inside the furs, trembling in shock. Trelan's threat held her immobilized. Did he have the power to slaughter an entire kingdom?

She chuckled softly. "I almost believed you."

He raised his eyebrows and relaxed. "I will send my brother with you and a sufficient force to ensure your safety. If my brother is murdered, then I will react in kind."

Valerie nodded, thinking of her brother's recent death. "The loss of a brother is unbearable. You should not risk him casually."

Trelan pushed her hair away from her face and tucked it behind her ear. His fingers reached behind her neck, caressing her skin. She met his gaze.

"Are you prepared to accept my offer? I will come with you if you desire." His pupils dilated.

She blinked, averting her gaze. He had offered to give her a child. She shivered with revulsion at the thought of submitting to him. However, he had implied he did not want her submission.

"I've never enjoyed the act," a tear coursed her cheek, "until I married Darrin."

Trelan's naked desire pinched with confusion as his thumb swiped away her tear. "He found something in you. My wife did the same for me."

A flame ignited at the edge of the field surrounding the castle. Other flames joined the first to form a great arc. The only opening lay toward Stone Bridge.

Shouts stirred the mob surrounding the castle. Chaos ensued among them. Women gathered their children and fled toward the bridge.

The torchbearers in the two arcs stepped from the tree line into the fields around the castle. Hundreds of white-clad warriors trampled through the fallow winter fields in the last light of day. The arc tightened.

The men of the mob held their ground until the route of escape began to close. Their courage faltered and they ran. Debris strewed the ground where once an occupying force had besieged Stone Castle.

The clank of chains signaled the drawbridge lowering. Trelan's men opened the gates. George and Andre cranked the portcullis upward.

The flaming arrows of the dark-haired archers extinguished all at once. A lone man advanced toward the drawbridge. Trelan walked out to meet him. The two men embraced and engaged in amicable conversation.

Valerie eased her aching bones from the seated position she had maintained for most of the day. She entered the side door of the gatehouse and descended to the courtyard. Did the man bear any news of Darrin? Could she go out to look for his body?

"Dantyn, meet the Crown Princess of Frenland, General Valerie of Bluebird Vale. She is the reason I asked you to meet with King Stephan." Trelan urged the younger man toward her.

Dantyn approached her and kissed both of her cheeks after the ancient custom of her people. "It is a pleasure to formally be introduced to the woman who saved my brother and his children's lives. Would that you had been able to save his wife and entourage."

The fresh smell of the man reminded her of crisp mountain air. His kisses had not been inappropriate. Strangely, she was not off-put by his demeanor of familiarity.

"I am pleased to know another son of the empress. Excuse me, my husband is missing and I must search for him." Valerie moved past the men to exit the gates and cross the drawbridge.

Dantyn followed her in youthful vigor. "The area is clear of bodies, though old blood was found on the ground in drips and pools within the trees by the river. Please," he took her hand, "you are cold. Come inside. Your husband is not in Danalan."

She stopped to meet his gaze, assessing that he told the truth. Grief cut a new swath inside her chest. Looking southward, she wondered what the enemy had done with Darrin's body.

"Why would they not leave him for me to place in a tomb? I need him, not they." It was the question of her heart and not meant to receive a reply.

"I am deeply sorry for your loss, Princess Valerie." Dantyn drew her alongside and guided her toward the castle keep. "It grieves me to burden you further with bad news, but I have been to the palace at Soniashi. Your mother is gravely ill. King Stephan asked me to deliver a letter to you."

Valerie absorbed the tidings in a state of shock. Trembling, she accepted the folded parchment. She broke the wax seal and read Stephan's handwriting. She recognized it from the many entries in the castle library.

"My mother may already be dead." She couldn't catch her breath. "Stephan warns me not to come, saying he cannot ensure my safety. He says the kingdom hangs by a thread." It took no more than a single erratic heartbeat for her to decide what she must do. "I will return to my home."

Chapter Fifty-Eight

Emerald enjoyed waking up warm. The arms that held her registered as familiar. She didn't open her eyes to the morning light coming in the partially collapsed roof of her grandparents' cottage. Liameo laid a kiss on her lips and rolled over to press his hip into her thigh.

She giggled. It seemed so silly to be this giddy. She wasn't a woman who giggled often, but her husband made her happy.

His hands roved her bare skin. She raised to cover him. With him on his back, she took a great deal of initiative in their lovemaking.

She had never thought to feel this way about any man. But Liameo had given her something she'd never dreamed existed. Now, she needed him, wanted his attention, and craved his touch.

She hadn't yet learned how to give of herself without reservation, but at least she felt no fear. She leaned down to kiss him. He wrapped his arms around her and held her tight. He hadn't finished but seemed to be in no rush. He took his time as if there were nothing more important than what they shared.

For once, Emerald let her cares go and simply enjoyed the moment. In a timeless haze of warmth and love, she existed as one with him, one body, one sensation, one thought. She gave her all to his happiness and received everything from him in return.

Such tender, attentive, actions she had never experienced from anyone else. It inspired her to greater heights of trust than she had dared before. She allowed Liameo to roll her on her back and press himself upon her. She received him, gave to him, and never once did she fear him. Something wonderful happened and the explosion of pleasure consumed her strength. Suffusing her with heat, it stole her breath.

Liameo withdrew and lay by her side. They both struggled for air. He recovered quicker than she did and kissed her forehead, her cheek, her lips, her neck, and the space between her breasts.

"I love you, Liam." She had nearly caught her breath now.

He met her gaze. "What happened this time?"

She smiled, shaking her head. "I have no words."

He found her breast and cupped it. "I've loved you for so long without knowing what any of this would be like. Sometimes, I think it's a dream." He met her gaze. "But I never imagined anything like this." He laid a kiss on her breast and slid his hand to the flat of her stomach.

Emerald sensed his turn of thought and faced her husband, enjoying the feel of his body along the length of hers. "I am the shoal upon which you have shipwrecked your life, Liam, but I am no siren. I did not want this life of turmoil for you. I never made things difficult for you because I wanted to hurt you. I did everything I could to escape the trap I'm caught in, but now I've ensnared you along with me."

She worried about the mob from Andolin. As of yesterday evening, they still surrounded Stone Castle. Her concerns about her responsibilities to the Creator, the fulfillment of the Legend of the Stone, and the expectations of the people of the empire troubled her.

Liameo wrapped his arms around her and held her tight. "I would pay any price for your love as long as I have you like this. The children we've adopted are the only other people in the world I care about. I'm yours to command, no matter what happens." He raised his hand to trace her forehead with his fingertips. "Don't worry. You'll think of something to save us from ruin and despair."

The flip manner of the last bit made her laugh. "Oh, sure, I'll think of something." She shook her head and rolled her eyes. "I can't think of anything when I'm with you." She leaned forward to take a kiss from his lips. "I've never felt this way." She met his gaze. "I'm not usually this optimistic."

He chuckled, then lowered his gaze to her breasts. "Optimism knows no bounds."

She kissed his lips, finding her way to places only she had permission to touch.

Chapter Fifty-Nine

Emerald and Liameo rode to Stone Castle. No longer besieged, the castle's drawbridge lay extended and the gates open. Urging Dusty into a gallop, she rode across the field to enter her home. Liameo rode into the courtyard right behind her.

Andre ran from the stables. "Where have you been?"

She dismounted and hugged him. "At my grandparents' cottage, waiting for the mob to disburse. Is everyone well?"

George exited the gatehouse. "Darrin did not return from hunting on the day you left. Soldiers from Andolin carried many bodies south. He is not to be found."

The news struck Emerald to the heart. "He can't be dead. What happened?"

"Valerie saw him follow you and Liameo when you rode out four days ago. She's grief-stricken. She kept saying that he didn't look back." George rubbed his face with both hands. "Trelan sent her to Frenland to marry Stephan. The people of the Mountain Realm believe she is the only person who can end the war and save him from assassination."

Emerald's jaw hung open. "She's gone to marry Stephan?" It couldn't be true.

Liameo led the horses into the stables and Andre followed. She watched the two of them care for the animals. Their simple act of service laid a balm across the raw wound of her grief. Darrin could not be dead. She knew that, but Valerie didn't. Emerald ached for her friend's suffering.

"Trelan is the oldest son of the empress. Valerie took great pains to make sure I understood her limited language skills well enough to relate his plans to you. He wants to rule the Modutan Empire with you at his side...as his wife." George stuttered his way through the news with flushed cheeks.

Emerald raised her eyebrows. "Then we must keep Liameo safe because I have no intention of obliging him. Does he seem like a violent man?"

George met her gaze. "Valerie says, yes. He's here and wishes to speak to you. You'll find him in the library."

Emerald scowled. The man had no right to invade her home and behave in such a manner. She noticed many more people of the East Ice in her castle than had been there before. All of them were warriors. Each of them was armed.

"I will meet with him. Watch over our family George. Do not trust these people." She touched his arm as she strode past him to enter the castle keep.

Tarah greeted her as she entered the main room. Nina and Marta ran to embrace her.

"We were worried," Nina said.

Emerald touched her face. "All is well with Liameo and me." She kissed Marta's soft curls. "I must speak with Trelan. Is he still in the library?"

Nina nodded.

Emerald ascended two flights of stairs to knock on the library door. It swung open. Trelan stood there holding it with a satisfied look on his face.

"I'm happy you returned unharmed. Have you heard the unfortunate news about Darrin of Wolfe? You have my sympathy. I know you cared for him as Valerie did." Something akin to sorrow clouded his expression.

"Is it certain that he was killed?" Emerald strode into the room and warmed her hands by the fire in the hearth.

"No, but it is probable. He did not return. I'm certain that if he were alive, then he would have escaped by now. I'm sorry for your loss." Trelan came to stand beside her.

Emerald met Trelan's gaze with suspicion. "George has told me everything Valerie communicated to him about you. You do not have my support in your ambitions. If you kill my husband in hopes that I will be yours, then you mistake the matter. The laws under which I am subject bind me in marriage to Liameo's younger brother as a stand-in should Liameo die. The boy is fourteen."

Trelan frowned and stared into the fire. "I would never kill Liameo to make way for myself. I lost my wife four years ago and have no plan to marry again unless it is to secure my place. I did not know about the custom you feel obligated to honor. I'm sure it is not as you would wish."

Emerald watched him closely. "No. Indeed, it is not. I hope Liameo outlives me because I have no desire to accept a man not of my choosing as a husband ever again."

Trelan knelt to stir the fire with a stick of wood before placing it on the coals. "Will you rule the Empire in my stead one day? My mother is elderly. As a member of Parliament, she is influential, but merely a figurehead in other regards. I don't think Valerie understood that. I have ambitions, but not to the extent you have been led to believe."

Emerald doubted that he spoke the truth. "I have no intention of ruling any land other than Danalan. I don't know how the Creator plans to reunite the Modutan Empire. You spoke of a Parliament and said your mother is a figurehead. Your society is not a matriarchy or patriarchy? I find the concept of equality of the sexes intriguing. Is your government representative of the people? Do they vote? The monarchy is hereditary, but is the rest of your Parliament elected?"

Trelan offered a genuine smile and climbed to his feet. "You are exactly right. We elect our representatives. Men and women vote on all issues. I am a direct descendent of the second son of Dana and Krelor. Thus, I would become emperor one day if not for your direct descent from their oldest son."

Emerald tensed. "I see."

He fingered a narrow braid of hair stemming from his right temple. "I don't think you do. I don't mind making way for you one day if that is what you choose. Of course, I would like to become emperor, but I will not be disappointed if I cannot."

Emerald pondered his words. "As with most things concerning the Creator, patience is in order."

Trelan glanced her way. "Wise words." He tucked the braid behind his ear.

"Why have your people commanded Valerie to marry Stephan?" Emerald grew bold in her questioning.

"Because they love each other." Trelan leaned against the mantle with his backside to the fire and his arms crossed over his chest.

"How can this be? My brother never knew Valerie. She would have told me." Emerald walked away to the far side of the library.

"She keeps matters of the heart private. I have sent a contingent of protectors, including my younger brother to keep her safe. Let us pray it works." Trelan walked to the table in the center of the room and placed his palms on its surface. "I don't know what else to do to end the conflict with Frenland."

Emerald faced him. "You are at war with my brother?"

"The empire is at war with Frenland because of him. He ordered his men to impersonate my people. They stole horses to fund his war efforts against Salicor. They slaughtered the noblest of them and incited Salicor's army to invade the ice. Seventy-two of my people were killed in the conflict. We cannot forgive his actions easily, but the real threat is that his people will discover the circumstances that made him king. They will burn him at the stake." Trelan rubbed his left hand through his short, dark hair. "We do not want that to happen. He is bringing civilization to a nation of savages. We support him. That's why I suggested we send Valerie to help him."

Emerald shook her head at the bitter news. "You know how much she loves Darrin. I saw it. Her happiness is all wrapped up in him. She won't give her heart again, not even if she loves Stephan. But if she loves him, then she will support him. I know her at least that well."

Trelan held Emerald's gaze. "Then we must pray for peace and keep her safe. Will you permit me to keep you safe as well? I don't want you to think my people are here against your wishes. The mere threat of force caused the mob from Andolin to disperse, but they will be back. You asked about my people. Would you like to visit them? We have much to teach you." He toyed with the braid again.

Emerald considered the inherently dangerous proposition. "Not at this time, but thank you for the offer." She pointed at the thin braid in his hand. "What is the significance?"

He came closer, his pupils growing large. "You are the first to ask. It is an ancient tradition. I'm sure you will read accounts of it in the volumes contained in this library. Unmarried adults braid a small patch of hair at their right temple. The marriage ceremony of the empire includes the cutting and tying together of the couple's braids." He reached for her curly hair.

Emerald moved away from him to draw a book from a shelf. "I have much to learn about our shared history. This library is a priceless resource. I intend to study the law now that I can read. If the Modutan Empire is to be reunited, then a higher form of governance must be established."

Trelan bowed low. "I'm happy to be of service to the Creator's child."

Chapter Sixty

Valerie stepped from the litter that had carried her to the Imperial City inside the Sacred Mountain. Celeniurisa strode forward. Deep concern etched her features. A mother always knew when something wasn't right with her child.

"Daughter, where is my son?" the lady asked.

Stunned by the intimate term of familial bond, Valerie's eyes misted at the realization that this woman had truly considered the marriage binding. "I have disturbing news, my lady. It is believed that Darrin died defending Emerald. She lives, but no one knows where his body was taken."

The lady's face went ashen. She stared into a void of nothingness that Valerie knew well. Celeniurisa extended a hand containing a circle of yellow-gold.

"My son requested this be made for you." The lady met Valerie's gaze. "Do you have a gift for me?"

Valerie intuited the woman's meaning. "It is too soon to tell."

The lady blinked and two tears streaked her cheeks. She swiped them away. Trembling, she placed the ring on Valerie's finger.

"You are my last hope." Celeniurisa met Valerie's gaze. "I know you loved him."

Valerie stared at the delicate craftsmanship of the ring. A rose of gold crowned the token of Darrin's affection. He had remembered the story about the yellow frosting rose her father had made for her when she was a child.

Emotion overwhelmed her and she embraced Celeniurisa. They wept together. Nothing existed outside their grief.

VALERIE PASSED THE night in the kitchen of her bakery. She arose early to perform her favorite task. The ring on her finger brought tears to her eyes. It reminded her of the man who had taken unabashed enjoyment in devouring the pastries she sometimes baked.

"He appreciated many things about you, Daughter." Celeniurisa entered the kitchen from the storefront, handing Valerie one of Emerald's embroidered handkerchiefs.

The gesture comforted and at the same time deepened the jealousy in Valerie's chest. She accepted the cloth, wiped her tears, and blew her nose. She had wept ugly tears for the past week.

"I thought he would outlive me." Valerie extended the handkerchief to Celeniurisa.

She shook her head. "It belongs to you more than it does to me. You saved Emerald's life when I could not."

Valerie stared at the stitching on the handkerchief. "I did not know what the cost would be." Valerie met the lady's gaze. "I cannot carry a child into the north. Yet, I am compelled to return to Frenland."

Celeniurisa frowned. "Who compels you?"

"Trelan is the eldest child of the empress of the Mountain Realm with a great army at his command. He seeks to rule the entire Modutan Empire with Emerald at his side. He has ordered me to marry the king of Frenland and threatened the lives of everyone in my homeland." Valerie looked away in shame.

"You must comply with his wishes."

Valerie's gaze snapped to meet Celeniurisa's. "I will not bear his offspring as he desires."

The lady's jaw fell open in an indelicate display of shock. "He would not dare."

Valerie flushed. "He has made his intentions known."

"I can see that his advances are unwelcome. How can I help you, Daughter?" The lady composed her features.

"Is there a way to know if I carry Darrin's child? I need to know the baby is his. I will not be in a position to deny Trelan if he insists on bedding me in the future, though I dread the encounter." Mortification overwhelmed Valerie, but she would submit for the sake of her people.

The lady frowned. "Trelan's pretenses of enlightenment seem to have been false."

"His people are good. They must not suspect him capable of this. Grief over the loss of his wife has triggered his downfall." Valerie had pieced together an understanding of the man over the past couple of weeks.

The lady scowled. "If Trelan loved his wife, then he will honor your choice in the matter. Do not fear him. Do not consent. As for a pregnancy, I can examine you. It is possible to discern signs this early if one knows what to look for."

Valerie numbed at the realization that the examination would require an invasion of privacy dissimilar to anything she had permitted before. "I delivered a child on my own because I could not endure people seeing my body. Your son saved my life last summer. He had to sedate me to clean and stitch my wounds." Valerie trembled. "I don't know if I trust you to keep my secrets."

Celeniurisa touched Valerie's arm, drawing her gaze. "I will tell no one of your suffering, your secrets, or your child. You owe me nothing. Go north and live in peace if you can."

Valerie left her dough rising on the table and closed the kitchen door, lowering the latch. "I must know if I carry Darrin's child before another man comes between us. I promised him I would never kiss anyone except him. The rest of my body will be surrendered as circumstances require. It has always been this way."

Celeniurisa closed her eyes, weeping. "Daughter, I hope it does not come to that. Will you undress and lay on the cot?"

To her eternal shame, Valerie complied.

Chapter Sixty-One

Half-frozen in a blizzard, Valerie huddled underneath a heap of furs to no avail. She just couldn't create enough heat to warm herself in this severe cold. If she could run alongside the litter, then perhaps she would be better off, but she didn't have the wind in her lungs to run. Furthermore, the jostling wouldn't allow anything she ate to settle.

The conveyance halted abruptly. She pulled the furs from over her head and looked between the woolen barrier covering the litter. A figure obscured by the weather pounded a wooden surface. The thud of each impact echoed. Snow blinded her.

"Admit us to see the king. We are an envoy from the Mountain Realm." Dantyn's words thundered upward in the language of Frenland.

Valerie clutched her furs and stepped from the litter. "The government of the Mountain Realm honor's King Stephan's request for an envoy. Dantyn, second son of the empress, will now grant him an audience."

A soldier hung a lantern over the battlement and nodded. "I will send word."

Dantyn urged Valerie to return to the shelter of the litter. Two women piled inside with her and opened their fur coverings to admit her into the bosom of their warmth. This was the indignity she had submitted herself to in making this journey in her condition. The flood of warmth brought on a healthy fit of shivers, though her feet did not thaw.

The creaking of hinges brought Valerie out of an anxiety-riddled dream of hatred and fire. The two women exited the shelter, taking their heat with them. The procession moved. The unsettling undulation of her litter churned her stomach.

Another set of hinges groaned in protest. That would be the offset entrance to the inner-city. Later, the well-oiled hinges of the doors of the Royal Hall yawned. They closed behind the litter as it entered the sheltered space.

Valerie took a deep breath. This was it. Stephan would be here.

She stepped out of the litter into the torchlit chamber. She had been destined to rule this kingdom. Frenland was her home.

That future had died when Stephan became king, yet Valerie had made way for him. She had enabled him to become the ruler of her homeland. She strode forth with confidence, casting back the hood of the shaggy white fur covering that had preserved her life in the frigid cold of a northern winter. Lifting her snow visor onto her head, she lowered the caul of her woolen clothing.

"You came." Disfigured by scarring on his head and neck, Stephan rushed forward from the dais. "Sarialla said you would come, but I didn't dare believe—"

The East Icers drew their curved copper swords.

Valerie strode forward. Stephan was many things, and some of them were unforgivable, yet she forgot everything at the sight of him. A spark of hope rekindled the flame of attraction between them.

"Permit him to come to me. He is the king." She spoke the mountain language, not wanting the smile on Stephan's face to end, though at the threat it abruptly had.

The king's guards had drawn their swords and moved between the monarch and the threat.

Dantyn lowered the tip of his sword. "We came in good faith under the premise of peace, your majesty. You are perfectly safe in our presence. We would suffer death before the dishonor of breaking such a trust."

Stephan proceeded through the throng of armed warriors to stand closer to her than she had expected he would. His sky-blue greatcoat with silver buttons and ash gray trousers spoke of his return to the traditions of his heritage. To her unnerving, he kissed her cheeks, gently brushing her skin with silky warmth.

"There's no time for pleasantries. Your mother is gravely ill. Until now, I haven't left her side for a week. Please, come with me." He looked deeply into her eyes.

A tightness gripped her chest as she met Dantyn's gaze. "I'm going with the king to see my mother. You need not follow."

"Your attendants will accompany you, Crown Princess Valerie." Dantyn signaled to the two women traveling with the party to follow her.

Stephan took Valerie's hand and led her from the hall. They crossed the Grand Way to the palace gates. The guards admitted them without question. Stephan's urgent pace had her breathless or was that his touch. Was mother dangerously ill? The woman was more robust than Valerie these days, especially since crypts disease had damaged her heart. Despite the cure, she had not recovered as much as she had hoped to.

Surprisingly, Stephan did not escort her toward the royal residence of the palace in the east wing. Instead, they climbed to the second floor of the west wing to the lesser quarters. These rooms were closest to the stables.

"You keep her amidst the servants?" Upset on her mother's behalf, Valerie pulled her hand from his.

Stephan never slowed. "She's in my quarters."

Valerie hesitated at a familiar door. "These are my family's rooms." She had grown up here, enjoying the proximity to the horses with the bonus later on of being far from her uncle's royal chambers.

Stephan rushed into the well-lit living room. "Close the door behind you, you're letting out the heat."

She obeyed, but leaned against the closed door from the inside of the living room, catching her breath. The two women with her remained vigilant. Through the open bedchamber door, the ashen visage of Valerie's much-aged mother startled her. Sarialla had wasted away in the weeks since they had resided in the Imperial City.

Warmer in the room than inside her furs, she cast the coverings off, leaving only the white wool of her leggings and high-necked tunic. She even stepped out of the fur overshoes to reveal her brown leather riding boots. She was stalling. Mothers couldn't die.

"Your daughter has come to see you, wise one." Stephan gingerly gathered the elderly woman's hand from the thick coverlet. "You knew she would."

Sarialla stirred. That was all the prompting Valerie needed to cross the room.

"Mother."

Stephan made way, placing her mother's hand in Valerie's.

Sarialla opened her eyes only a little. "Your hands are deathly cold, Ree. Are you well?"

A brief smile and a flood of tears overwhelmed Valerie as she bent to hug her dear mother. "I am well. Thank you. Your love has healed me. Oh, how I've missed you." The words tumbled out thick with emotion.

"I'm so relieved." Sarialla's lips upturned in a short-lived smile. "You will miss me more before long, but we will be together in the eternities." Sarialla went limp and her eyelids fell closed.

"Mother?" Valerie looked to Stephan in desperation. "Is she—"

He embraced her. "No, not yet. Sarialla does this when she tries to speak. It's too much effort at this stage."

Valerie stiffened with shock at the terrible news of her mother's decline. The warmth of Stephan's chest and the comfort of his arms eased her suffering. His wool greatcoat smelled of horses. She shut out everything but him, forcing her fears to hover outside the halo of fire within which the two of them stood.

She tilted her head to look into his eyes, not having fully embraced him. He leaned in to kiss her. At the last instant, she turned her face. His lips caught the corner of her mouth.

Never in her life had she been more tempted to capture a kiss than this one, but she dared not. Her heart raced in her chest. Gasping for air, her vision narrowed.

"Just hold me." It was the only comfort she could accept without falling into old habits of conquest, or worse yet, new desires for true intimacy.

"As you wish." He hugged her close with his cheek pressed against hers, his breath on her ear.

The servants in the room postured in a hostile fashion. She observed their deepening unease, as did her attendants, judging by their defensive stances. Mother had called Valerie by her childhood name, a shorter version of her given name, but some unfriendly servant must have recognized her. Perhaps they all had. Now the animosity of the women in the room and the four men at the door darkened with every whisper that passed between them.

Valerie took a half-step backward. "My king, might I request a meal?" She looked downward and to the right, toward her mother, yet not at her.

"Of course." He moved as if to request a servant's aid.

"Will you fetch it, please?" She glanced to see if he understood her true meaning.

He met her gaze, then took in the hostile posture of the people around them. "I'll be back shortly." He caressed her cheek. "Have no fear, these are loyal subjects, as are you."

His naiveté reminded her of why she had instantly cared for him when they met last summer. He left the room and the sound of his bootheels receded. With an East Ice attendant at each elbow, Valerie faced the audience of justifiably angry people. She laid a hand on the hilt of her East Icer attendants' curved copper swords, discouraging them from drawing their blades in her defense.

"I am who you believe be to be. Yet I am more loyal to Stephan than any of you." Valerie unbuckled the belt that held Queen Dana's sword and let it fall to the floor. "Slay me if you must. But know this, I have come to save him."

One of the guards charged forward, leveling a crossbow at her chest. "Your look of innocence and declaration of loyalty does not fool me, General. You are a viper." His trigger finger began to squeeze.

She met his gaze without guile. "I will lay down my life for him." The absolute truth.

The man hesitated. "His enemies almost have him now. Are you not one of them?"

"I once was. They will reveal their plots to me. As a rival for the throne, I could serve Stephan well by flushing out those who secretly seek to betray him. He cannot know why I've come. But I promise you, I will protect him." She meant every word.

Stephan entered the living room with a tray of steaming soup and buttered bread. "What goes on here?"

"Nothing, sir." The guard lowered his weapon and returned to his position beside the door.

"Good." Stephan booted the living room door firmly shut, balancing the tray. "I love her and she is welcome here." His cheeks flushed as he glanced at his bedchamber at the other end of the living room.

Charmed by his declaration, Valerie wanted to smile. But she could not save him if he knew her true intentions. "You mistake the reason I have come. Mother sent for me because those who support me asked her to. I am the crown princess. Step down from the throne, Stephan."

"What?" He rooted in place, sloshing the soup.

"Abdicate. The empress will receive you into the Mountain Realm to face justice for their dead." Valerie met Stephan's gaze with an unflinching calm.

"Sarialla wants you to be queen?" His gaze shifted to the woman sunken into the bedding.

"Yes, your majesty. I seek a union between the two of you. Appease the people of the East Ice and marry my daughter." Sarialla went limp.

A partial smile contorted Stephan's confused expression. "Marry me, Valerie. I declared my intentions last summer. I renew them now." He slid the tray into a servant woman's hands, went to one knee, and drew a sapphire ring in a silver setting from the breast pocket of his greatcoat.

Torn by the fulfillment of her tenderest hope for the inevitable union, she wished she was free to accept him. But she carried Darrin's child and had not seen her husband's dead body. She came to her senses. If she married Stephan, he would die. They both would.

She wrenched her gaze from his, retrieved her sword, and belted it around her waist. "I did not come to marry you. I returned to rule my homeland."

The adversaries who sought Stephan's life were deeply embedded in the new government. His innocence prohibited her from allowing him to know the truth of his peril. The only way to save him was to draw out his enemies with deception.

"Take my hand, Valerie." He reached toward her.

Surprised that he had not rescinded his offer as most men would, she sought strength because hers was utterly spent. Clasping, the hilt of the arcane sword, the thrum of its power energized her. Crushingly, the cost was far higher than anticipated. Her tender feelings for Stephan were trampled by the sword's obsession with vengeance.

Stephan wore the mate to her sword. The Ancient King Krelor had betrayed his queen. Valerie knew full well that Krelor's sword influenced the bearer to serve the one who wore Dana's sword as penance.

Perhaps that was the source of Stephan's devotion. It was possible that he did not love her as he claimed. Yet, part of her still remembered he had loved her before he possessed the sword, or it possessed him.

"Receive my life into your hands," he said. "By your admission, I am the king of Frenland. As such, I will not abdicate my responsibility to my people, nor face the justice of a foreign power. Marry me, and rule over me if you wish, because my heart is yours."

The strength of Stephan's convictions held Valerie in sway for a moment too long. He rose to his feet, sliding the ring onto her finger. He stopped short of pushing it into place, frowning at the ring already there.

"What is this?" His expression held confusion.

She withdrew her hand, leaving the coveted ring he offered behind. "I am already married," heat flushed her cheeks, "or at least I was until he died."

Stephan's shocked expression broke her heart.

"Who died?" His voice cracked.

"Darrin of Wolfe." She couldn't manage more of an explanation because the words simply wouldn't come.

Stephan covered his mouth with the hand that held her future pinched between his thumb and forefinger. His gaze searched her as he backed away. With one final blink of disbelief, he departed.

She stood her ground, gripping the hilt of Dana's sword in an effort not to run after him. The sound of his boots on the marble floors receded. Only then did she allow the agony of her devastation to escape her body in a sob. She crumpled beside her mother's bed and wept in shame for the pain she had inflicted on an innocent boy.

Her mother's trembling hand touched her head. "How could you do it, Ree?"

Chapter Sixty-Two

Stephan returned to the Royal Hall in anger. Striding directly at the group of fur-clad foreigners, he drew Krelor's sword.

"Face me, Dantyn." He spoke their language, so there would be no misunderstandings. "I was promised a wife. Now I find she has married a man who was promised to my sister. Explain this betrayal."

Dantyn stepped from the midst of his people. "King Krelor's sword has chosen you. Queen Dana's sword fell to Valerie. Fulfill the mandate of the blades and the fractured empire will be reunited. No one has betrayed you, King Stephan. Her marriage to the oath breaker, Darrin, was not legally binding, and now he is dead. She will marry you."

Stephan stilled. "Did you threaten Valerie?"

"Parliament threatened every living soul in Frenland." Dantyn met Stephan's gaze with remorse showing on his eyes. "I am merely a messenger."

A shiver strummed Stephan's spine. "Valerie is mourning the loss of a lover, her husband, she says." He sheathed Krelor's sword as compassion stirred his heart. "Her mother will soon pass from this life and she will need time to grieve. I believe that patience is in order. Wouldn't you agree?"

Dantyn held Stephan's gaze, extending a roll of parchment. "You must accept our terms publicly, your majesty. Otherwise, I have orders to return to the mountains immediately."

Stephan accepted the parchment and read it. He could feel the blood drain from his face. He cast his gaze around the Royal Hall. To his surprise, the majority of the representatives from each province had gathered around him. Helen's concern creased her brow. To his knowledge, none of them spoke the language of the mountain people and could not have understood the exchange.

Stephan addressed them in the Frenland tongue. "The government of the Mountain Realm has decreed the terms of peace between our lands. The empress' second son, Dantyn, has delivered her offering. I must accept an arranged marriage if I wish to end the conflict."

"No, my king. You must not accept the terms." Helen scowled.

"I must marry the woman who saved the empress's eldest son's life." Stephan drew out the revelation because once the name was given, Helen would not consider further.

"Your majesty, are you saying the empress of the Mountain Realm is asking you to marry the former crown princess?" Jarales of Soniashi smirked. "That is ironic."

Dantyn scowled. "You disrespect the king with your insinuations. The empress wishes for peace. She hopes the union will be blessed with happiness. A balance must be struck in Frenland that leads to a resolution to your troublesome conflicts. Otherwise, the armies of the east will descend from the glaciers like a scythe to cut you down. You have been warned."

A hostile silence prevailed among the representatives.

Stephan faced Dantyn. "I accept the empress' terms. Peace is my pledge. The wedding will be held in ten days and it would honor me if she officiated at the ceremony."

Dantyn bowed low. "Your request will be conveyed, your majesty."

Chapter Sixty-Three

Valerie stayed at her mother's bedside. Sarialla's illness progressed rapidly toward an inevitable conclusion. There were many things Valerie would have said had she been free to speak in front of a throng of onlookers, but her mother did not prompt her to say them.

Intelligent to the end, Sarialla seemed to have thought through what must be done without the need to voice her questions. The only thing Valerie did say, more times that night than she had in a lifetime, was how much she loved her mother. Sarialla returned the affectionate words as often as her failing strength permitted.

"Arlon." Sarialla opened her eyes.

Valerie lifted her head from where she sat bent over the side of the bed holding her mother's emaciated hand. This was the sign she had waited for. If her father had come from the other side of the veil to retrieve his wife, then it was nearly time for her passing.

No amount of coaxing had succeeded in compelling the elderly woman to eat and drink. The last attempt had almost been the end. The liquid had entered her lungs because she lacked the strength to cough. That had been an hour ago.

"Please send for the king." Valerie met the gaze of a servant woman attending the room.

"Right away, General." The girl curtsied and hurried from the bedchamber, closing the door.

The gesture of respect was odd from someone who supported the king. Perhaps the servants had believed Valerie's words to them in private while Stephan had been out of earshot. He hadn't returned after discovering she had married Darrin.

The heart-wrenching conversation with Stephan compounded the grief of her mother's inevitable death. It couldn't be long now. He would come, wouldn't he?

Exhausted, Valerie lay her head on the coverlet and gazed at her mother's gaunt features. Holding her hand, she wished they had never been parted. If Salicor had not murdered Arlon and captured her and Byron at such an early age, then everything would have been different.

Valerie had grown up in the palace kitchens with her father. She'd hidden in her mother's skirts as she attended Stephan's royal parents. Valerie remembered their infant son playing at their feet. She would have grown up with him if not for Salicor's betrayal.

She had spent countless hours in the royal stables as a child. Stephan was five years younger, but he would have found her there eventually. To be sure, he would have been annoying at first, but dear nonetheless. She would have loved him. Her mother had confessed that she cherished Stephan from the moment she delivered him into the world as the queen's midwife.

"I thought seeing you would bring her back to us," Stephan said from the doorway.

Valerie hadn't heard him enter the suite of rooms. The tenderness of his tenor bespoke tears. She faced him from her chair, still holding her mother's hand with one of her own.

"I commanded her to recover, but she doesn't take orders from junior officers." Valerie had meant it as a joke, but the mention of authority caused Stephan to visibly bristle.

"I told her the same thing." He walked around to the other side of the bed.

"Ah, well, she must be obeying a higher command then." Valerie did not doubt her mother's faith.

"The Creator will take me home." Sarialla watched both of them through barely open eyes.

Valerie's throat swelled with tender emotion at her mother's declaration. Perhaps if Emerald had been the one to come, then Sarialla would have listened to her. But then, Emerald wasn't the Creator. She was merely the Creator's child, and wasn't everyone?

"Don't go yet." Stephan sat on the edge of the bed on the opposite side, clasping Sarialla's free hand in both of his.

The elderly woman smiled. "I must. My work is finished. Help has arrived." With each broken statement she drew the hands she held together until she left Stephan and Valerie touching. "You are one." She faded away.

Unbelieving that her mother could be gone, Valerie watched for breath to rise again in her chest. It did not. Unaware of the comfort she was taking in Stephan's touch until he withdrew his hand, she hadn't held onto him.

She had no right to touch him, but she needed him. In her grief, she had forgotten to distance her heart. He captured her gaze, then turned away. Through a fresh wave of tears, she realized he was angry.

He wrung his hat in his hands. It was a gray beret that slouched to conceal the burn scars. "You didn't come to help. You came to rule."

Uncovered, the scars were vivid evidence of the fire that had nearly claimed his life last summer. She had saved him then. There was nothing that could prevent her from protecting him now.

"We'll invite the citizens of Frenland to decide the matter." It would buy her time to root out the enemies of the new government.

"An election? For a monarch?" He nearly tore the hat. "You plan to contest me instead of accepting our marriage? What is your reasoning?"

She stroked the back of her mother's hand with her thumb. "I will not defile you, Stephan. I told you that last summer."

"Yet you gave yourself to Darrin?" He glared at her.

"What do you know of passion? You are a child. Darrin offered me something you cannot give. And he never committed the unthinkable acts you commanded to be perpetrated in the name of conquest." She hadn't meant to be cruel.

No evidence of surprise registered on his face, nor on any of the servants' faces either. They must realize that she referred to the slaughter of the sacred horses. Their loyalty was far greater than she had suspected.

Stephan scoffed. "What could Darrin have possibly offered you that I cannot give? He is a shadow. I am a king."

Valerie looked away embarrassed that he would belittle Darrin and inflate himself. It was immature. Though, that was to be expected, since he was only seventeen years old.

"My mother told me you did not intend to remain a king." The idea that

Stephan had been swayed by power oppressed Valerie. "Sarialla said, that like Queen Emerald, you do not believe in an absolute monarchy. Mother left me with no doubt that you have no intention of fathering an heir. I have spared you the troublesome dilemma. You may avail yourself of my body as you wish, now that I am already with child."

A servant woman gasped and clapped a hand over her mouth.

Stephan flushed a deep red. "You're pregnant?" Skepticism dripped from his words.

Valerie lay beside her mother and closed her eyes. "We can call the office we both seek a presidential posting as opposed to a monarchy."

His weight lifted from the side of the bed. "You took another man into your bed because you believed I would not give you a child?"

She wished to die beside her mother. "You cannot father a child. I understand your reasoning, but I happen to disagree."

"So, you defiled him, as you call it, and now you say I'm free to use you as well? Here? Right now, I suppose. In front of these people and with your mother right there?" He wept great tears and heaving sobs.

"You may not believe me, but I rather like your idea of a representative government and will adopt it after I defeat you in the election." Her voice held dispassion, but her chest was crushed by guilt.

His jaw dropped and he stared. "You would defeat me and send me to the Mountain Empire?"

"You must go." She couldn't stay awake much longer.

"You want me dead?" he asked.

Her eyes popped open. "No." She hadn't intended to admit that.

His disfigured face registered his understanding. "You're trying to take my throne. But you don't want me dead. The empress has no intention of killing me, does she? You think I'll be safe there. But I won't go, Valerie."

She met his gaze. "You must go and the sooner the better."

He shook his head vehemently. "I can play your political game. I agree with your proposal for an election. I will beat you at the ballot box, then you will go safely to the mountains. But first, you must acknowledge that you have married me. Your mother's last words were legally binding. All we need to do is accept." He swallowed and faced Sarialla's body with renewed grief shadowing his features.

Valerie checked her mother for signs of life. How could she be gone? It didn't seem real, yet the inanimate hand of the woman who had given her life was already growing cold.

"I accept."

"So do I."

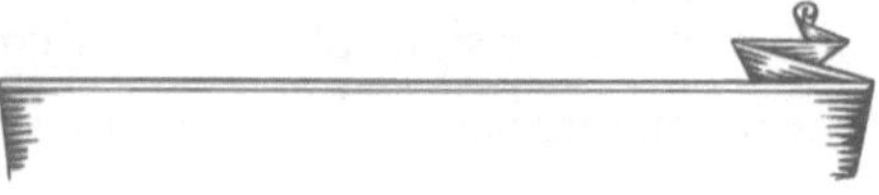

Chapter Sixty-Four

Stephan rubbed his face with his hands, realizing he must act. Sarialla was dead. Valerie lay beside the body as if she would never leave.

He strode around the bed and lifted Valerie in his arms. She was ice cold as if she too had died. Startled, she met his gaze.

"What are you doing?" she demanded.

"I'm availing myself of your body. Are you rescinding your permission?" he asked.

She trembled, though it was more like a shiver. "Your reputation will be ruined."

He scoffed at the notion. "The decree has been issued. Your mother bound us. You have agreed. Thus, the official ceremony with the empress is a mere formality." He carried Valerie to his bedchambers on the other side of the living room. "Leave us."

The guards who had followed him sputtered objections. Valerie's two, female, East Icer attendants were right on his heels. He slammed the door in their faces. He sat Valerie on the edge of the bed, knelt in front of her, and removed her boots. Unbuckling her sword belt, he inadvertently touched the hilt. A jolt of pain caused him to yelp.

"What is that?" He stared at the blade. "Why do you carry Dana's sword?"

"Why do you carry Krelor's?" she asked.

"That sword has never shocked me before, and I've handled it many times." Suspicious of the blade's transferred loyalties, Stephan wondered what it meant.

Valerie cast the weapon to the far corner of the room. "There is enmity between Dana's blade and Krelor's. Can you not feel it? For centuries, it was believed that Dana betrayed him with her shadow, but that was a lie. Records in the Imperial City revealed that he was the one who cast off his completely faithful wife and their eight sons in favor of another woman who could give him the daughter his people desired to be their ruler."

Stephan met Valerie's gaze and unfastened his belt, tossing Krelor's sword into an opposite corner. "I am not your enemy."

"You are not my lover yet, either." She held his gaze.

He searched the depths of her brown eyes by firelight. Dawn's first hint of light had not yet penetrated the gap in the curtains at the window. There couldn't be more than a few hours before the ritual viewing of the body must begin.

"The oracle hours commence at sunrise. You must rest." He could see the weight of her grief in the lines of fatigue on her face.

"Do you have a request?" Her gaze held him bound.

"Oracle of the Creator, will you be mine?" His request was outrageous, even by the standards of the custom.

"If you win my heart with your devotion, then on the other side of the vail, when we are both made whole, I will love you forever." She caressed his face.

He clasped her icy hand. Closing his eyes, he kissed the palm. "I'm sorry I'm so ugly that you can't stomach the thought of loving me now."

She unbuttoned his coat. "You're just tired. Come to bed."

He met her gaze, his breath catching in his throat as his heart pounded. "What of my reputation?"

She quirked a wicked smile. "How long do you think it takes to lose such a fragile thing?"

He had no idea. "A bit longer than this."

She turned down the bed and slid under the covers. "Not for most men."

He crossed to his side and slipped off his boots. She hadn't undressed. He followed her lead and entered the bed fully clothed.

"Are there exceptions?" He certainly didn't want intimacy with her to end after only a handful of minutes.

"I've only been with one." She snuggled next to him and rested her head on his shoulder like she had the night they met.

He hugged her to his side. "I've missed you as if part of my soul had been divided from me." He covered her hand on his chest to warm it.

She didn't reply. He glanced at her. She was already asleep.

Chapter Sixty-Five

Valerie rode Rumsfahail beside Stephan on his horse, Marcin, at the head of the honor guard leading her mother's funeral procession. She wore a white dress uniform, including a silver helm with a white horsehair plume. Valkyrie had come from near and far, wearing glossy black calf-hugging boots and the red and black combination of parade dress uniforms. Many joined the procession, but most were interspersed within the crowds that lined the Grand Way.

Stephan wore a silver helm with a white feather plume signifying respect for the dead. His greatcoat was sky blue and his trousers light gray. The colors symbolized the return of his line to the monarchy. He rode at Valerie's right side.

She had taken comfort in his closeness all day. He had lent her his throne to sit on and stood beside her in the Royal Hall. A long line of mourners had come to view Sarialla's body as it lay on display.

They had approached Valerie during the oracle hours with their requests of the Creator. Drained as she was from the intensity of her grief, she had often given the polite replies everyone expected. On occasion, however, she had felt a prompting to say something specific. The words she had spoken to Dantyn had surprised them both. His future encompassed the empire, bringing prosperity and peace. She had warned him to remain pure of heart, or else he would be passed over in favor of another.

Instances like this had taken place all her life. Only during the oracle hours of a funeral when the bereaved family was expected to have impressions from the beyond was it acceptable to share the whisperings of the Creator. However, Valerie had received a continuous stream of enlightenment ever since she could remember.

None of the inspiration had ever benefitted her. It was directed toward others, and she had acted on the urge to help from the time she was big enough to be of service. Her mother had recognized the rare and valuable gift. To Valerie's knowledge, Sarialla had never breathed a word of it to another living soul, not even to Arlon.

Sarialla's ornately carved casket rested on a wagon drawn by four white horses at the head of the procession. Valerie and Stephan rode directly behind it. Two columns of officers, women on the left, men on the right followed behind them.

Crowds lined the main thoroughfare of the city. If it had been anything other than miserable winter weather, then the mourners would have offered flowers and greenery. As it was, there were only somber looks of grief, or apprehension, interspersed with bridled hostility.

Valerie relied on the power of Dana's sword to keep her sharp. She hadn't had much stomach for the oracle hours because most of the people who turned up were not there to pay respect to her mother. Too many had been currying favor with Valerie because she stood as a rival to Stephan's righteous rule. There were deep undercurrents of danger in his court.

Rumsfahail snorted. The interruption of her thoughts reminded her to acknowledge the mourners' words of sympathy. She patted his neck, taking comfort from his companionship.

She made eye contact with individuals in the crowd. If someone spoke to her, then she nodded as she rode past. She hadn't spent much time in the capital over the past few years and the unfamiliar faces outnumbered the ones she could put a name to.

Numerous men and some women made rude gestures, or spit epitaphs in Valerie's direction, but none attacked. Honoring the fallen was the most sacred ceremony of her culture. The detractors would wait to offer violence until she attempted to reenter the city.

The return trip was likely to result in a civil uprising. She needed to do something. At the moment, however, her spirit was so oppressed that she hardly cared.

What in the name of the Creator would she say to the people gathered at the catacombs? Did the site need to be guarded against retaliatory actions by those who might desecrate her mother's resting place? Would Stephan be willing to stand beside her? Could she allow him to face such ire on her behalf?

She glanced at him, captured by his intensely pained expression. The cold air hurt. She remembered that much from her recovery after the burns she'd received in the fires of Scion. The helmet he wore did not completely shield his sensitive skin from the wind.

The longer she looked at him the more she wished to comfort him. The desire to touch his wounded face and draw his attention from the hostile gazes of the crowd increased. She gripped the hilt of Dana's sword fiercely to put a stop to the impulse. Sure enough, Dana's tumultuous influence ended any tender feelings Valerie had for Stephan.

He caught her looking at him. She righted her attention forward, her posture straight as the soldier she had been for much of her life. With the power of the sword heightening her level of awareness, she noticed the mood of the crowd increase in hostility.

A scowling man caught her full attention. He elbowed his way through the onlookers and raised a crossbow. Valerie reacted quickly enough to grab Stephan by the arm. She pulled him toward her, leaning over to shield him from the bolt that would have taken his life. It ricocheted off her helmet to land harmlessly amidst the crowd, leaving her stunned by the impact, but unhurt.

Soldiers from both columns behind Valerie and Stephan moved to apprehend the man. The assassin fled, but the crowd reacted of one accord to cut off his escape. He wounded three men before he was run through by a royal guard.

Stephan clutched Valerie close to his chest. Having lost her seat on Rumsfahail, if he hadn't held onto her, she would have fallen under the horses' hooves. Stephan pulled her into a seated position across his saddle.

Meeting her gaze, he calmed his breathing. "I thought…" He blinked quizzically as the hint of a smile upturned the corners of his lips. "You can't hide your feelings from me."

She touched his jaw on the scarred side. "I came here to rule." She repeated the lie.

His expression saddened. "Then rule my heart because I cannot pretend that I don't love you."

He held her body in his arms and her heart in his hands. Warmed by his brown eyes, she nearly succumbed to her overwhelming desire to kiss him. The intrusion of the crowd broke through her fixation with a slow build of clapping.

Coming to herself, she assessed the situation and withdrew her hand from Stephan's face. Flushed with embarrassment, she leaned for Rumsfahail's reins. Stephan grasped her around the middle and shifted her onto Rumsfahail's saddle.

Surprised by his strength, she gawked for an instant. It was long enough to elicit a smile from him and more than one amused expression from her Valkyrie. Unsure of what to do, she urged Rumsfahail to follow the funeral wagon.

Her mother's voice entered her mind. 'Love will prevail, Ree.'

Chapter Sixty-Six

Stephan rode to the palace stables with Valerie. Exhausted by the events of the funeral, he handed the reins to the stable master without a fuss. The grieving woman he had spent the day with, would not stop. Clasping Dana's sword, Valerie uncinched Rumsfahail's saddle.

"Please, let me do that." Stephan entered the stall.

Rumsfahail snorted in his face.

"I can do it myself." Valerie's eyes rolled back in her head.

Stephan caught her before she hit the clean straw of the stall. He carried her home. Laying her under the covers in her mother's bed, he stripped off her boots, sword belt, and coat. After doing the same for himself, he slid in beside her to embrace her chilly body.

She did not awaken. He didn't mind. Exhausted, he should have slept too. However, he could not take his eyes off of her delicate features. Her lips were inviting, but she could not consent, so he resisted the temptation to kiss her.

Sometime in the night, he felt her stir.

"I'm sorry." Valerie met his gaze with watery eyes.

A dam of emotion broke inside him and he drew her closer. "What do you have to apologize for?"

"I left Frenland." Despair echoed in her words. "My brother faced Salicor alone. It's my fault that he died. I should have been the one to lay down my life for justice."

Stephan understood that kind of guilt. "I'm glad you lived. I'm grateful you helped Emerald. She would have died without you. Your mother told me everything."

Valerie lifted her head to meet his gaze. "I went to the mountains and found a happiness that was unlike anything I've ever known. I took what didn't belong to me because I was selfish." She closed her eyes and tears splashed his neck.

He didn't understand, except maybe part of it. "Darrin didn't belong to you. Is that what you're saying? Dantyn has explained things. Darrin made his choice. You did nothing wrong." It was hard to say but true.

She opened her eyes, drawing Stephan into their dark depths. He wanted to run his hands over her body. He had longed to have her like this ever since they'd slept beside one another last summer. Not to mention yesterday morning when she'd fallen asleep without so much as a kiss.

"I will not defile you." She touched his scars.

He clasped her hand and brought it to his lips, noticing the ring on her finger. It was a yellow-gold rose. Darrin must have given it to her.

"You married him." Stephan righted the ring on her finger from its off-center position.

"I trusted him." Her tone was sad, angry, hurt.

"He betrayed you?" Stephan had not believed Darrin capable of that, yet the man had cast Emerald aside over a misunderstanding.

"Darrin left me to follow Emerald." More tears filled Valerie's eyes.

"Dantyn believes Darrin lost his life in Emerald's defense. That is the oath a shadow takes. How can that be a betrayal?" Stephan's heart went out to Valerie for her loss, but he could not understand her resentment.

She pushed him away. "Darrin didn't look back. I watched him, but he never turned to consider his promises to me. He chose her."

Stephan sighed in frustration and laid on his back, resting on the pillow. "You think he lied about his feelings for you?"

She stared at him.

Stephan met her gaze. "You think he used you?"

She blinked, sending two tears in a race across her face. "I used him."

Stephan realized at that moment that she desperately needed to be loved, held, and cherished. She deserved it because of what her uncle had done to her. He smoothed her blond hair out of her eyes.

"Mourn him, then be with me. I've always been yours." He retrieved the sapphire solitaire from his pocket. "This ring was my mother's. No matter how hungry we were, Emerald would never let me sell it. Valerie, will you honor me by wearing it?"

Motionless, she stared at him. "I will not defile you."

Stephan frowned, finally understanding what she meant. "Then I won't ask you to. Just be my wife in the eyes of the people."

She stiffened. "I will wear your ring, but I cannot take your innocence."

The finality of her words came home, creating an ache in his chest. The heat that quickened his pulse in her proximity abated by the sheer force of his will. Shifting his gaze to the ceiling, he clenched his jaw.

"I accept your terms." He slid the ring onto her finger next to the yellow-gold rose.

Darrin was a handsome fellow. Stephan understood why Valerie was attracted to him. She must find Stephan's scars repulsive to look upon.

"Leave my bed." Her tone was firm.

He scowled. "You are my wife. Everyone knows we have shared a bed. Gossip has already spread, especially after you risked your life for me on the Grand Way."

Agape, Valerie stared at him. Blinking rapidly, she shut her mouth. With a small frown, she lay beside him.

"And what do the gossipmongers have to say? Am I any good in bed?" She scowled.

He flashed her a mischievous grin. "Very."

She snorted a laugh. "Naturally. I have a reputation for excellence. I suppose they think you were helpless to resist my charms."

One of the guards standing inside the closed bedroom door shook his head. The other rolled his eyes. Both chuckled.

Stephan looked at her. "Is it all gossip?"

A worry line appeared in her brow and she met his gaze. "Why do you ask?"

Rebuffed, he stared at the ceiling and fought tears. "It isn't slander, is it? You sleep with plenty of men, but not me because I'm ugly."

She grabbed his hand and brought it forcefully to her breast. "Take me, if that's what you want. Far be it from me to keep you off me now that we are committed."

He relaxed his splayed hand to cup her breast through her shirt. He stroked the gentle curve with his thumb. Despite how inappropriate it was, he couldn't help smiling. He released her and lay back on his pillow with his hands folded behind his head.

"I can die happy now." He couldn't stop grinning.

She looked surprised. "I am a woman of my word after all."

His hand tingled with sensation. "An incredible woman." He too remembered the promise she made last summer.

Valerie snorted. "I wanted you to live."

He studied her face. "And now?"

She met his gaze. "I want more."

He absorbed the layers of implied meaning and tumbled into the depths of her remarkable brown eyes. "Everything I have is yours." A lump of unresolved emotions formed in his throat. "Take only what you wish."

Vulnerability broke through in her tone. "I promised Darrin I would never kiss another man."

Surprise washed over him. "You will never kiss me?" He had dreamed of her kiss and longed for her lips. He scowled, wounded by the deprivation. "Kissing is more sacred to you than other intimacies?"

"Your gaze has drifted," she said.

He flushed with embarrassment to be caught looking at her breasts. "Forgive me." He righted his gaze to meet her eyes. "You would allow me to make love to you?" He frowned. "Without kissing, I hardly think it could be loving." He shook his head. How would he know anything about it? He'd never done it. "I have no idea what I'm doing."

She watched him speak, but now her gaze fixated on his lips. Her pupils dilated in the firelight to become dark pools. Her breathing became shallow, and he could see her pulse in the hollow of her throat.

He reached out to touch her cheek. Her silky soft skin thrilled him. She closed her eyes and moved toward him, hesitating a hair's breadth from his lips. He couldn't breathe in anticipation of her kiss.

She opened her eyes and pulled back. He panicked and charged ahead. His lips connected with her jaw. She pinned him to the bed with a fierceness that surprised him.

"Leave my bedchamber." She spoke with a finality that left no room for argument.

"Fine." He cast the blankets off and grabbed his, coat, sword, and boots.

On the way to the door, he stopped and whirled around. "Why do you hate me? I'm in love with you."

She flung the covers off and marched over to glare at him. "You don't know what love is."

"Yes, I do." His chest heaved.

"Do not return to my bed until you can abide by my conditions." Her gaze lowered to his lips.

"Fine." He dropped his things. "You can't kiss me, but may I kiss you?"

She glanced at the men guarding the door. "No."

Shocked by her unwillingness to yield, his anger surged. "I didn't make any promises to Darrin. And he certainly shouldn't have asked this of you."

Color rose in her cheeks. "He didn't ask. It was my wedding gift."

Jealous, Stephan couldn't decide how to act. He wanted her, but not like this. He needed to kiss her.

"I know what love is, and it involves kissing. I will wait until you ask me, Valerie." He allowed the upset to leave him.

"I never will. I can't." She looked away.

The heart in his chest felt as though it broke. "I will prove my devotion."

"How?" She met his gaze.

"I will leave you untouched." No part of him wanted to go, but that's what he did.

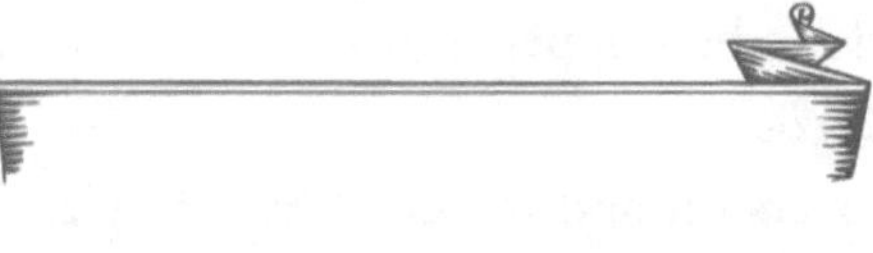

Chapter Sixty-Seven

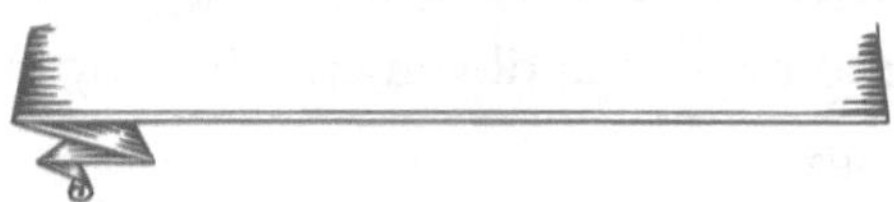

Aknock at the living room door of the suite startled Valerie. She had awakened early and come out of her bedchamber to read a book on the chaise lounge by the fire.

"My king, are you awake?" A military woman burst into the room. "The council has asked for you. I thought I'd deliver—"

Helen of Scion carried a tray of food. She stopped in her advance toward the bedchamber Valerie had occupied as a child. When she noticed Valerie, however, her expression swiftly changed from enthusiastic eagerness to dark hostility.

Valerie closed the book and drew her shawl around her nightgown. "He isn't here."

The door to the bedchamber opened. "Helen?"

Stephan wore trousers and nothing else. Valerie couldn't help noticing the extent of his scarring and the contours of his chest. Heat flushed her skin. She looked away, aware that she too was not properly dressed.

"Excuse me, I didn't realize..." Valerie fled toward her parents' old bedchamber embarrassed to think Helen had the right to enter the king's quarters with such casual intimacy.

"Seductress!" Helen deposited the tray of food on a table and crossed the room.

She spun Valerie around. Lifting her by the upper arms, she slammed her against the wall. Heart pounding and unable to catch her breath, the blow to the back of the head rendered Valerie unconscious.

VALERIE FOUND HERSELF in a heap on the floor. Helen and Stephan argued in the center of the living room. The military woman was keeping him from coming to Valerie's aid, but she considered that a gift since his bare chest would have influenced her thinking.

Angry, Valerie gathered herself off the floor and joined the fray. "Why are you in my rooms?"

Stephan shifted his gaze to Valerie. "I live here."

Shocked because his gaze had lowered to her breasts and she'd forgotten her shawl, she said the only thing that came to mind. "But these are my family's quarters."

He walked past her to retrieve his boots, coat, and sword belt from her bedchamber.

Helen scowled.

Valerie blushed at what the woman must be thinking. "Why aren't you in the royal residence?"

Both Helen and Stephan's noses wrinkled.

Stephan shook his head and righted his gaze. "That part of the palace is unlivable."

Valerie frowned. "Why?"

Stephan walked over to the tray of food on the table. "The stench became unbearable." He didn't touch the food. Instead, he walked into the bedchamber.

Both women watched him put on a clean shirt from a chest of drawers. Embarrassed to be slavering over him, Valerie walked to her quarters. She shut the door and dressed in white. It was a reminder that she was still in mourning, though she needed no prompting to grieve.

A chilling thought struck. It twisted in her chest like a shard of ice. What could have caused that part of the palace to stink?

Valerie lost sensation in her hands. In shock, she returned to the living area. Stephan too, walked out of his bedchamber fully dressed.

"When did the smell begin?" Valerie felt faint.

"I noticed the odor of decay on the fourth day, but we couldn't find where it was coming from." Helen sliced a loaf of bread and placed meat and cheese on it, taking a bite.

Stephan's nostrils flared. "I could no longer sleep after the fifth night. That's when I relocated to Sarialla's spare bedchamber."

A wave of nausea threatened to turn Valerie's stomach inside out. She collapsed on the chaise. Stephan strode over.

"What's wrong? You've gone pale." He guided her chin with a finger until she looked at him instead of at the dawn's light coming in the window.

"Tell me you found them." Horror washed over her like icy water.

Stephan's scarred face scrunched with confusion. "Who?"

Compelled to her feet, Valerie ran through the hallways of the palace to the royal residence. Trembling, she stopped at the bedchambers her uncle had occupied. A faint battlefield odor permeated the air. She turned the knob on the door and pushed it open. Her gaze leveled across the grand bed to the tapestry on the far wall.

No fires warmed this part of the palace. Valerie shivered uncontrollably, though not entirely from the cold. Stephan draped his coat around her shoulders. She glanced his way and covered the hand he'd left there with her own.

Tears flooded her eyes. "I can't do this."

He placed his other hand on her shoulder and drew her back until she rested against him. "Did Salicor hurt you here?"

She shoved away from Stephan. "You think I'm concerned for myself? They died in there." She hit his chest with a fist. "Why didn't you look for them?" She shook her head in agony. "You could have saved them."

Stephan's pained expression held deep concern, but no understanding.

Helen pushed Valerie through the open doorway. "What are you saying? We searched the palace from top to bottom, looking for anything suspicious. We found plenty, but no people."

Valerie's rage kindled. "They were children, Helen."

Stephan strode into the room. "Where could they have been hidden?"

Valerie pointed to the tapestry hanging along the wall. "Slide it aside, then press the circle in the wood molding in the corner. A doorway will open."

Stephan slid the tapestry as directed, then searched the ornate wooden façade in the corner. "I don't see it."

Helen stared at the wall. "There is an outline in the stones. It may be a hidden passageway."

Stephan pressed the circles along the ornate pattern until one depressed and the concealed door swung inward on silent hinges. Hit by the stale smell of decomposition, Valerie looked away. She had no courage to go any further.

Helen grabbed her by the shirtfront, knocking Stephan's coat from her shoulders. "What is that place? Your mother didn't know it was there. How do you?"

Valerie's eyes rolled back in her head. Helen slapped her soundly, snapping her back to consciousness.

"You're not escaping responsibility that easily." Helen dragged Valerie into the dark passageway.

"Be gentle, Helen. I don't think this was Valerie's fault." Stephan struck the flint on an oil lamp and carried it into the passageway to light the way.

Valerie dreaded what they would find. "I won't go in there." She broke from Helen's grasp.

Helen drew a dagger. "Lead the way."

"Helen, please. She's afraid." Stephan brought the lamp closer, illuminating the descending passageway on his right.

"We're the ones who should be afraid. This could be a trap." Helen's expression became murderous. "She is a killer. We should expect nothing less than treachery."

Stephan shook his head. "You're wrong about her. I'll go."

"No," both women spoke at once.

Helen looked from Stephan to Valerie with surprise in her expression.

Shaking so hard she could hardly walk, Valerie took the lamp and descended the steps to the iron door. She used the key hanging from a hook to unlock it. The stench caused her gorge to rise. Forcing it down, she mustered the strength to shove the door. It screeched on rusty hinges as it opened. She walked to the center of the room, knelt, and laid the lamp on the floor, weeping for the dead.

Footsteps descended behind her.

"Don't let him see." Valerie had no strength to say more.

"Stay here, your highness." Helen's booted footsteps entered the torture chamber. "Creator have mercy."

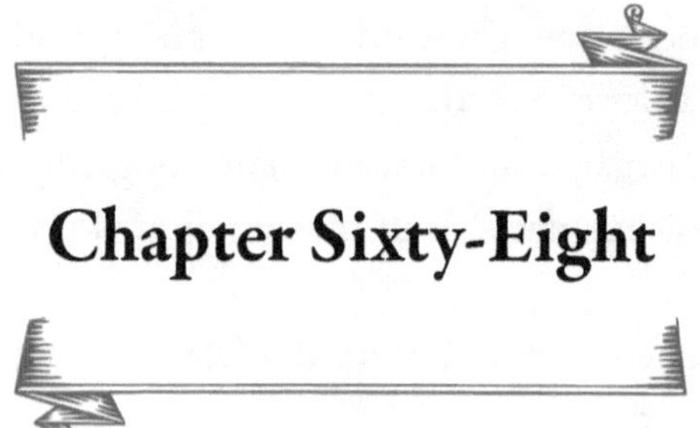

Chapter Sixty-Eight

Stephan hesitated at Valerie's warning not to enter the underground chamber. What didn't she want him to see? He had to know.

Inside the chamber, Helen retched her breakfast onto the dusty floor. Rats had scattered the bones, but sculls rested where young children had perished. Stephan counted more than a dozen.

"What is this place?" He drew Valerie to her feet, grasping her jaw when she would not look at him. "What happened here?"

Valerie's face was slick with tears. "What do you think?" She shoved him away. "You could have saved their lives. All you had to do was look for them."

Stephan's heart sank. "You're blaming me? I didn't know Salicor kept little children in a cellar."

"Babies, some of them were infants, your majesty." Helen held up a tiny skull.

Stunned, the only thing Stephan could say was, "Salicor the baby slayer."

Valerie shook her head. "He never killed them. Sometimes I did, but he—"

Helen rushed at Valerie holding the scull. "You killed innocent children? Oh, but we knew that about you. It's why you don't have any brats of your own, despite your proclivities."

Valerie's expression darkened further. "You would have ended their suffering too. The state he left them in could not always be mended."

Helen was taken aback. "Salicor tortured babies?"

Valerie laughed maniacally, turning Stephan's spine to jelly.

Valerie backed away, looking at Helen. "Why do you care? You've been a party to more of their deaths than I have. And you, your highness, your hands are covered in their blood, so don't look at me like that. This is your fault, not mine."

Stephan's fear mingled with his misunderstanding to anger him. "You're not making sense. I'll ask you one last time. Who are these children and why are they here?"

Valerie's hands dropped to her sides. "We are the jewels of the crown."

Chapter Sixty-Nine

Valerie knew she'd said too much, confessed more than she should. But in her grief-stricken anger, she had not been able to conceal her feelings. For many years, she had dedicated herself to rescuing Salicor's victims.

"You are one of these?" Stephan looked around the room crestfallen. "You are a jewel of the crown?"

Valerie couldn't speak past the emotions that caused a lump in her throat. Would he judge her for letting it happen? Would he despise her for sometimes doing the only thing she could to ease their suffering?

Helen scrutinized the scene as if solving a mystery. "During my investigations, I've heard of jewels. But I didn't understand they were people. Salicor selected them for their beauty and desirability. They have been described as being seductively alluring. How could children be viewed in such a manner? It doesn't make sense."

Valerie's bitterness bubbled forth in dark laughter. "You are incredibly naïve. He sodomized them. Surely, you've seen his brand on their bodies and the tallies on their backs."

Helen scowled. "You're lying. We check prisoners for Salicor's brand. He did not keep slaves."

The blood drained from Valerie's face and neck. They would not believe her. Long past shivering, there was nothing to save Valerie from suffering from exposure. Not since Helen had knocked Stephan's coat off of her shoulders in the bedchamber above.

"It doesn't matter" Unwilling to debase herself further, Valerie wanted out. "Let me leave this place."

She needed to escape. Her uncle had tortured her in this chamber for many years. She understood why Helen of Scion didn't believe her. Helen blamed her for the deaths of her family. Stephan's skepticism, however, wounded Valerie deeply.

Stephan's guards stood in the way.

"Let me pass." Valerie tried to squeeze between the men.

"Hold her, Aramis." Helen glared.

He grasped Valerie around the torso, preventing her escape. She fought him, trying to slide from his grasp. Her shirt caught in his grip and slid upward.

Stephan stood aghast with his gaze on her exposed skin. Helen retrieved the lamp. She inspected Valerie's lower back in the light.

"Release me." Valerie slammed her forehead into the guard's chest, panic rising as her inability to take in enough air made her vision narrow. "You're holding me too tight."

Helen lifted Valerie's shirt further. "What are these scars?"

"Nothing. Leave me alone." Valerie wrenched a hand free and pummeled Aramis' jaw until another guard stilled her fist in his iron grip.

Helen reached around and unfastened Valerie's belt.

"No. Please, stop." Tears coursed Valerie's face as the futility of her struggle became clear.

Helen lowered Valerie's trousers. "Salicor's mark. We found brands throughout the kingdom, but no slaves. We were looking in the wrong place."

Stephan strode forward, looking at Valerie's buttock.

Helen traced the faded brand on Valerie's backside. She shivered at the unwelcome touch. Helen slid her hand along the horizontal scars up one side of Valerie's spine and partway down the other.

"Release her," Stephan commanded.

The guards complied.

Valerie hiked her trousers, then slapped Stephan soundly. "Never come near me again."

She shoved the guards out of her way and plunged through the tunnels, heading away from her uncle's room. By feel, she chose a passageway that led beyond the palace walls. She needed to clear her head. Stephan's failure to defend her been a betrayal.

⤫

VALERIE FOUND THE TUNNEL that led through a subterranean arch built in the foundation of the palace wall. From there, she continued to move by feel until she found the ladder that led upward to the secret trapdoor in the floor of a storage building. She hoped nothing had been placed over it, or else she would not be able to exit here.

It opened. Cautiously, she made sure no one was in the dimly lit room. Crates and baskets surrounded her. She climbed out and secured the door. It locked. She would not be able to return to the palace this way without the key.

Angered by Stephan's treatment of her in the torture chamber her uncle had called his treasury, Valerie stalked from the storage room. She entered a narrow alley. Dantyn and the envoy from the Mountain Realm occupied the old whore house. The back entrance was nearby.

"My queen, I'm not surprised to see you here." A young man strode toward her with surprising confidence.

Valerie faced him, unarmed except for the knives in her boots. "Still lurking where you don't belong, Perry?" She held his gaze, weighing his intentions. "Why are you here? I thought you were safe in Skye."

He bowed low, opening his cloak to show he had drawn no weapons. "I am at your service, my queen."

She should not trust him, but couldn't resist touching his face. She had rescued him from Salicor. "Why come here?"

"You are deathly cold." His trousers bulged.

Valerie found the reaction to human contact not uncommon for jewels of the crown. "And this excites you?"

He unbuckled his sword belt and lowered his trousers. "Always at the ready."

She lifted her eyebrows. "Impressive display, but why show me?" She met his gaze.

"To prove my loyalty." He moved closer.

"How have you concealed your circumcision from the new regime? Surely, they must have executed everyone loyal to Salicor." Valerie didn't flinch, knowing it would be a sign of weakness and an offensive rejection of his misguided offer of pleasure.

Perry covered himself and fastened his belt. "They are soft-hearted fools.

Circumcision alone is not enough to condemn a man. They didn't even check before they hired me as a representative guard."

Valerie knew what that meant. "Then you have many allies. I think I will use you."

He came closer. "I require rewards that even your prowess cannot satisfy."

Valerie laughed. "Will a cellar of vintage wine suffice as payment?"

His lips twisted in a nasty approximation of a smile. "You know all of Salicor's secrets."

She tilted her head to the side. "Most of them. For the rest, I will rely on your assistance to uncover."

He clasped his fist and laid it across his chest. "I am at your command." He slowly met her gaze. "Don't upend the council. I have aspirations there. I will not return to being a worm beneath anyone's boot."

Valerie appraised the implications. "I may make changes, but I have a use for the council in my plans." She moved to walk past him.

He clasped her by the upper arm, yet bowed in deference. "The council's patience with the monarchy will end should rumors of your pregnancy be proven true."

Valerie shook his hand off her arm. The threat was plain. If she bore a child, then the council would kill Stephan and likely her as well.

"There is nothing to fear on that count. I'd as soon wallow with a pig than give that boy the satisfaction. Though, I hear there are already rumors giving me credit for seducing the young king into granting me his throne. Even I didn't know I was that good in bed." The left side of her mouth twisted.

Perry chuckled. "Ah, well, I figured as much. You've been off men for a while now. It makes sense that you would favor women. You have always surrounded yourself with enough of them."

The hair stood on the back of Valerie's neck. "And what do you prefer? Are you like my uncle?"

Perry chuckled. "I enjoyed Salicor after he was cold. I've had your mother too. Does that shock you, my queen?"

Valerie controlled the urge to draw her blade and plunge it into his groin, rip it upward, and gut him in the street. "I had thought to spare you from crypts disease. Did you know I contracted it last summer? Now that I know there is no danger to you, will you offer yourself to me again?"

He pressed her to the wall, his body hard against her. "I am at your service."

She led him into the storage room. He dropped his trousers and drew her hands to touch him. She wrenched his swollen member.

Writhing in pain, he knocked her to the ground. The weight of him pinned her down. He forced her trousers below her hips. She raised her knee and drew a knife from her boot, plunging it between his ribs.

He screamed. She'd missed his heart, but she jerked the blade to finish him. Gasping, blood frothed on his lips and colored his teeth.

"Why?" His eyes glazed over.

His last breath spilled blood across her breast. Sobs of relief and regret shook her body. She stroked his hair in tenderness. She had saved him from the treasury when he was a boy, but his actions today proved that she had been too late. He could never be normal after what her uncle had done to him. Even Skye could not heal him and now her enemies may know her most closely guarded secret.

Valerie slid Perry's body off of her. Trembling, she realized how close she had come to being re-infected with crypts disease. He had not come here to assault her but to do something else equally nefarious. He must have a key to the passageway. There was no other reason for him to be in the alley except to sneak into the palace.

She searched him, finding the key on a gold chain around his neck. She unlocked the trapdoor and shoved his body into the hole. He belonged with the other jewels who had perished in the treasury.

She draped the chain holding the key around her neck. Staring into the dark hole, she realized that she too belonged there. The blood on her chest chilled. She closed the trapdoor, locked it, and departed.

VALERIE STRODE FROM the storage shed into the alley. A woman stood in the doorway of a hovel. It was the only other door in the alley. She held a baby nursing at her breast.

"It had to be done. Perry served the enemy." The woman lifted the sleeve of her gown to reveal Valerie's brand. "Your secrets are safe with me, General.

Come inside."

Valerie followed the woman into the hovel and shut the door to keep out the cold. "The latch is broken."

The woman sat beside the hearth. "Just prop it closed."

Valerie moved the chamber pot to hold it shut. She reconsidered the choice since the next person to open the door would tip it over. Putting the chamber pot back, she selected a stick of firewood and wedged it under the gap at the bottom.

Shivering, she huddled by the fire. "Jane of Appleton, right?"

The Valkyrie bowed her head. "I miss the glory days, General."

Valerie shifted her gaze to the flames. "You were with me at Scion. What glory did we have then?"

"Saving you from their bonfire was glorious. What you became to all of us was glorious. Are we still part of your plans, General?"

Valerie rested a hand on Jane's shoulder. "Always," her lower lip trembled, "but the cost is so high." Tears spilled from her eyes, knowing what she must do to save Stephan from the council's assassins.

"Look to the Skye, General. Leave this place and take me and my baby with you." Jane popped the infant off her breast and stood as if to go immediately.

Jane's eagerness to shake the dust of Soniashi from her feet amused Valerie, lifting her mood. "Oh, that I could."

Jane gathered a basket and a crust of bread. "What stops you?"

Valerie stared into the coals of a dying fire. "A boy."

Jane slumped. "I've heard all about the king. He does his best, but he's not you. Are you going to marry him? Will you be our queen?"

Valerie considered Jane's words. "I have married him. It will cost my soul to save him from his enemies. If I fail, then I will betray your faith in me and cast the kingdom into a war we have no hope to survive."

Jane stared at Valerie. "Your soul? The only time you talk of losing it is when a child is involved. You must be pregnant. And here, Perry just threatened you over babies. Well, kill the serpents in the council before they carry through with the threat. You deserve the child you always wanted. Your boy king will forgive you for it not being his. Trust me, I'm a good judge of character."

Valerie stared at the baby in Jane's arms.

"Hold him, if you like." Jane held out her sleeping infant.

Valerie ached to receive the child, but it hurt too much. "I can't because if I do, then I won't have the strength to end the life of my own—"

"Pish." Jane thrust the baby into Valerie's arms.

He fussed at the shift. Valerie shushed him and held him close. Rocking the snuggly little boy back to sleep, she stared at his perfect features, beguiled.

"You were meant to be a mother." Jane smiled.

Valerie's heart stopped beating for just a moment. Painful as it was, the realization that she would never have the chance was worse. Darrin's child must die today.

Valerie laid a kiss on Jane's son's brow. She inhaled the infant scent of baby skin. There was nothing more lovely in the wide world than children.

"I have to go." Valerie handed the baby to his mother.

Jane frowned. "You're going to do it then."

"I forfeited my soul long ago. I was a fool to think otherwise." Valerie stood to depart.

Jane caught her before she could go. "Take this."

Valerie accepted a clean white shirt. She stripped her bloody one.

"You may wash here." Jane indicated a bucket of water.

Valerie used the bloody shirt to wash her chest and dressed in the clean one.

"You'll need this too." Jane handed her a red and black Valkyrie cloak.

"I will repay you." Valerie shrouded herself in the cloak and departed from Jane's humble home.

VALERIE MADE HER WAY to the apothecary. If she drank the tea there, then she would have just enough time to return to the palace before the cramps set in. Several days of pain would follow. It would become intense, and she would crave death, but terminating the pregnancy would end the threat to Stephan.

Entering the apothecary shop, Valerie removed the yellow-gold ring Darrin had given her. It was the only thing of value she owned other than the ring Stephan had put on her finger. Trembling with shame, she waited for an elderly shop keeper to shuffle from the back room.

"Haven't seen you in over a year." The woman's voice croaked with extreme old age.

"I thought your poor memory had been ensured by a ridiculous overpayment. I hope I was not mistaken in you, Myra." Valerie tested the woman's loyalty.

Myra chuckled and held out a hand.

Valerie parted with the rose ring with great reluctance.

"Cared about the father this time, did you?" Myra said.

Valerie couldn't find any words to reply. There was no need. Myra nodded and reached beneath the counter for a small paper packet. She dumped the contents into a mug and poured hot water from the kettle on the coal brazier over it.

"I am the worst kind of person." Valerie had no more tears to cry.

Myra grimaced a toothless expression of understanding. "Most of the girls that come in here don't know what they're doing will feel the way it does. They have a problem. I help them solve it. You've never been like them. You don't kill for convenience. You do it to be merciful. For you, it is always a sacrifice."

Valerie reached for the mug of tea. "You'd best forget that because the woman you see here today is making herself a murderer." Valerie lifted the mug to her lips.

Myra's hand shot out to stop her. "Then don't do it."

Valerie inhaled the smell of the bitter tea. "I have to."

Myra shook her head. "You can choose to have faith."

Valerie scoffed, angry at the Creator for leading her to this moment. "Merciful Creator."

Myra shuffled away, heading to whatever comfortable chair she had hidden away in the back room. "You've served him all your life. Don't stop now. He owes you this one, so hold him to it."

Valerie stared at the mug in her hands, letting it warm her fingers. Faith. Was it still faith, if she knew the Creator existed? Had she lost sight of him today when faced with that chamber of horrors beneath the palace?

Valerie poured the tea into the ash bucket beside the coal brazier. Sunlight caught on an object on the counter. Myra hadn't taken the ring. Valerie slipped it on her finger. With a sigh, she drew the hood of her cloak and exited the apothecary shop.

"Seize her." Helen of Scion commanded a force of ten representative guards.

They pummeled Valerie with their fists. She used her arms to shield her midsection, but one man kicked her hard enough to slam her against the side of the shop. Another man swung a club. She blocked it with her left forearm and a sickening snap sent her arm flopping at an unnatural angle.

"Enough. Burn her at the stake." Helen marched toward the place of execution.

"No. Helen, please," panic shot through Valerie, "anything but fire."

The man with the club leveled a final blow to the back of Valerie's head that laid her flat.

Chapter Seventy

Stephan stood stock still. His face stung from the slap Valerie had leveled on his burned side. She fled from the chamber where she had suffered repeated sexual assaults. He watched her go, but could not turn his back on what had happened here. He shouldn't have allowed Helen to touch Valerie's scars, nor should he have permitted her to be rough with her.

Helen looked upset. "Excuse me, your majesty."

Stephan waved his hand. "Of course, Helen, you may go."

She departed up the steps, leaving him with Aramis and three other guards. Stephan looked around the torture chamber. He found a plain-looking book laying on an otherwise empty shelf. Stephan set the lamp and the book on a stone altar.

He lifted the cover and the blood drained from his extremities at the sight of what it contained. Shocked, but determined, he read each page. Illustrations of the mutilation of male and female bodies sickened him. Instructions regarding female circumcision caused roiling revulsion in his stomach. He didn't know the names of the body parts to be cut away, but the stated purpose of ensuring the purity of females until marriage was preposterous.

He flipped the page. A detailed record of Salicor's victims was mingled with the names of men who had willingly submitted to his knife to prove their loyalty. Names and dates filled the rest of the book. Stephan read them carefully. He had been betrayed. Some of the representative council was on the list. There were others too, men who held positions of influence in Soni-ashi and throughout the provinces.

Evil men had come to this place and submitted themselves to mutilation to prove their loyalty to Salicor. It wasn't just innocent children who suffered here. Horrifying things had happened on this alter.

Stephan backed away from it. Bloodstained mortar held the stones together. His skin crawled.

A dozen innocent victims of Salicor's cruelty had perished in this room. Stephan hadn't known of their existence. He hadn't heard their cries for help.

What had they died from? Thirst. There was no water here.

Stephan resisted rubbing his face with his hands, fearing they were covered in the dust of corpses. With a shiver, he left the place behind. He took the hated book of cruelty with him as evidence to condemn the traitors in his new government.

CONFLICTED, STEPHAN led his guards from the palace. He couldn't shake the guilt he felt when Valerie had accused him of executing jewels of the crown. He had to know if he had unjustly condemned any of them. Could they be forgiven for their crimes because of what they had suffered at Salicor's hand? Unsure, a realization of his hypocrisy assailed him. He had excused Valerie, pitying her for her suffering.

"We're going to inspect the captives in the prison." Stephan slapped his forehead. "No, we can't. First, we must meet with the council."

The air outside had not warmed, despite the sun being directly overhead. It was colder than yesterday. Ominous clouds obscured the mountains from view.

Stephan departed from the vantage point that the palace grounds afforded and exited through the recess that led downward to the gates. The guards there saluted him with a fist across the chest. He returned the gesture.

Striding along the Grand Way in front of the Royal Hall, he entered the doors on the opposite side of the street. He anticipated a heated debate among the council members but found the Hall of Representatives empty. An orphan boy swept the debris-strewn hardwood floor.

"Sir, your majesty, my king." Martin bowed low with each iteration of honorific.

Stephan chuckled. "Enough, I'm not much older than you are. Answer me this, has the council adjourned for the day?"

Martin worked hard to earn his keep. He was an orphan, but rather than laze around, he'd obtained employment. Stephan approved of his industry.

"No, sir. They are visiting the prison in search of jewels." The boy scratched his head.

Stephan frowned. "Are there lice in the orphanage again?"

Martin smiled. "No, sir. We have fleas."

Stephan sighed. "If the children would quit inviting in every stray dog they found, that would not be the case."

Martin looked crestfallen. "Yes, sir."

Stephan chuckled. "Go about your work. There must have been quite a ruckus to create this much aftermath."

Martin nodded, staring at the dust, torn paper, and the odd abandoned item. "They argued like snowcats."

Stephan peered at a wet spot and a chunk of something in it. "Is that a tooth?"

Martin frowned. "Yes, sir. It came to blows before they stormed out of here. Is it true about the horses? Did you order them slain?"

Stephan's body drained of heat as he realized that his secret had been revealed to the council. "Yes. I was trying to save lives...human lives."

Martin nodded with deep concern etching his young features. "You should hide."

Stephan met his gaze. "King's don't hide from their mistakes."

Martin leaned on his broom. "They voted to uphold you. I guess that means they won't kill you."

Stephan weighed the boy's words. "Thank you for the information. I hope I haven't disappointed you."

Martin shook his head. "I've never even touched a horse. I don't know why they were so upset."

Stephan nodded to the boy and walked out of the hall with his guards close behind.

STEPHAN STRODE ALONG the Grand Way, departing it to follow the Lesser Way. The place of execution lay in a walled courtyard betwixt the Royal Hall and the prison. It wasn't visible from the street.

The guards at the main doors of the prison flung them wide to accept him and his four royal guards. They entered the stone building. Stephan's eyes adjusted to the dim lighting provided by torches.

He straightened his blue coat. Listening, he discerned the direction the representatives had taken. He plunged down the steps.

"They will all have marks like this if we spare the life of even one murdering, raping, thief because of it." Hilda, the plains' representative, clasped a handful of her long blond hair, letting out an exasperated sigh.

Cloe, a representative of the forest province, frowned. "You think they will brand themselves to escape justice?"

"Perhaps they will, but that matters little when they are guilty of the crimes that earned their punishment." Jarales brushed the dust from the sleeve of his shirt.

Two ragged youth, a boy and a girl stood shackled amid the well-dressed body of representatives.

"It seems only right that the jewels of the crown should be judged by one of their own." Stephan stepped boldly from the stairwell into the torchlight.

"Your majesty, no. Please, forebear. Valerie has committed some of the most heinous crimes of our day." Helen rushed toward Stephan. "Justice demands that she suffers a slow death. Marrying her means overthrowing the power you have invested in this council."

Stephan stood his ground. "You know I had to marry her."

Jarales stepped forward. "That is the only reason you have been excused from your wartime actions. I voted against you. General Valerie acted under orders from King Salicor, and it is only right that we forgive her. She would have been tortured and killed, if she had disobeyed."

Jarales was on the list of loyal servants in the book.

Commander Gentry pointed at the prisoners. "My king, would you make a woman more deserving of death than these nefarious youths our queen?" His gravelly voice rumbled from his elderly throat.

"She should be here with these vermin, not placed above us," Hilda said.

"She was once the crown princess and would have been our queen," Jarales said.

"All the more reason to kill her," Cloe said.

Stephan strode into their midst. "Valerie legitimizes this government in the eyes of a faction of the populace that seeks to take my life. With her at my side, the redistribution of power to the people will be ensured. After the summer solstice vote, Valerie and I will turn over the government to the newly elected representatives, then we will travel to Danalan where we may live in peace."

A hush fell over the room.

Commander Gentry lifted his head, straightening his bent spine. "It's too much too soon, King Stephan. Neither the people nor the members of this council have adjusted to the freedoms you have given us. You mustn't go."

Tears coursed Helen's face and she avoided Stephan's gaze.

Saddened, Stephan considered Gentry's words. "We will stay as long as we are needed, but you must accept the pair of us as your rulers and cease infighting. The empress of the Mountain Realm has agreed to a truce on condition of the stability my union with Valerie will provide. We must not disappoint her, or she will sweep the people of Frenland to the earth in a bloody swath."

Murmurs of fear and anger circulated the council.

"You're only marrying her because the empress commanded it?" Helen sounded incredulous.

Stephan held her gaze. "I married Valerie because I love her. The empress' approval matters little when it comes to my heart."

Cloe elbowed her way to the forefront of the group. "Turning away the ire of the ice is worthy of consideration. The throne will not be polluted with Valerie's filth for long. Her issue will never rule over us."

Stephan's cheeks flushed at the indelicate speech.

"I say we hold a vote," Jarales said.

"Here?" Hilda said.

"Now," Gentry answered.

Helen looked away from the lump of rotting straw she'd been staring at. "I call the council to order. All in favor of King Stephan's marriage to Crown Princess Valerie, indicate by the raise of the right hand and say aye."

Nine hands raised. "Aye," they said.

"Any opposed? Indicate by the raise of the right hand and say nay." Helen's voice was grave.

Nine hands raised. "Nay."

Helen was among them.

It crushed Stephan's heart to see her choose this path. "You carry my happiness in your hands, Helen. You have witnessed Salicor's depravity. You know about the lives he's taken. Innocence was lost in this land. Valerie is the only one to have successfully preserved life in the face of such evil."

He handed Helen the book from the torture chamber. She puzzled over the illustrations on the worst possible page for the book to have opened to. Blushing, she closed it. Shaking her head, she paced the room.

Stephan took a deep breath. "General Valerie rescued Salicor's leavings. She either fostered them out or put them to work in her army. She sheltered the innocent victims of his cruelty." Exasperated by the stony faces in the crowd, Stephan grasped for something to prove his point. "She taught the Valkyrie to read."

Helen's expression betrayed her surprise. Slowly, she closed her eyes. "I withdraw my vote in the negative and abstain. Thus, the motion carries with nine affirmative votes and eight negatives." Helen met his gaze. "If you intend to marry that scum, then you'd better hurry. She may be burning as we speak."

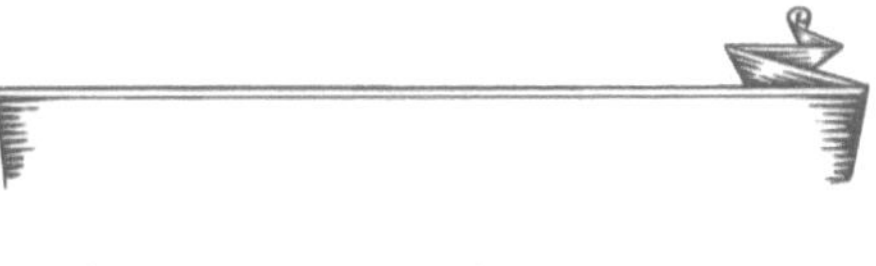

Chapter Seventy-One

Stephan departed from the prison through the side door that led to the place of execution. Across the cobblestone courtyard, he spotted a stake that had stood for many moons. It was a reminder of the old regime's cruel ways. Tied to the post was an unconscious, bruised, and broken woman. Dressed in white, Valerie was encircled by a heap of kindling and split wood.

"Stop." Stephan's heart pounded with panic.

He and his guards fought their way through a crowd of onlookers.

"Make way for the king," Aramis shouted.

A ring of men in representative guard uniforms carried torches toward Valerie.

"We have our orders from the council, your majesty. The murderer must burn." The man tossed a torch onto the pile.

Stephan lunged after it and flung it free of the kindling. Kicking the bit that had ignited away from the rest, he stomped out the flames.

"You cannot do this. The council has voted in favor of clemency." Stephan held up his hands, warding away the other torches.

"Kill her." A bent old woman with rheumy eyes leaned on a cane. "I witnessed the fires of Scion."

"I survived those fires." Book in hand, Helen came to stand beside Stephan. "I know of Valerie's atrocities and can never fully forgive her, but Salicor commanded her actions. Because of this, I must satisfy my need for justice with his death, and so must you. King Stephan's marriage to Crown Princess Valerie will unite the kingdom and secure the fragile freedom we enjoy."

The crowd absorbed the words without debate. "Kill her." The chant began, intensified, and was joined by many more voices as the gathering grew in numbers.

Stephan leaped onto the pile of wood and shielded Valerie with his body, holding her head against his shoulder. She still breathed. He kissed her forehead and wept tears of relief.

"Halt." Commander Gentry's gruff voice carried despite the cacophony.

The representative guards obeyed him and pulled back their torches before they ignited the kindling.

Gentry continued speaking, "I have spoken with the empress' second son, Dantyn. The ire of the Mountain Realm has been incited by our civil war. It spilled over into their lands and claimed the lives of many of their people. However, they respect General Valerie because she saved the empress's oldest son's life and the lives of his children. The union of our king and the general is important to re-establish peace. The mountains are no longer sealed. The Woman of the Stone has visited our land. Prosperity is within our grasp." Gentry reached into the air as if to snatch it.

"I will bow to no empire." The old woman said with a finality that rippled through the crowd.

"Kill her!" The chant resumed.

Galvanized, the crowd rushed toward the torchbearers. Stephan cut the ropes that bound Valerie's elbows. He carried her free of the kindling.

Shielded by his guards, they fled en bloc toward the palace gates. The palace guards admitted them and defended against the mob. Blood spilled around him as Stephan carried his unconscious bride toward their quarters.

He startled a servant woman coming out of his rooms. "Fetch a doctor." He reconsidered because of the clash at the gates. "No. Please fetch Randall instead. He's the stables head. Do not leave the palace grounds because it isn't safe."

Stephan rushed inside the suite to lay Valerie on her mother's bed. Her left forearm jutted at an unnatural angle. He covered his mouth with his hand, unsure of what to do next.

"Help me undress her." Helen rushed into the bedchamber.

She removed Valerie's boots and stockings. Strangely, she paused, running her hand over horrible scars on Valerie's ankles. The skin looked like ropes had charred indentations in melted flesh, but the burns were far from fresh.

Stephan's eyes filled with tears. Valerie had almost burned at the stake. Seeing those marks, he knew it must be her greatest fear come true. He understood her dread because he too was terrified of death by fire.

Randall entered the room. Helen stripped Valerie's clothing. The two of them inspected the injuries that littered her body.

"The bone break is clean," Randal said. "I think that it will heal if we set it properly. What concerns me is the bruising on her abdomen. She may lose the baby." He bandaged a bloody defensive wound on Valerie's other forearm.

Helen met Stephan's gaze with a stark expression. "She's pregnant?"

Stephan stood like a man marked for execution. Would the baby die? He shifted his gaze to Valerie's battered body.

"She should be conscious by now." Helen inspected Valerie's head, pulling her hand away bloodied. "There is swelling, but the skull is intact."

Randall covered Valerie with a blanket. He and Helen cleaned and bandaged the head wound, then set Valerie's broken arm and stabilized it. Randall checked for a pulse on Valerie's right wrist.

The stableman frowned. "Something is wrong. She's a young woman and her heart should be robust." He looked at Stephan. "Yet, it beats erratically as if it may fail."

Stunned, Stephan could do nothing except stare at the man. "She can't die. Don't let her die."

Randall looked at Helen. "I don't know what else to do."

Helen scowled. "Send for the sages."

Stephan blinked back his surprise. "The only sage I knew was her mother."

Randall stood from his spot on the side of the bed. "I can find at least one. She should be able to send word to the others. I'll fetch her."

Stephan grabbed the man's shoulder. "Be careful."

Randall nodded. "I can be in and out without anyone noticing. Have no fear, my stablemen and I guard the hidden passage well."

Stephan released him. "Hurry." It was one more secret he hadn't known until today.

Helen covered Valerie with additional blankets. "She's deathly cold, your majesty."

He met her gaze. "Will you stay with her? I don't have permission to touch her. I shouldn't even be here. I shouldn't have looked at her naked."

Helen shook her head. "I can't help her."

"Please? I'll never ask another thing from you." He begged, unable to face Valerie's ire when she awakened.

Helen held his gaze for what felt like forever. "I will warm her and watch over her, but it should be you doing this." She shucked her coat and boots, sliding into the bed. "This isn't your fault, Stephan."

"Yes, it is. I sent word regarding her mother's illness. I warned her not to come, but I should have known she would." He strode out of the room on his way to anywhere that might turn his thoughts away from what he'd done to the woman he loved and the child she carried.

STEPHAN CHARGED TOWARD the clamor of a hostile force at the palace gates. He carried Krelor's sword on his belt. Guards and servants alike poured from the armory with weapons. They wore solemn expressions. A crash and a clatter signaled the breach of the gates at the bottom of the incline.

"Do not die for me. Fight for Frenland." Stephan drew his sword.

A mob flooded through the broken gates, shouting for Valerie's blood. Untrained and armed with makeshift weapons, the invaders perished on Stephan's sword with a swiftness that sickened him. He loathed himself for having sparked the conflict by selfishly agreeing to the East Icer's terms.

Every stroke of his blade darkened his soul with a stain he could not see his way past. A woman dressed in red entered the fray from outside the gates and cut through the throngs. Running up the incline in his direction, she skillfully wielded a sword with a grin on her face.

Once she was near, she turned her back to him. He and the others with him fought alongside her, forming a barrier against the influx of new insurgents. The palace grounds had not yet been breached because the invaders were trapped inside the recessed passage that led to it. That gave palace defenders a tremendous advantage in combat.

The soldiers in red and black hacked down the mob from behind until the remaining attackers fled. The women in red shouted in exultation.

Laughing and embracing, they congratulated themselves on their victory.

Stephan did not share their elation, but he shifted his blade to his left hand. Approaching the woman who had formed the focal point of the rally, he extended his right hand. Ashlyn of Cairn clasped it and pulled him close to kiss each of his cheeks.

The custom still took him by surprise, bringing a flush to his face. "Thank you, Commander."

"It was my pleasure, sir. You saved the general from the flames. I would die for you now." She chuckled.

Mention of Valerie crushed him with guilt. "Protect her, not me. She was always meant to be your queen."

Sobered by the words, Ashlyn clasped her fist and tapped her chest in salute. "Stay with us, your majesty."

Smoke and the clash of steel emanated from the rest of the city. Chaos reigned in his stead and he could not permit that to endure. He transferred Krelor's sword to his right hand, preparing to face the fight.

"King Stephan, this mob at your gates was loyal to you. They craved Valerie's blood, not yours. Others in this city are fighting to take your life. Do not leave the palace." Her voice held undeniable conviction.

"We will defend you, sir." Aramis had survived.

"Defend the queen." Stephan knew the cost he must pay to keep Valerie safe. "My life is forfeit. I will not have anyone else die for me."

The blood and carnage that surrounded him had dealt a fatal blow to his soul. Weeping openly, he watched smoke rise from multiple fires across the city. Walking between the Valkyrie, he came to stand in the gap where once the gates had stood. When the angry men of the old regime came, he went out to meet them.

He struck down everyone who lifted a weapon against him. A hostile silence fell over the attackers. It would take all of them to kill him.

The instant before they surged, Stephan lowered his blade and walked into their midst. Outwardly stoic, he led them to the execution yard behind the Royal Hall. He climbed within the kindling and leaned against the stake. In silent prayer, he lifted his eyes to the sky.

"This man ordered the slaughter of horses as a tactic of war." Jarales grabbed a torch from one of several men who carried them.

Stephan looked toward the palace, wishing he could see Valerie. A woman in red and black stood on the wall, but it was not his wife. Ashlyn was within earshot and had likely heard the accusation.

"I am guilty. I accept my punishment." Stephan closed his eyes.

Jarales growled. "King Stephan ordered the slaughter of the great warhorses of our people. We have killed the council members who concealed his treachery. We showed them no mercy and we will show him none either."

Torches ignited the kindling. Fire licked at Stephan's legs, catching his clothing alight. He screamed as his flesh burned.

His last breath brought searing flames into his lungs. Blackened, his skin sizzled and split. He lifted Krelor's sword aloft and a sweet release freed Stephan from his suffering. The blade vanished like smoke as Krelor's debt was repaid.

Chapter Seventy-Two

A clash of steel roused Valerie from a dark slumber. The pain sharpened in her left forearm. With every jarring sound, a throb in her head increased. Helen wielded a sword to prevent a group of men from entering the bedchamber, but she wouldn't last long.

"What have you done? Where is the king?" Helen barked her questions between slashes, parries, and jabs.

Jarales laughed, sword at the ready. "He's dead."

Valerie's heart turned to stone.

Helen gasped. "No. It can't be."

"We burned him at the stake." Jarales knocked the sword from Helen's grasp, sending it clattering to the floor.

A disturbing brand of humor that sometimes took Valerie caused her to laugh. Everyone's eyes focused on her. She removed the bandage from her head, realizing she was naked.

That could be used to her advantage. She sat, exposing her breasts to their view. Casting aside the blanket, she stood to face them.

Forcing herself not to reveal her pain, she walked toward the gathering. There were six men and five women of the council, not counting Helen. As she passed through the bedchamber doorway, the surviving council members formed an arc in the living room.

"Reveal your loyalty." It was the act of obeisance King Salicor had required of petitioners who sought his favor and Valerie would do the same.

Jarales laughed. "You have your uncle's sense of humor." He unfastened his belt and lowered his trousers to reveal proof of his devotion to the former regime.

The female representatives exhibited alarm as the men followed Jarales' lead. Valerie surveyed their circumcisions. The last to comply was a man who took the time to strip down to the skin. Leering at her, he stood at full attention. The female council members gravitated to the far side of the room.

Valerie walked along the line of representatives at a deliberating pace. "I was the crown princess." Her backside became visible to each member as she passed. "I was the first jewel in Salicor's crown." She had traversed the room to stand before the light blue drapes of the second-story window. She cast her words over her shoulder. "And his favorite."

With her right hand, she parted the drapes, catching them on the hook at the side. An army of representative guards filled the palace grounds, surrounding a tight cluster of armed Valkyrie fighters. Commander Ashlyn of Cairn pointed at her, drawing everyone's attention to the window. Valerie hooked the other half of the drapes, showing the onlookers below her backside and the scars there.

Returning her focus to the representatives, she noticed that all of the men now stood at attention. "Your loyalty will be greatly rewarded, but I do not trust these women." She indicated the female representatives. "They must demonstrate their submission to my rule." Valerie's lips curled wickedly. "Assist them, won't you?"

Jarales laughed. "Gladly." He moved toward Helen.

"Not Helen of Scion. She's mine." Valerie said firmly, yet with languid ease.

"As you wish, my queen." Jarales seemed to realize that the other women had been claimed.

"Do you have a problem?" Valerie asked.

His enthusiasm lagged until she walked in his direction. "No, my queen. I am at your service." A lecherous grin formed on his face as he stared at her body. "I will be gentle since you are somewhat worse for the wear, though beautiful as ever, I must say."

She approached him. Rather than grasp his offering, she drew his dagger. Cloe screamed beneath the male representative from the plains. His assault was particularly rough and the female representative from the forest province fought in adamant opposition to the unfavorable turn of events.

Valerie took the two steps required to plunge the dagger through the man's back, killing him instantly. Cloe struggled beneath his dead weight.

She offered no thanks to her queen.

Valerie withdrew the blade and faced Jarales. "Have your fun while he's still warm."

Jarales smirked. "Yes, my queen." He obeyed with enthusiasm.

Valerie trembled with shock and fatigue. Stephan had suffered death by fire. He had saved her from the flames only to take her place. Tormented by the knowledge of what he must have suffered, she could endure the presence of his murderers no longer.

"Finish elsewhere. Leave my Valkyrie unmolested. I will grant you positions of power and influence on the morrow." Valerie watched a drop of blood fall from the dagger's hilt guard.

Grunting and grumbling, the men hiked their trousers. Sobbing and swearing, the women attempted to compose themselves. Some of the men lifted their unwilling partners over their shoulders. All of them departed from the residence.

That left Valerie, Helen, and the dead man. Valerie watched until the enemy had exited the hallway. Below, on the palace grounds, she observed the representative guards depart with the council members. Five Valkyrie had survived.

"You are a monster." Helen's voice held an anguished edge of horror. Her face was slick with tears and she collapsed to her knees.

"I know what they want and how to keep you from them." Valerie walked toward the bed.

Helen's gaze followed the blade in Valerie's hand. "I don't understand."

Valerie placed it on the bedside table and pulled back the covers, sliding gingerly between the sheets. "Stephan's killers will die by my hand. You have my word."

Ashlyn laughed as she walked through the living room to stand in the doorway of the bedchamber with her sword still drawn. "I've never seen the Creator do so much with so little. All we had was five Valkyrie and a naked queen, but we defeated an army."

"Tell me of Lily." Valerie's heart beat again as if for the first time in an hour.

"She is well and safely where I left her. I came as soon as I heard you were here. I apologize for not making it in time for your mother's funeral." Ashlyn bowed.

Valerie went numb inside. "Hide Stephan's remains in the catacombs as soon as you may safely do so."

"There's nothing left of him except this." Ashlyn entered the room to hand Valerie the hilt of Krelor's sword.

Valerie stared at the snarling wolves with the sapphire in their jaws. "The blade disappeared?"

"So did the king. I watched from the palace wall." Ashlyn's expression was grave.

Valerie met her gaze. "Take Helen to the blacksmith. She is to be the head of my royal guard."

Helen took to her feet, grasping her sword as she did so. "I will not serve you."

Valerie laughed weakly. "You are my slave and must become my lover."

Helen's jaw dropped.

Ashlyn rolled her eyes. "Not this ploy again."

Valerie closed her eyes completely. "I'm afraid so. I need Helen in Soni-ashi so that most of the Valkyrie can return to their villages and towns to recruit a loyal army."

Ashlyn harrumphed. "Loyal to what, General? You already know we're loyal to you."

Valerie opened her eyes to capture Ashlyn's gaze. "Loyal to Stephan's laws. Loyal to freedom from tyranny. Educate them to be leaders in the new republic. Arm them, train them, and send them to me. Defend the integrity of the Skye."

Ashlyn made a fist and clapped it across her chest. "It will be done."

Helen took a deep breath and let it out slowly, staring at Valerie. "You did love him."

Valerie held Helen's gaze for as long as she could. "As did you." With that, she closed her eyes, sinking into an overwhelming sorrow.

"Yet, he was your lover, not mine." Helen's voice held bitterness.

"I did not defile him." Valerie could no longer withhold her tears.

"Are you saying you never touched him?" Helen's tone held a complicat-ed mixture of emotions, chief among them relief.

"Return to my bed before nightfall." Valerie longed to curl into a ball and weep without restraint, but her wounds pained her too much for that.

Helen scoffed. "Why degrade my reputation in this way?"

Ashlyn slapped the back of Helen's head. "She's protecting you. Be grateful." Ashlyn faced Valerie and cleared her throat in a sad kind of way. "I'm sorry for your loss, your majesty. I'll leave three Valkyrie to watch over you."

"I need none. Helen is the last representative of the legitimate government. She is the one we must protect." Valerie closed her eyes, seeing nothing but fire.

Don't miss out!

Visit the website below and you can sign up to receive emails whenever S.V. Farnsworth publishes a new book. There's no charge and no obligation.

https://books2read.com/r/B-A-LKBI-MVYAB

BOOKS2READ

Connecting independent readers to independent writers.

Did you love *Monarch in the Flames*? Then you should read *A Rare Connection: Inspirational Romantic Suspense*[1] by S.V. Farnsworth!

Flirty, French, heiress Nicole Moreau takes her hard-working, American best friend, Andrew Leavitt, for granted, until he puts his education at UCLA on hold to serve as a missionary in South Korea for the Church of Jesus Christ of Latter-day Saints.

She can't understand his devoition, can't seem to be happy without him, and can't stop herself from interupting his mission. Intending to propose, she botches the question and leaves heartbroken.

Andrew is deeply in love with her but doesn't react fast enough to prevent a tragedy.

Caught in the crosshairs of the private war between her French Intelligence agent mother and a deadly North Korean unit of kidnappers, Nicole becomes collateral damage.

Can her well-meaning grandmother give her a second chance to chose

---

1. https://books2read.com/u/bpElxz

2. https://books2read.com/u/bpElxz

truth as well as love so she can heal from a #MeToo secret with the power to destoy her? Or will her mother's enemies exact the final revenge?

Read more at https://svfarnsworthauthor.com.

Also by S.V. Farnsworth

Modutan Empire
Woman of the Stone
Monarch in the Flames

Standalone
A Rare Connection: Inspirational Romantic Suspense

Watch for more at https://svfarnsworthauthor.com.

About the Author

S.V. Farnsworth is a linguist librarian who has spent time in Asia. Issues with grit give her novels the traction to move you.

A Rare Connection: Inspirational Romantic Suspense is about a couple who met as children and grew up to live worlds apart. Can a well-meaning grandmother move heaven and earth to give them a second chance at love?

Woman of the Stone is book one in the Modutan Empire series. *Monarch in the Flames* is the sequel. They are epic fantasy adventures with an appeal to readers who connect with #MeToo concerns and admire strong female characters.

S.V. Farnsworth graduated with a B.S. from SUU in 2002. She teaches ESL at Crowder College in southwest Missouri.

She is the 2020 and 2021 secretary of the Ozarks Writers League. She served as 2018 and 2019 president of the Joplin Writers' Guild, coordinated their conferences, and edited the guild's 2019 Anthology, *Seasons of the Four States*.

Subscribe to her newsletter for exclusive content and updates on her books at **svfarnsworthauthor.com**.

Read more at https://svfarnsworthauthor.com.